The Storm Knight II: Falling Mist

by Zachary Watson

Copyright © 2023 by Zachary Watson

For more information, address: z.watson.author@gmail.com.

Website: https://zachwatsonauthor.com/

Edited by Dana Morck, John Watson, Jordan Perona, Samantha Watson, & Catherine Hariton

Cover Art by Ed Bourelle

ISBN 979-8-9860285-5-2 (Kindle ebook)
ISBN 979-8-9860285-6-9 (Paperback)

For my family, friends, and everyone who told me I could do this.

Semper Victoria

Other Stories by Zach Watson

The Knights of the Compact

The Lost Knight
Awakening
Fealty
Ronin
Huntsman
Vengeance
Einherjar

The Storm Knight
Dark Skies
Falling Mist

Warblades of Saerda Novellas
The Amethyst Blade

Other Stories in the Knights of the Compact Universe

Welcome to Nowhere by Keven Karaki

Glossary of Terms

Caranat; Literally meaning 'The Language', Caranat is the primary spoken word of the Trahcon people and the Empire in particular.

Humanity; The newest addition to the Empire after Earth was conquered roughly a century in the past. Not particularly well regarded by most other species, they are increasingly being forced off of Earth and scattered across various colonial regions. An Imperial Human's term of conscription begins at the age of 15 Imperial (roughly 17 Terran), and lasts until they're 27 (roughly 30 Terran).

Imperial Intelligence; While its official main purpose is espionage and counter-espionage against foreign powers, the sheer size of the Empire ensures that most of its agents are dedicated to internal security and investigations.

Index; The record of an Imperial Citizen's life, used to determine both military promotions as well as to evaluate their progress through the technocratic civilian government.

Naule; A four armed, simian species counted among the five Humanoid races. Universally covered by long strands of hair, their small interstellar nations were overwhelmed and conquered by the Empire several centuries ago.

Sorcery; A range of telekinetic and pyrokinetic abilities focused on manipulating the same sub-reality that allows for FTL travel. Organized as 'spells', the difficulties in learning the more complicated spells ensures few Trahcon learn more than basics in the modern era.

Strike-Wave; The most popular sport in the Empire, featuring two teams of varying size playing on an oval pitch, a single large ball, and a goal at either end.

Trahcon; The founding species of the Empire, and the only Humanoid species naturally capable of manipulating energy without cybernetic enhancement. On average shorter than Humans, they have uniformly gray skin but extremely bright eyes. Unique in possessing a nearly three to one gender imbalance between females to males, and for having a five century long lifespan.

5

Prologue

Date: Day 5, Month 7, 2163 Imperial
Location: Transport *Blue-Stone*, Altair Sector, Empire of the Homeworld

I dreamt of fire.

A quiet inhalation was the only sound I let myself make when I woke up, teeth digging into my lip to make sure nothing louder got out. Thankfully I was on my back, which made it easy to clench my hands into fists without waking the packmate beside me.

It was a dream. Just another stupid nightmare. Not real.

But I could still smell...

Shuddering, I forced myself to swallow. I don't know when my mouth had gotten dry, but suddenly everything was too close. Everything was pushing in. The blankets, my pillow... it was too much. I had to get it off, had to stop that overwhelming terror of being smothered.

It was incredibly hard not to simply shove it all away. To calmly push the thick covers back. Cold air tickled my bare arms, making it even harder to not simply leap out of the bed to feel more of it.

Slowly. I had to be slow.

Carefully sliding myself out of the bed took every bit of my self control. The cold deck of the ship under my bare feet felt just as good as the air on my skin. My footsteps were silent as I padded to the door, feeling for the control panel.

Once I found it, a single tap had the hatch slide open, letting me escape into a dimly lit hallway.

"Aspects." I gasped the moment it closed behind me. "That was... a bad one."

Rerth called them Cursed Nights. Dreams several shades worse than a

6

casual nightmare, and almost always about some kind of trauma. The worst gifts of Vorep, Aspect of dark sorcery and nightmares.

I'd had my fair share of nights like this. In years past, the most common had been about my first squad confronting me, attacking me the very first night I'd met them. In real life, an officer had heard and arrived in time to stop them from going all the way. From doing more than giving me a beating, destroying what few personal things I had, and tearing my uniform apart.

In the dreams... he showed up late, if at all.

Those old dreams had been joined by new ones over the past few months. The latest came from Oshflara, where the mysterious priestess has just begun scorching off my face when she was interrupted. Convinced that killing me later would be more useful than torturing me in the moment.

She hadn't had me alone long. A few minutes of dismissive questions and sadism... but those few minutes had been the most agonizing of my entire life. A pain made all the worse by her casual tone, her complete dismissal of my sobbing answers to her questions.

And in these Cursed Nights... no one showed up to stop her either.

"Calm down, Ashe." I whispered to myself. "Calm down or you're going to throw up again."

It wasn't the pain that did that. It was remembering exactly what my own skin and muscles had smelled like when they cooked.

No sooner had that thought crossed my mind than my hand rose to my mouth, covering it as I fought down an involuntary heave.

Dammit.

I started walking without really thinking about it. Thankfully it was a very short trip to the nearest bathroom, and since it was the middle of the ship's night-cycle no one was there to see me staggering through the hatchway.

A thump of my fist turned the lights on once I was inside, and a few more steps got me over to the twin-sinks.

The mirror let me see a Human woman with brown skin, her dark

7

eyes haunted from a lack of sleep. The black fur growing from my scalp was getting longer every week, and it was a complete mess that covered up half of my face.

One hand rose, tugging some of it back to let me see the ripple-marks on my cheek. The physical memory of the torture that I'd get to carry for the rest of my life. Well, I supposed I could have it removed if I really wanted to pay for treatment.

But...

"I can't erase what happened."

The sight of the scars made my stomach turn over again, and I quickly let my fur fall back into place. I put both hands on the sink and closed my eyes, trying to fall back into a calming routine. Tried to focus on just my sense of hearing, to blot out everything else.

The quiet hum of the fan. There was a tiny hitch to it... a little warble. It probably needed a bit of maintenance. Quieter, far more distant, was the rumble of the ship's engines pushing us at faster-than-light. Protecting us from the rolling chaos of hyper-space. Some people didn't care for how pervasive that noise always seemed to be aboard ships, but I'd always found it strangely comforting.

It was a sound that told me that I wasn't alone. That I wasn't adrift in the void of space.

Metal creaked behind me; the door was opening.

I could guess who'd walked in even before her steady voice filled the air.

"Another one, then."

My head bowed in shame, "Sorry, Rerth. I didn't mean to wake you."

A quiet sigh preceded feet lightly moving across the deck, then warm arms wrapping around my waist. The oldest packmate I'd ever had gently pulled me against her, face resting against my shoulder as she hugged me.

"Just because I'm two centuries older than you doesn't mean you can't talk to me, Ashe." She said.

8

I nodded. "I'm sorry, it's just... weird. You're a Guide, and you're my superior officer. And I still kind of resent you."

Far from being upset, my blunt honesty made her chuckle quietly. "I know. Did the meditation help?"

"A little."

"Good. I'm glad Huvu'rith taught you that trick." Her grip tightened for a moment before she slowly let go. "Open your eyes, huntress. Tell me what happened this time."

Taking a deep breath, I opened my eyes and turned to face her.

Rerth'riah, Imperial Agent, my latest packmate, was a little short for a woman. She made up for that with her bright blue eyes, attractive features, and muscled gray skin absolutely covered in swirling tattoos. Most of those were covered at the moment; whoever the ship's captain was liked to keep it damned cold, and her sleepwear was as covering as mine was.

She was everything I wasn't. A beautiful, determined Trahcon woman excelling in her career.

I was... just me. A Human conscript one misstep away from being discharged to a penal colony. Who'd screwed up so many times I'd forced Rerth to burn through most of the favors she'd collected from Army officers just to protect me.

"Ashe." She said gently. "Come on."

Right.

"The priestess again." I said, focusing on the present. "What she did to my face. Except... except no one interrupted her."

Her tarah lowered, pulling her face into sorrow. "You don't have to say more."

"No, it's all right. Talking about it... it kind of helps." I still had to pause there, taking another few breaths before saying, "She, um, kept going. Ran her hands along my scalp, the other side of my face, and then my chin. I woke up just before she could start on my nose."

9

Rerth closed her eyes, shaking her head. "Cursed Vorep. At least it wasn't the traitors you had to kill this time."

The reminder of my *other* common set of nightmares had me wincing.

It had to be a Human thing. I'd never heard of anyone being particularly troubled about killing someone, especially not in the circumstances that I'd had to. Practically every conscript I'd ever met had been desperate to be assigned to combat zones, and those who'd actually managed to partake in skirmishes or battles had universally seemed to enjoy them.

Ashahn's blood, I'd been just as hopeful and eager. I'd even seriously tried to get myself assigned to Huvu's unit again. To join them in the quasi-war with the Chezzek in the Contested Zone. I had wanted nothing more than to fight beside them, to kill the enemies of the Empire, to feel like a normal Imperial citizen.

Then... I'd started dreaming about how I'd killed those two guards in the bathroom.

How I'd shot one through the throat from less than a foot away.

How his blood had sprayed into my open mouth.

Rerth's voice yanked me out of the deeps I'd started to spiral into once again. "The smell get to you again?"

My weight shifted, but I stopped myself from going to the nearest stall to vomit. "...always."

"And you're sure you don't want to try medication?"

"...I don't know." I admitted. "They're not as bad now as they were right after we left Oshflara."

She gave me a rather flat look. "Liar."

"I am not." I insisted. "They're not as common."

"But they're just as bad." Rerth countered. "Tell me that they aren't."

"They're not as common." I repeated sullenly.

10

That earned me another tired sigh. "What is it about Humans and getting so stubborn so early in your lives? Come on. Let's go back to bed, I can talk to you until you fall asleep like last time."

That sounded a lot better than splashing myself with water and trying to meditate alone.

Turning the light off, I followed her back to our cabin. Thankfully she'd left our own lights on their dimmest setting before she'd left, making it easy for both of us to climb back into the broad bed.

With just the two of us there was plenty of space, and usually she made me sleep much farther away than I was used to. Guides didn't need as much contact as Hunters did, and it was... a bit of an adjustment. For both of us, I thought.

I waited for her to get settled before curling up against her side, resting my head on her chest. The steady, twinned rhythm of her hearts filled my ear until she began quietly speaking.

"We're aboard for another eight days." She murmured, telling me things I already knew. It was a routine she'd picked up from somewhere on the DataNet, a way to calm children.

I'd been a bit embarrassed when she'd told me that, but I was too relieved that it worked to really complain.

"Unless the currents change, or one of the deep storms forces us to go shallow for a while. Once we're at the penal colony, we'll head down to the surface for just a few hours. We'll stay long enough to question my contact, then we'll be back in space and headed for Altair to meet up with the others in my pack. Our pack, now."

"...what did your contact do?" I asked. It was a question I'd posed several times before, and one she'd never really answered.

Tonight apparently wasn't the night where I'd learn that. "It's enough to say that she's a murderer. One who went so far that she's now on a penal colony for the rest of her life."

"Will it be safe to talk to her?"

11

"Nothing in our career is ever truly safe, Ashe." The arm I was half-laying on moved slightly. A moment later I felt soft tugging on my scalp as she began petting my fur. "But this is fairly low risk. Killing us won't get her off-world, it'll just get her executed and she knows it."

I nodded tiredly. A penal colony wouldn't be fun, but I'd rather live on one of those than be executed. I had to assume anyone living on one agreed, or else they'd have died trying to avoid that fate.

"And she'll know something about the smugglers?" I asked.

"Possibly, but they're a lower priority than your attacker. Either way, we get what we can from her, then we regroup on the sector capital. The sooner we get home, the sooner we find out just who that priestess really was, and what she was doing on Oshflara."

I closed my eyes, doing my best to enjoy the warmth of the body beside me. "And tracking the automation parts they were selling."

"And that, among other things. Do you want to hear about my packmates again?"

"Please."

This was a conversation we'd had five times already... well, six now. But the familiar topics really did seem to help me relax. Help my breathing slow towards sleep.

"Holde has been my packmate since childhood. He's my bond, my partner in all things." Her voice turned wry, "He's also the most handsome man I've ever met, and I'm sure you'll agree when you finally meet him."

A huff of amusement came from my lips, my own words growing quieter. "Or you'll order me to."

"Or I'll order you to. We started to drift off from the others in our first pack in our early nineties, when we were stuck doing garrison work on Abantia. Sector capitals are even more boring than normal assignments, so we started going around trying to find mysteries to solve. Our first adventure came when we ran into a Regnon exile, he was trying to sell..."

The old story carried me along into the waves of sleep... and kept the dreams far away.

12

I

An Imperial Penal Colony wasn't the last place I ever wanted to visit... but it was pretty close.

"Are you sure we don't need to be armed?" I asked, nervously stepping out of the shuttle that had brought us to the planet's surface.

It had put us down in what looked like the middle of a small forest. Blue-green leaves surrounded our landing zone, and stopped me from being able to see much of anything else.

"We'll be fine." Rerth replied, already walking off without me. "We're a hundred miles from the nearest settlement. There won't be anyone around apart from my contact and her pack."

And thank the Aspects for that.

Penal Colony Seventy-Five-R was a low-support, low-technology world. The kind of place where the Empire sent those criminals who hadn't quite deserved the punishment of execution, but also didn't deserve the mercy of exile. They had to grow their own food, build their own shelters, and generally live as though the last five or six thousand years of development hadn't happened.

I really didn't want to see what that was like in person. What kind of packs deserved that fate.

Shaking my head, I jumped down onto the ground before moving to catch up. "What about the woman we're here to see? You've said she's a murderer."

"And she very much is, do you have a point to your repetition?"

"You're way too calm about this." I muttered before speaking clearly. "And you're still not going to tell me exactly what she did?"

"To what end?" Rerth glanced to her right, her bright blue eyes meeting mine. "Why do you need to know?"

13

"I..." I hesitated, trying to think of a reason beyond my curiosity. She'd made it clear that wasn't a good enough reason. That I had to grow beyond merely *wanting* to know things. There had to be a justification, a practical one that would give me reason to *need* to know the answer.

"...because it might tell me how evil she is." I said as we both slowed to a stop. "How much trust I could put into what she says. If she's anything like the priestess who attacked me, then I don't know if questioning her will give us anything we could use without spending a lot of time verifying."

Rerth flicked her right tarah, humming. For a brief moment I thought she wouldn't answer, but then she smiled slowly in approval.

"You have been paying attention after all. Good. To answer your repeated question, Tia'mok was formerly a member of a planetary security force, assigned as a detective. She helped uncover a broad criminal conspiracy and was sent in to infiltrate it."

I perked up at once. That sounded a lot like the kind of mission I'd have enjoyed supporting. Not really doing, the infiltration part left me a little uncomfortable, but I'd have loved analyzing whatever information came out of it. "She was?"

"Yes." She nodded. "However, her old superior retired, and was replaced by someone with less patience. They began to arrange for a mass-arrest of everyone she had identified. Her warnings that they had agents within their organization went ignored, and the criminals were well prepared to vanish into the mists. Not about to let that happen, she assassinated them."

"Oh." I bit my lip before asking, "Um, how many?"

"By the time she was done?" Rerth turned away and began walking once more. "Twenty-seven people believed to be criminals, and another fifty believed to simply be in the wrong place at the wrong time."

I winced, again hurrying to keep pace. "She used bombs, didn't she?"

"Yes. She had a respectable motive considering the situation and vile nature of her targets. Had she avoided the collateral deaths, she probably would have been given a minor punishment after a second investigation."

It was easy to picture how that particular trial had gone. The judges had probably berated her superior, praised her for dealing with the criminals,

14

and then verbally torn her apart for killing so many innocent people alongside them.

"That would certainly explain why she's here." I said quietly.

"Indeed. Now that you know, do you think we can trust her information?'

I thought about my answer for most of a minute before replying. "I think so. She sounds like she had a good reason for doing what she did, she just... let it get out of control. If we tell her that we're hunting other criminals, she might give us good intelligence. Right?"

"Generally speaking, that has been my experience with her." Rerth replied. "I have been using her information for the decade since her sentencing. Mostly as a means to clean up elements of her former group, and those others that they worked with. It has been largely accurate."

"And you think she'll actually know something about the smuggling ring on Oshflara? About the priestess?" I asked.

"The former is possible, but a bit outside of their usual range. I am more hopeful she might have knowledge of a priestess operating in criminal circles."

I swallowed. "You think so?"

It was Rerth's turn to lower her voice. "The group she infiltrated was one of the worst I've ever heard of. They had a great many contacts with others just as dark, and many others who didn't realize just who they were working with. In my century of work in this field, I can honestly say I've never dealt with a more vile group. A priestess who gets off on torturing aliens would fit in among them."

"Oh." I said quietly. "Um, have you been able to...?"

There was a tiny nod as she led me farther down the narrow path. "Most of them are dead, or on colonies like this now. It has been my primary focus when I wasn't watching over you."

By 'watching over you', she really meant, 'micro-managing your assignments'. Not something I liked remembering, but this wasn't the time or place to repeat that particular argument.

15

"So you've had to talk to her a lot before." I guessed. "Um... is talking to convicted murderers something Intelligence Agents have to do a lot?"

Rerth rolled her right shoulder, both tarah lifting slightly. "Not as often as you're clearly worried about, but it's a port we have to pull into more than I'd like."

I swallowed and repeated a bit of the wisdom she'd been trying to teach me. "Sometimes the worst people know the most."

"Exactly." Her sigh was heavy and genuine. "Sadly Mok knows quite a lot, and she hasn't been so foolish as to give it all up at once."

"Which is why she wasn't executed for blowing up fifty bystanders." I guessed.

"That, and the people she killed were so terrible that even the judges weren't sure there was a better way to deal with them. Quiet now, her home's not far, and remember what I told you on the way down to the surface."

It was pretty easy to remember considering it had happened just a few minutes ago. And an hour before when we'd first gotten onto the shuttle. And the hour before that when she'd gone over the plan. *And* yesterday when she'd first seriously described Tia'mok's personality, if not her crimes.

Sadly that seemed to be pretty common in my new relationship with Rerth. Her idea of 'training' me involved a whole lot of repetition mixed with sudden tests of my intelligence and memory.

According to her, it was because that combination was the only way to get things through my thick skull.

Personally I thought that incredibly unfair, but I wasn't in any position to talk back. Not after what had happened on Oshflara. Not with how I was one misstep away from ending up on one of these colonies as a long-term resident.

So instead of replying, I closed my mouth and focused on following her through the forest.

For the next ten minutes or so we trudged along, the only sound our boots crunching through the dried leaves covering the dirt. The trees began to

16

thin out pretty quickly, and I saw the clearing ahead long before we actually walked into the open.

Rerth's contact was waiting for us outside of a wooden shack on the far side, neat rows of tall crops filling the space between us. Their leaves rustled quietly in the gentle wind, and made it a bit hard to see if there was anyone else present.

I was certain there was, I could feel eyes on me... but I couldn't tell where they were.

"Rerth'riah." A rolling Twins' accent colored the voice that greeted us, lengthening each vowel. "I was wondering when I would see you again."

"Tia'mok." Rerth replied. "You know you could be moved to a nicer colony if you actually told me more during our little talks."

Tia'mok was... not what I expected. Not at all.

She was honestly kind of bland, especially wearing nothing but the bright green pants of a prisoner. It was hard to tell at a distance, but I guessed she was average height for a Trahcon woman. Not overly muscled, not overly tattooed, not overly anything really. Even her green eyes looked a bit dim.

I could have walked past her on any street and not even noticed her.

"I prefer my privacy." Gray arms crossed her bare chest as she stared us down. "As does my pack. What do you want this time?"

Rerth only walked a few steps into the open before stopping, a single flick of her near tarah telling me to stay behind her. I did, turning to one side to keep Mok just in view to my left, and letting me watch our right for anyone trying to approach.

"Information, as usual." Rerth called back.

"On my old friends? I thought you'd finally cleaned up the last nest of them."

"Not quite. There's a smuggling group that's causing me some problems."

The other woman didn't look impressed. "Smugglers. That's far

17

outside of my currents, Riah. That was contract work, and drudge level contract work at that."

"I know, but this group has an asset that I thought you might be familiar with." My packmate said. "A tall woman who claims to be of the Order of Velshen. Extremely dismissive of non-Trahcon. And her right hand is covered in-"

"-burns from the wrist down." Mok finished for her.

I swallowed, doing my best not to reach up to touch the burns on my own face. The painful legacy of my one encounter with the fallen priestess.

"You know her then?"

"Unfortunately." Mok replied. "Your pet's face. Her doing?"

Rerth glanced back at me, her expression telling me it was all right for me to speak.

"Yes." I said, raising my own voice to carry. "She... would have done more if she hadn't been stopped."

We were too far apart, but I thought she grunted from the way her head bobbed before she spoke. "Bitch is a sadist, that's for sure. She gets off on torturing aliens with sorcery. Must not have had you long or you wouldn't be speaking without pain. Or able to speak at all."

It was far too easy to imagine just what a full priestess could do with sorcery to a mere Human.

I swallowed again, saying nothing more.

My elder packmate saved me from having to. "We need to know who she is, why she would be working with smugglers, potential locations... the usual suite of information."

"I'm sure you do."

"Mok..." Rerth's voice carried a warning.

A hand waved dismissively. "You have nothing to threaten me with besides exile and death. One would be a mercy, and you don't have the authority to order my execution, so spare me the theatrics and allow me to consider my response in peace."

My packmate's tarah lowered... but she backed off. Physically backed off even; taking a few slow steps back to stand beside me.

"Um..." I whispered. "Is she wrong?"

"No." She scowled. "Well, I suppose I could send her to an even worse no-support colony, but that's not much of a downgrade from her perspective. She might even *like* the change of scenery since they've been here a while."

And exile to the Reaches would be an improvement compared to being stuck on a planet like this.

Speaking of... "Where are her packmates?"

"Watching us."

"I know. Where?"

Rerth sighed. "Use your eyes, huntress. The whole point of this is for you to learn, not to rely on me for all the answers."

I felt my face heat up in frustration and embarrassment. Another quick look around didn't let me see anything out of the ordinary, or as ordinary as a brutally-basic cottage with its own plot of crops could be.

Taking a deep breath, I forced myself to calm down and focus.

It took a minute, but I found someone in the field to our right. Two blue eyes were staring unnervingly at us from between the grains. Their face was mostly hidden, but I thought it was covered in dark tattoos.

As soon as I saw them, focused on them... they drew back, the plants rustling for a bare moment before going still.

I couldn't see any of the others, but that feeling of being watched didn't go away in the slightest.

A little half-step moved me closer to Rerth. It wouldn't have done anything to save me if the locals turned violent, but it made me feel a little

19

better. She'd at least be able to cover me if anyone started throwing sorcery around.

Eventually Mok spoke again. "We called her the Burned Hand. She never offers an actual name, and so far as I can remember, used different versions of that designation for each job that she took. My organization used her twice, and I know of at least one other contract she took on the side before she moved on to another region."

"What kind of jobs?"

"Contract killer. Prefers assassinating aliens, but if you pay her enough, she'll get rid of anyone." A note of warning actually entered her tone. "Rerth, she's not cheap. Any smuggling group that could call her in isn't a small one. You're dealing with a serial killer who far exceeds my own body count."

My packmate crossed her arms. "I need a lead, Mok."

"I just gave it to you. Follow the money, and follow the burnt corpses that she's left in her wake. She demands plenty of the former, and has left a great deal of the latter." Mok started to turn away, paused, and then called, "And know this. She's not alone. Some of the jobs she did were too clean for anyone without a very large pack."

"Just a pack? Or an organization?"

"I cannot say for certain. And..." Another hesitation, then she sailed on. "I spoke with her once. Observed her. My personal theory is that the Burned Hand is someone's pet thug. Someone who even she doesn't dare disobey, and who she runs back to after each contract. Someone who controls her. Directs her."

"Who?"

Mok didn't reply. She just vanished inside the broken looking shack, leaving us standing there.

I licked my lips once, "Do we follow her in? If she's met her, she has to know more."

"No." Rerth said at once. "She's said as much as she's going to. If we tried, her packmates would attack us, drive us away, and I'm not in the mood

20

to deal with that. Come on."

We departed, trudging back into the forest towards the shuttle. That feeling of being watched lingered for a little while, so I waited to say anything else until we'd been walking for at least five minutes.

Only when I was pretty sure no one was following us did I ask another question. "She didn't give us much, did she?"

"It was vague." Rerth agreed. "But this wasn't a wasted stop. We learned a few things that will help. List them."

"Her alias." I said at once, that one was easy. "And... she's pricey, and she doesn't like aliens. I already knew that last one."

A hand waved flatly. "Only her price was news among those three. I highly doubt that a tiny group like the Keres or their Human puppets could spare the cash for a professional that even Mok thought expensive. That means we're looking at a far broader conspiracy than I thought, which could help or hurt our efforts to find her. Try again."

There was only one other thing that Mok had said. "Does knowing that she's one of a few others really help? I don't think all of them would burn their hands."

"No, but you must consider the context." Rerth's tarah rose, flexing outwards once. "I told you that Mok was forced to live among some of the worst beings in the Empire. Yet even she considered the Burned Hand dangerous. Worrying. She sounded afraid of her, even here, and refused to give us more than a few drips of water."

"Oh..." I bit my lip for a moment, "Um, what does that mean for us when it comes to finding her?"

"It means that this could be far more dangerous than I thought." She admitted. "Far worse than just tracking down the loose ends of a smuggling group."

"Oh." I said again. "Does that change the plan?"

"No. We're still going home, and we're still pursuing this project. But we're going to be far more careful about what seas we sail on. The last thing I need is you being smug that I kept you out of a combat assignment only to put

21

you in just as much danger."

"I wouldn't be smug about it." I said at once.

"Liar."

"Maybe."

She snorted once, and we walked the rest of the way back to the shuttle in silence.

II

I'd been through Altair a few times before. Never for more than a few days at a time, the first of which had been in between my first and second assignments. It had been a badly needed rest period during the worst part of my career. A reminder that the Empire was more than just girls being taken from their childhood packs, more than supremacist bastards attacking her for not being like them.

It was where I'd met Huvu and her pack, before we'd rotated to a quieter colony. When they'd learned what had happened to me, they'd taken me out drinking, partying, to theaters, to concerts...

Altair was the most diverse of the regional capitals, and prided itself on having something for everyone. Trahcon, Naule, Human, Meshicon, Regnon, Chezzek, Vekki... few here cared what species you were. They didn't care if you were a native citizen or an immigrant from the Reaches.

No matter who you were, or where you were from, there was somewhere on Altair ready to accept you.

I'd loved it then, and I loved it now.

"Ashahn's blood." I groaned as we walked down the streets of the capital city, the riotous color all around as comfortable as a warm blanket. "I missed this place. How long has it been since you've been here?"

For once Rerth was in a good mood as well, her tarah uplifted in amusement. "Ten months. It's good to be home, and better to see the rest of the pack again. Still, don't get too excited. We aren't staying."

That drew another groan from me, but a far less happy one. "I know. Do we at least have a few days to rest?"

"That will depend on how well the others did with their research while we were acting as bait in the shallows." She replied. "Speaking of the others, Holde!"

I followed her gaze to an outdoor cafe, where two men in gray Intelligence uniforms were playing something on a fold-out board. Drinks and

23

snacks were scattered to either side of the little pieces, and a waiter had apparently just dropped off some more.

"Rerth!" The Trahcon of the pair bounced to his feet the moment her shout reached him. He vaulted the little railing surrounding the tables in an extremely athletic move, and met my superior officer midstride.

Both were laughing as they hugged, Rerth picking him up off his feet for a brief moment before letting him back down.

Holde'riah was, to my surprise, exactly as handsome as Rerth had bragged.

He was quite shorter than her, maybe a bit over five feet. Bright blue eyes were accented by tattoos high on his cheeks, drawing even more attention to them. Below the neck he had the slender, toned frame of a man who put effort into his build, which pared very well with delicate features and wonderfully long tarah.

The two of them kissed for a long moment before breaking apart, their tarah and expressions utterly content.

"Oh good." Another man's voice reminded me of his presence; the Naulian officer silently appearing at my side. "I'll finally have someone to commiserate with when they do that."

Jet of Clan Roll was a bit taller than Korokek, which still left him far shorter than anyone else present. Unlike the man who'd helped me in the past, Jet had striking red-orange fur, but sadly shared the flat features and sunken eyes of every other member of the species I'd met.

"Jet." One of his upper hands rose, "You must be Ashe."

"I am." I took it, shaking it once. "She's told me a little about you."

He looked amused at that, "Did she? Must have been in a good mood, normally she doesn't tell anyone anything if she can help it. What did she say?"

"You set the record at Abantia's Intelligence Academy for clearing every exam." I replied, honestly impressed with what he'd done. "You did a three year course in just under two, and excelled in practically all of the classes you could take."

24

"Not quite all of them. I'm useless with a gun, passed those tests by one percent." His sharp grin was pleased all the same, and I didn't feel worried about chuckling.

"Um, did she tell you about me?" I couldn't help but ask.

"Yup. She says you're either going to break my record for getting into and out of the Academy, or you're going to spend the rest of your life miserable on a penal colony."

Well, that first part was flattering even if the second part was worrying. I wasn't really sure how to respond, so I went with my familiar strategy of saying nothing in that situation. Thankfully I was saved by Rerth and Holde breaking apart just about then, the two of them turning their attention to us.

"Good, you're all introduced then." Rerth said, "We'll have a proper reunion later. Duties first."

"As always." Jet drawled, already turning to amble back to the table. "You're a workaholic, Rerth."

"Tough talk from an overachiever." She retorted. "Come on. And get that game cleaned up, we all know that Holde was cheating anyway."

Her bond put a hand to his chest, "I would never cheat at something as trivial as a board game."

"Liar." Rerth and Jet said it so perfectly in unison that I couldn't stop a giggle.

I followed our eldest as she herded everyone back to the table the men had been sitting at, the two of them quickly cleaning up everything while we ordered glasses of water for ourselves.

Honestly I expected the banter to go on for a bit longer, this was the pack's first reunion in most of a year... but instead everyone just looked serious and stayed silent.

I could only sit quietly between Rerth and Jet, feeling out of place in my mottled blue-gray conscript's uniform.

25

When it had just been Rerth and I it hadn't seemed so strange, but now that I was with the others...

"Right." Rerth spoke after the waiter brought over two glasses of water. "Holde, Jet. What is our status?"

Holde leaned back in his seat, negligently flicking a hand. "We fished around for as much as we could on the smuggling ring. The trail goes cold after Dys'becix. We can be sure it ends in the Near Reaches, but none of the Agents operating in that region have gotten back to us yet."

That drew a scowl to her features. "It is hardly difficult to do a quick search on farming automations."

"True." He chuckled. "I think they want us to owe them a few favors, and are keeping their anchors settled until you call them personally. They're using the usual excuses of their projects having priority, lack of personnel, and so on."

Her scowl deepened, both tarah lifting in anger before she got them back under control. "Useless driftwood. Were you able to find anything from here?"

One of his hands rose, bobbing left to right a little. "Maybe. After you messaged us about the Burned Hand we tried to explore anything like the attack on our new packmate, with... well, mixed results."

I started to reach up to my face, only barely forcing myself to take a sip of water instead of touching the scars. "Um, there's... been other attacks like mine?"

"Sort of." He glanced to Jet, who folded all four of his arms across his chest before speaking.

"I've got seven different cold cases in the Empire pertaining to aliens being tortured with fire before being killed." His low voice got a bit rougher. "Naule, Humans, Meshicon, and even a couple of Chezzek. Several match the attack on you directly, Ashe. The victims were tied to a chair in an isolated area, and were probably toyed with for a while."

I swallowed more water, "...no one caught the attacker?"

Jet shook his head, orange fur rippling. "Cold cases, like I said. They were too good to leave evidence, and the attacks were in the Altair, the Stormshroud, and the Shield regions. Nothing connecting the victims, no reason for the local authorities to even think it might be a cross-imperial killer."

Rerth pursed her lips for a moment. "Ashahn's blood. How far back?"

"About forty years from the first one I found." He replied. "The crime reports didn't give us much at all, but there was a comment in one of them about the precision of the sorcery used. The local investigator thought the killer had to have been a high level Disciple of Velshen. A *very* high level one."

Holde bobbed his head, "We added Temples of Velshen to our search parameters alongside automation imports, but still didn't get anything. Then we got smart and remembered we were dealing with smugglers, so we looked for colonics that started to decrease or cancel their legal automation trade after the factories on Oshflara got started."

"And you found something?" Rerth pressed.

"We did." Jet's grin was full of sharp teeth. "The Group of Five used to have an Imperial Exception for farming automations, but they let it lapse five years ago. Even better, they have a significant Trahcon population who are supposed to be the most devout in the Near Reaches."

I felt myself straightening a bit, the wariness fading into excitement. "So we have a lead?"

"We do." Holde gave me a grin that I couldn't help but return. "Jet? The map?"

We all quickly pulled our glasses out of the way, the men doing the same with their snacks. As soon as the table was clear Jet pulled a small projector from a pocket and settled it in the center. After a quick link to his wrist-comp it hummed to life, displaying the Near Reach's mess of independent colonies, outposts, slivers of Imperial control, and the Ascendancy.

Well, the increasingly shattered fragments of the Ascendancy at least.

"Zooming in on our target sector..." The image flickered, then snapped in to a much smaller section of space well outside of the Imperial

27

borders. "...there, good. This is sector Trinity-Four, including the Group of Five."

Rerth leaned in, tilting her head a little as we all looked over the map. "Interesting. Jet, give the little shark an overview of the area."

He glanced at me, nodded once, then brought a hand up to point out the differing stars as he spoke. "We've got several Ark Fleet mining operations right through here, then two of ours that support Trinity nearby. There's an Ark Fleet farm-world here, and a collection of Thondian exiles have settled right next to them."

"Please tell me we aren't going that way." I said, more to Rerth than him.

There was a quiet snort from my elder. "Don't worry. We'll be avoiding *that* blood feud as long as we can, and the Ark Fleet in general. There's plenty of Agents already dealing with the operations those exiles like to run, and they wouldn't appreciate us sailing into their waters."

Good. The very notion of meeting Humans from the Ark Fleet made me shudder. From everything I knew, they made even the most extreme members of my species within the Empire look positively restrained when it came to views on people like me.

"That leaves this collection." Jet resumed, his hand slowly moving in an arc to cover each of them. "They're supposedly trying to make their own little nation out there called the Group of Five, and that's where our only lead on both the smuggling operation and your mystery attacker is."

I'd never heard of them, but then I'd never studied the Reaches much. "Who lives there?"

"It's a mixed Thondian-Trahcon group." One of his fingers tapped one system, then another. "These two are Trahcon majority, the other three are Thondian, but all five are mixed-species. They're stable enough that the Empire has an arrangement with them. So long as the Group of Five doesn't allow pirates to operate from their territory, the fleets out of Trinity will protect them from outside attack."

"Meaning," Holde provided, "We stopped the Ascendancy from invading a few times, something the local government is supposed to be pretty thankful for."

28

"Oh. So do we just go there officially then?" I asked.

"No." Rerth said at once. "I'm sure that we could go in as ourselves, but it is wiser not to. Our usual cover as merchants will do, I think, but we're still going to have to be circumspect in our operations."

"Meaning?" I asked.

Jet glanced at me, "She staying on the ship?"

Rerth nodded, "You both will be, at least at first. If I recall correctly, the locals don't have fond memories of the Unified Clans, and the last thing we'll need is more attention. We'll set up a real time network so the two of you can listen to our conversations and provide analysis."

That didn't sound nearly as fun as being able to go out and do actual investigations with them... but then, I'd never had to deal with people from outside of the Empire before. Or Thondians in general.

It would probably be better to observe at a distance first, to see how Rerth and Holde handled things. A nice easy mission to break me into the pack's routines. Plus it would get me a chance to know Jet, work with him on a one-on-one basis.

That would be good. I was more than ready to work with someone besides Rerth for a while. As much as I respected her skills, her rank, and her age... well. She was still Rerth. The person who'd been controlling my career from the start, and not doing a very good job of it.

I liked her, yet I didn't at the same time. Working with Jet would definitely be a nice change for a little while.

"I get to sit around while you two do all the work?" The man in question drawled, "And my only job will be to teach Ashe how to handle a communications suite? I'm not hearing a downside for me."

Holde snorted. "Just remember we'll shave you if you try to make her do all of the work."

"What about *most* of the work?"

"Acceptable." Rerth replied.

29

I glared at them all, my acceptance of my task fading quickly. The expression only made Jet smirk and the other two quiver their tarah in amusement. "Really?"

"Really. Are you complaining, Huntress?"

"...no, sir." She reached over, hand patting my head before ruffling my fur. "Hey!"

"Are you complaining, Huntress?"

"About my task? No, sir. About you yanking my fur out of the tie?" Getting my own hands up, I yanked the little band the rest of the way off and started trying to gather the dark strands behind my neck again. "*Yes*, sir."

Rerth grinned. "Good. Personal complaints are fine, duty ones are not."

"I know." I grumbled, shaking my head a little to make sure my fur was secure. When it merely tickled my neck a little, I called it good. "You don't have to repeat *everything* to me."

"Perhaps, but you're a stubborn little shark. Listen to Jet, do what he says."

"Yes, sir. Where are we going first?"

Rerth turned back to the map. "That is the question. Jet, which one had the most sightings of priests?"

"Rurasflara." He replied at once. "It's got the second largest Trahcon population. Aiming for the Burned Hand first?"

"She'll be our priority, but we won't be ignoring the smuggling completely. I want maps, local data, our usual assignment package for all of the colones in the Group. You're on that duty." When Jet nodded, she glanced to Holde. "Your usual as well."

He nodded, "What do you want to equip Ashe with?"

"Conscript standard, nothing she hasn't used before."

Oh. He was going to be getting our arms and armor then. I could assume that was a just in case thing, and I rather hoped that we didn't end up needing it. I was still having trouble sleeping some nights. The last thing I wanted was to end up in another firefight, even one I was properly equipped for.

Which was... not very Imperial of me. Or very Trahcon of me.

Too Human...

I shook off the unpleasant thought, focusing on Rerth telling us what she'd be doing. "...for all of the packing. Ashe? You're with me still. We need to arrange a ship, and I want you to learn just how many forms that's going to take."

Forms. I sighed, nodding obediently as we all stood up. "Yes sir. Um, are we going to have any down time at all?"

"It will depend on if there is a ship ready for us or not."

I sighed, and wasn't at all surprised when we boarded a shuttle for orbit just six hours later.

III

My arms burned as I pulled myself up once again, trying to keep pace with Rerth.

Sweat ran down my elder's face, her lips set in a grin as we both let ourselves slowly drop back down. A silent three count hanging from the support bar later and we both labored through yet another pull-up.

After five more she finally let go, dropping back to the hangar's deck with a huff. "Done."

I immediately let go as well, staggering when I landed. I think Rerth tried to laugh at me, but she was so out of breath it was more of an exhausted wheeze.

We both shuffled over to the water bottles we'd left on top of the shuttle fueling station, guzzling them down without a word. It was warm, unflavored, and I couldn't have cared less.

"Ashahn's blood." I finally managed to gasp. "I'm not going to try and keep up with you again."

Rerth made a choking noise, shaking her head as she tossed her empty bottle aside. "That's my line. I'm getting too old to try and keep pace with huntresses."

I shook my head before downing the rest of my own water. "...you say that like you aren't one of the most built women I've ever met."

There was another huff, but her tarah flicked to show her pleasure at the compliment. "Flattery won't get you out of your training routine and you know it. And before you say it, yes, I know you're annoyed that Jet is slacking and I'm not letting you do the same."

"I'm not annoyed."

"Jealous, then."

My arms rose above my head as I stretched them out, a quiet groan escaping ahead of my words. "I'm not jealous either. I just... wish he had to do more physical training."

Rerth's lips twitched, arms mimicking my stretch. "You mean you want to see him suffer for his less than tactful commentary about your scars this morning."

Even more heat rose to my face. "...maybe. Is he always like that?"

"Generally."

"And... it never annoys you?"

"Only when he manages to spectacularly ruin a delicate situation." A grimace made me think she was remembering such an occasion. "One of the many reasons we don't allow him to engage in anything requiring diplomacy anymore."

I managed to show some tact myself by not pointing out that Rerth could be just as uncomfortably blunt. "Am I going to be getting training on that too? Diplomacy, I mean."

She shrugged as best she could with her arms held nearly straight up, "Later. That's far less of a priority right now, compared to everything else you need to work on."

And there was a *lot* to work on. We'd been aboard the *Posa'vilt* for less than a day, and nearly every minute of my time was already planned for.

Physical training with Rerth, first thing every morning. Then, the moment I was cleaned up, I would be joining Jet in a conference room, learning how to both read and file Intelligence reports. I didn't get free time after dinner either; that was Holde's allotted time with me, where I'd apparently be learning proper investigation procedures, organizational rules, and so on.

In other words Rerth had moved from controlling my life from a distance to directly guiding every moment of it.

I... appreciated the fact that I was going to start learning proper investigative procedures. There would be actual, real Intelligence work for me to do in the near future.

33

I just kind of wished I'd... I don't even know. Hadn't screwed up so badly that I didn't have a choice in any of this. Ruined my relationship with a pack that had actually welcomed me.

I missed them. I missed Jal, I missed Ruru.

I... missed Fyth.

I shook my head, letting my arms fall so that I could stretch them laterally. And change the subject before I swam through my past mistakes for too long.

"Have you ever been this far outside of the Empire before?" I asked.

"A few times, but never as far out as Trinity." Rerth replied, keeping her own arms up for a few moments before lowering them. "The Near Reaches are anything but flat seas, so I'm not expecting prior experience to tell us much about what we'll see."

I bit my lip for a moment before asking, "What about meeting Thondians?"

Both of her tarah lowered as if she'd just smelled something unpleasant. "I'm hoping we don't have much to do with their kind."

"That bad?"

"I'm trained not to generalize an entire species." She paused, then growled, "That being said, every single one of those dead fish I've ever met has been a misogynistic, bloodline worshiping, authority-obsessed *ass* who was agonizing to interact with."

I blinked. "They're that bad?"

"Imagine the most supremacist Naulian you've ever met, who is convinced his clan is the greatest pack in the known universe, and thinks he has every right to dictate orders to you. All because he is obviously the most dangerous fish in the river, where you are a mere female who shouldn't even be opening her mouth in his glorious presence."

"Oh." I cleared my throat. That was certainly a vivid description. It made me wonder just how bad her prior experiences had been to draw that kind of reaction.

Rerth could be blunt, but she was usually a little more under control than that. "Um, so they're even worse than what I've seen in films?"

She took a long, calming breath before replying. "I'm sure there are plenty that aren't nearly that bad. But given the nature of the work we do? I haven't exactly had a chance to meet with a civilian pack living a comfortably boring life."

Which was a pretty good point, actually. "Because you mostly investigate smuggling and crime, you end up dealing with smugglers and criminals."

"Exactly. Not exactly ideal representatives of society." Her left tarah flicked out once. "If we have to deal with them, you can make up your own opinion. Try not to let mine taint yours."

I hadn't exactly been eager to meet the tallest of the five standard species, and I was even less so now.

"I'll do my best." I said. "Do the Academies have classes on alien culture?"

"Yes, both external and internal." Rerth nodded, turning a little and waving a hand. "Grab the water bottles, we can talk on our way to the showers."

I quickly did as ordered, scooping up the plastic and falling into step as we left the ship's hangar.

When we'd gone to arrange for our passage, I'd honestly expected us to be given some kind of pinnace. Maybe an FTL capable yacht if we were lucky.

Instead, after being told what the mission was, the Intelligence Transit Group had assigned us to a bloody *warship*. Well, an old Comet-type vessel; the smallest, fastest type of armed ship, but the key word there was 'armed'. It was the first time I'd set foot on one, and I was... kind of enjoying the novelty of it.

Especially since none of the crew seemed to care about my species, at least so far.

I was definitely enjoying that part, and hoping it continued.

"Most academies will make you take several courses on internal diplomacy, particularly the integration of alien cultures into the Imperial system." Rerth told me as we left the hangar, turning down a narrow corridor to make for the lifts. "If that's actually a field you want to focus on, then you'll probably want to apply at Gathahn."

"They specialize in internal work?" I guessed.

She nodded, "Most of the internal security types come from there, but I don't think that's going to be what you favor."

I wasn't really sure. "What kind of internal security?"

"How do you feel about infiltrating possible rebellious groups? Getting to know them, sympathizing with them, meeting their packs, their blood-children." She gave a knowing look when I grimaced. "Didn't think so. If you survive the next three years following orders, I was going to recommend you go to Zulflara."

That nearly made me stop moving in shock, and I had to skip a step to catch up. "The Homeworld? I don't have nearly enough honors to even try for that Academy!"

"You might, and you lose nothing by applying." Slowing to a stop when we arrived at the hall's end, she tapped the lift controls to summon one. "Their courses are more... aggressive than many of the others. I think that would suit you."

"...aggressive how?" I asked. "I'm not, um, really an aggressive person."

That earned me an amused little snort. "No, you're not. I mean in terms of aggressive investigations. The kind where you're on a time limit until the waves strike the beach, where speed and tenacity is key."

"...you really think I'd be suited for that?"

The quiet chime of our lift arriving kept her from replying, at least until we'd both stepped inside and I pressed the button for the next level up.

"Yes. You managed to botch both of your last assignments thanks to

36

your inability to let things go," I had to fight back another wince, "But in both cases you did quite a lot of work in a fairly short period of time. Extremely short periods of time if I only count the hours spent investigating compared to the time you spent on your duties. Even better, you did most of it alone, with minimal support from your packs."

"Oh." I said quietly.

"Do you think I'm wrong, little shark?"

"Um... I just never really thought of it like that." I admitted. "It always seemed like my investigations took a lot longer than I thought they would."

Her head dipped, "A combination of how little time you actually had to work on them, and probably your species. Humans always seem impatient to me."

I pouted. "I'm very patient."

"At times." But her normally commanding voice had a teasing lilt to it. "You assuredly aren't in the mornings when you're dealing with your fur."

Ugh. She had to bring that up. Just mentioning it made me remember that it was still growing, and tickling the back of my neck where I'd roughly tied it to keep it out of my face.

"You're sure I just can't shave it off again?" I tried not to whine, but I was really tired of having to wash it. And tie it. And tie it again when it mysteriously escaped the band. "It's so annoying."

Another chime sounded, heralding our arrival on the next deck. Rerth rolled her eyes at my complaints, tones still amused as we got moving again. "No. If we run into a circumstance where you have to leave the ship, having the fur will let you blend in. Human females outside of the Empire don't shave it so far as I know."

I had no idea why not. I could deal with the fur on the rest of my body, it was easy to clean and was covered by my clothing anyway, but the stuff on my scalp just got so annoyingly *long*. It was so much easier just to keep it shaved. The fact that it made me look a little less alien was just a pleasant bonus.

Rerth nudged me as we approached the small restrooms. "Get our clothes so we can shower, and be quick about it. You've got a lot to learn in a very short time."

When I nodded, she gave me a gentle pat on the shoulder before vanishing into the showers.

She may have also removed her shirt in the process of walking through the doorway, exposing her ridiculously muscled back in the process. I may have also been a little too invested on enjoying that particular horizon before forcing myself to keep walking, which was probably why I didn't hear anything as I approached the turn to our cabins.

I had just begun to move around the corner when a young man in a conscript's uniform came around from the other direction. There wasn't even enough time to brace myself before his head rammed into my shoulder, both of us recoiling in surprise.

"Sorry, sir! I wasn't-oh!" He blinked rapidly, long tarah rising as he got a better look at me."Oh. You're a Rifle-Experienced... wait, that's an Agent's marker, isn't it?"

"It's all right," I cut in before he could keep going. "Rifle-Experienced, assigned to Intelligence."

Bright green eyes blinked one more time, "Um, so am I? Assigned to intelligence, I mean. I'm only a Conscript."

"Directly." I amended. "I'm in Agent Rerth'riah's pack."

"Ahhh. I don't have to salute you, do I?"

It was my turn to blink. "I don't think so? Neither one of us is an officer. I'm still a conscript, I'm just in a separate chain of command now."

"Oh, good." His tarah abruptly pressed against the sides of his head. "Sorry for running into you. I'm Noro'thun."

"Ashe'lori." I replied, taking another step back to get a better look at him.

He was... well, pretty cute. A full head shorter than me, with the most delicate tarah I'd ever seen on a man. Very slender features went with an

38

equally thin body that made me think he hadn't been a conscript for very long.

The fact that he hadn't even graduated to Rifle yet, and didn't have merits on either of his shoulders, could have told me that as well.

Thun seemed to be looking me over in turn, and his nerves seemed to come back when he eyed the number of honors on my uniform.

"How long in?"I asked.

"Two years. You?"

"Six."

His nerves seemed to come back at once. "You did all of that in six?"

Lifting a hand, I coughed into my fist. "Um, Humans don't live as long. That's half my entire conscription period, so they fast-track us for both honors and demerits."

"Oh. Oh good." The young man looked entirely too relieved. "Ashahn's blood, I thought I'd already wasted my career or something."

I had to smother a smile. "This is your first major assignment, isn't it?"

Thun slumped a little, clearly embarrassed. "Yeah. We just finished our basic training last year, and were assigned here after. This is the first time we're even leaving orbit. I was just on my way to get ready for faster-than-light."

"You won't even notice." I assured him, "Not unless your cabin has a window... and I don't think any of them do, since, you know. Warship."

"Oh." He said again, blinking once. "You've traveled a lot, then?"

I was about to reply when the bathroom door slid open, revealing an annoyed looking Rerth wearing nothing more than sweat-soaked shorts.

"Ashe." She growled. "Stop chatting and retrieve our clothes. Conscript? Return to your duties."

"S-sir!" Thun stammered, managing a quick salute before darting past me.

When Rerth merely continued to glare at me, I sighed and gave her my best drill-ground salute. "Sir. Be right back."

"Good." Her eyes flicked to the retreating back of the young man, then returned to me. "I know it's been seven months, but you're better than an unblooded conscript. At least try to seduce an officer if you need sex."

My cheeks burned. "I wasn't flirting with him!"

The hum told me she didn't believe that. "You're a Huntress, and like I said. Seven months. I know better."

"I'm not *that* desperate Rerth!"

She didn't look any more convinced. "My clothes will be here in two minutes, or you'll be doing another exercise regimen after Holde is done with you tonight."

Throttling the urge to groan, I saluted one more time, then marched off to retrieve our things.

IV

The advantage of the *Posa'vilt* being our ship? It got us to Rurasflara nearly a month faster than I'd expected. That was one less month of drowning in information as my new pack tried to teach me an entire year's worth of Academy courses over a five week period.

The disadvantage of having the *Posa'vilt* as our ship? As small as it was, it was still a warship. It wasn't designed to enter atmosphere, especially when it was broadcasting the identity of a merchant barge.

So instead of getting to relax in a comfortable cabin or the ship's sole conference room, Jet and I were setup inside of one of the cargo shuttles. Holde and Rerth had piloted us down to a small landing field, then sealed us inside as they headed out to investigate.

"They've paid off the locals." Jet reported from his seat behind me, "Just the routine questions for visiting merchants. Any luck on a hotel?"

"I think so." I leaned back in my own chair, trying to keep track of everything in front of me.

I wasn't used to having more than a single screen on my console, and the advanced suite had *four*. The two on my right were smaller, showing live feeds from the cameras that my packmates were wearing, while the one on my left had a map of the local colony up.

That gave me the one in front of me to actually look up information, which would have been easier if motion from the video feeds didn't keep distracting me.

"Signal it." Jet prodded.

Right. A quick tap of my thumb opened a channel, "Best cost per night for the service is Grassland Suites. Sounds like the kind of place two merchants on a budget would want to stay at. It's two blocks in from the outskirts, there should be a bridge connecting to the landing fields."

"I see two bridges." Rerth's murmur was perfectly audible. *"Which one?"*

I glanced at the map. "Right side, closer to you."

"Very well. Update when you have potentials."

Jet spoke for us, "Confirmed, I've got one already, we'll have more by the time you make your room."

A quiet click of her tongue served to end the conversation, and I quickly stopped transmitting. "Potentials are investigative targets, right?"

"Mostly. We use it to mean any person or event that we have reason to think might be related to our project, but that we don't have direct evidence on."

I nodded even though he couldn't see it. "Right, and our potentials here are the local temples and any big names in farm equipment."

"Exactly. That gives us a respectable list of targets, but I want you to start with House ul Tradok. Either they own most of the farmlands to the south, or they picked a very strange place to build an estate. Check which it is."

Not the most complicated research, but at least he was starting me on something I could definitely handle. "Starting with the smuggling then?"

"Most temples don't give out much information on the DataNet. It'll be on Rerth and Holde to handle those investigations directly. See what you can find on that House, and we'll surge on from there."

"On it."

The local DataNet was surprisingly quick for such a small world in the middle of nowhere. Maybe this Group of Five was actually decent about paying for infrastructure.

I shook my head and focused as the House's information page came up. They were apparently invested enough to have a rather professional looking page

"Houses are like clans, right?"

"More or less." He replied. "A lot more structured, but that's everything Thondian. There should be a... Tararth, I think that's what they call their leader."

It was pretty easy to find him; he had his biography right on the starting link. "Vol ul Tradok. Elder, says he's a fourth generation settler here... huh. They openly brag that he bought out nearly all of the farmlands on the colony and consolidated it under his control."

Jet grunted. "It means he's got power because he controls a large section of the food supply."

I got what he wanted me to look into. Leaving Tradok's personal information, I started jumping through the various pages to see if there was any mention of Imperial automations.

Thankfully they did have a section dedicated to what kinds of food products they grew, what kind of herd beasts they raised, and even several pages on some kind of fish-farm they'd created farther outside of the main colonial city.

"...nothing on automations." I said after a few minutes of checking, reading, and then re-checking. "A lot of oblique references to streamlining food production. Plenty of charts on how Rurasflara went from needing to import to actually exporting agricultural product after they started buying up the smaller farms... nothing direct."

Creaking sounded as he spun his chair around. A moment later his head was poking over my shoulder as he stared at the same information I was reading. "You're sure?"

"Yeah." I thought furiously on the steps of investigation that Holde had been running me through.

My first attempt had turned up no direct evidence, so we had to look for something more indirect. If there wasn't anything obvious on the automations themselves... then what about the things that the large machines needed to operate? I'd seen plenty of their storage units on Oshflara, and plenty of farms laid out to take advantage of how they operated.

"Maybe... we can check the orbital maps for the kind of housing they need?"

"Regular farm equipment needs that too." He countered.

43

I nodded, "Yeah, but from what I've seen they don't need nearly as many people as a small-time farm. They just need enough mechanics to keep them running. That means they probably won't have houses nearby, just road access or parking for aircars. At least, that's what it was like on Oshflara, so it'd probably be similar here."

One of his hands patted my shoulder. "Good thought. I'll check for a central hub in their territory, then I'll double-check your work. I want you to move on. Check local car dealerships for Imperial models. If they're smuggling automations, they might be branching out. Might give us an excuse to call in an Agent from Trinity to check their records for us."

That search was just as fast, and just as easy.

"Are we seriously the first people to investigate this planet?" I asked a few minutes later. "We can't be the first ones to notice that the only cars they're selling are all from the Empire. I can't even find one model that's local, or not obviously produced by a Delne'lir."

Jet's voice turned dry. "The Intelligence branches out here aren't exactly well staffed. Or funded. Rerth might be the first Agent to ever actually visit this specific colony."

I scowled at my screen. "Someone out of Trinity should have noticed then. You said yesterday that sometimes they stop over and take leave here. At least one of them should have been paying attention."

His chuckle was grim and not at all humorous, his chair turning again so he could glance over my findings. "You're adorably confident in people's ability to spot things, Ashe. Most people don't question little things like why the hover-car models in a far-flung polity are the same as the ones back home. I doubt more than a few would even find it odd, and the rest would just assume they're purchased legally."

Before I could reply, he went on, one hand reaching out to tap the dealership on my screen. "Which they very well might be. Plenty of places out here do legal business, buy exports from the right merchant houses on Shaidan and Alum. We'll need to do more research to figure out if this is all above the surface or not."

My scowl didn't ease up. "...I'd have noticed that it was odd."

44

"And probably started an interstellar war in the process." He said cheerfully, either ignoring or not caring at the way my shoulders hunched at the comment.

A month with him had sadly revealed that my first impression of my new packmate had been a direct hit. He had no concern at all for what he said, and as a result could praise me in one breath and bring up a horribly painful memory the next.

Politely asking him to, well, *not* do that hadn't resulted in any particular change. The fact that he was the same way with Rerth and Holde meant he wasn't doing it specifically to me, but... well, that didn't make it any less fun to deal with. A month of daily training with him hadn't been *bad*, but I hadn't been looking forwards to our first mission nearly as much by the time we'd arrived.

The next few years seemed like they could end up being far more wearying than I'd hoped they would be.

I didn't even notice he'd returned to his own screens until he spoke again, "Sending a map screenshot and a few images to your console, confirm that looks like your last assignment."

Shaking myself, I focused on what was in front of me. I wasn't used to seeing farmlands from a sky-view, but after a few moments I thought I could just about make sense of it. There was definitely a large central barn in the dead center of a massive circle of crops, with neat dividing lines like the spokes on a wheel.

The second set of pictures was easier; apparently photographs from an immigration page, showing how excited various beings were to have moved here.

"Not sure on the map." I admitted after a moment. "But those automations in the background are definitely Delne'lir Noroth models. Images two through... five. I don't recognize what's in six."

"You're sure?"

"I helped deliver parts of them on a weekly basis for a few months." I reminded him, my own voice dry. "I'm pretty sure."

"Good. Then this may not be a wasted first port to pull into. Run a

45

few searches on local employers, see if you can spot any production to be safe while I verify something. There should be a few job-hunting nets that you can use."

The local network didn't quite have that level of detail, sadly. Or the local government didn't feel like making that kind of information public. Twenty minutes of wasted effort trying to find anything had me abandon that course, and instead I went back to looking into the distributors themselves.

A slower, more careful check still left me confident.

"No local production factories that I can find, and I double-checked that the stores only offer Imperial and Alum models." I reported when Jet asked for an update. "Prices for aircars and hovercraft seem high from what I know, but groundcars are pretty cheap. I think."

"We'll check later. Send me your list of the dealers, I'll report it in."

That was as simple as copying names and addresses into our shared text chat, and within a minute he had the locations of all five major car distributors in the local city.

"There's probably more in the smaller cities and villages. Want me to check that as well?"

"Make a note for now, we'll have time later. Going live again." He paused just long enough for me to copy him and open my microphone before speaking, "Good news. We've got one Thondian House and... five local dealerships for you to search for smuggled goods."

"*Estimated value?*"

"I'd put good money on the House. They've tripled their wealth in the last few decades, and Ashe confirms Oshflara-produced automations in a few pictures that I found. Since that model was never approved for export, I'd say we've found at least one harbor our smugglers have been using."

I glanced at Rerth's camera feed to see her already in a small hotel room. She and Holde were both prowling around it, checking for listening devices or cameras I thought.

Holde looked even more attractive than usual in casual clothing, something I was doing my best to block out. I was *not* going to give Rerth the

46

satisfaction of being right about all of the teasing she'd started giving me during this trip.

"Ground and aircar sales look viable as well." Jet went on. "Harder to tell if they're legal imports, but Ashe hasn't been able to find any local production being offered. Going to start her on the outlying settlements soon, unless you want us to switch to looking into the Temples."

Rerth was silent for a moment, then her feed swung around. She paced over to the room's small window, staring out at the quiet city stretching away from the hotel.

"...focus on the House. I want an infiltration plan as soon as possible. Our cover as merchants will only last until someone realizes the Posa'vilt's engines are throwing off way too much power. The moment they swing a telescope around to get a good look at it, we'll have complications."

"All right, we'll see what we can find. You have a plan?"

"We're going to eat, then rest. After that we'll do a casual swim and see if there's anything obvious. Save contact for emergencies, otherwise we'll do a full conference tonight."

"Got it." Jet closed the channel before groaning. "Want to know the downsides of getting a quick hit?"

"No rest?" I guessed.

"Nope." He confirmed. "Don't expect sleep anytime early today. Still, I need to stop staring at these screens for a bit. You?"

My empty stomach rather agreed, even if it had the courtesy to remain quiet. "Lunch and tea?"

He heaved himself out of his chair, "You had me at lunch."

47

V

Living inside of a shuttle wasn't exactly pleasant. Especially when most of the interior was taken up by our consoles, communications equipment, and storage lockers. Our 'beds' were sleeping rolls stretched out over the hard deck. The bathroom was both cramped and lacked even a basic shower, and our meals were limited to military rations we heated up.

Jet claimed he'd done missions like this before... but he'd done them alone, and he wasn't used to having company.

My little habit of talking to myself had gotten on his nerves by the second day, just as his constant fidgeting in his sleep had started to get on mine. By the fifth day the casual chats we'd managed in the first few were gone. We replaced them with silence and a constant focus on spearing all of the data that Rerth needed.

On day eight, she finally decided that getting anything from the Temples would take too long. So instead they would be doing a break-in of House Tradok's estate to get what we could from the best lead on the Oshflara smugglers we had.

The fact that she wanted Jet with to do field-hacking brought as much relief that I'd finally have some time alone as it brought jealousy that he got to leave and I didn't. Both feelings were probably more Human than I'd have normally liked... but for once I couldn't bring myself to be upset about it.

It was just too nice to shove his chair out of the way, loosen my uniform, open the fans on full blast, and not get told to shut up whenever I accidentally spoke my thoughts out loud.

"Or when I do it on purpose." I hummed, typing away as I kept live notes of what I was watching on the video feeds. "They're really taking their time."

Rerth's camera was perfectly steady. That gave me a good view of the mansion in the distance, its exterior lights just enough to make it visible against the night's sky. In contrast, Holde's camera was bobbing and weaving as he completed a second circle to make sure they hadn't missed any sentries or camera locations.

48

"*Ashe.*" The man in question murmured across comms. "*Confirm markers.*"

A slight turn let me check the map of the estate; complete with little yellow crosses that I'd been adding each time he'd found one. I counted them all to double-check, then gave him the results. "There are nine exterior cameras, five of them on the city side, only four are covering the rest of the exterior wall."

"*Good. Rerth? Ready.*"

She replied at once, "*Ashe, confirm you have the security channel open.*"

In response I leaned to one side, then turned up the volume on the line that Jet had cut us into before he'd left. A deep Thondian voice promptly began speaking in tones that sounded like gravel breaking, the translation running across my central screen.

"*...team to the corner of Fifth and Bluestone, more drunks for pickup.*"

"It's up, translation is running." I quickly turned it back down before the reply could drown my voice. "They're still cleaning up drunks downtown."

"*Good. Keep your eyes on that harbor. Jet? Up. We're moving in.*"

My heart felt like it skipped a few beats as a real Intelligence operation began to unfurl in front of me. The camera views to my right began to shift as my packmates advanced. Rerth's stayed perfectly focused on the mansion directly ahead, while Holde's swiveled as he looked for anyone who might spot them.

"*Right here, opposite the gardens.*" Rerth whispered when they reached a bend in the wall. "*Jet, settle. Ready?*"

His voice was anything but eager, one hand adjusting something on his armor. "*Shields off, ready.*"

Rerth and Holde both turned to face him, which was more than a little strange to see on the screens, and then... Jet began to quickly rise off the ground. The two Guides levitated him up until he could grasp the top of the wall, then our smallest member heaved himself over.

Apparently not needing to speak, Holde braced himself before Rerth made a sharp gesture to float him up as well. She began backing up the moment he was out of sight, turning to run when she was a few yards back.

"Moving to cover. Constant updates."

"Moving through the garden." Holde replied at once. *"Heading for the secondary entrance. Any news, Ashe?"*

I winced and quickly got my attention back to the security channel. The running translator didn't have anything that screamed about an alert, sparing me from ruining the entire operation in the first few minutes.

"Nothing yet, think you're clear."

Keeping my attention split from that point, I kept glancing between everything I had to keep track of instead of just sitting back and watching Holde's display. Even if that was a lot more interesting than several local officers complaining about someone throwing up in his vehicle.

Rerth's feed wasn't any better; she had a rifle out and was crouched in the farm field they'd used to approach the buildings. Apart from the tiny motions of her breathing, she was practically motionless.

"I wish I could be that still right now." I murmured to myself, doing my best to stretch my fingers out. It was hard not to rock my chair from side to side just to spend the nervous energy flowing through me. "Dammit. I really wish I was out there."

Well, with Holde and Jet's part of the mission.

Rerth kept watch as the two men breezed through the outer door nearly as quickly as if they'd had a key. After that I got to actually do something again; relaying directions from the building blueprint that Jet had fished out a few days ago.

I had no idea how he'd gotten something that detailed just from the local network... but it made me appreciate his skills, even if I wasn't sure if I liked him that much.

50

Or at all, after the last week.

"First right after the entryway." I provided when asked, "Service stairwell to the basement should be the second door on your right after that."

"Thanks." Holde murmured, a pistol just barely visible in his hands. *"Quietly, Jet."*

The other man didn't reply, but presumably followed Holde as he walked through the dimly lit hallways.

Another glance to my front saw that the security channel had gone quiet, which I took as a good sign. "Still nothing on the local radio."

"Good." Rerth said. *"Any ship traffic?"*

"Uh... one moment."

Twisting around in my seat, I leaned over the back to get a look at the data on Jet's screens. I raised my voice a bit to make sure that my microphone still picked it up, "Standard traffic. Nothing's flashing at me."

"Understood. Prepare for the data link."

"Preparing." I replied, stretching out to tap the icons Jet had indicated. "Channel is open."

She made another low sound of approval as I got settled back into my seat, just in time for Holde to whisper another request for directions. Adjusting the map of the building to the appropriate floor, I quickly pointed them to the space labeled as the server room.

There were dim lights in the basement, letting them make better time as they moved through the narrow hallways to the right doorway. Inside proved to be several racks of devices, coolant feeds and heavy fans humming away.

Most important was the small control-console that had been jammed into one corner, and Holde quickly motioned for Jet to get to work.

"Give me a few minutes to start the transmission. Preplanned order?"

Rerth hummed loudly enough for her own mic to transmit the sound.

51

"Yes."

Communications records first then. According to Jet those were pretty easy to find on nearly any system. He'd search for anything financial he could spear if nothing went wrong, and anything referring to temples or priests if there was any spare time left at the end.

I honestly didn't expect to make it that far, but in the end... well, nothing ended up going wrong.

It was honestly kind of strange.

"All data secure." I reported nearly two hours later, when the last of it came across. "Still no strange air traffic, still no alarms."

Holde sounded amused, *"Don't sound so disappointed, little shark. Withdrawing."*

"I'm not disappointed." I said, though I made sure I wasn't transmitting when I did. "I'm just confused. Nothing ever goes this well for me."

Apparently Khash was in a giving mood that day, because that great river of nothing just kept flowing.

The two men slipped out of the mansion without seeing another living soul, and got back up and over the garden wall without raising any alarms. Rerth watched them jog to her position, staying in place until they were past her.

Then she turned around, apparently acting as the rear guard as they headed back towards the rented ground car they'd been using.

She gave me more orders in the process. *"Closing the line. Start the pre-flight list that we showed you, and signal the ship. We'll be departing as soon as we return."*

"Understood, sir. Closing the line."

The channel closed, both camera displays snapping to black a moment later. I still made sure to shut everything down on my side all the same, and double-checked that I'd closed Jet's system too.

Covering a yawn, I walked over to the ladder against the forward bulkhead and climbed up to the shuttle's second level.

"Why am I so tired?" I complained to no one, stepping into the cramped little pilot's chamber. "I didn't even do anything besides read, watch, and talk."

And apparently stress myself out in the process.

"Why though? How? This was... professional, and quick, and supported."

The exact opposite of pretty much every attempt I'd ever done on my own. I should have been relaxed. Thrilled to be part of something so clean.

Instead I just felt like I wanted a strong drink, to be quickly followed by crawling into bed.

I could only sigh, reading the instructions Holde had relayed before slowly tapping the various buttons in the right order. Somewhere far behind I heard the generators change their pitch, starting to warm up in preparation for takeoff. Far closer were the control screens flickering to life; each one scrolling through start-up data before settling into standby mode.

Making sure each one was showing the right information delayed the call I had to make for a minute or two... but not much longer.

Then I had to sit down and prepare myself to talk with the Captain of the *Posa'vilt* for the first time.

"Ground team reporting."

A deep man's voice answered at once, *"This is Captain Anahc'koru. Status?"*

"Objective complete, sir. Ground team preparing to depart world, and system."

"Good." He said, surprising me a little by not asking who I was. *"Does the Agent have a destination in mind?"*

"Any nearby system. She wants time to analyze our data." I said in reply.

"We'll be ready. Orbital Asset out."

"Ground team..." The line cut before I could finish, leaving me to speak the last word only to me. "...out."

I bit my lip, briefly wondering if he'd done that because I'd been the one to call, or if he was just naturally brusque... then I got out of the seat, and started heading back to my station.

I'd monitor the security radios until everyone came back.

VI

In the aftermath of the mission on Rurasflara, the *Posa'vilt* had moved to an uninhabited system. At Rerth's order the Captain had pulled the ship into orbit around a local ice giant, waiting for us to go through the data we'd just acquired.

Well, while Jet and I did. Our elders were busy pouring over the information we had on the other worlds in the Group of Five, specifically seeing what they could find on the temples. True to Jet's predictions there apparently wasn't much, but Rerth wanted options in case the current we were chasing ended up leading nowhere.

The work wasn't too bad, overall. With Holde's help, we'd set up a pair of consoles in the ship's small conference room, turning it into our research den. It honestly reminded me a bit of the quiet DataCenter on Oshflara where I'd had to do my own research last year.

Just without the threat of supremacists coming in and beating me.

Sure, I was still working with Jet, and I... well. Wasn't really sure I liked him all that much, but at least he didn't have any problems with my species.

"All right." Jet opened our fifth day of research by settling into his seat, one pair of hands comfortably resting behind his head. "Rerth wants our preliminary findings tomorrow. You've had most of a week of independent work, so what have you come up with?"

Getting myself comfortable across from him, I pulled my chair a bit closer to the table. That gave me enough time to collect my thoughts and avoid stuttering when I replied.

"My first round of searching and organizing is done." I replied. "I have a list of three potentials assembled. Two are pretty solid, I think, the last one is a little hazier."

He grunted, tapping his console to life without looking away from me. "What was your focus?"

55

The one good thing about working with Jet was that he didn't try and micromanage what I was working on. He'd just given me a category and told me to get back to him when I had my findings written up and ready to go. Our only real communication had been when we'd needed to ask the other if they had any data to help explain things we saw.

I'd gotten the giant mess of letters and chat logs, while he'd focused on all of the financial data. I'd have been lost from the start if he hadn't also given me his collection of analysis programs, though I really hadn't needed his comments about how slow I was to get used to their commands.

"My primary focus was the automations and anything connected to them." I replied. "On day three I realized that several important people were traveling a lot, so I started looking for more records of that, which led me to start including any of the other planets in the area into my searches."

"Logical. Lay it out like you would for Rerth. What did you find, and where did you start from?"

"Um, I found three potentials like I said." I hedged. "Uh, where I started... right. From what I can tell, House ul Tradok are big investors in Rurasflara, or at least they're trying to be. Their attempts to monopolize the agricultural production is just step one of a long term plan."

There was a tiny shrug. "Not surprised. Thondians are rarely unambitious. How does that relate to our project?"

Tapping at my screen, I flicked three files over to his device. "I think it's related because members of the House are constantly traveling to other planets in the Group. They aren't doing it in yachts either, these letters definitely imply that they're taking freighters."

Jet nodded. "Meaning you think they're picking up the automations elsewhere in this little state."

"And maybe more beside. Look at the third one. The Tarath was berating one of his people for buying an Aliko groundcar. I ran a search and confirmed it; that model doesn't have an export license."

Leaning in, he read what was on his screen before replying. "Delne'lir Aliko.. they operate out of the Icar Region. That ties into our search results on Rurasflara."

"Confirming that the smugglers are moving more than just automations from Oshflara." I said firmly.

He hummed, "Likely, but don't say confirmation. Rerth hates that unless she's got physical evidence in front of her."

I grimaced at the reminder. "Right, sorry. Uh, I've got more on that point. Enough to convince her, I think."

"Good. Keep going."

Dropping my eyes back to my screen, I opened another to reread a few lines quickly. "Here. I merged a dozen letters from about an eight month period. It's hard to get through the language, but there's a lot of references to Varur'fluro and one of the Tarath's daughters. Something about purchasing product there."

"Same planet the other one got berated for visiting?"

"Yes." I confirmed.

"Send me the file." He ordered.

I did, and he took a quick moment to glance over the first sections. "Hmm. Reinforces your point, but I don't like that they're using the word 'product'. It's vague, could mean anything. You didn't find anything more specific?"

"I ran out of time. It's definitely not automations though, they talk about that one pretty openly."

That drew a slight frown. "You don't use generic words like that in internal communications unless you're extremely paranoid. Probably not Imperial exports... hard to say if they're talking about animate or inanimate product just from the context here."

I blinked, then grimaced when I got what he meant. "Slaves? Isn't the whole point of automations to remove the need for manual labor?"

"It's not about the labor, it's a status thing." Jet rolled his shoulders. "I don't claim to understand it. Regardless, your first potential is confirmation that they're tied into a broader smuggling ring?"

"Yes, and from the travel logs, I think its port of call is on Varur'fluro. Everything I've seen says they're making numerous trips there every year."

Jet reached up, stroking the fur around his chin as he thought about it. "That matches a lot of the financial transactions I've been finding. Payments with no descriptions going to groups on Varur'fluro."

"What kind of groups?" I asked.

"House ul Grator seems to be their main supplier. I checked the DataNet, and supposedly they run an import-export business on that planet." That fang filled grin appeared once more. "With the Ascendancy only, mind you. Not the Empire."

A little tremor of excitement ran through me. "Do you think they're the ones doing the smuggling?"

"Directly? I doubt it, we're too far removed from the Imperial borders. If I had to guess, they're just the local distributors. Either way they'll be a target when we hit Varur'fluro. Make a note to keep working that product angle, we need to know what else they might be moving."

"Got it." That had been my plan anyway, but it was good to know I was in the right waters. Even better, I'd get to do more research instead of struggling through Jet's lessons.

"What do you have on your second potential?" He asked.

My second... right, right. Shaking myself a little, I focused on the notes and reports in front of me. "A lot of the same, but they're also a lot more open about it. Talking about picking up new models, spare parts, that kind of thing."

"Still on the same colony?" He pressed.

"Mostly." I hedged, "Uh, all but one of the trips where they picked up shipments was on Varur'fluro. The outlier is the very first one chronologically."

Jet frowned a little, one hand drumming fingers on the table. "Odd. Reason?"

"That's roped in with my third potential. Can you read something for

58

me? I don't want to bias you first."

When he waved a hand in permission, I sent the report form that I'd filled out with excerpts from several letters and a chat log.

I watched him read it once, frown, then lean forwards in his seat to read it a second time. "...need to move pick-up operations to Varur'fluro. They were not pleased at our proximity."

"Something scared them off of doing business on Yashun." Unable to wait, I elaborated on my thoughts regardless. "I did a full search. There's no other references to Yashun after that date in any of the files that you grabbed. In better than four years worth of logs... nothing."

His sunken features grew more so as he frowned. "You think the Burned Hand or her pack told them off for being there."

Well, that's what I wanted to think. I wanted her to be there, I wanted her to be stuck with Tia'mok on a penal colony. I wanted my first project with the pack to be fast, clean, and a success.

As much as I hoped for those things, I needed to keep it under control. I'd made the mistake of twisting facts to suit theories in the past, and Rerth would make me run laps until I passed out if I did it again.

"I don't know." I said instead. "But something or someone, definitely scared them away from doing business there. Unless you found investments in that direction?"

Jet shook his head slightly. "I don't recall any, but Yashun wasn't my focus. I'll add it to my own research."

"What do you think it could be?" I asked.

"Could be anything." He hummed, "A proper House from the Ascendancy, local rivals, criminals, maybe even a mercenary band with a grudge. Assuming it's the Burned Hand is a bit of a toss."

My shoulders hunched a little. "I wasn't assuming anything."

There was a quiet snort. "Uh huh. Be more convincing tomorrow, and don't reach for your scars like you always do."

59

I started to do just that on reflex, clenching my hands into fists to stop myself. "I wasn't assuming anything. I'm hopeful, but I know it's not likely and that it could be anything."

"If you say so, little shark."

Somehow, coming out of his mouth, the nickname didn't sound nearly as endearing.

It was more dismissive, uncaring.

"What did you find?" I asked, trying not to sound as annoyed as I felt.

Two of his hands spread apart while the other pair started typing on his console. "Plenty of financial evidence to back up your first two potentials, and I've got another one on Kormok. You didn't find anything on that colony?"

I shook my head. "Not that I saw. Nothing on Aspic'tic either, but maybe I missed it."

"Maybe it's just tentative real estate deals then." He paused, humming again in thought. "That or it's something they're keeping quiet, even among themselves. I wonder if there was a private network we didn't find. Something the Tarath keeps to himself."

"They bought land on Kormok?" I asked.

"It seems like it, but it may have just been a cover payment for something else." Jet shrugged. "Only way to tell will be to go there and find out if the listed seller exists or not. DataNet is less than helpful in this case."

"Oh." I replied. "Um, What about Yashun?"

Jet rolled his dark eyes. "It's added to my research list. I'll tell you how the Burned Hand isn't there whenever I get that far."

I glowered at him. "Thank you, sir."

If my nettled tone bothered him he didn't show it. As usual there. "Anyway, your forms look fine, and I agree with your potentials. I'm merging my data with yours for tomorrow. You can be done for the afternoon."

Before Rurasflara I would have asked if he was sure, if there wasn't something else I could learn or practice on.

Now? I was already standing up before he finished the last word, locking my console with a final keystroke. "I will see you tomorrow."

He made a vague sound of acknowledgment, but otherwise didn't so much as react when I left the room. It felt far too relieving just to get out into the ship's hallway, a closed door between us.

That wasn't a feeling I should have been having about a packmate.

My hands rose, rubbing tiredly at my face. I wasn't even sure I could blame this one on my species. I just... ugh. The worst thing about working with Jet was that we could have several hours of productive time together, but then he'd say just one thing that would make me feel pathetic, defensive, or any combination of unpleasant things.

I needed to figure something out though. We were packmates now, and I wasn't going anywhere until my term of conscription was up.

Taking a few deep breaths, I let them out slowly. I had an hour before my training session with Holde. That would be more than enough time to relax, calm down, make myself presentable.

"Well, that's an expression."

Or Holde could find me before I could do any of those things.

"Hey, Holde." I quickly dropped my hands, trying to not look as exhausted as I felt. "Jet let me out early."

Holde's grin made me feel better, as usual. He casually approached, hands in his pockets as he looked me up and down. "I figured, since you're out here looking like a hurricane just ruined your day. Jet say the wrong thing again?"

"No, uh..." I trailed off, unable to really deny it. "...kind of. Is it that obvious?"

One tarah flicked, his expression sympathetic. "A bit. Come on, walk with me. We can talk about how annoying he can be."

61

"He's not that annoying." I couldn't help but *try* to make it seem like I didn't mind him. "He's an incredibly skilled researcher, and I don't think I could reach his hacking or lock-picking skills if I lived as long as you will."

"But you can't stand his personality?" He asked, almost teasingly.

"...I'd have never picked him as a packmate." I said, trying to be as diplomatic as I could while still telling the truth.

"Mmm." The hum came with a grin that told me he knew exactly what I really meant. "Come on, walk with me. It'll help."

Blowing out a final sigh, I got my legs moving. Soon enough the pair of us were randomly wandering the halls, speaking quietly as we did.

"You'll have to adapt to his personality, I'm afraid." He said after a few silent minutes of letting me burn off some energy. "Rerth and I have known him since his early conscription more than twenty years ago now. He's always been... less than tactful, but he's also rarely wrong."

I sighed. "I've noticed both. Trust me."

"Are you going to be able to tolerate him for the next three years?"

My heart sunk a bit toward the deeps. If I couldn't, then what would happen? I was on my last chance. I couldn't lose everything just because of a few annoying comments. "Of course."

His right tarah flicked out once. "If you say so. Just remember that we can find other work for you, if the two of you can't get along for the entire term you're with us. You don't *have* to be here every day of every project."

"I'm all right. I really am." From his expression he knew it was a lie, so I quickly sailed on before he could call me on it "Um, is *he* complaining about me?"

"Do you really think he'd avoid saying it to you directly?"

"No." I admitted at once. Jet was anything but quiet in his opinions. "Sorry, just kind of surprised by the conversation."

Holde rolled a shoulder in a lazy shrug. "Rerth and I noticed that his voice has been cutting you a bit more than we expected. Just wanted to be sure you're doing all right, that you weren't being a stubborn fish and not telling us if you had a problem."

"I can ignore a lot of it. Just... eight days alone in a shuttle with him was a lot." I paused, then added emphatically. "A *lot*. When it was just training I didn't mind him so much, but... I didn't really like being stuck in a metal box with him."

That earned me another chuckle. "Fair enough, little shark. Ideally our next stop will not require that kind of strategy... but it tends to be how we operate, given our skill-sets. Maybe we can have you remain on the ship and support from orbit."

"I can handle it." I said again.

"You can, but you don't have to." His grin returned, "Just because we're all far older than you doesn't mean we're any less your packmates."

"I know, I know. I don't mean to be... standoffish." I hesitated before pushing on. "It's just an adjustment, I guess. You're all so mature, and it's really weird sleeping in a separate bed every night."

"Having only three of us?" He guessed, "And all three of us being Guides who don't need constant company?"

I glanced away, looking at the walls, "...yes."

A quiet sigh came before his words. "You miss your old packs, don't you?"

"...sometimes." I admitted. "As... badly as it ended, I really liked the Vet. And I've missed Pack Ithi since Rerth took me away from them."

One of his tarah flicked at the reminder that, as much as I liked Rerth, I still hadn't forgiven her for that. "I can see the difficulties. Likely not helped by how little time to adjust you've had, given how involved we are with this project. You seem to be holding up all right, but that may just be me not being used to Humans."

"I am holding up all right. Just... adjusting, like I said."

"You're sure?"

63

"I swear by Ashahn."

His head tipped slightly. "All right. Well, remember you can talk to us, and feel free to call anyone you like. Do you want to start on our session early?"

"If we can?"

"We can." A hand patted my shoulder. "Come on, let's get some tea. I've got a few new ideas that you should have fun with."

That sounded wonderful, and I followed him without hesitation.

VII

Overall, I liked my training sessions with Holde far more than my research ones with Jet.

Especially because Holde turned out to be the kind of person who couldn't abide sitting becalmed all day. You had, at best, a three hour window before he simply had to get up and start moving.

So instead of sitting around memorizing the Intelligence regulations and organizational charts in a conference room or our cabin, I got to repeat them back to him while we walked laps around the ship.

Even better, he breezed through the basic rules and regulations as quick as he could, which let him start me on the lowest levels of field work. Most of it was pretty simple stuff, how to not ruin a crime scene by blundering around, but he also liked to have me pretend to be an Agent running an operation.

Which was far more enjoyable than anything Jet or Rerth had me doing.

"All right, you're sure you've tracked down the person leaking information to the Concordat and Federation." Holde provided as we wandered the lower decks, warm cups of tea in our hands. "What's your order of action?"

"I position my packmates to watch for an escape attempt." I replied, doing my best to both remember what he'd been teaching me, as well as simply using basic logic. "Uh, do I already have a full remit from the local Operative?"

"No."

"Then I send them a priority request for one, and I contact the local garrison to have a team on stand-by to support me when it shows up."

"Winds are strong so far. Keep going."

"Uh..." I sipped some tea to buy myself a moment to think. "If I don't

65

get a response within three standard days I have to make a personal call about going in directly with my pack, or holding in place."

He nodded. "Can you call in the garrison or security assets in that situation?"

That one I remembered. "I can request, but not order. It would be up to the local officers."

"Good. You've at least got the core of it, and most of the rest you won't need to know for a while."

I smiled. "It's not that hard really. It pretty much all goes like I would have thought, except for the whole Agents not cooperating thing."

"Oh, we *cooperate.*" He stressed before chuckling, "By certain definitions of the word, at least. Rerth complains about the budget, and she's not entirely wrong, but mostly it's a lack of personnel."

That wasn't something you heard everyday. Not in the Empire. "Strange problem to have."

Holde rolled a shoulder, feet finally slowing when we entered a small mess hall. It was empty at this time of day, and we quickly settled down at the nearest table.

"Intelligence work isn't for everyone, you know that." He paused to sip some tea before setting it aside. "There's a lot of travel, a good bit of mystery, but for every six months we get to spend planet-hopping there's a year's worth of reading reports a decade old. Usually about subjects that are either utterly boring, or utterly disgusting."

"Which isn't fun." I murmured. I hadn't had to deal with the disgusting yet, thank the Aspects, but there hadn't been much exciting in my research sessions so far.

"Which isn't fun." He agreed. "There's also the fact that we're not exactly encouraged to have large packs for security reasons. Worse, those same packs often have to split up for months or years at a time. This is the first time I've seen Rerth in most of a year."

Sipping more tea hid a wince. "I... don't know how I'll deal with that."

66

"We'll work on it." He promised. "I think Rerth's plan is to keep you with us until you can apply, then gently get a pack of your own together while you're there. And before you ask, no, I'm not going to let her hand-pick them for you like she has been."

I didn't like the idea of leaving yet another pack in my wake, but... I did like the idea of finally being able to make one on my own. To not have it be Rerth's choice.

"Thank you."

His grin was infectious, "Don't worry about it. Anyways, like I was saying. All of that is a pretty big detriment to recruiting, especially to young Guides who are still used to life as hunters and huntresses. It gives the Intelligence courses some of the highest drop-out rates once they hit field training."

I wasn't really surprised by that, not like I once might have been. As a Huntress myself, I was definitely struggling with the whole sleeping alone thing. And with how small my new pack was. And just how... mature and focused they all were.

I was doing my best to keep up, to act wiser than my years, but there were plenty of moments where I felt like a child trying to impress my teachers.

Wrapping both hands around my cup, I brought it to my lips to enjoy the flavor of my sweetened tea. It was a pleasant enough distraction to break me out of the dark waves, and left me free to reply with another question.

"And the network security teams steal all the best recruits, because they get to stay together and work in luxury?" I asked.

He snorted, "Jet's been complaining again, has he?"

"Yeah." I confirmed. "We ran into an encoded file that his program couldn't open, and I made the mistake of asking him if he knew anyone who could crack high level encryption. He started going on about some hacking bastard who was getting paid too much, and something about a woman?"

Holde rolled his eyes, "He's got a feud with an Agent assigned to DataNet security. They were both trying to date the same woman on Altair, and since Jet has to travel and the other man doesn't, she didn't pick Jet."

"Ah. That would definitely explain a lot of his complaining."

"It really does. The man's obsessed with romance, has been since he was a Hunter. Have you seen his suite?" When I shook my head, he snorted. "He's got more posters of scantily clad Naulian women than the most lust addled Half-Sword you've ever met."

I blinked several times, honestly surprised. "I... wouldn't have expected that from him."

"Probably because I'm lying."

"You-what?"

Holde threw back his head, laughing. "Sorry. I couldn't resist."

"I...you... why?" I stammered.

"Partly to tease you," He admitted without any shame. "Partly to see just how quick you are to believe people that you don't actually know that well. I thought about a more elaborate story, but I decided to be gentle with you since you're still new to this."

I could only groan. "Was the part about the DataNet Agent true?"

"Perhaps." Holde grinned at my exasperated look, "Welcome to an Intelligence pack, Ashe. Everything between us is a test and a game. It's how we keep our skills honed, how we make sure we're always ready to question rather than accept."

Here I'd been hoping that Holde would be different than Jet or Rerth; a man who challenged me to dig up his past, and a woman who constantly made me figure out just what she was up to.

Well, he was a little different. He was much nicer about it. That was something, I supposed. He'd waited a while before starting on this little game, which meant...

"You've been going easy on me?" I guessed.

His shrug was modest. "Rerth guessed you'd have issues with Jet, and we didn't exactly get the calm seas she was hoping for to start your time with

68

us. Still, I think you're as well adjusted as you can be. Figured it was past time."

"...thanks, I think." I said. On the one hand, it sounded like he was accepting me as a member of the pack. Which was great!

On the other hand, it sounded like I was going to have to start wondering if anything he or Rerth told me was true or not. Which was... far less great.

"So," He took up his cup of tea again, giving me a serious look over the top of it. "Tell me about what happened on Oshflara."

I blinked, not quite getting it. "We've talked about Oshflara. Several times."

"We have, but I want to see how well you can lie about it. If you can't deceive someone about your past then you're going to have a rough time acting like a proper Agent." He waved a hand slightly, "And no, Rerth's gambit of bouncing you from pack to pack after Oshflara doesn't count."

"Why not? I wasn't bad at it."

"Because inserting someone into a pack of Hunters and Huntresses is taking advantage of biology, not skill." He shook his head. "Your situation is more complicated by your species, but Rerth had you in, what, six units in six months?"

"Yeah."

"And only the last one even started to suspect you?"

I grimaced. "Yeah."

He waved his cup in a 'see?' kind of gesture. "If we gave you a fake Index, picked out an accepting pack, we could probably insert you anywhere even with your lack of training. It's not exactly moral, but it's effective. The problem is that very few things we investigate can actually be approached by inserting someone into a conscript unit."

That sounded true enough... most of the packs I'd been through hadn't liked me because of my species. My curiosity and need to investigate only became problems later. If I'd toned that down, if I hadn't starting swimming

69

around looking for smugglers and answers to questions... I probably would still have been on my fifth assignment, or my sixth.

A brief memory of Fyth glaring at me made me shake myself a little.

"All right. I can try. Just Oshflara?"

"Yes."

"Should I pretend like I've got a fake index?" I asked.

He grinned, apparently pleased by the question. "Yes. Adjust anything about your past that you want. Now, tell me what happened there?"

I took a deep breath, took one more sip of tea, and tried to make a story out of nothing but sand. "Right, um. I'd just been removed from Pack Ithi because they were assigned to a combat zone. I was upset and angry, but got lucky in being sent to join Pack Vet. Um, we were assigned to Oshflara, a planet we didn't know anything about."

Holde leaned to one side, resting an elbow on the table as he watched me. "Keep going. What happened when you arrived?"

"I started dating Jal'vet. We went fishing together, and he helped me practice Strike-Wave." I tried to muddle things between what was sort-of true and what wasn't. That was what they always said you should do in films and novels. "Our packmate, Fyth, was too curious for her own good. She started looking into why we were stuck on Del-cycle while a lot of alien formations were all on Ah-cycle. That led to us being targeted by a local group of Notables."

I went on to accurately describe us getting howled at by our Arsenal Commander, but tried to keep replacing my role with Fyth, and Fyth's role with Jal. I kept going until the end, completely avoiding the subject of my capture and torture at the hands of the insurrectionists.

"And that's what happened on Oshflara." I paused, then self-consciously asked, "Um. How did I do?"

He hummed, brilliant eyes meeting mine for a long moment before he shrugged. "Better than I thought, but not as well as you could have. Mixing true events out of order can be effective, but it's dangerous. It's very easy to trip yourself up since you'll be fighting against your actual memories."

70

"Did I?"

"Somewhat. You had a hitch in your voice when you spoke about Fyth'vet, but not Jal'vet. That was minor, only a trained person would have likely noticed. The larger gaps were when you mentioned *your* argument with Ruru'vet, rather than *Fyth*'s argument with her."

I bit my lip. "Oh. I could have sworn I said it right."

"You likely thought of the lie, but what came out of your lips was the truth. Like how someone writing a report can't spot the missing word no matter how many times they reread it, because their brain *knows* what they intended to put there."

I nodded slowly. "So... if I want to try that, I have to rehearse it a lot? Make it reflex'?"

"If that works for you, yes." Holde agreed. "When creating a cover story, you have two options. Mixing the truth with lies, as you did, or simply stringing so many lies together that no one looking can find the truth lurking in the depths. Rerth is better at the first, I'm better at the second."

"Jet?"

He snorted. "Terrible at both. The man's incapable of being anything but blunt. The best he can manage is to avoid talking about himself at all, which is of limited value. Sooner or later someone always asks questions, and all he can try to do is be even more evasive."

Meaning Jet probably wasn't any good at infiltration, despite his training and apparent skills. Unless Holde was lying about that too...

Ugh. This was going to make me paranoid in a hurry... which was probably the point.

"So I should practice both options then?" I asked. "See which one I'm better at?"

"I think so. Now that you have the basic regulations down we can really start on the fun parts of the job. Every day when we're together, I want you to invent stories, or mangle your own history. I want you to become so convincing that even though I know the truth, I start to wonder."

71

"I'll try."

"You'll need to." He replied. "Think of how much smoother Oshflara would have gone if you'd been able to fake being a resentful Human, despising the sea she'd been thrown into. How much more information would that have gotten you, how much faster?"

A lot, and a lot.

"I knew that even then. I just..." My head shook, some of my dark fur escaping the tie behind my neck. "...I got to know some of them. I didn't like lying to them."

Holde's voice turned gentle, his eyes turning to stare at nothing. "That's the pain of this career, little huntress. Unless you want to be a dedicated analyst, or join the DataNet teams... sooner or later, you have to befriend someone. Have to lie to them every day. Have to gently cut open their chest to find their secrets, and smile while you do it."

I tried to imagine it. Spending more time with Ramos. Talking sports with him. Accepting his invitation to meet his bond. To meet his child.

Faking complaints about the Empire, to see what he said in reply.

Learning who he was working with. Working for.

Tried to imagine sitting at the bar, laughing with him the moment the army stormed in to arrest him based on what I'd learned.

"I'm not sure I can." I admitted. "I mean, maybe if they're really terrible people? But I'm just..."

"Not comfortable?" He supplied.

"Not comfortable."

"Good."

I blinked. "Good?"

Holde nodded without looking at me. "If you were comfortable with that level of deception, then Rerth was very wrong in her profile of you. If

72

infiltration and betrayal is easy for someone, that someone isn't a person we could ever trust. There's places in Intelligence for people like that, but not with our pack."

"Oh. But... will I have to do it?"

"Honestly I couldn't say. We're all trained for it, and we do little games like lie to one another to stay in practice." A faint smile came and went, "You should hear Rerth and Trell when they get together. They're constantly trying to come up with the smoothest deceptions, it's quite fun to listen to. But infiltration like that is fairly rare, overall. It's easier to use paid agents."

"...but when we have to do it ourselves, we *really* have to?" I guessed, voice quiet.

"Exactly." His right hand rose, patting my shoulder once. "Don't worry too much about it, this operation doesn't seem like it will require it. Treat it like a game among packmates, and it'll make things easier on you."

"I'll do my best." I promised.

"All we can ask. I think that's enough heavy waves for tonight. I'm going to find Rerth. I want you to finish your tea, relax for a while. Don't stress about presenting to Rerth tomorrow."

"Thank you, sir. Um... can I ask one more thing?"

He gave me a final smile as he stood up, "Of course."

"Am I going to be going out on any of the missions? Not just staying in the shuttle, I mean."

Holde chuckled, "Impress me with your next few sessions, do well with your half of the research presentation tomorrow, and I'll talk to Rerth about finding you something to do on Kormok or Varur'fluro. Deal?"

I bobbed my head at once. "Yes sir."

"Good. Take the rest of the evening off and relax. I'll see you in the morning."

"Good night." I watched him go before lowering my eyes to my cup, staring down into the dark liquid within. Even though the ending had been a

73

little rough, I'd still rather enjoyed the session.

And his promise to talk to Rerth, if I could do well enough in his training. That would be... that would be lovely. I could work with Jet, but I didn't want to end up in a shuttle with him for another week. Not if I could help it.

Not when I was certain we had a strong wind behind us. We had such good leads pointing to Varur'fluro, and maybe even Yashun. There had to be something more that I could do to help the investigation when we got there.

Something I could do... something that even my terrible luck couldn't help me screw up.

"Learn fast, focus, don't disobey any orders. Not even by sticking to the letter and ignoring the intent. Do it right." I whispered to myself. "Do it right, and you can do more than be stuck in shuttles."

Any other words of encouragement I could give myself were cut off by a young man calling out in excitement. "Ashe!"

I looked up to see Noro'thun beaming at me, practically skipping over to my table. Right behind were two women, probably his packmates from how quickly they followed. Both proved to have bright teal eyes, and were about my height. The closer of the two lifted her tarah as she approached, a rather fetching smirk appearing.

"There really is a Human on board." She earned an honor for not using a nickname or slur, her eyes shamelessly moving from my arms to my legs. "And she's a fit one."

Noro'thun groaned as he took the seat Holde had just left. "Really, Uru?"

Uru'thun, I assumed, merely turned her smirk on him. "Jealous Noro?"

"N-no!"

Both of them giggled at his stammer, while I felt a bit of heat rise to my cheeks. While the unnamed woman took the seat beside Noro, the more flirty one quickly slipped around the table to sit next to me instead. Her eyes had become locked onto my fur, so I wasn't terribly surprised when she

74

reached out to brush her fingers through it.

"You're a bit forward, aren't you?" I asked.

To my surprise she blinked, hesitating while her tarah briefly angled to show embarrassment. "Oh. Is touching it a... *thing?*"

"Of course it is." The other woman rolled her eyes, "It's attached to their head after all. It's probably like if you just walked up and started stroking someone's tarah."

Uru immediately pulled her hand back, her flirtatious demeanor cracking entirely. "Sorry!"

"It's all right." I spoke quickly, "It's, um, not *that* intimate. Just... kind of an awkward thing to do before we've even exchanged names."

She cleared her throat, desperately trying to reel her confidence back in. "Uru'thun, and anyone as toned as you can call me Uru."

"Ashe'lori," I smiled to show her I wasn't terribly offended. "Ashe is fine."

A relieved smile came and went, then I turned to face the others. Up close, the woman beside Noro proved to be a bit more muscled than Uru, though her tarah were longer and almost masculine.

"Tevi." She provided, lips quirking on one side. "Personal names are fine with me too. Sorry for Uru. She flirts before she thinks."

There was a low growl from the other girl, which just made Tevi smirk. "And you know Noro thanks to his usual clumsiness."

Noro groaned. "I'm not *that* clumsy. Could you stop embarrassing us in front of a Rifle-Experienced?"

I huffed out an amused little breath. "An RE isn't an officer, Noro. I'm a conscript the same as you three."

"Not the same." He shook his head, "You're lucky enough to be assigned to Intelligence, a real pack even. Um... that Agent isn't on her way here, is she?"

75

"She was meeting with the Captain, and the rest of the pack is relaxing for the evening." I replied. "I just ended a training session, finally have some time to myself."

He slumped in evident relief. "Oh good. She was, um, kind of intimidating."

"She can be." I agreed. "Do you all have the rest of the night off as well?"

Tevi nodded, "Yeah, not that there's many duties to do as is. Seems like all we do is alternate between exercising and helping the crew do basic maintenance. Not nearly as fun as what you probably get to do."

"Definitely not." Uru had apparently recovered, because she casually leaned a bit against my side. "Swap stories with us? We've never met a Human before, and we've definitely never heard good stories from an Intelligence operative."

"We can get you some drinks." Noro quickly spoke up again. "If you want. If you've got time."

Sitting around, sipping tea or beer with other conscripts? Ones that seemed more intrigued than disgusted by my species?

"That sounds fun." I smiled. "Do any of you like Strike-Wave?"

VIII

I didn't end up going down to the surface on Kormok. That was less out of special treatment, and more how Rerth wanted to handle that mission. Jet had stayed in orbit as well, the two of us still poring over the information from the estate burglary while Holde and Rerth pretended to be prospective colonists below.

Sadly, aside from confirming that there was a strange amount of Imperial tech laying around, they didn't find anything particularly important. None of the temples had struck them as the kind to work with the Burned Hand, and the more rural nature of that colony had made investigating more difficult.

Worse, Jet's lead on the real estate finances hadn't ended up going anywhere. The people that House ul Tradok had worked with had seemingly vanished, or had never actually existed in the first place. Besides telling us that it probably been a pay-off of some kind, we really had no idea why they'd dumped a million Imperial credits into the world.

Varur'fluro was a different matter.

It was far more urban than the prior worlds we'd visited, and had a sprawling spaceport complex in its largest city. Complete with hangars, fueling stations, passenger terminals, conference suites...

And security cameras.

Jet and Holde would be doing a break-in, just as they had at the House on Rurasflara. They'd pull all of the archived footage they could and transmit it back to the ship. With a bit of luck, we'd spot the automations being moved through, maybe even members of House ul Tradok meeting with their suppliers here.

After that everyone else would be back in orbit while Holde stayed on the surface, posing as a would-be Acolyte for a local temple. He'd find out as much as he could about House ul Grator, and maybe more if our search of the video footage turned up anything.

Me?

I got to undertake my first real field mission; covering Rerth's back when she met with an Intelligence Asset in a local bar. She hadn't said much about the Asset, besides the fact that he apparently worked for another Agent who specialized in counter-Ascendancy operations.

It had taken a favor, but the Agent in question had given her permission to question him and task him with helping us investigate things on Varur'fluro. Rerth had been happy about that, even if she was less happy to have me along.

True to his word, Holde had talked her into it, and to say that I owed him was a massive understatement.

If only my hands would stop shaking from a mix of nerves and excitement...

"Don't be so nervous." Rerth murmured as we walked towards the dimly lit bar. "Holde is confident you can handle it. Just remember that this isn't anything you didn't do on Oshflara."

I did my best not to grimace at the memories, and to not tug at the loose clothing I was wearing. We'd replaced our uniforms with casual slacks and shirts, which in my case were a bit baggy and ill-fitting. About the only comforting thing was the weight of the pistol on my belt... which wasn't all that reassuring considering everyone else I'd seen had been armed as well.

"On Oshflara," I whispered back, "I was a nervous wreck, but at least no one in the Riverside Cantina was carrying a shotgun while they ordered drinks. I don't think any of them were considering shoving a slave implant into my neck either."

She chuckled, but there wasn't much humor in the sound. "No. They were just considering making you a martyr for the cause."

That time I did grimace at the reminder. "Yeah, but... I knew something about them. I don't know much of anything about the people here, even with our quick lessons."

"Welcome to the Reaches. You'll learn fast, or we'll be shooting our way out of here." My wince had her patting my shoulder once. "Focus, Ashe. Be casual, chat about whatever anyone wants to. I'll handle the actual sand-sifting, all you have to do is watch my back and play up your cover as a deserter."

Exhaling heavily, all I could do was nod.

Rerth grunted once in approval. "Good. Now stop picking at your shirt, remember our story, and stay in my wake. Let's get this done, and see what the Asset knows about our project."

"Yes sir." I made sure to say the words under my breath; we were too close to the entrance for anything louder.

The bouncer leaning next to it was the first Thondian man I'd ever seen up close, and he was... exactly as intimidating as his job probably required.

He had at least two feet on me, probably more, and looked like he could have casually picked up Rerth and I in either hand without effort. The armored cartilage over his jaw and throat was the color of fine sand, standing out against his nearly jet-black skin. Both contrasted wildly with the bright green uniform and the golden rings in his pointed ears.

The worst though, were his eyes. Dull brown irises were concealed by the black sclera around them, making them look... shadowed and vicious.

He looked even more intimidating when he grinned, showing off especially sharp canines in the process.

"Two alien women at this hour?" His Caranat was clipped, precise, and delivered in a rumble I thought I could feel in my chest. "A gray and a short-fur, without a man to protect them even. You two are bold little whores, aren't you?"

Rerth let out a barking sound, and when she spoke her casual farmland accent was replaced by a perfect match to my languid Altair tones. "Fuck off, sand giant. I'm thirsty as hell, and we both know your knob couldn't fit between my legs."

To my surprise he belted out a laugh in return. "Bold indeed. You get drugged and chipped, not the house's problem. You cause problems? I crack your tiny skulls together. You can't walk that off, get chipped? Not the house's problem. Only warning you're getting."

"Whatever." Rerth drawled as she walked past, leaving me to keep

79

pace just behind her... and leaving me to keep my very real concern to myself.

Only my second official trip on an Intelligence operation, and I was already walking into a place where being enslaved was a very real possibility if I fucked up.

No pressure.

The interior was far nicer than the rough exterior. It was still a bit dimly lit, but it was very clean and smelled pleasantly of wood smoke. There were about two Thondians for every Trahcon inside, split between booths and tables. A raucous group was playing some kind of table-game in the corner, while others were simply bantering loudly.

Rerth strode over to the bar proper, taking a stool next to the only Trahcon man seated there. The Asset, I hoped. She hadn't told me what he looked like so I could only guess.

Of course her choice of seats left me to sit on her right, next to a Thondian even taller and broader than the bouncer had been.

My packmate promptly turned her back on me to engage her fellow Trahcon in conversation, leaving me alone as said giant turned to loom over me. His entire body leaned oddly to the right, which was... dammit. I knew this. Right angles meant... a show of dominance. He was looking down at me.

Literally and figuratively.

He wasted no time in growling something in his own tongue, which I didn't understand in the slightest.

"I don't speak your language." I replied, reaching up to tap my right ear. "No translator, either."

The man blinked slowly, then replied in surprisingly elegant Caranat. "How does a short-fur know Caranat?"

"Imperial born." I told him. "They didn't let me learn anything else."

Those intimidating eyes narrowed. "Not Ark Fleet?"

I didn't have to work very hard to bare my teeth in a grimace, though I made sure to try injecting a bit of anger. "Those deadwood idiots are the reason everyone thinks I'm a bloody pirate. I want nothing to do with them."

Holde's lessons must have paid off because he chuckled, straightening his body out a little bit. "You're a deserter, then?"

"We're heading for the Far Reaches." I avoided the question, "Just making a short stop while our ship takes on provisions and fuel."

There was another rumble in his own language, followed by an amused sounding snort. Then he again switched back to a language I could understand, "Short-furs. You lot always try to lie by not lying. It makes you sound weak."

I blinked. "How does just directly lying make you less weak?"

"Because," He slowly leaned forwards until I was seriously fighting not to either hunch down, or draw my gun to make him back off. "If I lie to you directly, woman, it's because I know you wouldn't dare call me out on it."

"I... see." I clenched my jaw when he didn't back off, and took a gamble based on how Rerth had acted outside. "You want to stop looming, or do I have to draw my gun to make that happen?"

He glanced down to spot my hand on my pistol... and then there was yet another rumbling chuckle. His retreat was slow, deliberately so, but I started breathing more easily as he straightened up.

Before he could say anything else, another figure strode over and put down tall glasses of beer in front of us.

"Your drinks." The bartender, yet another Thondian man in the same green uniform as the bouncer, announced.

I was about to say that we hadn't ordered anything when Rerth let out a mocking laugh. It was loud enough to get the attention of everyone sitting at the bar, and we all watched as she casually grabbed them both, leaned over the bar, and dropped them.

The sound of glass shattering drew even more attention from the tables and booths, several Thondians letting out strange whistles before a partial silence fell.

That sudden quiet made it easy for everyone to hear Rerth when she

81

spoke again, "If you're going to try and drug us, put some Aspects-damned effort into it."

Evidently the bartender didn't have the same sense of humor as the others. He snarled at her, looming as best he could from across the bar. "You dare accuse me of trying to drug you, gray bitch? With how pathetically tiny you are, I could break you over my knee without effort."

"I accurately stated that you didn't even try to hide the fact that you were." Rerth sneered right back at him, "Wander off trail, sand-walker. We'll get our own drinks. Try it again and I'll snap your neck without moving my hands."

The bartender shook with anger as several men chuckled or openly laughed, clearly far more amused by Rerth's insults than sympathetic to him. I think he was about to say something else when the man to my packmate's left cut him off.

"The deserter's not wrong, Grosh." He flicked his tarah sharply up. "Get out of her sight, before you look weaker than you already do."

Evidently that was enough, because he stomped away with more snarling under his breath. For my part I could only watch as Rerth casually leaned over the bar, poked around for a moment, then pulled two unopened bottles up.

"Here." She offered one to me. "Covered and in sight at all times."

"I remember." I told her as I took it. "And I wasn't about to drink the first one."

Her grin was approving before she turned back to her own conversation. Leaving me to carefully twist the top off of my bottle, and take an experimental sip.

"Hmm."

The man I was apparently stuck talking to glanced down at me again. It was stranger than I make it sound; he didn't turn his neck at all, instead turning his entire body to face me directly.

Odd, but better than looming. "Not to your taste, short-fur?"

I was getting really sick of hearing that slur, but I didn't want to threaten to shoot him again. That was probably the only threat I could seriously make, and I didn't think it would go well for me if I overused it.

"I'm used to mixed drinks." I replied. "This is... kind of watered down, and there's not much flavor."

"Good to know that even your kind can't stand your own product."

Blinking once, I picked up the bottle to inspect it more closely. Sure enough, while there was a tiny label in Caranat facing me, a turn let me see a far larger one on the other side. I couldn't read it, but I recognized the alphabet as a Human one.

"Huh." I shook my head. "I'd call you out for being a supremacist, but I think you've got a point."

His laugh was deeper, and more genuine sounding that time. "Oh, I am a supremacist, little short-fur. Your species is pathetic at the best of times, but I am in a good mood this evening. Plus I heard the hatred in your voice for those Ark Fleet pirates."

"So I'm more tolerable than most?"

"Indeed." He brought his glass up in a kind of vague salute. "That and you are properly polite. The last of your kind I spoke with offered insults with every other breath, and arrogantly made demands of me."

Good to know he was more than a little hypocritical, considering how many times he'd called me a short-fur.

"How did that conversation go?" I asked.

His grin turned sharp. "I broke both of his arms, chipped him, and made a tidy profit selling him to an Ascendant House."

I couldn't hide my wince. "Oh."

"Remain polite, short-furred woman, and that will not be your fate tonight." He sipped from his drink as if casual threats of brutality and slaving were nothing of particular note. "What employment do you seek in the Far Reaches?"

Taking another pull from my own bottle didn't really settle my nerves. Telling him the rest of the cover story strangely did... at least a little. Probably because of how many times Holde had made me practice saying it during the trip here.

"Mercenary work, I think." I replied, sticking to my planned speech. "Combat and support is all I really have any training in, so might as well stick to my strengths."

"Wise. Terminus bound?"

I shook my head, "Ashahn's blood, no. You couldn't pay us enough to go there."

That earned me a more honest looking grin. "Wise indeed. I have been there on business, twice. I have never been to a more unpleasant world. An excellent place to conduct profitable enterprise, but I would never elect to live there."

"What about Alum, or Xentha?" I listed the only two other worlds in the Far Reaches I actually knew anything about.

"Alum is nearly paradise." He paused to drink more, a quiet, almost seething whistle coming out once he'd finished. "But the grays who live there are powerful, dominating, and sneer at all others. Even those Houses of my kind that live there struggle to expand their power."

I blinked. "There are Thondian Houses there?"

"One even of the true Highborn. Rumor states that they even hire your kind... so perhaps there is some value to you after all. Consider House Shaaryak, should you choose Alum."

"We will." I covered the lie by drinking more of the unpleasant beer. "I'm sure they'll pay better than being a conscript."

He let out a heavy snort. "Undoubtedly. I shall never understand the Imperial system. It is... so pathetically inefficient."

Apparently I'd hit the right button, because that turned into a nearly thirty minute rant on the superiority of the caste and ranking system compared to the Imperial technocracy. A sneering dismissal of the Ark Fleet's mixed oligarchic-democratic system as 'even worse' led to me asking just how

84

pathetic it was, and got me another solid twenty minutes of vicious mocking.

He got in a few probing questions about my own past, which I deflected with the truth of my less than pleasant experiences. I didn't think he cared in the slightest that I'd been nearly raped, or disparaged for my species, but he seemed to believe that I was angry enough about both to desert.

All in all I managed to draw out the conversation for nearly two hours before Rerth tapped my shoulder, and we made our exit after leaving some credits for the beers we'd drank.

"What did you learn?" She asked once we were a block or so away, walking mostly alone down the dimly lit street.

"Thondian culture makes no sense, I'm pretty sure the man I was talking with would have been just as happy to enslave me as chat, and I have a few potential places we could get jobs as mercenaries on Alum."

Rerth snorted. "Are we being followed?"

I started to look back, caught myself, and instead stretched my arms above my head. After a few steps of that I lowered them, then twisted at my waist like I was trying to loosen up after sitting for too long.

"...not that I can see." I reported after a few quick twists let me glance back. I kept up the stretching, just in case. "Did I pass?"

"We're alive, not slaves, we didn't have to call in backup, and you didn't inspire him to try and break your limbs." She replied dryly. "Obviously you passed, little shark."

I blew out a breath, "Right, sorry. That was... really stressful. And the constant slurs were really annoying."

"I'd say you get used to them, but you really don't." The Agent sighed, shaking her head once. "Let's get back to the shuttle and see how the others did."

"Yes sir. Oh, did you learn anything?"

Her tarah lowered. "Possibly, but... no. I need confirmation before I say anything. Quiet down, keep your eyes on the horizon. Don't assume we're safe until we've got armored doors shut between us and the locals."

I swallowed, nodded sharply, and stayed alert the rest of the way back.

IX

Going over security recordings was pleasantly dull after the terrifying excitement of Varur'fluro.

Not that there was really all that much to go over. According to Jet, the starport was cheap. They didn't keep their security feeds for more than a year before purging them to make room for more.

Unfortunate for our investigation, but we still had a little bit to work with.

Going from the information he and I had managed to put together from House ul Tradok's files, we picked out a few dates where we thought we could recognize someone. Jet let me handle that; a mixture of running facial recognition software and personally watching the recordings to see what was there.

On the second day the software found something, and after watching the file in question, I thought I'd found something too.

"...and there she is." I paused the recording, pointing out the Thondian woman striding down a busy hallway. She was easy to spot thanks to the ring of Thondian men shoving bystanders out of the way, keeping a bubble of open space around her.

"Heading into that conference suite with two assistants, and two guards staying just outside. She's going to stay in there for the next couple of hours."

Rerth leaned in, her right tarah quivering for a moment. "You saw no one go in ahead of her?"

I shook my head. "I only ran through four hours before this point, didn't see anyone. There might be another way in or out though."

The Agent nodded slowly. "There likely is, but... hm. Who else goes in through this entrance?"

"Her first guest arrives in seven minutes, and then another one shows

87

up four minutes after that."

"Fast forward to each one."

Tapping the appropriate controls, I skipped ahead to the next arrival. He was another Thondian, well dressed, but from what I could tell he was a bit on the shorter side. At least for his species. He'd have towered over me from how he filled the doorway.

"Jet says that's a member of House ul Grator, the Tarath's eldest son." I paused again, "Uh, he's still working on getting more information on him. What information he found already says that Grator likes to send him out on important business deals."

Her lips twisted a little. "That is not surprising. What concerns me is that the woman you spotted is House ul Tradok's eldest female child. Is this strictly business, or negotiations for one of those strange bloodline unions? Their warped version of bonds that somehow creates an alliance?"

My own mouth mirrored hers. Just because I was Human didn't mean that I understood the bizarre custom either. "I don't know, but their next guest isn't a Thondian if that helps."

"Perhaps." She hummed for a moment before sailing on, "Add researching how Thondians do those bond-alliances to your list. I want to be certain we're not wrong on this."

"Yes sir."

"Skip ahead to the next arrival. Is that the one you called me down to see?"

"Yes sir." I repeated, again doing as ordered. The screen quickly updated, and I paused it the moment the man I'd spotted walked into view.

He was almost comically small against the massive Thondian bodyguards at the door. The thick robes he wore made him look more comically round than bulky and imposing, and on my third view I was certain I could see the guards sneering the moment he slipped past them and into the room.

"...a priest of Velshen." Rerth murmured. "What is a disciple of Dark Sorcery and Nightmares doing sitting in on a Thondian House negotiation?"

I could only shrug. "That's part of why I called you down here instead of just asking Jet. It gets... weird when they leave."

"Be more descriptive, little shark."

Biting my lip for a moment, I tried to find better words but could only shake my head. "*Weird*, Rerth. I don't know Thondians, but they don't look right after this. I wanted your opinion on it."

She was silent for a long moment, then made a vague sound of approval. "Good that you've learned to ask for second opinions. How long does he remain in there with them?"

"The full two hours. "

Pressing down my thumb, I set the fccd to sixty times speed. Rerth watched in silence as it ran all the way until the first visitor left the conference room. Slowing it back down again, I didn't say anything as the man from House ul Grator boldly strode back out of the room.

"Pause." When I did so, she asked, "Where does he go?"

"Uh..." I had to change over to the note form I'd been keeping, "...Hangar Twenty-Four-Mu. Jet has to get back to me on what ship was in there, and where it came from."

That earned me a single flick of her tarah. "Resume."

I did, but back at the normal playback speed. The priest and the woman both came out together, the Thondian woman's bodyguards following behind.

Unlike the man from Grator, the Thondians around the priest didn't... look right to me. Well, more not-right than usual. Their normal stiff posture was absent, all of them moving with slumped shoulders, their heads bowed slightly. The priest was clearly speaking as they walked, his own tarah raised high in either anger or irritation.

"...your behavior was intolerable." Rerth's murmur made me blink. "You will... dammit, he angled his head. Do you have another camera angle?"

I could only shake my head, "No sir, sorry. This is it for this hallway

89

until they get to the intersection. You can read lips?"

"It's not as difficult as many make it seem. You'll learn in your third Academy year. Where does this group go?"

"They walk together for a little while, then they break apart. That's the next weird thing."

Her eyes narrowed. "Show me."

A few quick adjustments let me do just that. Within a few seconds I had another video feed up, showing the moment that the little group split apart.

The priest drifted off, heading to his own hangar, while the woman and her followers turned right instead.

"...the moment they break apart their body language goes right back to normal." I held my hands palm up, baffled. "All of them in unison, like someone flipped a switch."

Beside me, Rerth leaned in, head tilted. "Replay it."

I did, then I did it three more times at her order. Each time it was just as strange as it had been the first time I'd seen it.

One moment they were shuffling, heads bowed, shoulders hunched in, and with no particular expression to their features. Then the priest moved away, and within a single step all five were confidently stomping down the hall, spines as straight as a ship's mast, visible sneers on their faces.

"What in Velshen's fiery name..." I didn't think she meant for me to hear that particular mutter, but she was so close I couldn't miss it. "...that is..."

"Weird?" I provided.

There was a quiet huff. "Yes. Unsettling is another. A good catch either way, little shark."

I tried not to smile at the rare compliment. "Jet was able to get me the hangar records for their ships already. The ul Tradok people are headed back to Varur'fluro, and the priest went to a public liner. Next stop was Yashun."

Her only response was a quiet hum, eyes sliding back to the screen.

"...can I know what the asset told you now?" I asked.

"Do you have a reason to know?"

Groaning at the reminder, I leaned back in my chair. "Yes sir. If it's related to the local priests I can expand my search of these files to see if there's a lot of traffic through the starport. If they're doing a lot of sailing around, maybe there will be a pattern that can tell us something."

That earned me another of those low, approving noises from her throat. "At least you were prepared this time."

"Thank you, sir."

She rolled her eyes before settling back in her own seat. "Your ability to be perfectly obedient in word and yet sarcastic in tone is something I do wish you'd lose."

I immediately blanked my features as if I was standing at attention. Folding my hands in my lap, I was the very model of an obedient Human conscript awaiting judgment from a senior officer.

"Brat." She growled, but her tarah flicked outwards in amusement. "That Asset is classified above your level, but I will admit that some of what he had to say is related to what you've discovered."

"A lead on the Burned Hand?" I asked, trying not to sound eager.

Rerth eyed me, wordlessly telling me that I'd failed in that. "Perhaps. Save these files and your notes. You'll have time to put the appropriate forms together later, for now you'll be coming with me."

Blinking a few times, I quickly started saving and closing everything. "Uh, yes sir. Where are we going?"

"To collect the others and discuss our next move. You'll learn what is relevant when we have them with us."

As soon as my console was locked I followed her into the hall, where she went the further step of locking up the tiny room I'd been working in. That was something we'd never bothered doing, something she hadn't even hinted

91

was needed considering that we were aboard a warship.

I was equal parts nervous and excited by the time we dragged Jet out of his own room, rescued Holde from a meeting with the Captain, and then gathered in our elder's cabin. At Rerth's order we all got settled sitting on spaces of the broad bed occupying most of the space, the two men looking as serious as our leader.

Doing my best to copy their expressions and postures, it didn't take long for Rerth to get started.

"We need to get to Yashun as quickly as possible. Holde, what is the ship's supply status?"

If the question surprised him he didn't show it. "It's running a light crew, and it was fully stocked before we left Altair. I'd have to double-check with the Captain, but I'd assume we've got another two or three months before we have to put in."

"Not good enough." Her head shook once. "Tell him we need an immediate resupply and refueling. We're going to be doing a long-term insertion and I want them to be able to linger in support for as much time as they can."

He nodded once. "You and I are becoming priests then?"

"Yes. Jet? You will be focused on House ul Grator. Pose as a small time merchant from Shaidan. I want confirmation that they're the distributors of the smuggled goods. Take as much time as you need to determine what they're bringing in."

Jet nodded in turn, one of his hands stroking the fur below his chin. "Do you want anything on the smugglers themselves, or are we just hitting their harbor?"

"We aren't hitting anything yet. Get me that information and we'll go from there." Her gaze snapped to me. "Ashe? You'll be on the surface as well on this one. Pose as Jet's hired bodyguard."

"Yes sir. Um..."

"Out with it."

I winced, "Um, are Humans or Naule common there?"

"Not likely. You wish to know how long you will be on the surface?"

"Well, yes." I admitted. "If you're infiltrating a temple, won't that take weeks?"

"Months." Holde said.

Rerth tipped her head toward him, "As he says. You two will likely have only a few weeks before you draw attention. Jet will determine the overall length of your stay. Do as he says, assist him in any research, and provide armed back-up in case of an emergency."

My mouth went a little dry at the idea of engaging in a firefight. "Yes sir."

She kept staring at me for a few breaths, probably making sure I wasn't going to ask anything else. When I didn't, she resumed. "All three of you have been asking about my discussion with Fyvn'trell's Asset. To let you see past the surface, he did not have much of anything on the smuggling ring. Well, beyond the obvious fact that the local economy is filling up with Imperial goods."

Jet huffed. "And he didn't bother telling Trell?"

"He didn't think it important, or relevant to his deal." She replied, her tone making it clear she wasn't happy about that. "He only provides her with information on the local political situation, and that was all he would give me."

Our only Naulian member frowned, all four arms dropping into his lap. "I'd say that wouldn't give us much of anything on our project, but your tone says otherwise."

"You know me so well." A single shake of her head. "Several Thondian Houses, powerful actors, have begun to behave erratically over the past few years. Elders are feuding with their children in public. Houses once focused on chasing monopolies in specific industries are investing in unrelated fields. What's more, there has been a complete turn around on the notion of accepting refugees from the Ascendancy."

I could only join the men in frowning, speaking up, "They were

93

against that?"

"Until very recently, yes. Now the official government line is that they will welcome any and all fleeing the civil war. The Asset thought it significant that several major politicians have all begun to reflect the same words offered by senior priests."

"...like priests of Velshen?" I asked.

She tipped her chin towards me, "Perhaps. He was extremely certain that the local temples are becoming major political players, but he had no idea why. As recently as nine years ago they were entirely apolitical, yet now nearly every leader in the Group of Five is wary of upsetting them."

"Even the Thondians?" Jet was already shaking his head. "That makes no sense. I've never met one of them who didn't worship their stones and ghosts. They sneer at Aysh and the Aspects."

"Until a few years ago, the Asset would have agreed with you." Rerth paused for a long moment, then let out a frustrated breath. "Ashe discovered something in the recordings that... I do not know what it means, but my instincts say it isn't something we can ignore. We need to find out what is happening in those temples."

Holde grimaced. "That's beyond our project, Rerth. Trinity's Director will drown us if they find out we're doing a drifting investigation in their territory."

One of her hands waved dismissively. "The Burned Hand is a priestess, probably of Velshen. We have every legitimate reason to infiltrate their temple. This will give us an opportunity to sift through both."

"If you're certain." He certainly didn't sound it. "Are you all right? You're normally not this quick to decide something like this."

"You'll understand when you watch the recording." His bond replied. "And you know that I was already contemplating following this current. The video was simply the final marker."

Holde frowned before tipping his head. "True. Once I'm done with the Captain, I'd like to see this video for myself."

"Go now, then. I will go there and view it again, see if there is

94

something we missed. Jet, Ashe? Go to the mess hall and pick up food for all four of us, then meet with me. Consider our usual schedules dismissed until we have collected every scrap of evidence we can from our existing data. Understood?"

All three of us nodded once.

"Good. The sooner we discover what is going on, the sooner we can create a plan of action to remove a potential threat to the Empire. Let's move."

X

Getting supplies for the *Posa'vilt* required leaving the Group of Five entirely. According to Rerth, there were a few hidden depots in the area, but they were reserved for ships operating out of Trinity. We didn't have the authorization to use them, and would be turned away unless we showed up literally starving and out of fuel.

Since we weren't even close to that level of dire emergency, we instead headed back the way we'd come. Two weeks of slow cruising brought us to the stable lane connecting Trinity to Earth, and let us reach one of the Waystations on that route.

Where I was promptly told to help the rest of the conscripts get everything loaded.

"It's kind of depressing really." Tevi called over from her cart, the pair of us idling while we waited for the next shift of locals to show up. Once they arrived and loaded the overly long vehicles we'd get to drive them over to where the ship was docked.

Then the rest of Tevi's pack would get to unload them while we got the easy drive back here for more.

"You get to be in a pack with an Agent, and she doesn't even get you out of things like this." She went on.

"I didn't really expect her to." Stretching my arms out a bit, I tried to find a more comfortable way to sit. If the driver's seat had ever had cushions, they'd long ago given up their battle for survival. "Honestly it's kind of a nice change of horizons right now. I'm tired of watching security footage six hours a day."

Her head bobbed in agreement, "That does sound pretty dull. Is that most of what intelligence work is? Watching boring things?"

"It's... hmm..."

"Hard to describe?" Tevi asked dryly.

96

I huffed, "Just trying to think of a comparison that will work. It's like being a regular conscript, except the rotation cycles are shorter. Instead of Ah-Cycles I get fun missions, but for every one or two days of those, I end up doing a few months of... watching security footage."

Or reading endless forms on the Group of Five's political body, trying to pinpoint the rate the priests had been acquiring power. Or digging through DataNet pages, looking for inconsistencies in their economic data.

Neither of those had been any more fun than trying to pick out priests using the starport on Varur'fluro, noting their times of arrival and departure, and trying to see if anything weird happened around them.

Tevi snorted in amusement. "I'd probably think that was an incredible analogy if I'd ever been on an Ah-Cycle. First mission off of Altair, remember?"

...right. Ugh. "Sorry. My mind's filled with fog from everything."

That drew a quick grin to her lips, both tarah lifting up. "I'm pretty sure that Uru or Noro would be very happy to help you focus."

A bit of warmth rose to my cheeks. "You think so?"

"Definitely. Uru thinks you're the most exotic thing she's ever seen, and Noro agrees with her. They've started arguing about which of them you like best."

I blinked. "Since when?"

"Last week or so." She paused, then snickered as she seemed to remember something. "Well, they argue as best as Noro can. I think either of them would be happy to join you in your cabin if you asked them."

I hadn't even really thought about it... but now that she'd mentioned it, I started to.

Uru was definitely attractive, and very forward about being interested in me. I'd taken that to be harmless flirting the last few times we'd spoken, but if she was serious... hm. I probably wouldn't have said no if she attempted to lure me to bed, but I didn't think she'd be all that interested in spending time with me beyond that.

97

Noro probably would. He was adorably in awe of me, treating my higher rank and status as an Agent's packmate as something far more important than they really were. Well, that and he was just adorable period. I wasn't sure he'd ever work up the nerve to ask me directly for anything, but if I approached him...

Huh. Since when was I the woman with romantic options?

I was about to ask her exactly why they both were into me, besides my apparently exotic species, when the next group of local conscripts finally showed up to help. The full Half-Sword entered the warehouse together, chatting quietly as they did.

Until one of them saw us waiting, sharply elbowing the woman next to him, and nodding... directly at me.

My mood began to descend into the deeps in an instant. I knew exactly what that expression meant; I'd seen those tight lips, lifted tarah, and narrowed eyes too many times to count.

Across from me, Tevi slowly settled her hands on the wheel, a frown wiping away her own good humor. When she spoke it was in a murmur, "What's their problem?"

"Me." I whispered back. "Don't respond to anything they say with anything but our orders."

She blinked. "What?"

Ashahn's blood. I was about to try and explain when the Half-Sword Leader, an unusually tall man, strode forward from among his pack.

For the moment my luck held; he ignored me entirely and directed his attention to Tevi. "Which ship are you supplying?"

Still looking confused, Tevi replied, "The *Posa'vilt,* it should be in your order docket."

He nodded once, pulling a tablet out from his uniform pocket. After a quick check he turned it around for her, "Twenty-four pallets of stored food. Sign at the bottom, Rifle-Experienced."

"Uh..." She tugged at her uniform, clearly pointing out the Conscript

98

rank badge she was wearing. "That's Ashe, not me."

I met his cold stare when he reluctantly turned to his left, clearly unhappy that he had to hold it out for me.

Taking it without a word, I glanced over the form before nodding once and signing with a finger. The moment it chimed with the verification, I started to hand it back, and nearly fumbled it when he yanked the thing out of my fingers.

"Get your carts set up in zones three and four." His voice dropped to an unpleasant growl. "We'll start loading."

Shaking my hand once to get the sting out of my fingers, I used my other one to shift the cart into gear. A quick glance at Tevi had her shake her head but follow my lead, her cart sliding in behind mine when I gently accelerated out of the waiting area.

A very short drive past enormous stacks of containers let me pull into the marked spot on the ground, Tevi doing the same to my right.

"What in Ashahn's bloody name is their problem?" She said the moment we had our vehicles quietly idling once again. "The morning Half-Sword was hungover and they were still more polite than those dead fish."

"Keep your voice down." I shot back, far more quietly. "They're supremacists is my guess."

"...wait, they're giving you those looks just because you're Human?"

It was both sad and kind of reassuring that it was only just now occurring to her. "Yes, Tevi."

"You've dealt with people like that before?"

Constantly. "Yes, Tevi."

Her jaw worked for a moment, but her voice finally dropped down to a murmur again. "Are they going to try anything?"

"We're on duty." I reminded her softly. "In my experience they'll settle for glaring and insults. If they start anything there's cameras in here, and they'll get demerits."

99

"...if you say so. What do we do?"

"What I said. Don't be loud, don't confront them. Repeat our orders to get back to the ship if they try to delay or harass us. I'll help with unloading and have someone else drive back with you on the next run."

She nodded, but didn't look happy about it.

Pushing out a breath, I tried to settle into the uncomfortable seat. Rerth's presence, and her rank badge, had protected me ever since I'd left Oshflara. It had been a pleasant break from what I'd been used to dealing with, but now it seemed like it was time to return to the familiar seas.

Regardless if I wanted to or not.

Despite their attitude it didn't take them very long to start hauling the heavy containers over with their own mini-carts. Each one had a small lift on the front, making it easy for them to slide the large boxes into the backs of our vehicles.

At least the first dozen. Once those were in place and locked down, the next set had to go on top of them.

I started to get nervous when they didn't bring out the heavier vehicles that the morning team had used to stack them. Instead the entire Half-Sword grouped up to use sorcery to lift them, the air filling with the ozone scent of their talent when they lifted the first into Tevi's.

That one had glided up and over as smoothly as if it had been on guidance ropes.

The one they loaded into mine... was not so controlled.

My fingers tightened around the wheel as it bobbed and weaved drunkenly far too close to my head, and kept wobbling once they got it up above. It wasn't until it was directly over the others that they got their control back...

And neatly put it into the very back instead of the front as they had for Tevi's.

My friend hissed the moment they all moved off to get the next pair.

100

"Those drowned assholes, you don't lift something that heavy over someone like that!"

"They're just trying to rattle me." I whispered back. "They want to make me dive out so that they can laugh at me, and the fact that I can't call up a barrier spell to protect me."

"This has happened to you before?"

"Yeah." More than once on my third assignment. "Steady, Tevi. Just a bit more and we're out of here."

I think she was going to reply, but the return of our hosts had her clenching her jaw instead. Just as before, her cart was loaded smoothly, while I was threatened by being crushed with a refrigerated container for the better part of twenty seconds before it moved into place.

That pattern repeated itself until it was time for the last of them to be brought over.

In hindsight, I should have taken a bit of the humiliation. Reacted a little, not enough to really set them off, but I could have flinched once or twice. Something to let them laugh among themselves and feel proud that they'd cowed a miserable Human.

Instead they started to get irritated that I wasn't giving them anything to work with.

I realized that something new was going on when they roughly, but cleanly, loaded the last container onto both of our carts and waved for us to move out.

Without going back inside. All eight of them glaring at me in particular.

Taking a few, slow breaths to calm myself, I carefully released the brakes. There was plenty of unpleasant things they could do once I was moving, things that only Tevi could attest to if they stuck with sorcery.

Accelerating as slowly as I could, the cart was practically crawling as I turned it to pull past Tevi's. That drew a visible snarl to one of the women's faces, and told me that my guess had been right.

If I'd tried to pull out quickly, they'd been planning on hitting the top-heavy cart with a strike or five. Enough to tilt it, knock it over, and make it look like I'd been driving recklessly in my rush to get out of there. With only Tevi's word that they'd used sorcery, and my demerit history, it probably would have worked in most of my past assignments.

I don't know why I slumped in relief as I straightened the wheel out. Why I gave them that visible sign that I knew I'd beaten them.

What I did know was that it was a stupid thing to do.

"Ashe!"

I jerked my head around at Tevi's shout just in time to see the same woman's tarah flexing out from her head. The Strike spell that slammed into my ribs was no less painful for being invisible, driving me sideways and making my hands yank down on the wheel.

The cart's pathetic speed was the only thing that stopped it from instantly tipping. Gasping in panic, I slammed my foot down on the brake at the same time as I let go of the wheel, jerking the thing to a shuddering stop.

I felt it leaning for several seconds before settling back, leaving me to sink back in relief.

At least until a pair of shouts had me whip around again, just in time to see Tevi finish crossing the distance between her cart and my attacker... and deck her full across the face.

"Shit!" Ripping off my restraints, I barely had the presence of mind to lock the brakes down before I got out. "Tevi! Stop!"

My voice was one of too many; the woman's packmates were already mobbing my friend. Fists and hands shoved her back, then sorcery slammed her into the side of her vehicle.

"Sto-"

A teeth-rattling *boom* cut off my shout, and made every Trahcon in the area grab their tarah in agony. While they tried to recover, I turned to the warehouse's entrance to see that two more carts had just pulled in.

Two other conscripts from the ship who I knew by face if not name were driving those.

And Rerth and Holde were riding in the back of one.

From their expressions as they leaped down, neither was anything less than livid.

"Attention!" Holde's shout had everyone straighten on reflex, though the movement made me grimace and clutch at my ribs.

The movement drew Rerth's attention at once, her features growing more thunderous as she stomped over. "So that's what this is about. The usual problem, Ashe?"

I winced. "Something like that, sir."

"I see." Her eyes turned to glare at everyone else. It was apparently just as intimidating for everyone else as it usually was to me; everyone, Tevi included, dropped their tarah in submission when she looked at them. "Holde? Deal with the locals. Conscript! Are you fit to drive?"

Tevi looked like she was already bruising, but nodded once. "Yes sir."

"Good. Back into your cart, follow us back to the ship. I will be speaking with your Sword Leader about a suitable demerit." Tevi proved her youth by wincing, but she still managed a sharp salute before limping to her vehicle.

"Ashe." Rerth growled, an edge still in her voice.

I gave her a salute of my own, then turned around and marched back the way I'd come. Settling back into the driver's seat, I waited until Rerth had taken the empty seat beside me before carefully accelerating away from yet another unfortunate incident caused because...

Caused because I had been born Human, instead of Trahcon.

XI

The supply outpost was a hollowed out asteroid, meaning space was at a premium. Even once we left the warehouse I didn't get the cart up beyond a walking pace. While it didn't take us long to get back to the tunnels connecting us to the docking ring, the trip through the narrow spaces took a lot longer.

Rerth was quiet until we made it that far, speaking up as I made the turn. "What happened?"

My right shoulder rolled a little. "Supremacists tried to intimidate me into a reaction, then tried to get me to tip the cart when I didn't give them what they wanted. One of them snapped when I avoided what I thought was their last attempt and tried... something more direct. Tevi reacted."

"Hrn." Her grunt was as quiet as it was angry. "Details."

Sighing, I relayed what had happened. The arrival of the new Half-Sword to handle the afternoon shift, their reactions to my presence, and how they'd enjoyed threatening me with being crushed to death. What they'd probably been planning to do when I left, and what one of them had done when I'd managed to forestall that attempt.

And how Tevi had reacted when she'd heard the spell hit me.

She listened silently until I finished.

"Why didn't you send a message to us that you were being threatened?" She demanded. "You had more than an hour of them swinging crates over your head. I could have sailed in to deal with it a half hour ago, if not earlier."

Her tone made some rebellious waves curl around my heart. I worked my jaw for a moment, but managed to keep my tone both civil and respectful. "Because it wasn't anything I haven't dealt with before, sir. On every assignment I've ever been on since you conscripted me."

My unspoken comment, that *she* had been the one to personally pick out my assignments, couldn't have been more blatant.

From the way her tarah briefly lowered in shame, she got that message loud and clear.

"I had thought your packs would have sheltered you from that." She replied, voice quieter. "At least on your more tolerable assignments."

I twitched my shoulders, the motion drawing a bit of pain to the new bruise on my ribs. "Having protection just gives the supremacists an excuse and a grudge. They tell themselves they could have put me in place if not for a real citizen blocking them, and a lot of times they lurk on the horizon until they know I'm alone. Then it gets worse."

She let out a furious little breath, shifting as best she could in the passenger seat. "Your officers should have dealt with it."

"Few cared." I said, carefully turning to follow a curve in the tunnel. "Or believed me. And even when I was in Huvu's pack it's not like I was with her constantly. Usually it didn't happen on duty like this, but I've charted those seas pretty well. I know where I made my mistakes today, what caused them to attack."

That growl came back into her voice at once. "You didn't make any mistakes. You're a citizen of the Empire, that they *attacked* you with sorcery at all is enraging."

Coming from anyone else and I'd have appreciated the sentiment. I suppose I even liked it a bit from her, but... she was still the one who'd put me on all of those past assignments. Who'd picked out my first pack. My third, fourth, and fifth. Who'd so often left me surrounded by people who loathed my very existence.

I knew, on some level, that my resentment of her was irrational. There was every likelihood my term of conscription would have been just as awful without her interference in my career.

"Permission to speak as a packmate, sir?" I asked.

Her left tarah flicked outwards for a moment. "Yes."

"Part of me really wanted to punch you when you said that."

Rerth went still, eyes widening a little. That clearly hadn't been what

105

she'd expected me to say.

"I appreciate the sentiment, Rerth." I went on, speaking quietly. "I really do. But you're the one who kept putting me on assignments where I had to deal with Humans hating me, Trahcon hating me. I've even run into Naule who enjoyed mocking my appearance every morning. I want an Empire where I won't be attacked just for being born the wrong species, but... that isn't the Empire I have."

"Ashe, I've apologized-"

I pushed on, speaking over her, and for once it was the Agent who quieted down instead of me. As I told her things I'd never actually admitted to her before.

"Rerth. Today was nothing. One bruise, not even a real crisis. On Oshflara, my second best assignment before this one, I ran into a group of locals who beat me until I could barely walk. All because I was alone and they felt like it. *That* is closer to my normal routine than being sheltered in an Imperial Agent's pack."

"...how many times?"

"Have I been used as sorcery practice?" I asked, shrugging. "Enough that I haven't counted how many times those waves struck my beaches."

Her eyes closed for a long moment. Then she exhaled, reached up to her collar, and carefully pulled her rank badge off. I blinked in surprise as she settled it onto the dash, then leaned back once more as I drove slowly down the dimly lit tunnel.

"Packmate to packmate." She murmured, "I will never not regret my choices when it came to your assignments. And yes, Ashe. I am sorry I pulled you off of Huvu'ithi's. You weren't rated for combat, and I was terrified you would die before I could make amends for what happened with your first pack. I was rash, and I made a decision without consulting with you or her about it."

I swallowed, glancing between her and the tunnel to make sure I didn't crash us. "...that doesn't make me any less resentful."

"I didn't expect it to. You've made it clear you aren't about to forgive me for that, and I am not about to ask for such mercies. I'm just... ugh." Both

106

of her hands rose, running lightly along her tarah before she sighed again. "I was assigned to investigate how you ended up on Alzuc, one lone Human, because I happened to be there to close out another project. Going from the triumph of shutting down a criminal guild, to holding a terrified child as she sobbed into my neck was the single most awful moment of my life. I..."

I bit my lip, focusing very hard on the road. I didn't like to think about that day. Not even a little bit.

After a moment, she found her voice again, sounding too uncertain to really be Rerth. "...I felt responsible for you. I don't know why. I don't have Closed Nest, or any romantic interest in you. You were someone I should have simply dropped off before moving on with my actual work. But... when it came time, I couldn't just let you be randomly assigned. I had to pick out the best place for you. To... I don't know. Make up for the pain I caused when I took you away."

A gentle wave reached my mind. "Ashahn's blood... I'm still a child to you, aren't I?"

"You're not even thirty." She replied. "Of course you are. I know that physically, mentally, you're a huntress. Intellectually I know that. But every time I had to pick you up after your pack turned on you, or because your determination to investigate caused problems... you're still that tiny child whose tears stained my uniform."

"I'm-"

"Let me finish." I closed my mouth, and did. "I'm not giving excuses. You've told me you resent me before, and I will always admit that it is justified. What I am saying is that... I will never stop trying to make things right, even if I can't tell you exactly why I feel that way."

"...yeah." I said softly. "I know, and... dammit. I *do* appreciate you Rerth. I'm happy to be your packmate, I'm thrilled to finally be trained in the one thing I seem to be good at. I just... Ashahn's blood. Every time I start to relax, start to think I'm in a good place, something like today happens."

My elder sighed, "And everything you buried under the ice erupts. If you were Trahcon, I could name any three mental conditions for that. All of them stemming from the fact that you've never had a stable pack in your life. Even as a child, you had to have known that you'd be separated from the others."

107

Fingers clenched around the wheel, "I did my best to pretend that day would never come."

"For which no one can blame you, but you still *knew*. In your entire life, you've never had a stable pack. One that you could honestly believe you'd be with for the rest of your life."

Her saying the words out loud made my heart ache, my head bow. The cart slowed further as I let my foot off the accelerator, letting us glide forward.

"...no." I admitted without looking up. "I've... never thought that."

A warm hand came to rest on my shoulder. "I can't promise that with us either, Ashe. I'm not blind. I know you and Jet don't really like one another. What I can promise is that, when you arrive at an Academy, I will do everything I can to make sure you have a choice in what kind of pack you build for yourself."

I swallowed, glancing at her. "Do you mean that?"

She nodded firmly, eyes meeting my own. "If you want to be attached to Huvu'ithi then, I'll arrange it. If you want Pack Vet to support your investigations, I will find a way to transfer them. If you truly like the conscripts we're working with now, I will do the same."

And for a few long breaths... I imagined it. Stealing Fyth from her pack, earning her forgiveness. Supporting Huvu as the intelligence officer assigned to her formation. Cutting through the waves of the Contested Zone, discovering the secrets of the Holy Concordat. Discovering enemy agents, then sending in my friends to clear them out.

Being respected for what I could uncover, instead of derided for my fur.

It was a dream I'd nearly given up on. A dream I could lose at any moment if I made one more great mistake. But...

"Even with as many times as I've fucked up, you still think I can make it?"

There was no hesitation in her reply. "You would not be in my pack if

I did not, little shark."

I let out a ragged... breath, sob, gasp, I couldn't even describe it. All I could do was reach up with a shaking hand to grasp hers. "...thank you, Rerth."

"You have no need to." The seat creaked as she leaned over, planting a gentle kiss on my temple before slowly drawing back. "Are you all right to drive us back?"

Nodding, I checked my face for tears and rubbed away the moisture under my eyes. Rerth patted my shoulder again, then got her rank badge back in place when I shifted the cart back into motion.

Ashahn only knew what Tevi was thinking behind us.

"Um..." I cleared my throat, desperately trying to sound professional again. "...I think it would be best if I changed my duties for the rest of today, sir."

"I quite agree. In fact I think we should both avoid that warehouse for the remainder of our stay here."

My foot gently pushed back down again, getting us rolling in the right direction. "Both of us?"

Her voice dropped to a furious growl. "Yes. The only thing that stopped me from hammering those dead fish into the ground was my self control as both an Agent and a Guide. And the fact that you've been literally beaten in the past makes me want to start a personal project to track down everyone responsible."

That little spark of resentment was still there, still flickering... but that time it lost the war to the small smile that creased my lips. "I wouldn't mind seeing either of those things, sir."

"Of course you wouldn't." Rerth's grin was quick and vicious. "Sadly it would be unprofessional of me. So I'll have to restrict that to my imagination, and focus on training you properly instead."

"As you say, sir. Um, what kind of training did you have in mind?"

She hummed, clearly considering it as we drove along. "Considering how little I trust Jet's ability to pose as a merchant, we'll need to work on your acting if you're to loom appropriately behind him. Holde says you've been improving significantly in that area."

A tiny bit of heat rose to my cheeks. "He exaggerates."

"We'll see if he does, or does not." She paused, then smiled once again. "I recall a rather amusing drill from the Academy that you might enjoy. We'll need three of your fellow conscripts, ones you haven't spoken of your past with."

"I thought I was better than unblooded conscripts?"

Rerth blinked, then huffed out an amused little laugh. "You are. There are at least two officers who would love nothing more than to run their hands through your fur while you caress their tarah. Find them or continue to go without."

I rolled my eyes a little. "Yes sir, thank you for controlling my sex life in addition to my career."

"Brat." She growled, but it was more playful than angry. "Regardless. The point of this will be to test how well your lessons in creating versions of your past have sunk in. You'll be giving each of the conscripts a different tale of your life, and they will then have to try and piece together what you were lying about."

That... did sound kind of interesting. Not my favorite area of training, but interesting all the same. "What if I lie about the entire thing?"

"Then you will win the game if they think more of it was true than false, but I doubt you will travel that river. You prefer partial lies like Holde does, do you not?"

"I do." I admitted, picking up the speed at bit more as we finally reached the docking ring. Stone floors gave way to metal, and the narrow confines opened into the broad halls. "How long do I have to prepare?"

She glanced around, then shrugged. "Ten minutes until we arrive at the ship, and perhaps that many again for me to find three off duty soldiers to listen to your lies. I would get started now if I were you."

I felt another smile come and go.

In spite of everything, Rerth was still Rerth... and even if I would never tell her, I did love her for caring about me more than I resented her for screwing up my assignments.

"Yes sir. I'll do my best to impress you."

"I know you will, little shark."

XII

Eight weeks later I was sipping tea on Yashun, staring down from our hotel balcony at the neighboring Temple of Mahkhas.

The shrine to the Aspect of Light Sorcery and Nightmares was a beautiful spire that towered over our hotel. It was absolutely covered in windows, making the entire structure glisten painfully in the sunlight. I couldn't look at it for more than a minute, and let my eyes fall to the carefully tended grounds surrounding it.

They were both far easier to look at, and far more important. Those green spaces was where the local disciples were laboring through their daily training.

"The tea is good, thank you." I said after my third or fourth sip.

Jet stirred from his place on my right, his own glass cradled in his upper pair of hands. "You're welcome, and thanks for not falling over in an allergic fit."

A faint smile tugged at my lips. "You're just happy you've got someone else who can drink your tea, so you aren't stuck finishing an entire box on your own."

"True." His sharp teeth appeared. "Anything interesting this morning?"

"No." My smile faded into a sigh. "Just the same trainees out doing their morning routines. No one from other temples today."

There was a quiet grunt of disappointment. "Holde?"

I leaned forward just a bit, then nodded to the left. "He's in the corner. I think he's been pretending to screw up something simple from how many times one of the ranking priests has come over to try and coach him."

"That or he's abusing his supposed handsomeness."

"There's nothing supposed about it. Don't be jealous."

Jet scoffed. "Aliens. He's as ugly as a slab-sided rock. Still, if he can seduce his way into secure quarters, we might be able to trim this down to a short visit. Otherwise we might be here for a few more months."

That didn't sound particularly appealing to me. Mostly because Jet and I wouldn't be on the surface nearly that long; our cover as traveling merchants was already wearing out. Two days from now and we'd be back in orbit, supporting the others from a distance while we tried to piece through what little we'd discovered.

Not that I minded the crew or anything. I'd started to become friends with a few packs, particularly the Thun. But liking them, and wanting to be stuck with them and Jet on a ship the size of the *Posa'vilt* for months on end, were two entirely different seas.

I had no idea how sailors went that long without seeing sunlight, but I was finding that about a month was my limit before I needed real ground under my feet.

"Do you think we'll really be anchored here for six more months?" I asked.

"It's possible." Jet admitted. "It's even likely it might take longer."

"Really?" I tried, and failed, to keep the dismay from my voice. "You think they'll wait that long before they try to acquire information?"

He huffed. "Rerth would definitely want to. She's been cruising at top speed through this whole project, and I'm sure it's getting to her. Worst case, the ship runs low on supplies, we'll probably head to Trinity to wait for a call to come back and pick them up."

I blinked. "And what? We just... leave them here without support?"

His lower pair of hands rolled to be palm up, in what I was pretty sure was a shrug of some kind. "Wouldn't be the first time I've had to. Rerth's usually thorough about this sort of thing, like I said."

"Oh." I bit my lip, turning to look down at the various acolytes once again. "Do you think it's the video that's making her move so fast? Or is it the Burned Hand?"

113

"Probably all of it." He sipped more tea. "The smuggling ring we found on Oshflara, and here, is massive. Bigger and more spread out than any I've ever heard of, and I know that's offended her. Toss in the Burned Hand, too many unsolved murders, and the strange behavior we saw in the security recordings..."

Enough problems were all swirling together that she felt pressured to figure out what was happening sooner rather than later.

"Makes sense, I guess." I brought my own cup to my lips, enjoying the flavor before asking my next question.

Despite more than two weeks worth of work, and plenty of evidence that there was far too many Imperial products here, Jet hadn't quite managed to find the distributors. Well, besides House ul Grator. They were definitely involved, but they didn't seem nearly wealthy or numerous enough to be handling *everything* we were finding.

We'd expected to find cars and farming equipment, and we had. We'd also found heavy vehicles, travel gear, liquor, sculptures, artwork, and furniture. There'd even been a rather unscrupulous looking Thondian who'd offered an Kalladahn made FTL capable shuttle-craft.

About the only thing we hadn't found was guns. I wasn't sure if that was just because we hadn't found them yet, or if it was because there weren't any here. Jet firmly believed it was the former, and I couldn't bring myself to disagree.

Of course, knowing that it was all for sale here didn't really do us much good. Not if we couldn't figure out who was actually bringing it all in, and who was paying them to do so.

"Do you think the smugglers know we're after them?" I asked.

"Smart ones always think someone is after them, and they're almost always right." Fur rippled as he shook his head, betraying his own annoyance at our lack of progress. "Either people like us, pirates looking to expand who they steal from, or criminal guilds looking to forcibly recruit them."

I fought the urge to roll my eyes. "You know what I mean, Jet. Rerth and I were playing flicker-fish for most of six months after Oshflara. Do you think that made them dive deep before we even got here?"

"It's possible, but I doubt it. Worst you probably did was scare a few smugglers off of their usual routes, or pushed them into other regions." He glanced at me. "Annoyed that we haven't caught them?"

"...a bit."

There was a quiet huff. "You're not alone. Rerth won't be happy if we don't come up with something. She's embarrassed enough that such a large group was operating in a sector we're assigned to, and we didn't have any idea they existed."

Yeah, that would definitely bother her. "What's our next plan then?"

"Not much we can do while we're here to be honest. I don't want to risk hacking anything while we're on site like this, too easy to trace back. We'll save that for when we're on the ship."

I nodded, "I'll be on data analysis again?"

He rose with a quiet groan, all of his limbs stretching out. "Not like you can help me with the hacking, or checking out that eastern distributor. I'm going to handle that this afternoon."

Fighting the urge to scowl, I turned back to look down at the temple grounds again. That particular warehouse had refused to talk to him simply because I'd been present. It hadn't escalated, thank the Aspects, but it hadn't improved my mood any.

"Did you get our analysis on the local economy compiled yet?" He asked as he walked behind me.

Huffing in irritation, I turned as he did, following him back into our room proper. It wasn't much; two beds, a dresser, a nightstand, and a working desk. Still, it was more comfortable than the shuttle, so there was that.

"You know I did that this morning, you saw me finishing it up." I said. "Complete with all of your target recommendations if a raid is going to happen."

"I hadn't had my tea yet. You're lucky I remembered who you were."

I rolled my eyes. "It's compiled and a copy was sent up to the ship, just like Rerth ordered the last time she managed to call in."

Which had been a few days ago, and we weren't expecting another message from her anytime soon.

Holde had gotten the lucky side of that particular coin flip between them, getting to infiltrate the Temple of Mahkhas. None of us were particularly sure if that Aspect's disciples were up to anything, but there was a very unusual number of temples devoted to that Aspect here.

Just as there were too many devoted to Velshen... which was where Rerth was similarly posing as a would-be disciple.

In her single chance to call us, she'd confirmed that there was a lot of anti-alien sentiment among the priests. That was a little worrying, but it became alarming when she said it was being matched by a lot of anti-Imperial sentiment within their sermons.

I was nervous for both of them, even if neither had seemed particularly worried about their personal safety.

"All right then." Jet set his mostly empty cup on our desk, then started ambling around to grab his things. "I'll check those warehouses, see if I can't figure out who actually owns them. I'll be back by the evening meal, then we can start packing for our departure tomorrow."

"What's the plan?" I asked.

He gave me a proper shrug that time, walking between our beds to grab his wrist-comps from the nightstand. "The security guard on the western side is a kid. Going to bribe him, not try any breaking and entering."

"Just don't get arrested, please."

There was a quiet chuckle. "No guarantees. You've got our emergency plan if that happens. Follow it and don't do anything stupid."

Leave him in jail, send a priority message to Holde and Rerth, then get myself back up to the ship, he meant.

"I remember. I'm not going to try and arrange a jailbreak entirely on my own." I sat down on my bed, stretching my legs out a little. "Do we have enough work to last us six months?"

Jet hummed, tugging the mesh sleeves over three of his forearms. "Probably. Why? Bored?"

My back tightened up defensively. "We've done all of our analysis, and found everything we can on the DataNet. How much more will you really find once we're back on the ship?"

"I'm sure I'll find something. As for you, there's always more research to do."

"And I've been doing it." I crossed my arms, blowing out a breath before going on. "It just seems like we've already found everything we're going to find that way. There's nothing left on the public servers, and I don't have your hacking skills. That leaves me just going over the same limited news reports we can pull from the DataNet."

For once he looked like he agreed with me, lips twisting in displeasure. "You're not wrong, and we'd be making more progress if Rerth had let us pick a better cover. We could linger and search more rivers, question more of the locals."

Our cover was the reason we were already leaving. Posing as a merchant and his Human bodyguard only worked for so long if you never actually bought anything.

It would also help if he wasn't terrible at the questioning part, even if he was very good at the searching half.

I, at least, had the tact not to say that to his face.

"Especially if she'd let me go out without you. We'd cover more ground if we could split up, pose as something else."

There was another wave of his hand, "I don't disagree, but you're still her personal whirlpool of guilt. She's not going to risk you unless she's standing next to you at every moment."

Truth. After the bar trip on Varur'fluro, and our talk on the supply station, I'd kind of hoped that I'd be able to do a little more. But instead... instead that was apparently a one-off, and now I was back to being just a supporting member.

A younger, more foolish me with fewer severe demerits might have

117

tried to convince Jet to let me go out and explore anyway.

The me that never wanted to have to live on a penal colony was too scared to do more than complain once in a while.

"Good luck today." I told him, pushing down more complaints that wouldn't change anything. "Let me know if you need any quick research done. Or directions if you get lost again."

Jet snorted, waving two of his arms my way as he made for the door. "You get lost one time in a foreign city, and suddenly conscripts think they can tease you about it."

"Three times!" I called to his back.

The door shut on his grumbling, leaving me alone in the hotel room with... well, not all that much to do really.

Like I'd just told Jet, I was pretty much done with my analysis of his findings. Not that I'd really done much 'analyzing'... it had really just been translating his notes into the proper forms to be filed when we got back to the Empire, which had been just as much fun as it sounded like.

We had every bit of public information we could get on the local temples, and the temples throughout the Group of Five. There wasn't a public member list, but the sheer number of groups dedicated to the Aspects hinted that the locals were either extremely devout, or they were trying to train up a sorcery-focused military force.

We had our rough analysis of the local economy; it was unusually strong, and had far too many blatantly Imperial goods to not be reliant on smuggling. Especially since the official records didn't have nearly enough ships coming in from the Empire or Alum to account for it all.

We even had a compilation of local death records, taken from public news sites. Among that we'd picked out three that fit our old pattern of non-Trahcon brutally murdered by flame-based sorcery. They'd all died in a narrow stretch of time about nine years ago, but it made me think that the Burned Hand had once been here.

We'd done all of that over the past four weeks, and now there was... well, not much left for us to do given the constraints of Rerth's orders.

118

"So now what?" I asked, walking back out onto the sunlit balcony. "Is this another test of hers? Seeing how I handle the monotony of all this?"

I'd have thought so, but she'd been clear I was to follow Jet's orders while she and Holde played infiltrator. And Jet had kept me busy up until we'd simply run out of things we could safely check.

"Can't exactly research his past. Or call my old packmates. Or even chat with anyone on the ship."

I stared down as the morning training apparently wrapped up; the various disciples, Holde included, were already filing into the tower. Within a few minutes they'd all vanished inside, leaving me with nothing to watch.

Sitting down in one of the chairs, I let my head fall back with a groan. "Let's see. I wrote a letter to Huvu last night. Wrote one to Yora the day before. Can't send either until I'm on the ship. I guess... I could go back to searching through the records for something we've missed."

That didn't sound very interesting. Or likely to result in anything new.

Sighing quietly, I reached down and unlocked the recline function on the seat. All I had to do after that was lean back and enjoy the sunlight on my skin.

Sheltering my eyes with one hand, I made sure my wrist-comp's volume was set to high before letting my arms fall and my eyes close.

It's furious chiming five minutes later had my eyes snapping open to let me stare right into the noon sun.

Yelping louder than I should have, I ducked my head and blinked as quickly as I could to try and clear the spots.

"Ow, uh, Ashe'lori!" I managed to tap to accept the call.

"Rifle-Experienced." Captain Koru's voice came from near my wrist. "Am I interrupting training?"

Ashahn's blood. "Uh, no sir! I was startled by the call, it's been a quiet morning sir."

I couldn't tell if he believed me or not when he spoke again. "I see. Is

119

your packmate still unable to communicate?"

"Yes sir. Two of us will be returning to the ship on schedule."

"Very well. Should she become available, inform her that her latest report has garnered attention from Trinity. A reinforced battlegroup is being dispatched to chastise the local citizens for their illegal trade."

My mouth went dry even as my heart plummeted into the depths of my soul. "What about our investigation sir? We believe it may take months!"

"Then you have fifteen days to increase your speed." He replied. *"Inform your superior as soon as possible. There is nothing I or she can do to countermand the orders."*

"But-"

"Orbital Asset out."

"Sir, please..." My voice trailed off as soon as I realized that he'd ended the transmission. "...dammit."

An entire Imperial battlegroup was on the way here... by the holy Aspects, this was going to be a mess.

Swallowing, I got myself upright and staggered inside, finally getting my eyes clear enough to see the screen floating above my forearm. A few quick taps started up another call... and got it ended by rejection almost at once.

"Dammit." The word came with a sharper tap on the priority icon, turning it to the highest one we had. "Pick up, Jet."

Thankfully he did, though he didn't sound happy about it. *"If this isn't an emergency you are going to be in trouble."*

"We have fifteen days until an Imperial invasion starts."

Silence.

"Does that count?" I asked, unable to help myself.

"...fuck! Hang the towel from the railing to alert Holde we've got a

120

level one problem. Soon as you've done that, start packing. We need to get to orbit as soon as possible."

"On it."

XIII

Rerth waited until the day before the projected invasion before fleeing the temple, making her way back to the starport, and then getting back up to the ship. She didn't even stop to change, and was still wearing her black and red disciple's robes when she arrived.

Not that the outfit did anything to detract from her anger.

"Which storm-wrecked idiot thought this was a good idea!?" The shout made me, along with everyone else, flinch. "Where the fuck is the Captain?"

"Bridge." Holde quickly moved to block her path, hands spread as if he hoped to placate her. "Rerth, he didn't request this. Please don't cause an inter-service incident while we're in the middle of a bloody storm."

Her fully lifted tarah told me that she didn't really care about the circumstances. "He should have maintained communications silence! We're not even within Imperial borders, what was he thinking routing reports!?"

"Yes," He allowed, "He should have known better, but we didn't *order* him to stay silent. He was within his rights to relay the reports we've compiled to the archives on Trinity."

"If you're trying to calm me down you're failing miserably!"

"I know better, I'm trying to distract you. Our bigger problem right now is Ashe's theory."

Rerth's terrifying glare snapped to me at once. "What theory?"

I swallowed nervously, not having expected him to actually mention it. "Um, it's just a theory I came up with last week. I didn't think he'd mention-"

"Out with it!"

Another flinch. "Right. Um, Holde says that reports from an Agent shouldn't have drawn much attention this quickly. They should have just been

122

archived, maybe looked at in a few months once priority-"

She interrupted me again, this time by swearing. "Iriahn's fucking blood. You think the Burned Hand knows we're after them, and they have an agent on Trinity?"

"Well..." I shifted my weight, "I didn't quite go that far, but I thought it was very strange that there was a battlegroup sent so quickly to start an invasion over smuggling."

Jet gave me a vague wave. "Smuggling that we haven't even confirmed yet. We've got one unproven distributor and no actual smugglers, so as far as Intelligence is concerned all we have is educated guesswork. That means either our Avatar of Khash is living up to her name, and they were preparing to invade anyway..."

I glared at him, but finished his thought. "Or they recognized us from when we were sailing around after Oshflara. And they're fine with starting an invasion to cover up their activities."

Our leader's jaw worked, both of her tarah quivering angrily for several long breaths. "There are problems with your theory. Starting with the fact that you presume the Burned Hand has high level contacts inside of a major Imperial outpost. Even more, that they'd go so far to conceal their presence in the Group of Five out of fear of a single Agent's investigation. That combination is beyond unlikely."

"Yes sir," I admitted, "But, um, so is a sudden invasion of a client state on nothing more than unconfirmed economic reports. Especially after the Empire has supposedly been supporting them for decades without any real problems."

Holde tipped his head, "You've got to admit, Rerth. The seas are a few degrees beyond murky. Even if Ashe's little theory is wrong, there's definitely *something* seriously odd going on out here."

"Obviously Holde!" She snapped. "We wouldn't be here otherwise."

His normally polite voice turned annoyed as well. "You know what I mean."

Her grunt said that she did, but that she wasn't about to apologize. "Fine. If someone at Trinity is behind this, they'll be moving to cover it up.

123

Holde, Jet. Compile all of our reports, including what I just sent you about the temple this morning. I want local copies kept secure in case someone out there felt the need to adjust what we sent in order to cause this."

"Got it." Holde replied, "You want a duty list of the Agents and Operatives there as well?"

"Yes. If you can also grab the Network teams, I'll take them, otherwise we'll have to wait until we arrive to track them down." When he nodded, she turned to me again. "Ashe? You're with me. I have a Captain to interrogate and give orders to."

"Um, me?"

"Yes!" The bark made me jump. "You're the witness to anything that useless idiot of a deadfish says!"

"Sir!" I saluted on little more than panicked reflex, and then quickly raced to fall in beside her. Despite the fact that I was taller it was a struggle to keep up with her furious stalk towards the bridge.

I may not have been the wisest woman in the Empire, but I was wise enough to keep my mouth shut for the entire trip.

"Captain Anahc'koru." I had no idea how, but she managed to sound civil when we arrived.

Well, mostly civil, given that she still looked like she was an instant away from violence. Both of her tarah were quivering without pause, and the distinctive ozone of impending sorcery was filling the air.

"Agent Riah." The reply came as the Captain turned around, facing us from the center of the bridge. To his own credit he didn't look perturbed in the slightest, and waved for the crew to focus on their duties when they started to glance over.

It wasn't my first time in the ship's command center. I'd come with a few other times that someone, usually Holde, had visited to speak with the various officers.

Not that there was really all that much to see. The room was basically an armored box in just forward of the ship's center, buried as far inside the hull as possible. It had just enough space for a dozen command stations, along

124

with a central position for the Captain.

"Before you speak," Koru fell into a casual at-ease stance once he was sure his officers were focused. "You did not order communications silence, and it is protocol to dispatch all reports on a weekly basis for backup."

"Considering that you have been assigned to Intelligence activities for the last forty years, I should not have had to." She snapped back, "Not when fifty percent of our assets were attempting fully submerged infiltration on a non-Imperial world."

He snorted, right tarah angling outwards for a brief moment. "I learned my lesson about presuming the whims of Agents long ago. If you'd wanted silence, you should have ordered it."

Rerth's jaw clenched while I did my best to blend into the background. "You're clearly in no danger of being assigned to a Void Fleet anytime soon."

I flinched at the sharpness of the comment, but the Captain merely flicked his tarah again. "As I have no desire to join those impulsive fools, your insult misses the mark. Doubly so, as it is those same fools who are sailing at full speed to disrupt your project."

"Can their orders be countermanded?"

"The dispatch was signed off by Chahshti'tahza Obdel'rilem." His voice turned dry. "It implied this operation has his personal approval and attention."

A Void Lord was responsible for this? My throat went a bit dry at the thought. That was... a level far beyond even a veteran Imperial Agent.

From the way Rerth grudgingly shook her head, she wasn't about to try to countermand the orders. As angry as she was, she at least had enough control to recognize sheer stupidity when she saw it.

Not that it didn't take her nearly a minute of steady breathing before she managed to speak again. "...very well. What is the operation plan? Full conquest or merely chastisement?"

"Chastisement of Yashun to begin with, to be followed up depending on the initial results."

125

Rerth growled. "Irritating. Very well, we'll have to weather this particular storm. I will be taking personal command of your infantry compliment."

He straightened slightly. "I presume they will not be merely raiding warehouses to look for Imperial goods?"

"No. Direct assault of the Temple of Velshen, located in the outskirts of the colonial capital." There was another deep inhalation, then she slowly let it out. "We'll time it to coincide with the full invasion. Have all three shuttles fully prepared, and have the ship similarly ready for a fast transit to Trinity upon conclusion."

"Very well. Should I prepare a space for prisoners?"

"Yes. Time of the fleet's arrival?"

"Latest report had the initial battlegroup arriving tomorrow by the sixteenth hour. Based on the latest reports from the FTL buoys, I'd expect them by the twelfth hour, if not earlier."

My packmate nodded tightly. "I want Sword Leader Seru'hoth in the conference room within the hour to discuss the plan of attack."

"She will be alerted."

A final sharp nod preceded Rerth storming right back out, forcing me once again to hurry to keep up with her.

I was ready to stay quiet the rest of the way back to our cabin, but Rerth didn't quite make it that far. Instead the moment the lift doors closed she brought both of her hands in front of her mouth, and... well...

Screamed so loudly that my ears rang.

"Those storm-wrecked, shark fucking, cursed by the Aspects idiots!"

"...ow." My own hands rose to rub at my ears, but apparently even that quiet noise was enough to remind my elder that I existed.

She whirled on me, taking a step forwards to get right in front of me. "Swear to me, by the Aysh itself, that you didn't do anything stupid with Jet."

126

"I swear, Rerth! I stayed in the hotel and just did research."

Her eyes narrowed. "...you never left it?"

"Just to the shuttle and back, and only with Jet." I swallowed, weight shifting. I knew I probably... well, I definitely deserved the doubt, but it still hurt a bit. "I know better than to risk my last chance, Rerth."

"...you do." Rerth's little nose flexed as she took more deep breaths. "Dammit."

"...do you think someone would start an invasion just to stop us?"

Rerth's jaw worked for a moment, then she reached out and jammed her thumb down on the hold control. The lift obediently beeped, locking in place just before it could arrive on our level.

She stayed like that for a little while, seemingly mulling it over before she finally spoke. "I cannot rule it out as a theory, but like I said before. It is beyond unlikely. A percent chance, if that, and you know better than to offer theories without evidence."

I winced, glancing down at my feet. "I know, but... I knew you'd be frustrated, and the suddenness of it doesn't make any sense."

"It may, if there is pressure on Lord Obdel'rilem. With no active wars, and the Torlah forbidding intervention in the Ascendancy, he may be jumping at the chance to win glory."

"Yeah, but... I thought of that." I defended my theory as best I could. "If that was really what this was about, why didn't they send an Agent anytime in the last few decades? The Group of Five has been around for a while, and from the scale of what Jet and I were finding? I don't think them filling their economy with smuggled goods is new."

Her right tarah twitched sharply. "A respectable point, but the Torlah may have issued direct orders against that kind of action. We simply do not know the details."

Well, when she put it like that... ugh. My very first project and I was already breaking rules that I'd been good about sticking to when it had just been me doing the investigating.

127

"No theories without direct evidence." I sighed, repeating the rule out loud. "Or else you start seeing the rivers going to the destinations you want, instead of where they actually go."

The sound she made was vaguely approving, one finger reaching up to tap my chin. "It's not the worst theory, even if it is both far too paranoid and egotistical. There *are* other factors involved in the Empire beyond our project, little shark."

I winced. "Sorry."

Rerth snorted, finally looking like she was calming down a little. "It's all right. You're at least half as frustrated as I am, and you were looking for someone in specific you could blame for costing us our best leads."

Now that was a change of subject that I could get behind. "We didn't find much in specific though, apart from the Noroth machines on Rurasflara. There's no direct proof of anything else, not from anything recent at least."

"Hmm." She hummed, finally letting go of the hold command.

"...what? I thought that was pretty good."

"Too obvious, too desperate." The words came with a little smile. "But to answer your unspoken question, yes. I do think that the Burned Hand, or one of her pack, is actively involved at the temple I was within. That is why we will be attacking it when the invasion begins."

I remembered what she and the Captain had said. "You want to capture the priests? Interrogate them?"

The door pinging open stopped her from replying, at least until we were walking down the hall towards the conference room. "Yes. Few of the disciples were capable of much, I expect them to submit to the shores of reality easily enough."

"But what about the priests themselves?" I asked. "And the smugglers?"

"There are only two. Holde and I should be enough, especially with a full Sword formation backing us." She paused, grimaced, then added. "Even if that Sword is nothing but fresh conscripts."

"And the smugglers?"

"Will be aborting their runs to Yashun as soon as news gets out, and it *will* get out. If Trinity is declaring this a full raid, that will mean they will also be taking over direct control of any local investigations."

My mouth fell open slightly, "They're... just going to take over our project?"

"I'm sure I could get it back, they won't actually *want* it. They'll want concessions about my time and energy once it's over. Want me to work directly on some of their own projects." Her head shook. "No. They caused this mess, they can deal with it. We will focus on the Burned Hand, and the priesthood's influence."

"Yes, sir." Hesitating, I found my next question after a few steps. "What about Jet and I?"

"Jet will be with us to access any secure systems we can find, preferably before any of them can find the intelligence to wipe them. *You*," And there was a very heavy emphasis on the word, "will be remaining aboard the ship."

"I can handle combat." I said defensively.

"Your elders will keep their own counsel on that front." Her tone was final.

"Yes sir." I replied dutifully, if not enthusiastically. Not that I *wanted* to see combat. I... really didn't, if I was being honest with myself. My stupid Human mind just not looking forward to it like it should have.

But that didn't mean I wanted my pack to go into peril without me either.

"How will I be supporting you?"

"Tomorrow morning, report to the ship's medical team and assist them in preparing their facilities. You will be under their command for the duration."

"Yes sir."

129

XIV

I didn't have to help bring the wounded to the medical station, thank the Aspects. Not because there weren't any when the shuttles returned, there were quite a few, but because there were more than enough crew to handle that duty.

Instead I got to help move the prisoners, which I was far less thankful for. None of them were happy about their situation, and they were even less happy to discover that there were aliens aboard.

"Don't touch me, short-fur!" One of the disciples spat when I started to move up to direct them. I was pretty sure she tried to flare her tarah up at me as well, but the nullification bar connecting them kept both weighted down. "Aspects damn you Imperials!"

The comment earned her a sharp punch to the side from Holde, the armored man snarling right back at her. "Quiet! Move, all of you!"

"Move!" I copied his shout if not the snarl, using the carbine I was holding to point the way. "Down the hall!"

All six of the captured priests shuffled along dutifully, if still blatantly disgusted by my presence.

None were foolish enough to try and make a grab for our weapons, so there wasn't much excitement to herding them. Just a lot of shouting, mostly from Holde, and a lot of glaring, mostly from the prisoners. I did my best to echo the shouts and ignore the glares, and was mostly successful at both.

The ship's brig was tiny, consisting of a single barred room with a bed and toilet. Fortunately it was both fairly close to the hangar, and it was *just* large enough for all six of them, though I doubted they'd be comfortable.

I had no idea where they'd put the wounded prisoners I'd seen being hauled off; it would be close to standing-room-only if they tried to shove them in.

The lot of them had enough to complain about as it was. No sooner had we gotten there, and the sailor on guard duty had unlocked both the outer door and the cell, than Holde had barked for them all to strip down.

I could have done without seeing that, and without having to also shout for them to take their robes off. I mean, I knew the logic of it. Just because they'd been searched didn't mean they didn't have anything hidden in their clothing.

It wasn't the nudity that bothered me, I'd seen plenty of that in barracks and locker rooms. There just was something about naked priests giving me death glares that made my weight shift in discomfort.

"You'll be given prison clothing soon enough." Holde told them once the cell door's locks clanged into place. "Along with food."

One of them, a much taller woman than the one who'd insulted me, spoke. "And the senior priests?"

"Will be kept separately, presuming they survive their wounds." He replied, already turning away. I followed him through the outer cell door, where there was a tiny space just large enough to fit a duty station.

The sailor on duty had already returned to her seat, glancing between us and the door, "They're going to start shouting, aren't they?"

Holde flicked his left tarah. "Probably. You can close the outer door, but keep a constant watch on the cameras. Make sure they don't kill themselves. We can't question corpses."

"Sir."

I kept a hold of my patience for the twenty or so steps it took us to get back to the main hallway on this level... and then I couldn't keep the questions in anymore.

"How did it go?"

There was a soft chuckle. "You made it farther than Jet when he had to stay back for the first time."

"That doesn't surprise me." I said. "You also didn't tell me how it went."

He shrugged, armor creaking with the motion. "We took all of the

131

disciples at that particular temple alive, as you just saw. Both of the senior priests are wounded. One should survive to be interrogated, the other's fate is less certain."

I waited for him to say more, and pouted when he didn't. "That's good, I guess, but that doesn't tell me how it actually went."

"True."

If I hadn't been holding a gun, I'd have thrown my hands up in frustration. "*Please* Holde. Rerth didn't even let me listen in on the radio traffic this time. I know there's wounded among the ground team, but you yanked me away before I could see if any of my friends were hit!"

"Because we had duties to attend to." He replied, "And now we're heading to speak with Rerth. She has more orders for you, and you'll be able to check on that conscript pack then."

"Holde..."

"Patience, huntress." For the first time he sighed, tarah lowering. "I honestly don't know if they are among the wounded or not."

"But-"

He shook his head tiredly. "The battle was exhausting. Peace, please."

I had to bite my lip to stop from saying anything more. It was so very hard not to demand answers, not to simply lengthen my strides to walk ahead of him.

Thankfully whatever Delne'lir had designed this particular ship had shown unaccountable good sense; one of the medical bays was next to the hangar. Ideally positioned for emergency cases to be quickly hauled over from the shuttles to be stabilized.

Rerth was just outside of it, still in her form-fitting armor, scowling as she used a hand-cloth to wipe blood off of her arms.

"Rerth." Holde called before I could, "The lower ranks are in the brig, and Ashe is about to explode with questions."

"I am not!" I protested immediately.

Our Agent huffed without looking our way, "Go lay down, get some rest. You overdid it today. I'll handle the little shark."

I came to a stop next to her, Holde slowing down just enough to kiss her chin before heading to the lift.

To my immense frustration, Rerth kept cleaning her protection without saying a word. An attempt to open my mouth had merely earned me a sharp enough glare that I'd snapped my teeth together, falling into an at-ease position until she finished.

"One of your conscripts was wounded, but not killed." She said finally. "Uru'thun took an arm hit. Minor wound so far as I know, and I expect that she will be fine."

I let out a relieved breath. "Thank you. What about the rest of the Sword?"

"Less fortunate." Her voice was flat. "One Half-Sword took full casualties. Three dead, the other five are in critical condition inside the medical station."

How fast my relief turned into a depressed squall. "...the priests did that?"

A tiny nod. "They had charges rigged in the temple that I did not know about, which they backed up with far more talented sorcery than I expected. Both HSL's are wounded, though lightly."

"The Sword Leader?"

"Needs a promotion." Rerth blew out a long breath of her own, "For a conscript with no merits, she was exceptionally collected. Directed the recovery of the wounded, set a perimeter, then jumped my opponent from behind and beat him unconscious with her rifle."

I felt my eyes widen, genuinely impressed. "Wow."

"I just hope she didn't give the bastard brain damage. Holde held the other off long enough for me to assist, but we had to wound her more severely to bind her. I doubt she'll live considering she's at the back-end of triage."

Cold. Logical, it was far better to save the lives of the wounded soldiers first, but it was still a bit harsh.

Swallowing against my turning stomach, I went with my next question. "Um, what about the invasion? How is that going?"

Rerth flicked one hand dismissively. "The invasion is none of our concern, little shark. Our project, what is left of it, is our focus."

"Right, sorry. Um, where's Jet? Did he manage to get data?"

"He's already at work trying to see if he did or did not. I had no wish to linger given the chaos unfolding on the surface." There was a sharp exhalation. "Irritating. I attempted to request a direct attack on the Temple of Mahkahs as well, but the useless fish commanding that sector is apparently more devout than is good for her."

I grimaced. "She refused to attack a temple?"

"And castigated me for even asking. The bitch."

Another grimace. Rerth so rarely swore that it was a sure sign she was in just as foul a mood as she had been yesterday, even if she'd managed to come back with prisoners. And maybe even useful data.

When I said as much, she snorted and gave me an honestly amused glance. "I'm not another huntress whose spirits need buoying, little shark. Help me get this armor off, then secure our weapons."

I nodded once. "Yes sir. Orders after?"

"Go find the pack you've befriended." She shrugged, already reaching up to loosen the armored plates on her chest. "You have the remainder of today off, tomorrow you will be back to assisting Jet."

"I'm not distracted, I can handle duties."

She snorted. "I have a confidential call with an Admiral that you cannot witness, Holde overdid his sorcery to the point where he must rest, and unless Locol dared to interrupt Khash's playing with your soul long enough to grace you with hacking skills, you won't be of any use to Jet."

"I..." I earned myself another look, and immediately surrendered.

134

"Yes sir."

Between us we got her armor off fairly quickly, even if organizing it into a pile that I could carry took a little longer. I ended up slinging her weapons belt over one shoulder, my carbine over the other, and then carefully balancing her own rifle on top of the plates cradled in my arms.

At least the sailor in the armory didn't laugh when I gingerly made my way inside, and he even helped me get it all put away.

With that finished up, I started wandering around the ship looking for Pack Thun.

I honestly expected them all to be in their cabin, and was a little surprised when I found three of them in the mess hall. Well, I was surprised by two of them being there.

Ekan was showing her usual care for decorum by laying out on top of a table, a tablet held up so that she could read whatever mystery novel she was on now. Noro and Tevi were both seated in chairs, like normal people, and all three had clearly just come from showering from the way their off-duty uniforms clung to them.

"Ashe!" Noro smiled on seeing me. "Hey."

"Hey Noro. Was Uru...?"

His tarah lowered, but that only made Tevi huff. "Stop being dramatic. She's fine, complaining about being kept in medical for another few hours, *and* she's already bragging that she's the first in our pack to get a battle scar."

I couldn't help but let out an amused sound of my own. "That... sounds a lot like Uru. She really is fine though?"

Tevi reached around with one hand, tapping a spot six inches above her left elbow. "It cracked her armor right here, but the plates slowed it down enough that it didn't even reach her bones. Ship's doctor said it will heal up quickly, they didn't even take her into surgery."

"...that probably won't scar much then." I noted.

"Oh I know." She grinned. "But I'm not going to be the one to tell her

135

that. You want the full story, or did the Agent already tell you?"

My arms spread. "I have the rest of the day off for you to regale me."

"Great! Noro will waste half of that stuttering around flirting with you, so that might be enough time to talk about the fight."

Said Hunter pouted as ferociously as he could, and managed to look about as threatening as a member of my childhood pack.

Laughing, I padded the rest of the way over and pulled out a chair of my own near Ekan's head. She shared enough of Uru's features to make me wonder if they had a blood relation, though Pack Thun's bibliophile had a constellation tattoo covering her left cheek.

When she didn't react to my presence, I glanced at Noro over her, and then pointedly back to the woman occupying the table.

Snorting, he reached up and poked her sharply in the cheek.

"Yes, Ashe is here to talk about what happened." And she didn't even look away from the text as she said it. "Hello Ashe."

"Hello, Ekan." I said. "Not even combat can stop you from reading?"

"Oh no, it did." She said seriously, "I have to make up the time or I won't finish this series before we make it back to base."

I could only shake my head while Tevi rolled her eyes, "Ekan, could you please, I don't know, *try* to act normally around our friend?"

One finger rose... and then blatantly flicked her screen to the next page. "You also told me to be myself. This is me."

Tevi groaned. "Noro?"

"Why is it always my job?" The young man complained.

"Because I'm the noble one who gets into fist fights to protect Ashe's honor, which means you get to risk your very soul taking books away from Ekan."

I couldn't stop a snort while Noro rolled his eyes. Despite a few more

136

muttered complains, he eventually worked up the nerve to reach out and grab the tablet.

In spite of her obsession Ekan didn't resist when he yanked it away. She did glare rather ferociously at him when he jabbed her in the side with it, forcing her to get off the table and settle into a chair on my right.

"So?" I prodded. I wasn't all that eager to see combat again on my own, sure, but there was still something exciting about hearing what my friends had experienced. "What happened?"

Noro quickly launched off before either of the girls could, "It was incredible! We got to do an assault landing at the vanguard of an entire invasion! You could see all of the other shuttles coming down when we landed!"

I leaned in at once, "Was there anti-aircraft fire?"

"A little!" His tarah perked up, his slight stutter entirely gone in his excitement. "I think it picked up later, but we were engaged by then so it was kind of hard to tell."

"Engaged." Ekan grumbled. "Most of those robed idiots were too busy gaping to fight back when we jumped them."

I glanced at her, "Not many spells?"

"Not at first." She shrugged. "More of them tried to run, to get back to their packs, but we spread out quickly on arrival. I don't think any got away."

"They didn't." Noro confirmed. "Uru and I jumped one of them when she tried to sneak out through a side. We waited until she got just past us then jumped her from behind. She tried to throw us off with sorcery, but our shields..."

I smiled, listening as he went into a blow by blow account of a wrestling match that couldn't have lasted more than a few seconds. How they'd hauled their prisoner off to one side just before the explosives had gone off inside, covering the entire grounds in dust and debris.

When he got to how their Sword Leader had frantically reorganized them into a cordon, he'd started stuttering around how impressive she'd been. Tevi and I had promptly teased him about that, making his embarrassment

137

even worse, at least until Ekan pushed the story farther out to sea.

"Uru was hit by a stray round from one of the senior priests." She said, her own storytelling quick and concise. Probably because the sooner my curiosity was sated, the sooner she could get back to her novel. "I pulled her out of the line just before the SL jumped into the fight."

"I heard she beat one of them unconscious with her rifle." I said.

Tevi let out a little giggle, "She did! She even yelled at the Agent to stop wasting time and take the other priest down."

I blinked in surprise, trying to picture Rerth getting barked at by a conscript who wasn't even fifty years old.

The mental image made me giggle too.

"You should have seen the sorcery they were throwing around." Noro quickly jumped back in, "It was incredible! I couldn't believe how loud it was. You should have been there."

My own amusement faded into a quiet sigh, "Human, Noro. I can't hear sorcery, I can only smell it."

"Oh. Sorry." His tarah lowered in embarrassment, "Forgot."

"It's all right. What were they throwing around?"

Ekan huffed. "Everything that wasn't too heavy for their minds to handle. I'm pretty sure the priest and the Agent were both throwing out multiple Strikes at a time, and the handsome man in your pack pulled off a full Cloak of Ashahn."

I felt my lips part in shock. "Isn't that, like, insanely difficult to do?"

"Yeah. And incredibly draining. I'm surprised he could walk after." Ekan paused, then resumed just before her packmates could say anything. "They took the last priest down, burned and beat her pretty good, then we all got back to the shuttles. Book?"

"No." Tevi said primly. "You skipped too much, and you need to socialize more."

The theatrical groan and the way she slumped made us all laugh, and even Ekan couldn't stop a little smile.

And for a few more hours, we all relaxed together, talking about the battle at the temple grounds... and debated how many more such battles might be in the future.

And for a few hours... I felt like a proper huntress, eager for the fight, for the first time since Oshflara.

XV

Rerth's prediction came true; of the two senior priests they'd captured, only the male of the pair survived the trip to Trinity.

I had to keep my hand clenched in front of my mouth to avoid throwing up when the interrogation had started, desperately wishing that they hadn't brought me with to observe.

He'd looked... awful when Holde and Jet had dragged him into the interrogation room. I didn't think they'd been feeding him much of anything over the journey, or giving him much water. Just enough to keep him alive. Two weeks of that had been more than enough to leave a visible impact.

I also knew the storage room they'd used as his 'cell' aboard the ship hadn't had a bathroom. Or lights. His eyes were squeezed shut even against the dim panels in the room, and I'd had to help Jet hose his own waste off of him before we'd transferred down to Trinity itself.

"Steady, little shark." Rerth tapped a button on the control board in front of us, the broad window flickering once. Probably polarizing it so he couldn't see into the observation booth. "This won't take long."

"...it's already been too long." I whispered back. "This is awful."

"Yes." She replied without turning, "And it will get worse, but we need answers. This man is hardly innocent, it took me less than a week of listening to him to determine that."

I could only swallow, staring through the window as our packmates shoved him down into a reclined seat. He didn't resist as they strapped him down, or seem to notice when Jet wheeled over a heavy piece of medical equipment.

Holde's voice came through clearly when he finally spoke, his tones as polite and warm as always. "I would apologize for the rough treatment, but I'm afraid I've listened to recordings of your sermons."

The priest coughed once, twice, then found his voice and his courage when he rasped, "...die in a desert, Imperial."

140

"I'm afraid death isn't on today's agenda. Certainly not for me, and likely not for you either." Holde said as he began to pace a circle around the bound man. "This will be a simple affair. How many agents did you train for the Burned Hand, and when was the last time you saw her?"

"...who?"

A snort from my packmate. "A tall woman, with vicious burn scars on her left hand, who often claims to be a priestess of Velshen. I think such a person would be rather hard to forget."

"...who?"

Holde stopped his circling directly behind him. "You can tell us what we wish to know, and in exchange you will be given food, water, and a proper cell. If you continue to cooperate, we will remand you to a high-technology penal colony where you can preach in peace for the rest of your life."

Another rasping cough. "...I don't know what... you're talking about."

There was a heavy sigh. "Chemical interrogation it is then. I do hope that you cooperate. If that doesn't work, we will have to return you to a dark room, and eventually try again with... alternative means."

Jet got to work at that point. The priest didn't struggle when the injectors were attached to his upper arms, but he did start to thrash when Jet made to wrap another set around his tarah. It didn't last very long; between the restraints and his lack of energy, he went still rather quickly.

For his part, Jet simply waited until he was done, then got them fixed in place.

"It's about to get worse, isn't it?" I whispered.

"Yes." Rerth's voice was flat.

"Can... can I...?"

"No."

I flinched just as I'd been about to move for the door, rocking back on my heels as I aborted my flight to safer waters.

141

She let out a slow exhalation as Jet got seated in the other room, starting up his equipment. "If you're going to be an Agent, Ashe'lori, then you have to accept that there are unpleasant things that must be done. I don't enjoy this any more than you do, but we need answers."

"...I know."

But that didn't make it any easier when the priest's entire body shuddered violently, the first drugs entering his system. I had no idea what they were injecting him with, and quite honestly I didn't *want* to know.

His pained reactions told me enough.

"We'll start off easy on you." Holde, somehow, still sounded as polite and charming as ever. "Something to put you in the right frame of mind. Now, when was the last time you saw the Burned Hand?"

"F-fuck... you... Imperial."

A gesture had Jet fiddle with his controls... and the priest abruptly convulsed for a moment, arching back against his restraints. I had to clench my jaw as bile rose in my throat, agonized memories of my own time strapped down to a chair welling up from the depths of my soul.

"When was the last time you saw the Burned Hand?" Holde repeated patiently.

The priest's answer was another rasp. "...don't know her..."

"The tarah, this time, Jet."

The scream that followed snapped my self control. I made it the three steps over to the room's garbage before throwing up the breakfast I'd had on the ship. I was only vaguely aware of Rerth pulling my fur out of the way, holding it back as I kept heaving.

Pained howls from the room's speakers turned into whimpers, and Holde repeating himself once again.

Just like the Burned Hand had done.

The memory brought a sob, another heave that burned all the way up.

142

"I'm sorry." Rerth's voice was quiet, the hand that began stroking my scalp gentle. "But you have to face the memories, or else you'll drown in them the moment we find her."

I hacked a few more times, trying to get the disgusting taste out of my mouth. "...water?"

She handed a bottle over when I straightened, letting me use it rinse and spit a few more times before I guzzled the rest of it.

Rerth let me do it, but then firmly got a hold of my waist, pulling me back over to watch the rest of the interrogation.

Thankfully the priest's resolve seemed to have broken by then. He was crying openly, babbling answers almost faster than Holde could ask the questions, and they didn't need to inject more of whatever they'd been shooting into him.

He just kept sobbing, telling us that he'd only met the Burned Hand once. That he'd mostly spoken with her packmates who came through the temple once every other year to look for 'recruits'. Disciples with a deep hatred for aliens, for the Empire, who also had better than average talent with sorcery.

Finding out that they'd been due for another recruiting trip anytime in the next few months had seen Rerth snarling curses about the local commanders yet again.

More broken words told us that the senior priests had only begun engaging in politics over the last decade. That he had no idea why, only that he'd been ordered to not speak against Thondians in his sermons. Every other species remained a fair target, and he'd been given a full blessing to verbally attack the Empire.

Sadly he didn't know much beyond that. He wasn't a member of the Burned Hand's pack, or their organization as a whole. Nor was he high enough up the local ranks to have been told just why they'd started grabbing power, or just what might have happened with the Thondians from House ul Tradok.

He was just a like minded Trahcon supremacist who pointed the Burned Hand towards new blood for... whatever it was they were up to.

143

"Dammit." Rerth hissed when Holde made a silent gesture; telling her he thought we'd gotten everything we were going to get from him. "Fine. Ease him off the drugs, put him in a standard cell. Ashe, with me."

It was a blessed relief to get out of the interrogation cell, even if the cramped hallways of Trinity's Intelligence facility weren't all that welcoming. Rerth's angry stalk kept the few DataNet Security officers wandering the halls from getting in our way, and within a couple of minutes she'd led me to a residential hallway of some kind.

"Where is her fucking... here." Rerth jammed in a pass-code, a door opening to a well appointed suite. "She better have booze."

I cleared my throat, cautiously following her inside. "Uh, whose room is this?"

"Fyvn'trell's. Old packmate, we split apart when she got promoted ninety years ago." She replied, already in the small kitchen to the left of the door, yanking open cabinets. "She doesn't drink anything but the best, and I need something strong after that. So do you."

I couldn't bring myself to disagree, and found my legs carrying me over to help. A minute of searching produced black bottles without any marking near the small refrigerator, and glasses from another cabinet.

She'd just started to pour it when another woman stalked into the apartment, a knife in either hand and a ferocious scowl on her features.

At least until she saw Rerth, at which point her tarah promptly lowered from their threatening lift. "Ashahn's blood Rerth. Did you *have* to break into my apartment already?"

"Yes." My packmate said flatly. "You're lucky I waited until the first interrogation was done."

The woman grunted, shutting the door behind her. Somehow she made the knives vanish into her Intelligence uniform with little more than a twitch, her eyes jumping between us.

She... kind of reminded me of Tia'mok. Average height, average build, average looks. I couldn't see any tattoos on her face or hands, and her blue eyes were rather dark for a Trahcon. Even her accent wasn't one I could place.

144

"You must be Lori."

"Yes sir." I said at once.

A hand waved as she walked over, "Calm your waves girl, I'm not going to make you salute in my kitchen of all places. Grab me a glass so I can enjoy some of my own alcohol."

I did, and within a few moments we were all standing around the kitchen's small island with glasses of midnight-black liquor.

I only got a few ounces, as did our host. Rerth half-filled hers, and probably would have added more if Trell hadn't pointedly cleared her throat.

"That bad old friend?"

"Worse." Rerth growled before taking a heavy gulp of the drink, "You heard about the Group of Five?"

A nod came with a sip of her own, an action I mimicked, and...

Ashahn's holy blood. I had no idea what in Aysh's name this was, but it was... too many heavy flavors competed, with the gentlest of alcoholic bites following them. It was the best straight drink I'd ever had, and I couldn't imagine ever finding one better.

"Everyone here heard about the expedition. Ruined your investigation did it?"

Rerth's jaw clenched so tightly it was a wonder she didn't break something, and I hesitantly spoke for her.

"She and Holde had just started a long-term insertion that the invasion made us abort." I said, fighting down the urge to drink more of what was in my glass. "We didn't have the time to confirm the smuggling ring we were investigating... and we just found out that we'd have been able to try and grab one of our secondary target's packmates in the next few months."

The Operative hissed, quickly lifting her cup to her lips. "...damn. That certainly explains why you look like you're one breath away from detonation."

She was probably closer than that, but I wasn't about to say that. So instead I sipped more of the blessed liquor, going back to trying to be invisible.

"Get anything from the interrogation?"

Rerth flicked one tarah. "Confirmation of political bias among the priests, descriptions of the secondary's packmate, and confirmation they recruited from temples in the region. They made sure he didn't know more than that."

"Damn."

"Damn." Rerth's glass rose and fell, "Can you get me an audience with the Void Lord?"

"Are you going to scream in his face for smashing your project into the rocks?"

"Depends on how much of this I drink before the meeting."

A snort. "Then no, I can't. You *can* have a bed for you and Holde though. My packmates are all out on assignment so I've got a spare for you two to burrow into."

"Thanks." Rerth started to lift her cup once again, stopped, then visibly forced herself to put it back down. "Ashe is a huntress, you mind sharing yours with her?"

I blinked, a little confused, until Trell turned to look at me, then up and down me, and then at my fur. "Do you shed?"

"Uh... just a little?"

"Hm. Rerth talked you up a few times, and I read the report on Oshflara. You're interesting, for a conscript. Fine. You can stay in my bed." It was a fight not to cough in the middle of a sip. She definitely noticed, grinning for a bare moment before turning back to Rerth, "Jet isn't setting foot in my room, and don't even try to ask. He can take the couch or find a hotel."

Rerth rolled her eyes, "He's just as fond of you as you are of him. He'll find a guest suite."

146

"Good. You want to get the ranting done with now, or later?"

In response Rerth lifted her glass up near her face, mock-examining it. "Let me finish this, refill it, and then you can explain to me just what in the Aspect's bloody names happened."

"...fine, but you're paying for the bottle. Vekki Dark is expensive out here."

"Yeah, yeah. Ashe? This is going to include classified materials."

Meaning I was being kicked out. "Um, do you have any duties for me, or can I go exploring Trinity?"

She waved a permissive hand, "Tell Holde and Jet where I am, and make sure you can log in at the local DataCenter. After that, do whatever you like, just be back here by the evening meal. And I do *not* want to hear about another incident like the one at the supply station."

"I'll be careful, sir."

"Good. Go on then, have fun, and relax."

Nodding once, I finished off what was left of my drink, savoring the flavor for as long as I could.

Then I left to get my short list of duties done, to be followed by a hunt to see just how expensive that booze was.

Maybe if I drank enough of it, I wouldn't have nightmares about what I'd just seen.

147

XVI

I didn't get to do much over the next few days. Not because Rerth didn't want me to, or because they didn't need help with the analysis, but because the local Coordinator was far more severe in their classification of documents than the officers on Altair.

Everything Jet had taken, plus everything else recorded from the invasion, had been marked several levels higher than I had access to.

Rerth had filed an emergency request to get me temporary access... but she'd done it right after a heated meeting where she'd demanded to know why *our* reports had been unclassified and given over to Void Fleet officers.

According to Holde, the meeting hadn't exactly gone well after that.

Long story made shorter, I hadn't been surprised at all that the request had been denied as a result, or that I'd been barred from even going into the local DataCenter. Which meant I couldn't help with the smuggling investigation at all, and I could only look at Jet's old data about the Burned Hand.

In other words, I was becalmed and generally useless when it came to actual Intelligence work.

It was a little odd though. Not in the restrictions, I was kind of used to that. It was more that, for once, I was being denied something because of someone else. Not because of my species, or my own actions.

Of course that left me with very few duties to do, beyond acting as the pack's manual labor just to fill the time.

Since cleaning up Trell's suite, mailing information requests to Altair, and cleaning the pack's combat equipment didn't really take up much of my time... I basically got to wander around the city to see what was there.

I'd say this much; it was certainly unique among the colonies I'd been on.

Trinity was less of a single location and more a collection of space

148

stations, domed outposts, and shipyards spread across a trinary solar system. The Imperial Intelligence outpost was in the second largest of the ground-based facilities; a canyon valley on a dead moon.

Officially, I think it was designated Trinity-Base-Seven, but locally it was just 'Canyon City'.

The name was apt. They'd domed over the top with armored glass, and sealed off either end to create nine miles of livable space. It was... a lot nicer than I'd have expected. Most of the actual buildings were buried in the canyon walls, but there were plenty of bridges stretching across. Nearly all of which were packed with restaurants and open-air bars.

You even got to see the moon's green gas giant hovering far overhead.

"Do you think it's been long enough?" I asked over my mixed drink. "I really want to talk to her, or anyone else from the pack, but I'm worried they'll refuse the call. Then, you know, remember to be angry at me for even longer."

The bartender hummed, leaning against the other side of the bar.

Her name was Visi, and she'd lost an arm, an eye, and control of one tarah fighting Thondian pirates forty years back. Not that the extensive battle scars or missing limb stopped her from being able to make a very mean Emerald Wave. Or from being an exceptional listener.

"A little less than a year is pushing it a bit." Her single hand tugged at her shirt as she glanced down, making sure the tan cloth was spotless. "But you Humans don't have the years to spare like we do. Calling might be too much, but a letter wouldn't be bad."

"Are you sure?" I asked. "Letters always just feel so... impersonal."

Her better shoulder rolled in a shrug. "It tells her that you still want to talk, but doesn't put pressure on her to have to directly interact with you. Let's her work up to it, talk to her pack about how to respond. And if she does reply, it'll get her used to talking to you. Can work your way up to a call from there."

"Huh. That's a good point. Thanks."

She grinned, the expression twisting the scarring around her eye-

149

patch. "You're welcome, kid. It's what Guides are for. Now, you want something to eat today, or are you going down to the floor again?"

I hummed around another sip of my drink, "Food today. One of my packmates is supposed to be around to pick me up later, hopefully with good news about some real work to do."

"I'll pray to the Aspects for you. Your usual?"

"Please."

Giving me another smile, she slipped off to enter the order, then went down to the far side to talk with a pair of naval officers who were already on their second beers.

"But how do I start a letter to Fyth?" I muttered into my drink, letting the thoughts roll through my mind. "Sorry I'm a useless Human who screwed up on Oshflara, please beg for the pack's forgiveness for me, and how has your new assignment been going?"

It had the benefit of honesty, and it would probably make her laugh. For a second or two at least. Then she'd delete it and move on with her day.

A longer pull from my drink didn't give me any better ideas, even if it lightened my head a little. Maybe I could just call Huvu and ask for advice. If I was really lucky, we'd get through the entire call without her exploding in anger that I was in Rerth's pack and not hers.

Like she had the last two times I'd called.

Maybe if I... no. I couldn't even pretend to believe I'd avoid that.

I was about to try and type out something on my wrist-comp, in the vague hopes that it would help, when I got a serious case of mental reflection.

Three Humans sat down next to me at the bar; a woman right beside me, with two men taking the seats to her right.

I had to blink a few times to actually see them instead of Akari, her bond, and their friend. Once I'd managed that I found myself being stared at right back by all three of them.

The woman beside me could have been a blood-sibling of mine. We

150

shared the exact same tone to our skin, similar features, the same dark fur, and she was only a little shorter than me. Same conscript's off-duty uniform, same Rifle-Experienced rank, and even a similar number of merits.

I was so busy staring at her, and being stared at in return, that I nearly missed the two men just beyond her, at least until one of them chuckled loud enough for me to hear him.

The further of them was massive, with pale skin. Even seated it was easy to tell he was a full head taller than me, and his own conscript's uniform strained to contain his muscles. His fur was a pale brown, only a little shorter than mine.

But he was far less interesting than the man in the middle.

Not just because he was the closest thing to a handsome Human man I'd ever seen, with pleasantly slender features and dark skin. Or because of the shocking number of merits decorating his shoulders, or the intriguing storm tattoo covering his neck.

No. What made my mouth drop open in shock was the spotless white uniform he was wearing; one I'd never actually seen in person.

I must have had too much to drink already, because I actually blurted out my thoughts, "There's a Human in the *Watch*?"

He blinked once, glanced down at my own rank insignia, then mimicked my tone of voice perfectly. "There's a Human in *Intelligence*?"

Heat rose to my face at once as I finally noticed something else; the rank icon of a Dual-Commander on his shoulder. "I'm sorry, sir! I just didn't expect-"

Laughter from all three of them cut me off, one of his hands rising to stop me from finishing the apology. "You said the same thing, Nadia."

"I swore more." The woman next to me grinned.

"Understatement." The officer grinned. While I tried to collect myself, he glanced over my honors, nodded once as if he'd just decided something, and then reached around his companion to offer me a gloved hand.

"Anton'johanson."

151

"Ashe'lori." I took it, feeling... incredibly off balance. This was not how other Humans greeted me. Not speaking with an Icar accent while smiling and laughing. "Um, I *am* sorry sir. I didn't mean to sound like that."

He continued not acting right by rolling a shoulder in the Trahcon way, nodding towards my drink. "You're halfway through an Emerald Wave. I'm impressed you're coherent at all."

"...it's really not that strong, sir."

A snort. "Uh huh. We've tried Visi's drinks before, Lori. We know better."

I sighed, "I'm off duty, sir, and it's not like I'm drinking a Hurricane."

All three of them turned to stare at me, nearly identical expressions of disbelief making the fur above their eyes arch. It was the kind of look that usually came right before they demanded to know if I was being honest about not speaking any Human languages.

"What?" I asked, my back tightening a little defensively.

The fur raised some more, Johanson speaking slowly. "...you actually drink Hurricanes?"

"...yes?" I said hesitantly.

"And you can actually finish one? And be conscious after?"

"...yes?" I said again. "Sometimes I'll have two, if it's been a bad week. Not with extra rations though. One of those is enough."

He blinked again, far more slowly that time. "You're either a shockingly functional alcoholic, or scientists need to research your liver."

I was about to reply when Visi arrived, tossing down a coaster in front of each of them with practiced little flicks of her hand.

"Commander Johanson, Rifles Bauer, Ricci." The bartender greeted each by name. "On duty today, or off?"

Johanson sighed, "On, sadly. We have an hour and a half, then it's

152

more meetings all afternoon."

Visi nodded sympathetically, "One beer each it is. Your usual order?"

They apparently felt like changing it up. Each of them took a little time in figuring out what they wanted, bantering with her about the options. I didn't mind at all; it gave me time to try and collect myself.

What *was* a Human doing as an officer in the Imperial Watch, and what was one of their officers doing so far into the Reaches? The Airalon Wastes were a very, *very* long way from here after all. Watching over that dead stretch of space was supposed to be their only duty...

The little mystery of it intrigued me more than it should have. I blamed the fact that I couldn't work on the actual project, and I was desperately bored.

Considering the best way to ask about either of those things, I was a little surprised when the Rifle-Experienced turned her stool to face me directly.

"Nadia'bauer." She said, offering a hand just as her superior had. "Um, you're not from Turahshak, are you?"

I shook my head even as I shook her hand. "Alzuc, out by Altair."

"Oh good." Her shoulders slumped, "Here I was thinking my father had an affair or something. Were you born there?"

"No, either on Earth or on a World-Ship."

Her head cocked to one side, "Huh. How did you end up out by Altair?"

Sighing a little, I told her the usual story of my early life. I'd *definitely* had too much to drink already because I did it without a whole lot of prompting on her part. Even the arrival of my pasta didn't do much besides slow down the story a little, though it gave her more room to interject.

Or maybe it was just the fact that this was the first time I could ever remember a Human both hearing my story, and not considering me a traitor for it.

"At least you got consistency." She sighed, taking a long pull from her beer when I finished. "My parents fled to the Ark Fleet when I was eight, but apparently didn't feel like taking their fifth child with them. Going from having parents and blood-siblings to a childhood pack was..."

"Rough?" I guessed.

"Ashahn's blood, yes."

I nodded sympathetically, "Then conscripted at fifteen. I hated all of the Aspects for a while after that happened."

She huffed out a little breath, "Same. Still getting over it at times, I'm only twenty. You?"

"Twenty two now." When she took another sip of beer, I used the chance to quickly eat more of my pasta before asking, "Did you at least get to stay with one pack?"

Bauer shook her head, "On my second. First one was... all right, but there were issues with other packs in the Arsenal. I requested a transfer and got lucky. You?"

"Seventh."

I'd mistimed that, because she promptly choked on the beer she'd just swigged. Quickly grabbing her bottle before she could drop it, I awkwardly rubbed her back while she tried to clear her lungs out. After a few tries she managed to rasp out, "*Seven*? How?"

"...that's a long story." I said, a little more quietly. "And not really good lunch conversation."

"I... all right, that's probably fair. That part of the reason you're attached to Intelligence now?"

I nodded, then jerked my chin towards the officer behind her. "What about you and him? Packmates?"

Another shake of her head, "No, seconded to him as bodyguards while he and some other Watch officers are here. Don't ask me why, they won't say."

"Why he needs guards on Trinity, or why he's here at all?"

He must have heard me because he leaned forward to see around Bauer again. "Both. Really going to try and interrogate my bodyguard over beers, Lori?"

Well, not now at least. "No, sir."

"Uh huh." He drawled, thankfully looking more amused than insulted. "I'm sure you'll be able to figure it out. And stop it with the sir stuff, we're on lunch and in different branches anyway."

I really didn't think that was how it worked, but I wasn't about to argue with an officer. When I merely inclined my head, he gave me a final grin before turning back to his conversation with the other man.

"He's like that." Bauer told me. "But for an officer he's pretty fun to go out with, and he's from Colony One."

"Colony One?" It took me a second before I managed to remember the less than stellar name. "Wait, where Void Lord Delarah set up the Humans who sided with her in the invasion?"

A quick nod. "Yeah, down in the Iklahviah region. I've never been there, but from how he describes it... it's the closest thing to home that we have. I'm thinking about going there when my term is up."

"Not staying in the service?"

We chatted more about her thoughts about transferring to the navy for at least a term after her conscription was up. I told her a bit about my desire to go to an Academy to become a full Agent, maybe even on Zulflara.

She'd never made it to the Homeworld either, but she *had* been through Gathahn for a month in between her two assignments.

I was deeply enjoying her descriptions of the Imperial Capital when Rerth arrived, and the surprisingly fun meeting came to a regretful end.

XVII

"What is an officer of the Watch doing this far from the Wastes?" Rerth demanded the moment we were a dozen yards from the restaurant.

"They wouldn't say." I replied.

"Did you ask him directly?"

"No," I said defensively, "I tried to ask the guard I was talking with, but she had no idea."

And if he'd overheard and told me to stop asking, well, Rerth didn't need to know that. I knew I needed to work on my subtle questioning, hearing her tell me I was still terrible at it wouldn't tell me anything new.

Of course that meant keeping a secret from her, which was never a good idea... ugh. The others had probably been right about how strong Visi's drinks were. I wasn't drunk, but I was definitely more affected than I'd meant to be, even after eating.

"They did mention that they'd be in meetings all afternoon though." I added before she could question me further. "Not sure what about though."

Rerth huffed, waving for me to head towards the nearest bank of lifts. "Could mean anything from arguing about supply priorities, some kind of political conflict between the Void Lords, or just preparations to rotate their operational zones."

I started to ask which Lords were involved, and what they could be fighting about, when I remembered some of her other constant instructions. "Which is interesting, but doesn't have anything to do with our project. Right?"

Her grin was approving. "Correct. Speaking of, we're heading down to the canyon floor. We have an officer who lives on that level who needs to be questioned."

"About our reports?"

"No. *Those* were handed over to the Void Fleet by standing order from Lord Obdel'rilem. My theory was correct, not yours." Not that being right made her sound any less frustrated. "According to Fyvn, anything taken from the Group of Five is transferred directly to the Lord's staff, to be analyzed for an excuse to attack."

"Oh." In spite of myself, I was... a little disappointed. I'd have liked to have been right about that. Even if being right would have meant that either the smugglers or the Burned Hand had infiltrators here. "What are we questioning them about?"

She held a hand up, telling me to quiet down for now. Guessing that she meant to tell me on the way to the canyon floor, I kept my mouth shut.

Unfortunately for my curiosity, the lift that she picked was one filled with sailors heading down as well. A couple of them gave me rather dark looks that did a lot to bring me down from the high of my lunch meeting.

Of my first experience with other loyalist Humans... people I'd never honestly expected to meet in person.

The sudden return to disgusted glares and tarah flicks was all the more unpleasant in contrast. At least I wasn't alone; Rerth's presence stopped any of them from saying anything, much less doing anything. She gave me a tiny nod when I moved a little closer to her, returned the glares in kind, and let me stay right at her side when we got to the surface.

Canyon's City's 'floor' was a more traditional city than the cliff-side balconies and crisscrossing bridges high above us. Stores, homes, apartments, temples... all it was really lacking was proper parks. The locals tried with little gardens, but between the minimal agriculture and the darkness of the levels above, it wasn't enough to make it feel like a normal world.

My superior led me away from the lifts, walking with the foot traffic for ten minutes before turning down a side street.

"The officer we're questioning is one of ours; an Intelligence analyst. Give me your reasons why we might be doing such a thing."

I was used enough to her little surprise tests that I started thinking out loud almost at once, not feeling too self-conscious since there were very few other people on this particular walkway. "Is he assigned here?"

"Yes."

"Long term?"

One tarah flicked, the only sign of approval she allowed herself to show. "Forty years of service at Trinity."

"That tells me that it's a Trinity affair." I said at once. "My first guess would be that they unclassified something they weren't supposed to, but you already said that the Void Lord already has standing orders on that. So my next guess would be... that they *didn't* unclassify something they should have, or covered something up. Maybe something on the Group of Five we could have used?"

Her elbow knocked into mine, "No credit for partial thoughts, little shark. Your superiors will want details."

"Right." Swallowing, I stayed quiet for a few steps. Giving myself time to look around and think.

We walked past several restaurants, moving into a collection of built up apartments. None of them... well, none of them looked all that well built if I was being honest.

What was an intelligence officer doing living down here?

Pushing the curious thought aside, I focused on the test. "If it was smuggling related, then there'd be someone else going to interrogate them. So-"

"Why?" She cut in.

"First, because the smuggling project is a Trinity project now. Second, because the Void Lord *wanted* to invade the Group of Five." I replied. "And he just used smuggling Imperial goods as an excuse to do it. Put together, that means if someone was covering that up, they'd be in much bigger trouble with the locals than with us."

"Good. Resume."

"Yes sir. That leaves me with something to do with the Burned Hand. Either they found something about the Burned Hand herself, or one of her packmates, or they wrote reports on murders like the ones Jet and Holde researched on Altair."

"Good." She repeated. "And you're generally correct. They were seconded to a local security investigation of a murder that fit the Burned Hand's profile."

I perked up at once.. "Local? You mean it happened on Trinity?"

"Yes. Thirty-two years ago, a group of Naulians were found burned alive in their home." Her tarah rose in frustrated anger. "All of them were later determined to have been smugglers, and the investigation was..."

"Incomplete?" I suggested.

"Incompetent." She countered with a growl. "As was the death of a Thondian attached to an Ascendant diplomatic team ten years ago."

"...and that didn't turn into a crisis?"

"The diplomatic team had already departed. The man in question was a defector who stayed behind. I'm certain that you can guess what the authorities determined."

I shook my head. It was an easy guess that they'd simply assumed the Ascendancy had arranged for the murder, but that didn't explain why a larger effort hadn't been made to find the killer.

My back and neck began to tighten up right around the time I was going to ask if anything had been found. I knew the feeling; it was usually the only warning I had before a supremacist did something painfully violent to me.

Slowing to a stop on reflex, I started looking around to try and find whoever was staring at me. Worn, old buildings surrounded us, and I could only make out a handful of people in the distance far ahead.

Rerth was, of course, far closer. She was also turning to glare at me as she came to a stop of her own. "What are you doing?"

"Don't you-" Maybe it was because I'd just had a reflection moment of Oshflara an hour ago, but somehow I realized where my packmate was standing.

159

A half-step away from being silhouetted by an alleyway that was directly opposite another.

Exactly how I'd been ambushed on Oshflara, the day I'd been tortured.

I lunged forward and grabbed her arm before I could even think about it; hauling her back just as she was about to start walking again.

Her startled growl covered up any noise, but I saw something metallic flicker through the space her head would have occupied if I hadn't grabbed her.

Either Rerth saw it as well, or she heard the sorcery used to enhance its flight because ozone flooded the air as she called up a spell around us. The barrier had hardly begun swirling before it sent two more throwing knives ricocheting into the concrete, one of them shattering from the impact.

"Tight against me!" The barked order was immediately followed by her backpedaling further, pushing me back with her body as she tried to create some distance between us and the ambush point. "Check high!"

I glanced up immediately, "Nothing!"

"We need one alive!"

Wait, what!?

I dropped my eyes in time to see two figures cloaked in the heavy robes of Disciples of Ashahn, both just barely visible in the shadows of the buildings. One held another knife, the other a silenced pistol... but they quickly yanked it back when Rerth kicked off into a charge.

"Stay close! Move!"

An instinctive obedience to orders got my feet moving. Which was probably a good thing. With how hard my heart was pounding, I was sure I'd have locked up entirely if she hadn't snapped at me.

Of course I nearly tripped over my own feet anyway when she tossed a knife of her own over her shoulder. "Use it!"

Khash must have been with me positively for once; I caught the thing by the handle instead of slicing my fingers off. "I'm not good with knives!"

160

"Learn fast, run faster!"

I lengthened my strides, flinching on reflex as we charged. The knife thrower hurled another weapon that would have missed wide even without the Barrier as we approached, and then turned to bolt when Rerth turned to head straight at them.

It was a minor miracle that neither of us tripped with how close we were when we made it to the alley, and I couldn't help but look back when we made the turn.

The pistoleer was retreating as well; thank the holy Aspects. Even as I watched they vanished around the far side of the other building, something I would have reported if we hadn't caught up to their partner.

Sorcery collided in ways that I couldn't begin to keep track of when Rerth got within an arms length of the running figure. I only knew it was happening from the artificial wind ripping at their robes, at Rerth's uniform, and the cracking impacts of invisible blows against the apartments' walls.

Rerth must have gotten the worst of it because she stumbled, caught her feet up, then collapsed into a tumble.

I was saved from deciding to stop or not by the ambusher; they slid to a halt, and came straight at us with yet another blade.

I wasn't very good at melee combat, but I *was* most of a foot taller than the cloaked Trahcon ahead of me. And if Strike-Wave was good for anything, it was good for my reflexes.

Sweeping my left arm up under theirs slammed my forearm into their wrist before they could complete their thrust, saving me from being skewered. Sadly my own attack wasn't all that much better; they easily leaned away from the wild slash I sent at their chest, getting their balance settled.

Doing my best to mimic their pose drew a heavy snort, then a masculine voice spoke, "What am I doing? Pathetic beast."

It was the only warning I had before a Strike spell collided with my chest, hurling me off of my feet. The blow didn't hurt nearly as much as slamming into the ground did; Rerth's knife flying from my limp fingers.

161

Panic at the familiar attack set in, and I was scrambling back as fast as I could nearly the moment I landed.

A pained howl let me focus my gaze to see the robed man clutching at his leg; Rerth sweeping up with a long dagger in her dominant hand.

She slammed the hilt into his chin, bouncing his head off of the building's wall. When that only made him sway woozily, she did it again. Harder.

That time he dropped in a boneless heap while she stood panting.

"Ashe! Alive?"

"Yes!" The word was more of a wheeze, and I coughed a few times against the pain in my chest. "Ow. Bruised, alive!"

"Good! Get over here, help me get this idiot tied up in his own robes. Fast now! They'll realize we took him alive, and I doubt whoever sent him will tolerate that for long!"

Swallowing, I heaved myself up and quickly darted over to help. "Where are we taking him?"

"Back to headquarters, to find out who he is and why he did this." Her eyes were harder than I'd ever seen them. "And to find out just how they knew we were coming."

XVIII

Rerth decided to reward my instincts in spotting the ambush by not making me attend the next round of interrogations.

I appreciated that, a lot.

Well, at least until she clarified that my 'reward' included another test: she was giving me my first independent assignment. While she began a rapid questioning session with Jet, Holde alerted all of the appropriate authorities... I got to assemble the ship's Sword Formation.

Our mission? Get to the analyst we'd been going to meet in the first place, and drag him up to answer some rather pointed questions. Thankfully the SL was just as good at organizing as she was at fighting; she had the entire formation at the Intelligence Headquarters inside of an hour. Since I didn't have the light Intelligence armor yet, I'd scrambled into my conscript's bulkier protection and rushed out to meet them.

Technically, as Rerth's packmate and representative, that made me in command of the little mission as it formed up outside of headquarters.

Pragmatically, I drowned any misunderstandings before they could occur.

"This is your operation, Sword Leader." I said after I'd given her the plan, but before she could say anything in reply. "I'm just along to flash the Intelligence badge if anyone tries to interfere."

Sword Leader Seru'hoth had blinked a few times, then visibly relaxed. "Good, thank you for being sensible about this. Stay close to me at all times in case another ambush happens. Sword Formation! In line and move!"

Fortunately Trinity's status as a Fortress system meant that there wasn't any need to throw Rerth's name around on the run back down to the surface. We got a couple of vaguely interested looks, a lot of people clearing out of the way, but not much more than that.

From the muttering I heard it seemed like most people were taking pity on us. Probably assuming that we'd pissed off the wrong officer and had

163

to do a full-kit jog across the entire canyon.

The first people who knew better were the local security teams swarming the ambush site. They'd cordoned off most of the street, and were clearly questioning everyone who lived in the neighboring apartments. Fortunately Holde had called ahead, and we got waved through without having to slow down.

That came when we reached the far side of the complex, where a loose watch was being kept on the building by a dozen or so men and women.

"Soldiers." One of the Security Officials greeted us, his palm raised. "We've cleared out the citizens from the first floor, residential data has the Analyst living on the second."

I hesitated until SL Hoth gave me a bit of a nudge, reminding me that Rerth wasn't here to handle the talking "Uh, right. Thank you. Does it record any packmates?"

"Three."

"Any contact with them? Attempts to leave?"

His head shook once. "Nothing, their window is blacked out as well. We tried a loudspeaker call to summon them out, but got nothing. The other citizens were told to lock themselves in their apartments. We'd have moved in already, but orders were to let you handle it."

Swallowing, I tried to think of anything else we could do... and came up with nothing. "Thank you. Sword Leader? I think we need to do just that."

Hoth hefted her rifle up. "Pack Thun! You're on the bow-wave, secure the second floor. My pack! Stay out here, follow instructions from the local security to help blockade the building. Pack Korl, with myself and Lori. We'll hang back until the floor is secure, then breach the apartment."

The full coverage helmets made it impossible to tell, but I was pretty sure my friends in Thun were thrilled to get to take point. The moment she gave the signal they raced forward at a sprint, vanishing through the front doors without slowing.

I did my best to stay relaxed in the few minutes it took them to confirm the hallways were clear, and that there wasn't anyone lurking in the stairwells or the lifts.

At a gesture, I followed Pack Hoth into the lobby. That same feeling of... wrongness that I'd picked up on my trip with Rerth got stronger inside.

The apartment building was in bad shape. Old, so old I wondered if it had been one of the first built when this moon had been colonized. Its walls were battered, the lights were dim, and there was almost no art or color to even make an effort at making it feel like a home.

It was the kind of place you expected to find the poorest of aliens, not a pack belonging to Imperial Intelligence.

Making it to the second floor helped keep me focused; the analyst's door was right next to the central stairwell.

At Hoth's gesture, the other conscripts slowly spread out through the hallway, all of them keeping their guns aimed at the door. I did the same right behind her, covering the Formation leader when she cautiously approached.

"Fune'ythin!" Her fist hammered the wood. "Open the door, by Imperial order!"

I wasn't surprised that he didn't. Still, she gave him two more repetitions before she gave up and back off.

"Sorcery." She ordered. "Concentrated Strike on the door, left side. Four, three, two, execute!"

The door abruptly slammed open, what was left of the lock and handle flying in various directions. They'd hit it hard enough that two of the hinges went as well, leaving it hanging drunkenly when it finally stopped.

I started to move up only to be stopped when she side-stepped into my way. "No, you stay. Rahlic, Gyvin! Check it carefully!"

Two armored forms crept forward, sweeping their rifles left to right at the doorway. When nothing happened, they both moved inside just as slowly.

It didn't take long for one of them to shout back, "Ashahn's blood! He's dead!"

I swore under my breath, but Hoth didn't clear my path. "Check for

165

traps! Merlyn, watch the other apartments!"

The other Rifle ducked their head in embarrassment before quickly doing as ordered.

I could only shift uncomfortably at the genuine anger in her voice. She'd just lost most of an entire Half-Sword to a trapped building, of course she'd be worried about having that happen again. It was probably why she'd only sent in two people, and had spread the other two packs out as much as she could.

Several more tense minutes passed before the call came. "I think we're clear!"

"Right. Lori, with me inside. The rest of you, keep watch and stop anyone from leaving!"

Inside of the apartment wasn't any better than the outside.

Once we turned the lights on, it turned out to be a whole lot worse.

"By the holy Aspects..." Hoth apparently agreed, from the way she slowed down as soon as we were inside. "He *lived* in this?"

Swallowing as I gingerly stepped onto black and brown mold that carpeted the floor, I could only shake my head. "I don't think anyone could live in this. Something is off."

"No. Shit."

I grimaced. "There might be some of that on the floor too. Watch where you step."

I guess she had a weakness for gross things, because her only reply was a choked noise that made me think she was struggling to avoid retching. She let me take the lead as I picked my way through the living space near the door, following the tracks through the grime.

Two of my fellow conscripts were waiting just inside of the bedroom, staring down at the figure on the bed.

The corpse was just as out of place as the disgusting environment.

166

He'd dressed himself in his formal Intelligence uniform, with full merits on display on the left side of his chest. His rank insignia on the right was polished to a mirror shine, as were the Crescent-Waves of Intelligence on his shoulders.

If not for the neat hole in the center of his forehead, he'd have looked like he'd just gotten home from a banquet and needed to take a short nap.

"Call..." My voice cracked. I took a few calming breaths, thanked every Aspect I could think of for the miracle of fully sealed armor helmets, and then managed to go on. "Call the Security teams. Get someone who can tell us when he died in here."

"...Gyvin, get downstairs and handle that." Hoth ordered, apparently needing a moment as well. "Uh... do you need us in here, Lori?"

"I... no. You can head out. I'm going to, um..." It was really hard to think with the corpse just staring up at the ceiling. "...uh, right. I'm going to investigate."

She vanished so quickly it was as if she'd invented a new sorcery. The other two were out nearly as fast, leaving me with no one besides a dead man and grime for company.

Well, at least until I managed to get my wrist-comp up to call Rerth.

"Ashe." Her angry growl told me the interrogation probably wasn't going well. *"Tell me you have him on the way up."*

"Uh..."

"Ashe!"

I flinched, blurting out my words. "He's dead in his bed!"

That anger turned into stunned silence.

"Uh... the place is a mess. Like, rotting and falling apart." More words just tumbled out of me without any input from my head. "I'm surprised the floor hasn't collapsed. Uh, he's in his formal uniform, in bed. Pistol in left hand, forehead shot. Wearing his formal uniform. The bed is neatly made, why is it the only thing in here that's clean? Besides his formal-"

167

"Ashe! Stop!"

I did, only then realizing how heavily I was breathing.

"You're repeating yourself." Rerth said, tone far gentler than it had been to start the conversation. *"Stop, close your eyes, and focus on your hearing."*

Squeezing my eyes closed, I willed myself to not see the body laying in the bed. To not remember the corpses in the barracks on Oshflara. To not see anything but the darkness of my eyelids.

Listening. Listening was the only thing I had to do right now.

The quiet hum of my helmet's fans, circulating clean air behind my neck. The sound of Rerth's words coming from the speakers near my ears, quietly urging me to focus, to push everything else aside. My own breathing contained by the front of the helmet, ragged but slowing down.

According to the display, it took me about six minutes to calm down enough to open my eyes with a final exhalation.

"I'm back. I'm sorry."

"It's all right. Don't tell me what you see, I'll get that from the security recordings when they do their analysis. Tell me what you think instead."

I did. "Everything about this is wrong. The location, the building, the apartment. This isn't a place where an Intelligence analyst would live, or how they would live."

"Any sign of his packmates?"

"I'll check."

"Describe your thoughts as you do." She ordered.

"The grime in here is disgusting. Mold and rot and worse." My boots seemed to sink into the muck as I began picking my way through the room, looking for anything of significance. Besides the body. "I don't know what it is, and I don't want to know. There's no art on the walls, no pictures. Furniture is pretty bland too. That... that makes me think he didn't actually live here."

168

"Likely." Rerth agreed. *"And keep your helmet sealed. Don't breathe in whatever fumes are in there."*

That was an order I had no problems following. Carefully using the side of my hand, I nudged one of the dressers open before reporting. "There's clothing in the dresser, but I think some kind of insect has been eating them. Must be something that stowed away on a ship."

A noncommittal hum told me she was still there, still with me, but let me keep talking.

I kept up the babble as I moved from room to room, careful to disturb as little as possible as I walked around. Bits of Holde's training mixing with simple common sense making sure I didn't ruin any evidence more dedicated investigators might find.

The other two bedrooms had been converted. One was a work out room, complete with a multi-purpose weight machine. The other had a full Intelligence console with multiple screens, and at Rerth's urging I made an attempt to power it on.

"Nothing." I said. "This room's as disgusting as the others, maybe the power cables went."

"Check to see if the local memory is still there."

A gentle tug pulled a piece of the system's cover aside, letting me peer in. "It's already gone."

"Ashahn's blood." She sounded more disgusted than angry; she'd probably expected me to find nothing. *"Close it up, get back up here as quickly as possible. I'll need you as a witness."*

I swallowed. "For what?"

"The local branch has been compromised, and they're not going to want to hear it."

Oh dear.

XIX

I made it two steps through the doorway before a pair of Agents in full combat gear were on top of me.

"Ashe'lori?" One of them demanded through her helmet.

"Yes?" I said through my own, "Can I help you, sir?"

"We're to escort you to the Director and Agent Rerth." She replied, jerking her head to the right. "This way. Sail with speed, Rifle-Experienced."

"Sir." I'd hardly gotten the word out before each of them grabbed one of my arms, force-marching me out of the entrance lobby while half-a-dozen staff watched with interest.

Stumbling a little, I got my feet straightened out in time to keep pace. They led me down a hallway marked as restricted, then up a level via a secure lift that required a passcode to even open.

From there, we went through three more hallways, through another security door, and finally to an office guarded by two more Agents similarly armed and armored. They made a show of checking the rank badges of my escort, and myself, before nodding and opening the door.

Then I was gently nudged into the heart of Trinity's Intelligence headquarters. It was a big room, but one that was almost entirely empty apart from the broad desk in the center and a scattering of chairs. A painting of the Torlah hung in a place of honor on the back wall, while those of past leaders decorated the others.

Rerth was standing just inside with her arms crossed, her gaze firmly on the woman seated at the desk.

I didn't know her, but I recognized the rank insignia on her clothing.

Trinity's Director of Intelligence was a tiny little woman, her short tarah drooping with the same age that lined her face. Despite her obvious status as an elder, her posture was perfectly rigid. A natural compliment to the honor-laden uniform she was wearing.

170

"Close the door." The Director's voice was flat as ice, and about as warm. Not a good sign. "Step forward, Rifle-Experienced. Helmet off."

I took steps closer at once, my armor, and the muck still covering my boots, a sharp contrast to the fresh uniforms of the other women. A quick yank got the headgear off, and I tucked it under one arm.

The Director waited until I'd fallen into an at-ease position before speaking again. "You were the one to find Analyst Fune'ythin, yes?"

"Yes, Director."

"Describe the condition of the body."

I didn't hesitate for more than a moment before doing as instructed. "He was wearing his formal uniform in bed. One hand rested on his chest, the other held what looked like a standard light pistol. The impact wound was directly between his eyes."

Dark green eyes narrowed to slits. "An apparent suicide?"

Suicide among Trahcon was virtually unheard of, so I seriously doubted it. At least now that I'd had time to think about it on the walk back. Of course I couldn't say definitively, and I knew better than to offer an unsupported theory in this situation.

"I cannot say without evidence, Director."

She hummed, though if that was a good sign or a bad one I couldn't tell. "Describe the apartment."

"It was..." I struggled for a formal way to say it, then gave up and just went with brutal honesty. "Utterly disgusting, Director. Everything was rotting or covered in dark mold, apart from the bed and his body. I didn't see any extra boot prints in it, apart from mine and the conscripts who went in ahead of me. I have no idea how he made it from the door to the bed."

"I see." The Director's expression didn't change. "Your packmate believes that there was no way Analyst Fune'ythin actually lived at that location. Do you concur?"

My mouth got a little dry at the question. I entirely believed my

171

theory, but why was someone at the Director's level asking me about it? Especially with Rerth, a full Agent, standing next to me?"

Well, it wasn't like I had a choice about answering. "Yes, Director."

"I see." One finger began tapping at the wooden top of her desk, but apart from that she remained just as stoic as when I'd walked in. "Agent Riah. Results from the preliminary interrogation of your attacker?"

Rerth didn't bother to hide her disgust. "Nothing. He barely reacted to standard chemical interrogation. Spent the entire session mocking us, our questions, and the quality of the drugs. A level two run will be required at a bare minimum, probably higher."

"I see. I will alert a dedicated interrogation team that they will be needed. Have him ready for transfer within the hour, and delegate one of your packmates as your observer."

"Sir." She tipped her head in salute. "We'll have him transferred over. Speaking on the matter of the analyst and ambush, I formally request your permission to take over the full investigation. It is clearly related to my project from the Altair region. I also need my entire pack authorized for all files related."

That finally cracked the other woman's frozen features, drawing a sharp tarah-flick. "You are aware that it is against Intelligence policy, considering that you are not a Trinity assigned Agent?"

"Yes."

"And you make such a demand regardless?"

Rerth crossed her arms. "Yes. As I stated, this must be directly related to my ongoing project, and evidence indicates your local branch may be compromised. In that regard my status as an Altair assigned Agent may be advantageous to the investigation."

"You certainly do not lack for audacity, Agent Riah." Her fingers drummed along the wood once again. "Under normal circumstances I would never consider giving an Agent from another region direct control over local matters... but these circumstances are anything but ordinary. You will have full authority in this affair."

My eyes widened at the same time as Rerth's tarah perked up. Her voice was eager when she spoke again, "Will I be reporting to you directly?"

"Yes. I want this done quickly, and as quietly as possible. The last thing I need is for-"

The door directly behind me sang out an override tone a half-breath before it opened. A wall of bronzed armor began to come through, and I only barely got my feet clear before they could be crushed. The soldier in full power armor didn't even seem to notice they'd nearly ran into me, instead taking a place to one side of the doorway to free up the space.

I retreated to Rerth's side, gaping as another soldier carefully slipped into the room. While neither actually held a weapon in their hands, the heavy submachine guns mounted in each wrist, and double-technical launchers riding on either shoulder was arms enough.

Following them was a slim, older looking man in another uniform I'd never actually seen in person. The cloth was midnight black, with white flaring artfully scattered across the arms and legs. He had no merits on his shoulders or chest, no weapons on his belt. The only insignia on his uniform was the triple-mountain insignia of the Empire on his collar.

I felt my hands start shaking at the same time as I straightened on pure, panicked reflex.

Rerth was saluting even before I was, and even the Director rose from her seat at the Void Lord's arrival.

"Calm the waves." Grine'obdel'rilem ordered, his voice far softer than I would have expected. Up close he had nearly as many signs of age that the local Intelligence head did, but like her he didn't seem to let that affect the way he held himself. "Director."

"Void Lord Obdel'rilem." The Director did not sit down again. "We were not expecting you."

He gave her a cold little smile. "From the way your packmates attempted to divert me, I am certain you considered the possibility I would hear of your latest... misadventure."

I swallowed nervously. One of the eight most powerful beings in the entire Empire, one who only had to obey the Torlah, was standing less than

173

five feet away from me.

And he clearly wasn't very happy.

"It is an internal Intelligence matter, one that we are handling."

His tarah rose, "An internal matter that led to a shoot out in the streets, emergency interrogations, and a dead Analyst being found in his apartment?"

The Director openly scowled at him. "You do not need to flaunt the fact that you have people in this building reporting to you. Nor do you need to take up critical time. Agent Riah! To your duties."

Rerth started to take a step forward, then jerked to a stop when the Void Lord imperiously raised a hand. "No. You shall stay, so shall the alien."

I fought the urge to lick my lips, not liking the way Rerth's tarah had lowered in submission. Or... maybe genuine fear. Even as an Agent, she was nearly as far removed from a Void Lord as I was as a mere conscript.

"Sir." Rerth's voice remained strong, and confident. "If you have direct questions, please ask them quickly. There is a great deal of work to do."

The Third Void Lord gave her a flat stare. "Your elders will ask their questions in their own time, Guide."

My packmate's jaw worked, but she jerked her head into a tiny nod.

As if seeking to prove the point, he said nothing for more than a minute. The only sound was the quiet hum of the power-armor, and the heavy beating of my heart in my chest.

Lightning struck my nerves when he turned sapphire eyes to me, tilting his head a little to directly meet my gaze. "Identify yourself, alien."

Ashahn's holy blood....

"Ashe'lori, Rifle-Experienced, sir." I somehow managed to avoid stuttering, quickly getting back into a proper at-ease position. "Packmate to Agent Rerth'riah."

One of his tarah flicked. "You must have done something

174

extraordinary to have drawn the attention of an Imperial Agent. Tell me what that was."

"I... I helped uncover two smuggling rings during prior assignments, sir."

His tarah rose slightly. "Oh? Interesting. Normally I find little use in your kind, despite how much Sever seems to be fascinated by you all. You're always in a rush, so quick to make judgments without the wisdom of your packs."

I had no idea who Sever was, maybe he meant Void Lord Delarah, but I wasn't about to ask. This situation was far too similar to the interrogation on Oshflara... and just like then, I fell back into the best defense a soldier had against their superiors.

I said absolutely nothing.

From the way his gray lips twitched, he seemed to approve of my silence. Or maybe he was just enjoying the way I was struggling to maintain my formal posture.

"And this is the Agent who will be handling this matter?" He glanced to the Director, and at her nod turned back to me. "I see. Do you believe, Ashe'lori, that Agent Riah will be able to determine what exactly happened today?"

"Yes sir."

"Why?" He asked politely. "What gives you such confidence?"

"Agent Riah has never failed an investigation to my knowledge." I replied loyally. "She is cunning, determined, and extremely intelligent. She'll figure out what is going on."

He actually looked a little amused, finally sparing me his gaze and turning to Rerth. "You have certainly installed proper pack-loyalty into this one, Agent."

Rerth apparently knew the trick about being quiet too; she just nodded, keeping her mouth shut.

Lord Obdel'rilem stared at her for a few long moments before speaking again. "Tell me, Agent. How do you intend to proceed?"

"Full forensic sweep of the apartment and autopsy of the corpse to prove suicide." She said immediately. "As high of an interrogation level as required for the prisoner we took. Local assets will be able to handle both of those affairs. My team will focus on tracking Analyst Fune'ythin. Where he was, what projects he was involved with, and why he attempted a public attack on us when we came to interrogate him."

"I cannot imagine it was anything sane given the sheer stupidity of it." The Void Lord's voice was utterly dry. "I will expect your full report by the end of the month, Agent."

The Director didn't quite growl, but I thought it was close. "You exceed your authority, Void Lord."

"I am well within my rights to request she brief the both of us, rather than you alone." He countered. "I am not usurping your right to assign whichever Agents or Operatives you believe best suited to the task."

Her lips pressed into a thin line for a moment. "...this discussion is delaying the start of Agent Rerth's investigation at a critical moment."

Lord Obdel'rilem swept an arm left to right, "Very well. To work, Agent. I look forward to your findings."

Rerth saluted again, a gesture I echoed as quickly as possible. I was far more ready when she started walking, staying right behind her as we fled the office.

Six more of the power-armored guards made the hallway incredibly cramped, and none of the Agents waiting just past them looked happy about the Void soldiers' presence. The same two who'd escorted me brought us back to the lift, unlocking it so that we could get back to the base level.

It wasn't until we were walking down the hall, heading towards the interrogation rooms that I found the courage to speak again.

"Um, we're in... really deep waters, aren't we?"

Rerth's exhale was as long as it was exhausted. "Yes."

"...what do we do?"

176

"We finish our project. Call the Sword Leader, then get yourself down to liaise with the Security teams. I want every detail pulled from that apartment the moment it happens. It will take a few days, and I want you staring over their shoulder the entire time. Understand?"

I nodded at once. "I can handle that. Do you need anything else from me?"

"No, I'll call you if that changes." Her right tarah flicked outwards. "You did good today, little shark. The whole pack is going to be relying on you in this. Get it done."

Warmth rose in my soul, pride surging up somewhere inside my chest. "I'll handle it, sir."

"I know. Go."

XX

Shockingly, the local Investigators weren't all that happy to have to report to a Human.

I tried to use the same trick I had with Seru'hoth. Telling them I wasn't there to give orders, wasn't there to take control. I was only around because Rerth couldn't be in multiple places at once, and I was the one she'd picked to keep her up to date on their work. I wasn't going to tell them what to do, I just wanted to observe and report back.

They hadn't cared in the slightest.

Shoving my rank badge in their face had been the only thing to stop them from shoving me out of their building entirely, and even then they weren't giving me real access to their work. Just written copies of reports to go along with the occasional alert for a meeting... usually several hours after they'd already happened.

"Apparently the mold was especially toxic to Naule." I relayed to Holde over comms, my feet carrying me down one of Trinity's countless bridges. "Which most of the local security team's investigators and detectives are. Two of them are hospitalized, and they refuse to believe me when I say I didn't recognize it."

The tiny image of Holde hovering above my forearm shook its head, tarah angled in disgust. *"Why weren't they wearing full protective kits?"*

"They glared at me when I asked that, then they changed the subject."

"Of course they did." His little figure began shifting, he'd probably started pacing around whatever room he was in. *"Have they given you anything on his death?"*

I shrugged, carefully stepping to one side as a group of Conscripts in loose clothing jogged past while their Sword Leader barked at them. "Time of death was the same morning we went to interrogate him. They didn't find any evidence of anyone else in the apartment, but that mold and fungus that was seeded through the whole place made getting anything else nearly impossible."

"Nearly?"

My shoulders rolled front to back once again. "They think there's a few traces of his packmates, but nothing more than that. About the only thing that stood out was the mold. Based on its depth and known rate of growth, it was seeded several months ago."

His hum was barely audible over the general sound of the city, *"Could a Trahcon have lived in it?"*

"Not without getting incredibly sick." My mouth twisted a little, "It's not as fast-acting on Trahcon, or Humans, but it'll kill us if you breathe too many of the spores in."

"And Fune'ythin showed no sign of illness over the past few months."

"Did you find anything in his routine?" I couldn't help but ask.

"Your report first, little shark. What else is in there?"

Sighing, I gave him the rest of it. "They didn't find much. Minimal clothing, minimal personal effects, minimal food that was long expired. They're reasonably sure no one has actually lived in the apartment for at least six months, if not longer. That's why they're focusing entirely on finding his packmates."

Which was where I was currently going. They'd sent me a memo indicating they'd found a possible lead on where the Analyst's missing companions were. Two investigators had been sent a couple hours ago, and I was hoping to at least catch the aft end of their questioning.

I wasn't all *that* hopeful, but I had to try. Rerth had given me a job, and I wasn't going to let her down. Not when an actual Void Lord wanted to know what we'd learned.

Holde nodded. *"Good. Keep us updated on that. Was there anything else on the body?"*

"Nothing they thought of as important."

"No alcohol or drugs?"

179

I shook my head, slowing to join the line waiting for a public lift. "Toxicology was clean."

That drew a frown to his handsome features. *"I would have expected something there. Alcohol at least, if not something more powerful. What about the neighbors?"*

"The building was less than half occupied, and no one they talked to would say they even knew who lived in there." My shoulders rolled in a light shrug, letting me take a few steps forward. Ahead of me a tallish man in a navy uniform glanced at me, then my rank insignia, and quickly turned his attention forward.

I was pretty sure he was still listening, but there wasn't much I could do about that. Holde wanted an update, and this was the only time I had free today.

"A few of them said that people on the second floor kept getting sick, and that led to them finding other places to stay."

His frown stayed as he visibly turned, probably reversing course for the third or fourth time in his pacing. *"The ownership didn't resolve matters?"*

"Ownership is a Naulian clan who just finished a new building half a mile to the south. They moved the complainers out first, and planned to demolish the old building in two months."

"Interesting."

I was glad he thought so, because I wasn't seeing how we'd learned much of anything from the apartment. Or the corpse.

Pushing that thought out of my head, I shuffled up as the line shortened, eventually coming to a halt next to the controls. Tapping the button for the spaceport's level, I settled in to wait again.

"So... that's it. The Investigators can't figure out the purpose or reason for the mold, but the cause of death is a clean suicide as far as they can tell."

"Do you believe that?" He asked.

"I don't know enough about him to say." I said back. "What do we

180

know about his career?"

A quick grin told me he liked the quick response, and immediate demand for information. *"Fune'ythin was a valued researcher who specialized in code-breaking and the tracking of logistical patterns. Nearly all of his tasks revolved around using those to support anti-pirate operations, or in looking into Ark Fleet movements."*

Teeth worked at my bottom lip for a moment as I considered that. "I can't see either one managing to get to him. Not at the fortress system dedicated to hunting both."

"Which also makes it their most logical target." He countered. *"Just because we expect them to try such things doesn't mean they can't succeed. The enemies of the Empire are intelligent too, little shark."*

I ducked my head, "Yes sir... but still. Suicide? He wasn't even two hundred years old yet."

"I didn't say you were wrong." He replied dryly, *"I completely agree that someone got to him, but we cannot simply dismiss the two most likely suspects."*

"I guess, but I think the Burned Hand is more likely. She *is* the reason we're here, and we may have just ruined one of her recruitment operations. One moment."

A hand rose to tell me to go on, letting me focus on getting into the lift when it finally arrived. While there was still a short line no one else climbed in with me, leaving our conversation private when the doors shut.

Tapping the button for the spaceport, I felt the lift shoot upwards. "On my way to the port level. Did you have anything I should keep in mind once I find the packmates?"

"Keep an open mind." He said seriously. *"And tell me what you think of their careers when they are questioned on it."*

"Is there something in Fune'ythin's Index?" I asked.

"His career was... too clean."

I blinked. "...too clean?"

181

"Too clean, too average, call it what you wish." A shoulder rolled. *"He was well regarded in his niche, but from his Index's records he was never considered for promotion. Never made any attempt to rise to the rank of Agent. He had his small specialization and focused, almost exclusively, on those fields."*

I still didn't quite get where he was sailing. "Not everyone is ambitious. Maybe he was just holding in place while one of his packmates sailed up a different river."

That drew a rare scowl to his features. *"I doubt it, which is why I'm glad you're on your way to assist in questioning them."*

Saying I was going to 'assist in questioning' was a bit much. If I made it there in time at all, I'd probably be pushed to one side and left to just listen. And if I didn't get there in time... I'd be lucky to get a recording of what had already happened.

A quiet chime told me I'd arrived. Slipping out of the elevator, I side-stepped around the long line waiting to head back down, lengthening my stride to pick up the pace.

"Almost there. Anything else you can give me on his career?"

"Not much, it was entirely unremarkable. The only projects of note where when he was seconded to the investigations on the smugglers and the Thondian defector."

"Why did he even get those tasks if he's a pirate specialist?"

"He volunteered." His right tarah angled out for a moment. *"Make of that what you will. In either case, it seemed clear to Rerth that he either made no effort in his investigations, or else covered up what he found."*

"Covering for the Burned Hand." I guessed.

"That is a potential theory, but keep your eyes open." Holde looked at something out of view before shaking his head. *"I need to meet with the interrogation team. Contact Rerth when you have results."*

"Yes sir."

182

He gave me a final approving smile before cutting the line, leaving me able to focus on where I was going.

Canyon City's starport was massive. It had to be in order to handle how much traffic was constantly coming and going. Thankfully whoever had been responsible for its construction had thought ahead; there were about a million signs to direct everyone, and nearly as many maps.

One quick check had me darting over to get aboard a shuttle-train just before the doors closed. From there it didn't take more than a couple of minutes to get to the hotel block, where I paused to consult with my wrist-comp as to which one of them I needed to go into.

The line inside of the Green Horizon was long enough that it would have taken me twenty minutes to wait to speak with the host. Fortunately there was a bored looking security guard standing to one side of the lobby, and I wasted no time in approaching him.

His bored expression shifted to one of caution when he realized I wasn't just going to walk past him to get to the elevators, his tarah lifting slightly. "Can I help you, Rifle-Experienced?"

A hand rose to shift my rank badge, making sure he could see the Intelligence insignia attached to it. "On investigation, looking for two local security officials who should be here questioning someone."

"You have an official document on that?"

Not terribly surprised that he didn't believe me, I shook my wrist-comp down a little and spun it up. It was only after he looked over my orders, complete with Rerth's signet, that he waved me to go on ahead.

"Floor seven." He directed. "Room 722N, they arrived just ahead of you."

Just ahead of me? They should have been here for several hours already. Something must have delayed them...

Shaking my head, I forced myself to focus. I shouldn't complain if Khash was giving me a bit more good luck. The sooner I got upstairs and heard what was being said, the sooner I could report to Rerth about where Fune'ythin's packmates were.

183

"Thank you!"

He merely waved me on, already looking bored again as he resumed leaning against the wall. Not that I really blamed him. While there were probably the usual problems with drunken soldiers, or even officers stumbling back to their rooms, it was a little early in the morning for that kind of thing.

Another lift deposited me on the correct floor after a short ride. The decorations on the walls and the rich carpet made me think that this hotel catered far more to officers than to mere conscripts such as myself.

Which was a little strange. Not the luxury, but the fact that the investigators thought there might be a lead here. Sure, it was a nice place, and it has direct access to the starport, but... it was kind of the first place anyone would look. So if Fune'ythin's packmates were here, or if someone they knew was here...

Either they weren't all that intelligent, or they weren't involved, or both.

"Time to find out." I murmured, turning the corner to leave the lift space.

I'd apparently showed up just in time; two figures in the uniforms of Security Officials were emerging from a door at the far end of the hall. Both wasted no time in heading my way, the tarah quivering as they spoke in low tones to one another.

"Good morning." I called down the hall as we walked toward each other. "Finished already? They must not have known..."

My voice trailed off when both of them snapped their attention to me. The closer of them was a woman who'd been tugging at her uniform, but now her bright teal eyes were locked onto mine.

Which wasn't good for me, because both of the investigators I'd been coming to talk with had been men. Ones I'd met and spoken with, and who didn't look anything like the two people now walking briskly towards me.

"...all that much." I tried to recover, my heart speeding up as the nerves struck. I wasn't armed, I didn't even have a shield belt on me. If this turned violent I was in all kinds of trouble. "Heading back to write up the reports?"

184

The man of the pair nodded affably, but his tarah were quivering with suppressed emotion. "That was the plan, yes. You must be from Intelligence, sent to sit in then?"

I nodded, "That's right. Apologies for not being here on time, for some reason all of the messages to me seem to be delayed."

He tried for a charming grin, but it didn't reach his eyes. And the fact that his partner hadn't stopped glaring at me wasn't helping him either. "It happens. Care to escort us back?"

I didn't know what had happened to the investigators whose uniforms these two were wearing. What I did know was that nothing pleasant was going to happen to me if I went anywhere with them. Getting into a confined elevator was certainly a suicidal idea, which meant I needed both an excuse and an alternate route.

"Do you mind if I find a bathroom first?" It wasn't my best excuse, but it was the first one that I could think of in a hurry. "I had to rush here when the message finally caught up to me."

"Of course." That not-smile remained in place. "There should be several on the ground floor."

Right. This was a hotel. Dammit.

Back-up plan then. I needed one, and I needed it now.

"Sounds good." I started to turn, and my eyes caught on a nearby sign. That would do. "Wait for me in the lobby?"

His smile faltered when I took my first few steps, casually heading for the stairs. "Not in the mood to take the lift?"

"I don't want to wait for it to come back."

I hadn't turned my back on them, or really looked away. In hindsight that would have given me away even if they'd believed what I'd been saying. Which they probably hadn't, but the fact that I blatantly kept my eyes on them definitely ruined it.

The woman lost her patience when I was just about to push the door

185

open.

Her Strike spell caught me in the ribs, shoving me into the wall hard enough to make my teeth rattle. I reeled in pain, rallied, and lunged for the door only for the man to catch me with a fist to my stomach.

The two blows left me gasping for breath, trying to get my arms up to block anything physical. A quiet snort was his first response, while a quick Strike of his own was his second.

More pain blossomed across my chest when invisible pressure slammed into me once more.

I couldn't breathe. I couldn't shout for help.

Another punch kept my jaw shut, then a knee caught my stomach when I staggered away from the wall. Every attempt to get my arms up saw a spell drive them away. Every desperate effort to raise my voice saw a hit that stopped me from screaming.

I tried to counter. To throw a punch, to defend myself, but I just couldn't *breathe*. Could barely see through tears of pain, couldn't think as they separated, moving to either side, keeping me pinned against the wall, two predators amusing themselves by killing me quietly.

I tried to stay upright. Tried to get to the door. A side blow to a knee sent me down, a Strike to my face slamming my head into the wall, making my vision swim and ears ring from the impact.

"What in Iriahn's bloody name is this!?" The feminine bellow saw both of them jerk back, heads whipping around in unison. "Both of you identify yourselves at-"

They moved, driving through the doorway that I'd been desperately trying to reach.

"-cowards! Toj! Check that poor thing!"

I could only groan as a figure appeared just above me, gently tugging my fur out of my face. My blurred vision cleared up slowly to let me see an older man in the black uniform of the Void Fleets, his withered tarah lifting a little in relief when he saw me reacting to him.

186

"Easy there, young one." Warm fingers trailed over my face, touching my throat. "Can you breathe?"

A gasp was about the best I could manage. Every rib felt like it was bruised, and my throat wasn't much better.

"She needs attention." He reported to someone out of view. "They were trying to smother her with air, she's barely getting anything into her lungs."

More tears made things blurry. Ashahn it... everything hurt. It was...

"Supremacist pieces of driftwood. Probably saw her alone and thought they'd have some fun."

No. It was... I had to tell Rerth. I had to...

One shaking hand managed to rise, touching my rank badge. Trying to bring attention to it. The Void Officer noticed, then swore quietly. "Ashahn's blood. She's Intelligence, and a conscript at that. She must be on a mission here."

Another face appeared above his, but I couldn't make out her features through the sobs. "Fuck. Lizi! Sound the alert, now! Two security officials fleeing a crime! Toj, let's get her up and into the lift. We'll carry her down to the medical center."

Strong arms scooped me up as if I weighed nothing, the hotel spinning around me as I was carried away from yet another failure.

From another moment where luck had been the only thing that saved me.

187

XXI

Rerth came storming into the starport's medical clinic in time to see the doctor finish another pain injection.

I probably looked far more terrible than I felt given how many things he'd already loaded me up with. They'd pushed me down onto a medical cot and stripped off my uniform top, revealing the fact that I had more bruises than clear skin between my waist and my forehead.

"How is she?" My packmate demanded the moment the Naulian man stepped back from where I was sprawled, reveling in the ability to inhale without pain.

The red haired officer shook himself a little, all four arms busy putting his various tools away. "She's got five fractured ribs, heavy contusions to the rest of them, and ecchymosis over seventy percent of her torso. Fortunately she avoided major internal bleeding, but she also has a small rupture to her spleen. I've given her painkillers and two repair accelerators tailored for her species."

"Recovery?"

"A month or two with proper care and rest. No major physical exertions for at least three weeks."

Which wouldn't be fun, but I was too ecstatic at being able to breathe normally to really care in the moment. The number of shots and pills I'd be taking every day was a problem for future Ashe.

"She's on enough drugs to not care right now," He went on, probably knowing exactly what I was feeling. "But she's going to feel like she got hit by an aircar tomorrow. I've already pinged her comp with a full list of what she'll need to take every day. You know where to get them if Intelligence's medics don't have them in stock?"

"Of course." Rerth replied, jerking her head toward the door. "If you're done?"

He grunted, ambling out with a final word. "Her kind are stubborn.

188

Make sure she's on light duties for at least a month."

She didn't smile, or make a quip about already knowing that. She just waited until he was gone before shutting the door behind him. A quick flick of a finger locked it, leaving her free to walk over to stand next to my bed.

"Are you cognizant?"

I nodded, doing my best to focus. "Yes."

"What happened."

I told her everything that had happened after I'd ended the call with Holde. From my arrival at the hotel to encountering the two in the hallway. My voice faltered a bit describing the beating they'd given me, but I managed to stutter my way through to the point where the Void officers had rescued me.

"Did they find the security officials?" I asked when I finished.

Rerth's lips thinned. "Their bodies were both in the hotel room. They're still analyzing the room, but the wounds suggest they were hit from behind with some kind of poisoned weapon. Something fast acting and lethal, maybe Xenthan venom, maybe something more exotic. We'll know for certain after the autopsies."

I didn't know enough about poisons to ask any intelligent questions on that, so instead I went with the second question I thought important. "Did they capture them?"

"No." She didn't sound nearly as upset about that as I'd have expected, something that made her huff when she noticed my expression. "Interrogation hasn't gotten us anywhere with the man who attacked us. I doubt it would get us anywhere with those two either. As soon as we alerted them, the DataNet Security teams took control of the Starport systems and tracked them to their ship."

"Ohhh." Even drugged up I got where she was sailing with this. "We're going to follow their ship to try and find the Burned Hand?"

"Assuming she or her group are the ones responsible for this infiltration, yes."

I blinked. "Is there really a chance that they aren't at this point?"

189

One of her shoulders rolled. "There is always a chance, little shark. Not much of one at this point, the torturous way they attacked you compared to the quick deaths of the investigators is a rather large hint to their motivations, but we must keep our minds open. We still do not know if the Analyst was even involved with the Burned Hand."

"Right, sorry." I apologized.

"It's fine. I do not expect you to be at your best right now. Regardless, an Asset at the port was able to attach a beacon to their ship before it departed. It's designed to ping each time it passes an FTL buoy, but we must depart soon in case they discover it. Can you stand?"

I was sure that I could. Swinging my legs around didn't hurt or anything, neither did getting myself upright. My shoulders were stiff enough that I ended up needing her help to get my uniform top back on, but I didn't have any problems keeping my balance when she led me out.

She signed off at the exit station, clearing me to leave under her authority. After a short pause for her to check something on her wrist-comp, she led me back into the broad walkways of the starport. Though she'd kept her tones professional, she stayed far closer to me than usual, clearly ready to catch me if I so much as wavered.

"Jet and Holde are presenting the situation to the Director and Void Lord." Rerth updated me as we walked, my elder leading me deeper into the port rather than back towards the exit. "I'm taking you directly to the shuttles, then going to assist them in gathering our remaining things."

"I could-"

Her hand cut through the air, her left tarah mimicking the motion. "No. You are going to the ship to rest and recover. From here on out, you will never be alone unless you have at least a sidearm on your person. I've already requisitioned nullification grenades so that you will not be so helpless again."

"I..." My throat worked as I swallowed. The nice little buzz from the painkillers was fading fast, and I desperately wished that it wasn't. "...that's probably wise."

"You disagree?"

"No! No, I just..." Was going to have more nightmares about today. About being trapped, helpless, *again.* About Khash's blessings doing nothing but luring me into his punishments.

"...never used one of those grenades before." I said more quietly. "And I'm not very good with a pistol."

"Then you will choose another weapon, or you will learn until you are more than merely good." Rerth said. "I have been focusing too much on your direct Intelligence work, and not enough on your combat capabilities. I made a mistake in not working on that after the supply station. You nearly died as a result."

I winced. "Rerth, I-"

"Quiet." Her voice dropped to a hiss. "This was not supposed to be an investigation involving combat. I assumed you would be able to focus your entire Academy time on that, and that I would train you in everything else beforehand. I was arrogant and foolish. By all rights you should be dead. You would be if they had not elected to bat you around for their own sick amusement."

A low shudder ran through me, and my mostly empty stomach rolled dangerously.

She wasn't wrong about today. With their sorcery, the two could have killed me in an instant if they'd truly desired it. Snapped my neck, burned me alive, cracked open my...

I stopped walking, bringing a hand up to my mouth to stop myself from heaving in public.

Rerth stepped in next to me, one arm sliding around my waist while her other hand rose to cup my cheek. Her pull was as gentle as it was powerful, tugging me forward until we were pressed against each other.

She didn't say anything; she just held me as I got myself under control.

By Aysh and all of the Aspects... I was sick of feeling like this. Being like this. Breaking down right in the middle of the street, being stared at while my packmate kept a hold of me. Stopped me from making a scene.

Closing my eyes, I forced myself to listen. To calm down. To focus on the steady footfalls of people coming and going. The quiet clanks of doors opening and closing. Announcements about arriving and departing ships, reminders of the location of the secure shuttle bays, about the locations of the officer's rest stations.

I couldn't hear my breathing, or Rerth's... but I could feel the warmth of her body. After a few minutes I managed to calm down enough to speak without overly stuttering.

"What... what will I be doing?"

"You will be working with your conscripted companions every other day. I will instruct their Sword Leader to not allow you to rest until you can out shoot any of them with a sidearm, and until you are perfectly versed in nullification equipment."

"Yes sir."

She continued, "During your days with us, I will be cutting back on the time you are spending training under Holde and Jet. Instead you will be working on tactical awareness with me. You will be watching training videos until you can recite them in your sleep."

I nodded into her palm. "Yes, Rerth."

"Good. Are you all right?"

No, but I was good enough to start walking again.

Rerth resumed speaking as she escorted me to the waiting shuttle. Going over what few details she'd managed to hear on her way down to collect me. Besides the fact that the two investigators had been killed, stripped, and left behind, there wasn't all that much.

Neither of the killers matched the appearances of Fune'ythin's packmates, meaning they were still missing. The Director would be taking one of her local Agents off their current project to command a full sweep of Trinity to try and find them.

I wasn't confident that they would be located anywhere in the system, and from her tone Rerth wasn't either.

They were probably long gone, leaving us with nothing but questions.

"In you go, little shark." She gave me a gentle push, helping me climb up into the waiting shuttle. A Half-Sword of the ship's conscripts were waiting inside, their commander already waving me to take a the seat beside her. "Seru'hoth! Make sure she doesn't do anything stupid."

In response the senior conscript stood up, grabbed me before I could think about dodging, and gently pushed me down into the seat.

"I'm not an invalid!" I protested when she rapidly hauled the restraints into place, ignoring me entirely as she locked them. The other conscripts snickered, and I distinctly heard Uru's voice from one of the helmets. Heat rose to my face. "Rerth!"

"Behave, little shark!" Rerth called over her shoulder as she walked away. "And arrange her training schedule!"

"Sir!" Hoth replied, slapping the door controls. "Pilot! Ready to depart!"

I let my head fall back against the rest, fighting the urge to pout like a child as everyone else got settled into their seats.

Sure, I'd just had a near break down in public, but that didn't mean I needed to be... handled like this. I was debating whether to try meditating again or not when Hoth settled down beside me, speaking quietly as the pilot started the engines.

"Are you all right, Lori? We didn't get the details besides the fact that you were attacked. Everyone in Pack Thun was beside themselves."

I really didn't want to talk about it again. So instead I just reached down, tugging my uniform's collar enough to show that the bruising extended well down from my neck.

She winced, both tarah lowering. "You in pain?"

"Painkillers. A lot of them." I took as deep of breath as I could, feeling the strain in my chest even if it didn't actually hurt at the moment. "Everything is bruised down to my bones."

Another wince. Thankfully she seemed to understand my tone and

193

changed the subject. "The Agent says I'm to personally expand on your combat training. Have you had anything besides the basics?"

I shook my head a little. "Not really. I've only been on one Ah-cycle, and that was only for a couple of months. You?"

Her tarah flicked in embarrassment. "This is our first full assignment. I mean, I've had the extra training for an SL, but that's it. I'm not really sure why she wants me to handle this."

"You probably scored better than me. Any merits in shooting?"

"A few. You?"

"None." I sighed. "Basic competency with a rifle and pistol only. I nearly got the advanced marker with a carbine, but botched the sidearm drills pretty badly."

"Anything you particularly liked using?"

I could only shake my head again. "Not really. I mean, I guess rifles were easy enough to use, but they're not sidearms."

Hoth grunted, settling in properly as the shuttle began moving. "I guess we'll start by going through everything we've got on board. Maybe one of them will feel better in your hand. After that we'll focus on aiming in different situations."

That drew out a groan. "Not the bounce drills."

"Sorry, Lori, but they do work. If it makes you feel any better I'll make sure you have company each time. Plus you'll be doing it at a walk until the Agent says you're recovered enough to do them properly."

That made it only a little better. Bounce drills had been one of my least favorite things during basic training, even with Huvu being the one to run me through them. Maybe they wouldn't be as bad this time around...

Ugh. I was being so pathetic about this. Hadn't I just decided I was sick of being helpless as people assaulted me? Wasn't I sick of the nightmares those situations gave me?

I needed to be better than this. I needed to, or I'd just end up like this all over again.

"I'll do my best." I said. "Are we going to start when we get to the ship?"

"I was just ordered to make sure you behaved... so no. You're going to relax in your cabin if I have to put guards outside it."

Huffing quietly, and doing my best to ignore another titter from Uru's direction, I tried to stretch my legs out and relax...

And not think about what had just happened.

XXII

I groaned pitifully, laying face-down on the bed in Pack Thun's cabin. The cool blankets felt delicious against my forehead, to the point where I couldn't be bothered to even grab a pillow.

Rerth and Seru'hoth had started to ramp up my training sessions after the ship's doctor had cleared me for light activity. While I'd thoroughly enjoyed having a few weeks off of my usual drills, it had also been more than enough to leave me feeling out of shape.

End result? The fairly light training I'd spent the morning laboring through had wiped me out.

Fortunately I'd had the good sense to plan ahead for once.

"Kill me." The words were a pained rasp. "Please."

"Quiet." A heavy weight settled onto my thighs as Ekan got herself settled on top of me. Thankfully she followed that up with her thumbs pressing into my back, the rest of her fingers grasping my shoulder as she began to carefully feel around the area. "You are such a child about this."

"Says..." My words broke in a gasp as she slowly increased the pressure. "...says the woman only doing this because I stole her books."

"Which makes you a smart child who understands blackmail. I assume your Agent taught you that."

"No, that was...ohhhh..." I groaned in pure relief as her fingers really started to dig in.

Ekan wasted little time in methodically working her way around my shoulder blades, quietly reminding me to stop her if the differences in Trahcon and Human musculature made it painful.

My breathing evened out as she started along my spine, turning my head to rest my cheek on the bed.

Proving that she wasn't as content to float on the surface as she

196

usually appeared, Ekan waited for just a few minutes before asking a question. "Do you know where we are going?"

"You know I don't." I murmured, wincing a little when she found a knot by my spine. "Ow"

She hummed. "Your packmate has not told you?"

"No." Which meant she didn't know yet, or at least she didn't know for certain.

Three weeks aboard the *Posa'vilt*. Three weeks at faster-than-light, with each day that passed drawing us closer to the Ascendancy. To an ongoing civil war that the Empire was officially steering well clear of. I was just as hopeful as everyone else that we wouldn't be plunging into those waters, but there weren't all that many colonies in this region of space.

If the ship we were chasing didn't stop soon...

"...there's two colonies left they might be at, from the last pings we got." I relayed what little I knew. "If the local buoys don't have a marker, then we'll know they went into the Ascendancy."

Another hum came along with her hands continuing their gentle pressure. "Will we pursue?"

I shrugged as best I could while laying down. "Think so. A little lower."

Her hands obediently shifted to my lower back. Apparently that was enough conversation for her for the day; she didn't say anything for the next twenty minutes or so. She just adjusted the massage, moving it from one location to another while I slowly let myself utterly relax.

This was the closest thing I'd come to being intimate with someone since Fyth. I was still sleeping alone, apart from a few nights next to Fyvn'trell. She'd tolerated me curling up next to her, seemed amused by it even, but this was the first time I'd had someone willingly touching me like this.

I'd almost forgotten how much I missed it.

"Sorry for taking your tablet." I said when she migrated to my neck.

"I shouldn't have followed Tevi and Uru's advice."

"I would not have agreed to do this had you not." She replied. "In that your decision was wise."

"That's kind of what I mean. You're only doing this because I took something of yours. It wasn't something I should have done."

"No." Her agreement didn't make me feel any better. "Are you going to give me a better apology than that?"

Well, when she said it like that I didn't see what choice I had. "Yeah. Should I give you a massage too?"

There was a huff, then her hands slid up into the mess of fur on my head. Fingertips pressed lightly on my scalp, moving in gentle circles. "I need Arath'kuvo's second series in physical format. The new editions."

My personal account groaned along with me. I'd heard that she'd been eyeing those when we'd been on Trinity, and that she'd been lamenting just how much the price was. "That's a very expensive apology."

"Personal massages are expensive." Came her retort. "Purchase them and I will both forgive you, and give you additional massages after your training sessions so long as we are assigned together."

"...all right." I sighed. "Deal."

"Good. Now be quiet and allow me to focus."

I obediently shut up, letting myself relax once again. Ekan settled back into her rhythm, repeating the areas she'd already done but at a far slower, gentler pace. The pure relief on my aching muscles felt so good that I didn't realize that I fully dozed off.

It was only the feeling of the bed shifting that made my eyes snap back open, just in time to see the rest of Pack Thun climbing in around us. They'd finished showering after the morning drills then, meaning my allotted time was up.

"See?" A still damp Uru was grinning as she sprawled out next to us, "Told you she was the best at those. At least once you dragged her away from her little stories."

198

Ekan huffed, her weight vanishing behind me. "There is nothing short about the stories that I read, Uru. I am going to shower, and I expect my tablet returned by the time I get back."

Groaning, I rolled onto my back before waving at her. "Yeah, yeah. It'll be here. Sorry again."

Twitching one tarah, she gave me a final nod before slipping out of the room. For my part I heaved myself up, stretching my arms out to protests from both Uru and Tevi.

"Sorry." I repeated as I stood up. "Uru? Her tablet's in your locker, under your shirts."

My fellow huntress was pouting when I turned to look back at them, "You're not staying to relax with us? I even told you the secret to getting Ekan to actually pay attention to you!"

"First, Tevi told me that, you were too busy trying to convince me to let you massage me instead. Second, I still need to shower and meet up with my pack after lunch for an update. Do you want me to lay around, or do you want me to have answers for you tomorrow?"

Uru pouted while Tevi flicked her tarah and made a shooing motion. "Swim away then, but you'd better take care of Noro. He's extremely jealous that Ekan got to grope you before he could."

Said poor Hunter had just walked in, evidently having been volunteered to carry everyone's laundry back from the showers. "What!? I am n-not!"

It would have been more believable without the stutter, and the way his tarah immediately lowered in mortified shame. The combination drew amused laughs from the entire pack, and a smothered smile from me.

"Uh-huh." Uru drawled. "We keep telling him to do something clever and manly for you, but he keeps saying he can't think of anything."

"No!" He did his best to growl back at her, "I said I had, and *you* said that you'd be with her first no matter what I did."

"So?"

199

A chorus of groans came up from the other members of the pack, Tevi included, as the pair fell into another of their whirlpool debates. Rolling my eyes along with them, I gave Tevi a final little wave before slipping out while they were distracted.

Not that I was against two cute people arguing over who would get to take me out first. It wasn't... something that usually happened to me, and I was appreciating the novelty of it.

Far more the novelty than their timing. Both of them had already tried to get my attention after my injury, and they'd both managed to do it while Rerth was nearby. Her glaring at them, and icily pointing out that she wasn't about to let my recovery be set back by 'the stupid antics of children'... well. It had been rather humiliating for everyone involved.

Me especially, which had me more annoyed than flattered by their attention over the past week. Which was why I'd asked Tevi for a massage, and then gone with her idea to convince Ekan when she'd directed me that way instead.

"Maybe I should just date Ekan." I murmured, stretching my arms out a bit as I walked. "She'd be the least likely to do something foolish in front of my packmates, and book reading is a calmer hobby to have than most."

Evidently I'd been a little too loud in my musings. I'd hardly turned a corner before Holde's voice reached me, "That does tend to be a problem with forty-somethings. No self-control to go along with a crippling lack of patience."

I sighed on seeing him just outside of the officer's showers. "Is Rerth still angry about what happened?"

"She was never all that angry about it." He rubbed a towel over his head, carefully drying off both tarah, "But she wants you focused on the project, not on finding bedmates to play with."

Looking for bedmates was a bit of an exaggeration. Maybe... well, less of an exaggeration than it had been a few months ago, but I wasn't exactly desperate for company. Not yet, at least.

"You mean she still thinks I'm... what did she say?" I frowned, thinking back on it. "Oh, right. That I'm better than unblooded conscripts?"

Holde grinned, wrapping the cloth around his neck. "Sounds like something she'd say. We can talk about your prospects in that area later though. Rerth and Jet are already waiting for us in the usual conference room."

Puzzled, I glanced at my wrist-comp and confirmed I had another hour before the scheduled meeting. "Early? I was hoping to shower and get changed."

"Early." He confirmed. "We've got news, you can wash your fur later. Come on."

A quick walk and a short lift ride to the level above brought us to the conference room. Our other two packmates were already there just as he'd said; Rerth pacing back and forth on the far side, Jet rapidly flicking through a tablet he held in one pair of hands.

"Sit." Rerth didn't so much as look at us when we entered. Apparently she was too busy glaring at the walls, both of her tarah pressed flat against the sides of her head. "We have intelligence from the horizon and from the shore, and neither is good news."

Swallowing, I quickly took the seat to Jet's left, but Holde elected to remain standing near the door. The moment he sealed it, the lock chime sounding, Rerth resumed speaking.

"We have a confirmed ping from the tracking beacon. The ship has left hyperspace in the Nuova Genova system. I have ordered the Captain to bring us to the system's outskirts to drift for a few days so our pursuit will be not blatantly obvious." One of her tarah flicked as she slowed to a stop, turning to rest her hands on the back of a chair. "We will take the shuttle in to pose as refugees. That is our first problem."

I shrank a little when I realized she was looking at me in particular, "Um, not friendly to Humans again?"

"Opposite problem." Her lips pressed together for a moment before she went on, "It is a former Ark Fleet colony, abandoned during one of their conflicts with the Ascendancy. According to our reports, they tolerate Reach-born Trahcon and Mikira, but are principally Human dominated and disdain most other species."

201

Jet grunted. "Meaning I'm staying on the shuttle."

"Yes, as will I." Rerth flicked a tarah towards her bond. "Holde and Ashe will be our ground team, playing the role of deserters looking for work after fleeing the Group of Five. There should be plenty of jobs available. With the Ascendancy in full collapse, this system is drawing attention as a valuable harbor for pirates looking to raid the aftermath of battles. Be on your guard, trust no food or water, the usual routine at a pirate den."

Ashahn's blood. I was finally being given a real task for the pack, but it was happening in my worst nightmare of a situation. "Uh, do you-"

She cut me off before I could even start. "You will be fine. You will follow Holde's lead and use the same backstory you did when we did your training run on Varur'fluro. If you could forestall a bored Thondian pirate and convince him to speak with you, you will have no problems with members of your own species."

"But-"

"You will not think or doubt. You *will* perform up to my level of expectations. Understood?"

Her sharp tone had me respond on reflex, "Yes sir. Targets?"

"Holde will investigate the local temples, of which there are supposedly several. You will provide whatever backup he requires. I expect you both to locate those responsible for attacking you in the hotel at a minimum, and any evidence for the Burned Hand's involvement if possible. Any connection to the Group of Five's priesthoods will be a tertiary target."

Holde must have moved up while I was distracted because one of his hands came to rest on my shoulder. "We'll get it done, Rerth. Once we have that, what is the plan?'

Both of her tarah rose for a moment. "A battle-group has already been dispatched from Trinity to support us."

There was a long groan from both men, a sound I wasn't quite brave enough to echo.

"Not again." Jet shook his head. "A time limit?"

202

"Not a short one, thank the holy Aspects." Rerth exhaled. "They will lurk just outside of the system until we signal them to approach. Full logistical support as well. We should have at least six months before the Void Lord loses patience."

Jet huffed, not looking relieved at all. "I wouldn't put any money on that bet, Rerth."

"Which is why we're going to get this done as quickly and cleanly as possible." She retorted. "You and I will provide remote support and ensure there is an exit strategy if the winds demand it."

"Got it. Do we have anything else on this colony?"

"Plenty, but that will be discussed while we are on approach. For now our discussion must be on the news from Trinity." Pausing there, she took a heavy breath that was clearly intended to calm her before she managed to resume in a forcibly level tone. "Our prisoners are both dead."

My heart dropped into the depths, Jet snarling a curse while Holde's fingers tightened around my shoulder.

"How?" He snapped, all of his usual levity gone. "Which incompetent piece of driftwood managed that?"

Rerth's own scowl was as furious as I'd ever seen from her. "The Director did not say. Only that the attacker we subdued was able to kill the priest we took, and then was killed by the team attempting to subdue him."

Holde's voice didn't get any warmer. "That's an impossible systemic failure."

"Yes." Our leader agreed. "Which is why I already relayed a priority message back to Altair indicating something is wrong at Trinity. Keep that project in your minds, but not on the surface. I want all of us focused on our targets. Find Ashe's attackers, discover if the Burned Hand is behind these events, learn just what connections both groups may have to the strange acts of the priests in the Group of Five."

"Understood." All three of us replied.

"Good. Let us discuss the details, I want our arrival to go as smoothly as possible."

And with that we settled in for several days worth of planning in the hopes that this mission wouldn't slam into the rocky shores.

XXIII

I felt my feet slow to a stop as the bar itself came into view. Wood smoke trailed up from two chimneys while warm light glowed inside of circular windows. A promise of comfort and food against the light coating of snow on the pointed roof. Despite the early hour it was already doing a brisk trade.

Taking a final few breaths, I reminded myself that I had to do this. This was our best chance to get to know the local situation. I just had to go in, have a drink or two, and see if I could make it one night without inspiring my own species to hate me.

If I did it enough times, maybe they'd talk to me. Reveal something.

Hopefully.

Walking inside, I was struck by the confused rumble of conversations in at least four or five different languages. The lighting was flickering, coming from both wood and gas fueled fireplaces.

Oh. And nearly everyone inside was Human. Hard to miss that.

Swallowing, I started forwards, the dark skinned host glancing up at me as I approached. To my relief he greeted me in Caranat. "Good evening! Bar, table, or booth?"

"Bar, please."

He grinned and waved me on. "Smart to get here early then! They'll all be taken soon. Go on and find any of them that are open."

"Thank you."

Sliding past him, I weaved between several tables before I got to the square shaped bar in the center of the place. Broad screens above it were split between Human football and some kind of Naulian dueling sport.

About half of the stools were taken, but I found one that had several empty seats on either side. The bartender, a woman with skin only slightly

205

lighter than mine, held up one finger while her other kept filling a mug. I nodded to show I understood, and tried to force myself to relax.

The mental reflections from my first visit on Oshflara were so severe that I had to shake my head a few times. Had to blink to make sure I was actually seeing the woman instead of Ramos.

That was something the bartender didn't help with. She mimicked my first meeting with Ramos almost perfectly; resting an elbow on the bar as she leaned in toward me, a smile on her lips. "Evening. What's your poison?"

"A Dark Nova, please." I replied. "What kind of bread do you have?"

"Buttered rolls, or pita with hummus."

"Rolls please."

She nodded once, twitching her head to keep her thick curtain of dark fur out of her eyes. "You going to have dinner at the bar as well, or are you waiting for someone?"

"Getting out of the cold while I wait for a hotel room to open." I shook my head, "I wish someone had told me it was winter here."

"Ha! You and half the new arrivals. Be right back with your drink. Call for Sofia if you need anything."

Nodding, I managed to smile back before she moved off to start preparing the cocktail.

In any Imperial bar I'd have done a quick listening meditation to help calm down. Common sense, and Rerth's orders, kept my eyes open and watching the bartender as she mixed my drink, making sure nothing extra was being added.

Its arrival brought a quiet thanks from me, and another smile from her before she moved off to help someone else calling for her.

Only when she was gone did I close my eyes, resting a hand over my glass and focusing on my hearing. The sounds of voices speaking words I couldn't understand, the almost inaudible crackling of the nearby fire, the quiet clinks and clanks from the hidden kitchen. Lifted voices whenever the door opened, allowing the cold wind to rush in.

I'd found my calm lake when I heard the heavy thud of a plate being settled in front of me. Opening my eyes let me see the bartender giving me a sympathetic look, gently pushing the small dish with two rolls toward me.

"You all right?"

Taking a final breath, I gave her the mix of truth and lies that I'd been practicing with Holde. "Still recovering from a beating. A few officers thought it would be fun to see if they could strangle me with sorcery."

Whatever she'd expected to hear, it certainly hadn't been *that.* Her lips parted in surprise. "Oh God. Mercenaries?"

"Imperial." I wrapped my hands around my drink. "Not the first time it happened, but it was the last time I was going to put up with it."

A look of understanding came across her face. "You're a deserter."

"Is that a problem?"

"Not here." It was my turn to be surprised, one of her hands reaching out to gently pat my wrist. "Anyone who manages to get away from those bastards is welcome on Genova. The boss knows some people, if you want to get to the Ark Fleet."

"I... thank you." I said, the hesitation very real. "Um, right now I'm just looking for a job. Something to help me get some money before I decide on what I'm doing."

"Hmm. Well, I might be able to-"

A shout from farther down the bar interrupted her. "Sofia! Otra cerveza, por favor!"

Sighing, she gave me a helpless glance. I gave her my best understanding look in return. It seemed to help her relax, and she moved off to help the other customers.

Naturally I was just about to pick up my drink when my wrist-comp buzzed with a message, interrupting me in turn.

Status?

"Really, Holde?" I muttered, quickly tapping out a reply.

At bar, job hunting. Status?

Western Inns & Suites. Room 522. Do not stay out too late.

I rolled my eyes. He'd been entirely supportive of me being along with him on this mission, but now that we were actually here and alone he was being as overly protective as Rerth. I'd done this exact kind of mission on my own before.

Sure, I was nervous to be doing it on this particular planet, but I was far more comfortable lying to other Humans than I'd been lying to Thondian giants who could have snapped my neck with minimal effort. At least members of my own species would have to work at it, and I was more confident in my ability to talk them down or simply run away.

And besides. Holde was directly next door, and ready to come running if I needed him.

Yes, elder.

Brat. Remember your emergency call.

Yes, elder.

And don't drink too much.

Huffing, I stabbed my finger down to close the chat. Then, just because I could, I took a deep pull from the Nova in front of me. It was... well, a lot better than the ones I'd had on Oshflara, if not as good as the ones I'd had on Trinity.

I paced myself after that first mouthful. Carefully looking around to look over the rest of the customers.

Unlike the Riverside Cantina, which had clearly catered to the local elders, the Stone and Hearth was filling up quickly with people who... well, I'd have labeled them as off-duty soldiers if we'd been in the Empire. Their posture was rigid, few were old or overweight, and everyone was drinking heavily.

208

There were a handful of Trahcon in the crowd, but they seemed to be sticking together in a collection of tables in one corner rather than being spread among the Human majority.

Apart from that major difference in species, there was also the languages being spoken, and the general lack of uniforms. Well, mostly. There *were* some people in uniform, just not Imperial ones. They didn't match what I'd seen from Ark Fleet soldiers in Rerth's briefing before we'd landed either.

"Mercenaries and pirates." I whispered around another careful sip of alcohol, turning away from the Trahcon in their corner. All of them were wearing some kind of camouflaged uniform I'd never seen before. "Be careful in here, Ashe."

Movement had me shut up before I could talk to myself further, Sofia the bartender walking back over to me.

"Sorry about that." Her eyes rolled a little. "They're five beers in and not slowing down. Good for business, but I could do without the pick up lines."

I'd never heard serious flirting from other Humans before, but I was pretty sure drunken come-ons were ridiculous no matter which species was uttering them. "Are they bad?"

"Terrible." Her voice both lowered and deepened, clearly mimicking someone. "You've got such a fiery personality. Think you could use it to keep me warm tonight?"

I blinked once, then snorted. "Did they seriously say that?"

There was a groan and a nod. "That was one of the better ones. It's only going to get worse the more drinks they have."

"They aren't going to try anything, are they?" I asked, surprising myself a little by being honestly concerned for her.

"No, they know better. And if they get too drunk and forget, that's what the boss and the bouncers are for." Sofia waved vaguely toward the kitchens. "They'll be out and looming soon. Remind everyone that they really do have to pay for their drinks, and that none of the staff are on the menu."

That last one must have been another Human idiom, but I think I understood it after a moment.

"Do you think your employer would need more security?"

She blinked, leaning a hip on the bar. "What do you... oh. You mean as a job for you? Um... don't take this the wrong way, but I don't think you're what he'd be looking for."

"I'm tall, scarred, and I'm decently built." I noted, "Plus I'm trained as a conscript. I can handle myself all right."

"And that would normally help, but you're... well, a woman." She winced even as she said it. "Maybe if you were even taller and built like a Thondian, but even then..."

"Even then?"

Her weight shifted. "The boss is an old fashioned kind of man, if you know what I mean."

"...I don't." I admitted. "Is this a Human cultural thing?"

The poor woman was looking more uncomfortable by the minute. "Something like that. He might take you as a bartender or waitress though, we're pretty short staffed right now. How's your English or Espanol?"

"Non-existent. Grayborn."

That drew another wince. "I figured when you stuck with Caranat after ordering, but I didn't want to assume."

Which at least made her far more polite than nearly any other Human I'd met. "I'm guessing that kills my chances?"

"Probably. Sorry." She glanced around, and only after making sure no one was calling or waving for her did she go on. "You've got to be fluent in those two plus Caranat to work the front here. What other skills do you have?"

I started to roll my shoulder, forced myself to stop, then carefully moved it up and down instead. "Uh, I can drive almost anything, do basic maintenance on vehicles, that kind of thing. And I still have a few colonial records as a Strike-Wave goalie."

210

Sofia perked up at the last. "We don't have Strike-Wave leagues here, but there's a competitive football group. If you can make it to spring you can try out as a goalie, I think the skills translate pretty well."

"Would that be enough to live off of?"

"If you're really that good at it, sure. Plenty of the through traffic from the port loves to spend their money watching or betting on the games." She paused, then deflated a little. "But that's not going to start up for three months yet. Would you... want to take off world jobs?"

I brought my glass up, tilting it back to drink down the last of the Nova. "...ah. I'll need to sleep a lot more on that one, I think. Do you know any shops that might take me? I know my way around Imperial vehicles like I said. Maybe I could do maintenance."

She was happy to help me with that after making me another Nova. In between running off to take other orders, she ended up giving me a list of two local shuttle services, a rental facility, and the name of the repair shop that serviced her blood-pack's vehicles. After that she, far more quietly, gave me the names of two local groups who were always in need of soldiers, and who wouldn't mind that I only spoke Caranat.

Or that I was a woman.

The way she kept warning me about that made me feel like there was definitely context I was missing, but I appreciated the wealth of intelligence she'd just given me all the same. She topped it all off by giving me her personal number, assuring me she'd be happy to help me settle in if I needed any help.

Holde shook his head when I met him in the hotel lobby a few hours later. We both settled into a quiet corner on a couch, speaking in low tones as I reported on what I'd learned.

"Ashe'lori, charmer of bartenders." He chuckled. "I honestly don't know how you always manage to get so much information out of them."

"I talk to them like they're people?" I suggested.

"So do I, and I'm far more handsome than you." Holde countered with a grin. "Maybe you're actually an Avatar of Polvro, doomed to make everyone

211

who works in a bar swoon at the sight of your scars."

I tried to huff, but felt the warmth rising in my cheeks all the same. "I don't need another Aspect taking a personal interest in me, Holde."

"True, true. Leaving your personal connections aside, it sounds like you might have a few options when it comes to local work."

"Are you sure I need a job?" I bit my lip. "Do we have time for that, with our orders?"

His expression settled into a pensive frown, tarah lowered. "Honestly, I don't know. They could decide to move in at any time if they lose their patience... but there's nothing we can do about that, so we can't worry too much about it."

"But-"

He quickly lifted a hand, forestalling my protest. "We *will* be moving far more quickly than Rerth or I would like, but that doesn't mean we can risk being obvious. If I can't get into the temple, we'll both need local work to explain how we're affording this hotel. It will also help make us look like common deserters just trying to get by."

"If anyone gets suspicious about us asking questions, we're just getting to know our new home." I said.

"Exactly." He replied. "There are three local temples who are recruiting disciples. I intend to apply tomorrow, you'll support me from a distance. I'll do the same while you check out your own list the day after. Which one is your preference?"

"I... oh. Another test?" His grin told me that it was, so I settled back to think about it.

The mechanical shops wouldn't give me much of a chance to really learn anything during work. Well, it would probably tell me a lot about how much smuggled or stolen Imperial vehicles were present here, but that wasn't our focus anymore.

We had to find the two people who'd attacked me. Why they'd fled here, of all places. Had to learn what the priesthood in the Near Reaches was doing. How the Burned Hand was involved. If they even *were* really involved.

212

Sitting in a repair shop wouldn't help me with that, besides as a cover for why I was staying on world at all. Leaving on a pirate ship wouldn't help either.

"Shuttle services." I said after a minute of thought. "If they're piloted, that will let me travel across the colony every day. We could plant listening devices and have Jet filter them for anything interesting."

"Agreed. Let's get to our room and contact our packmates about our plans, and see how well they're adjusting to sleeping on the shuttle's floor."

"...would it be crass of me to tell Jet how comfortable the beds are?"

Holde laughed.

XXIV

According to both Sofia and my new coworkers, the most trustworthy arms dealer in the city was a man named Harshk. His little shop was on Canal Street, and proved to be surprisingly cozy for a building filled with guns, grenades, and ammunition.

I slipped inside after my fourth day of 'work'. I was still wearing the plain olive uniform, complete with cap, that marked me as one of the drivers for the ground-shuttles.

"Welcome, driver of ground craft." The voice that greeted me was as deep as any Thondian's, but... spoke very slowly, and with an incredibly thick accent. "What brings her here?"

Its owner came into sight around a display of ammunition, giving me my first in-person look at a Mikira.

He was, well, short. The top of his head might have come up to my chest. As if to make up for that, he was also incredibly wide, and his thick arms made the bouncer on Varur'fluro look scrawny. While his limbs and the front of his chest were covered in some kind of personal armor, his entire back was shielded by a bright blue and red shell.

The colors matched the quills hanging from his narrow chin, and the razor-sharp horn rising from the end of his reptilian mouth.

"Uh... I need a personal gun." I said after a moment to recover. From the depth of his voice, I'd honestly expected him to be a lot taller. "Some of my passengers have been leaving me nervous."

There was an almost avian-like chirp, then he spoke again. "This world can be unsafe. The driver of ground craft is wise to arm herself. Come. We shall assist her."

I followed when he turned around, lumbering his way with surprising speed back toward the counters. He slid through a gap and closed it behind him, leaving me to keep pace on the other side as he walked down to a display of pistols.

"Does the driver know which arms she prefers?"

It was a little struggle to get used to the odd way he was speaking, but I thought I adjusted fairly quickly all things considered. "I've used Strike pistols in the past, but I was wondering if you have any recommendations."

His alien features made it impossible for me to tell his expression, but the way his mouth opened slightly made me hope he was pleased to be asked all the same.

"A weapon is a tool." He rumbled, "A tool must be used for the right task. What tasks does the driver require of her weapon?"

I'd already told him I needed it for personal defense, but I didn't think he was asking me to repeat myself. "Some of the local priests haven't seemed to like that I was the one assigned to the shuttles they got onto. None of them have done anything yet, but I didn't like the glares they gave me. Or the muttering."

Another chirp came out of him, lower in tone. "Yes. Acolytes of the many-faced-god often speak against those of the savanna."

"Do you have recommendations?"

One of his hands, tipped in tiny claws now that I could see it properly, reached up to scratch at his chin. It made the quills there shift and wave like fur before settling. "The river sharks can be most dangerous to those like the driver."

I didn't know if I liked how he was referring to our species, but at least he wasn't using slurs. "Trust me, I know. I've been assaulted by sorcery in the past, and it's not fun."

"If the driver has the wealth, then we may aid her in stopping such from happening again."

"I should have enough credits. I think."

"Then let us examine my wares."

It turned out that buying a handgun was the easiest part. He quickly picked out a Strike configured to fire Imperial-Two rounds. It lacked most of the features I was used to; there was no linking system to make aiming easier

215

with a helmet for example, but that helped to keep the price down. Sort of. It still cost enough to more than wipe out everything I'd earned over my first few days of work.

Fortunately I had far more than that thanks to Rerth and Jet. Enough to afford everything else he wanted to sell me.

Well, within reason. "I know nullification grenades are ideal, but I can't afford to buy five of them. Especially not since I'm already getting a shield belt with a recharging nullification pulse."

"The driver speaks of costs," Harshk rumbled in reply. "We seek to protect her very life. The pulse is one use, then must recharge. It will prevent sorcery for not more than a dozen seconds. The driver should have a second option."

"You're not wrong, but I literally cannot afford *five.*"

I eventually conceded that I would buy one, which got him to stop insisting long enough to pick out the appropriately sized shield equipment for me.

It also gave me some time to question him a little bit.

"Do you know where the temples are?" I asked while tugging a shield belt on. It wasn't really a 'belt' so much as it was a full harness that covered most of my torso... covered it a bit too tightly for me to breathe even. "Too small."

He turned his narrow head a little, regarding me with just his right eye as I got to work getting it off. "Why does the driver wish to know such things?"

"Avoidance. Maybe I can request routes that don't take me anywhere near them."

"The driver is wise. Wiser than many of the savanna." His nod was more angular than directly up and down, but at least he seemed to approve. Even better, he answered. "The face of darkness has its temple in the east end, as does the face of light. The face of dreams and storms sits high upon the southern hill."

I had to take a moment to process his odd way of naming things. It sounded like the Temples of Mahkhas and Velshen were in the east, and the Temple of Ashahn was further south. That matched up with what Holde had learned earlier in the week.

I set the shield belt aside, taking the next size up when he gave me another nod of permission. "Which one is the most hostile to my species?"

"All of them."

His instant response made me pause, "...that bad?"

"The driver is not the first of her kind to come to us for the weapons to protect herself from them. The driver will not be the last."

Ashahn's blood. "How though? I mean, this is a Human majority world. Why don't they kick them out?"

Harshk's small eyes seemed to narrow. "A question many have asked, driver of ground-shuttles. A question whose askers have not returned to us the answer."

Well that was certainly ominous. I hesitated for a moment longer, then started pulling the next belt on. I wanted to keep asking him questions on the subject. Wanted to see what else he might tell me about the local situation. But... some instinct told me to stop pushing here.

I thought his voice warmed up a little when we got back to discussing the features of the shield-belt. He even let me quick-charge it with the equipment he had once I paid for everything, and gave me a substantial discount on a waist-holster for the gun.

By the time I left I had the shield belt on underneath of my uniform top, the pistol secure on my waist, and a small grenade in my pocket.

Honestly I felt pretty ridiculous, but also... a bit safer.

Sleet and snow crunched under my feet as I strode down the walkway, hunching my head a little against the cold air. Thankfully it wasn't far to the nearest shuttle station. The little alcove was both well heated and sheltered, and there was only a single Trahcon woman too busy reading to even look my way.

She didn't so much as glance up from her copy of Arath'kuvo's fifth

217

novel when I sat beside her.

"Status."

I stretched my arms out with a groan. "An unlinked pistol with 12 rounds, a category five shield-belt, and one nullification grenade. Cost all of my pay and half of what you said I could overspend."

Rerth grunted, turning a page despite the fact that her eyes weren't moving across the words. "Keep them concealed when you're working. If your attackers ever board, the surprise of your weapon and shields may be the only thing that will let you escape."

"Yes sir." I made sure to barely move my lips around the last one. I didn't see anyone watching us, but I knew to be careful even without her emphasizing it. "Are you sure you're all right to be off the shuttle?"

Her huff was just as quiet as my words. "According to Jet the starport security has been compromised by so many different hackers it's a miracle any of it works at all. This world looks far more civilized than it truly is."

My few days of driving around it had started to make me think that as well. Most of the local citizens, or at least people I presumed to be local citizens, seemed pleasant enough. Like Sofia they were incredibly polite, quick to thank me for driving them, and surprisingly understanding of the fact that I only spoke one language.

The people I presumed to be pirates or mercenaries were... far rowdier, less civil, and left me nearly as worried as when a trio of Disciples of Velshen had boarded my crawler.

"Did you learn anything on our project?"

I nodded slightly. "Harshk says all three temples preach against Humans, enough that more than a few have bought weapons from him for self-protection. He also said there's been a lot of talk about just why no one has tried to get rid of the temples for what they've been saying."

Her nearer tarah twitched. "Any answers?"

"No. It was hard to tell, but..." I hesitated. "...from his tone, I think he was trying to tell me to stop asking about it."

218

"You have a theory." She noted. "What proof do you have?"

"None." I said at once. "And I know better than to tell you the theory until I have proof. Permission to do research on it?"

My elder looked pleased as she turned another page. "You may, so long as Holde doesn't need your assistance for his own infiltration."

"Thank you. How is he doing?"

"He was accepted as a Recruit-Disciple of Velshen this morning. You will have the hotel room to yourself for the next few days, then I will be joining you full time."

I glanced at her. "Uh, I'm not complaining about having company, but what cover are you going to use?"

Her shoulder rolled, "My usual one as a minor arms dealer. Before we left Trinity I had several crates of obsolete weapons brought on board for the purpose. Jet has already inserted a false arrival slip, I will use that to return to the shuttle tonight. We'll lift off, link up with the *Posa'vilt*, and transfer the arms aboard."

"And come back in a few days with a new transponder tag." I guessed. "Posing as new arrivals, and I'll say I'm sharing a room to make up for the money I just dropped on guns and armor."

"Exactly, little shark."

I nodded slightly. "And then what? Are you going to try and sell guns to the priests?"

Rerth huffed. "If Khash is with us for once, that would be an ideal way to make rapid progress. It is more likely I will have to supply local stores like the one you just departed, or else the pirates who frequent the starport. Speaking of, we have another complication."

"Another one?" I groaned. "Really?"

A hand shifted away from the novel to pat my leg. "This one is not your fault, or anything we had control over. We have confirmation from the Far Reaches; war has broken out between nearly all of the Great Warlords."

219

I blinked. "Over what?"

"The usual feuding between the Scarlet Tears and Cathia, though Terminus and Xentha have both been dragged in this time." She rolled a shoulder. "Regardless, we can expect both refugees and the wiser pirates to come flooding into the Near Reaches soon enough."

The refugees I could understand. I wouldn't want to be in the middle of an interstellar war between people who openly called themselves Warlords either. But pirates? Wouldn't they want to stick around to raid whoever they could?

Rerth shrugged again when I asked her. "The greedy ones, yes. The wise ones know they will be conscripted quickly by their betters. To be used as flicker-fish and fodder. Better to migrate to the Near Reaches in the hopes of maintaining their supposed freedom to raid who they wish."

I grimaced. "And we're the nearest major port to the Ascendancy's civil war, and their warlords aren't strong enough to deal with pirates like the Great Warlords?"

"They likely are, but pirates who frequent the Far Reaches usually have unrealistic views of the Near Reaches. They think themselves the most dangerous beings in the sea, and the Near Reaches as a pond where they will easily dominate."

Meaning this entire area of space was going to turn into storm-fueled whirlpool sooner rather than later. "Um, what do we do?"

"Continue as we have been, little shark. This complication may work out to our advantage in the end."

"Uh, it could?"

"It could." She closed the book with a snap, leaning back. I took the hint and did much the same, turning to watch as snow started falling on the street once again. "If the priesthood hates other species as much as they claim, I wonder how they shall react to swarms of pirates looking for a safe harbor to trade their loot for supplies, arms, and luxuries."

"Ohhh." I got it then. "They might overreact, giving us a good chance to identify their leaders."

"Among many other things, yes." Rerth agreed. "That may take a few months, but I am hopeful it will give us options. Your crawler approaches."

A glance to the right let me see the heavy vehicle slowly coming around the corner. "All right. Will I see you again before you leave?"

"No. Be careful until I return, little shark." Warm fingers wrapped around mine, squeezing tightly for a long breath before letting go. "You will be alone for several days until I return. Be cautious."

"I will Rerth. I swear."

She nodded, opening her book back up to resume reading. I took a few deep breaths, trying to calm my nerves.

A few days alone. Holde was undercover, he wouldn't be able to respond to any sudden requests for help that I made. Rerth and Jet would be off world entirely.

I would, quite literally, be all alone.

"I can do this." I whispered, standing up when the crawler crunched to a stop in front of us. "I'll prove that I can do this."

Rerth didn't say anything. I wasn't sure she even heard me. But when I settled into my seat aboard the shuttle, glanced out the window, I saw her smiling at me for the barest moment before she looked away.

"I can do this."

XXV

I sipped tea that was just a few degrees off from boiling, one hand tugging my fur to make sure it covered my right ear. Well, not so much my ear as the communications device settled inside of it.

"Thank you for meeting us so quickly, Lyth." A distant woman was speaking in warm tones. *"I am told you're settling in very well already."*

Holde's voice was dry when he replied. *"It's too cold out to do anything else."*

She laughed. *"True enough. This place is truly miserable this time of year. Trust me when I say it is far more pleasant in the spring."*

"I certainly hope to see more of the city then. At least the..." He hesitated for effect, *"...more civilized parts of it. Is the Eastern Garden as pleasant as the other disciples say?"*

"More than pleasant." She assured him.

They bantered for a while longer, discussing just what the local parks would look like once the snow and ice was gone. It never quite got flirtatious, I was sure that the priestess interviewing him was at least as old as he was, but she seemed to be enjoying the casual conversation all the same.

I drank more tea and did my best to get comfortable. The cafe I was in apparently catered strictly to Humans, and they swore that the blend I was drinking was from leaves smuggled off of Earth.

That probably would have impressed me if I'd been a Human supremacist.

Or if I hadn't had to mix in copious amounts of sweetener just to make it palatable.

Exhaling quietly, I glanced out the window to watch the latest snowstorm ravage the colonial city. I knew it was important that I be ready to listen in on Holde's first interview with a senior priest. Where it would be determined if he'd be given permission to join as a full-time disciple or not.

222

But I also knew the kinds of things he'd likely have to say. The kinds of things the priestess was likely to.

I wasn't looking forward to that at all.

"...said that you came here from the Group of Five. May I ask why you left those worlds for a colony dominated by Humans?" She asked, their banter apparently drying up.

"Speaking honestly?" It was easy to imagine Holde shaking his head a little. "Too many Thondians. I know, I know. We're closer to the Ascendancy here than I used to be, but I know they aren't liked here."

Her voice turned intrigued. "You do not care for their kind?"

"Not especially. The constant looming got old rather quickly, as did the constant threats and power plays." He sighed loudly enough for his hidden microphone to pick it up. "I may not care for Humans much either, but I find them much easier to deal with. Do you disagree, honored one?"

The chuckle was just barely loud enough for me to hear it. "Not at all. Your words could have been from my own interviews four decades past. The furred ones can be just as blindly arrogant, do not get me wrong, but they're also far quicker to back down once we make it clear how inferior they are."

I closed my eyes and let out a heavy breath.

So it began.

"Yes. Some of them are properly respectful of age, and can be tolerable company." Holde let out another theatrical sigh. "Sadly it seems like all of those ones are born in the Empire."

"I cannot help but agree, disciple. I am told you traveled with one of their kind, one that is now driving shuttles about."

I swallowed, fingers clenching around my warm cup. Had Holde told them that, or had they learned it on their own? Yes, we hadn't really focused on stealth when we'd arrived. Hadn't hidden the fact that the two of us had arrived together.

But even if Holde had told them he'd come here with me, I couldn't

223

imagine him having told them that I'd stayed. Found a job. Was supposedly trying to settle here long-term.

Someone had been watching us, or at least digging into Holde's movements.

"I did, yes. A polite thing, terrified I'd kill her at any moment with sorcery." His snort came at the same time I had to close my eyes, reminding myself firmly that he was acting. That he had to in order to fit in.

"But why travel with her?"

"Because living as a disciple didn't offer me a chance to expand my accounts, and she was easy to intimidate into letting me travel with her." He replied easily. *"I'd have preferred other company, but I wasn't awash in options at the time. She was quiet, didn't shed much, and flinched whenever I summoned something to my hand."*

He was acting. He was acting.

"You didn't sleep with her?"

Holde sounded disgusted. *"I hope you don't mean sexually. Just because I can tolerate them, and didn't mind traveling with one that was properly respectful, doesn't mean I want to stroke their fur that way."*

I had to remember that he was acting.

The priestess let out a far louder laugh, sounding genuinely amused. *"I thought you'd respond like that, but I had to make sure. Sadly there are those of us who succumb to... idle fetishes."*

"I'm too old a Guide to bother with idle fetishes, and I like to think I'm too civilized to even consider having sex with an alien just for fun."

"That is very good to hear. Now, tell me how your first few nights at our temple have been?"

"More tea?"

I glanced up to see the waitress, a very pale skinned woman, smiling down at me. Forcing myself to take a single calming breath, I let it out and kept my tones polite. "No thank you. Perhaps that... confection that the man

224

over there is having?"

"It's been more than comfortable. The other disciples have been very welcoming-"

Green eyes looked to where I'd nodded. "Oh! I'd be happy to get you a slice of cake. I'll be right back with it."

"-senior priests have helped-"

"Thank you."

She bounced off, letting me focus on the aft end of Holde's speech. *"-particularly enjoyed last evening's training session. It's been too long since I've really had to strain my sorcery. It..."*

"Made you feel like a Hunter again?" The priestess suggested.

Holde sounded like he was beaming at her. *"Exactly. It felt fresh and new again. It was far more pleasant than what I was doing before. There it was all rote drills."*

"You won't find much of those here. We much prefer challenging our disciples, letting them prove that they can learn and adapt." She paused for a moment, probably for effect as well, then chuckled loudly. *"At least until you reach my rank. Then we need the drills and routine. Sadly there just isn't a better way to perfect the more advanced spells."*

After that they started discussing advanced spell theory, and exactly the kinds of techniques that they would be able to teach him if he graduated beyond being a mere disciple.

I went back to half-listening as the conversation turned ever more technical. Thanks to my species and complete lack of sorcerous skills, there really wasn't anything I could glean from that particular conversation. Besides the fact that the priestess seemed to really know what she was talking about, and that Holde was impressing her with his quick replies and questions.

They were still debating some kind of variation of the Strike when my cake arrived.

"Here you go. Chocolate cake with vanilla frosting." She smiled. "Both freshly baked from ingredients taken from Earth. Did you need anything else?"

"Thank you." I wasn't anymore impressed with the notion of smuggled cake ingredients than I was with smuggled tea, but hopefully it would at least taste better. "And maybe a glass of water, if you could."

"Of course!"

I waited for her to walk away before cautiously using my fork to cut a bite of cake for myself. It...

I fought the urge to grimace, chewed, and quickly swallowed.

Apparently all of the sugar that they'd forgot to put in the tea had been put into the cake instead. It wasn't *bad*, the actual flavor was actually pretty good, but I was pretty sure I could feel my teeth rotting even after the first bite.

"*...believe that we can fully welcome you here.*" I started focusing on what was being said when they finally left the topic of theoretical sorcery. "*Did you leave any belongings behind?*"

"*I wish that I had. It would mean I had more to my name than just my clothing and a lost pack.*"

Sounds of movement and shuffling made me think she'd stood up, maybe took his hand or rested her own on his shoulder in support. "*Many come here alone, but no one leaves that way. Don't worry, Lyth. We'll find you a proper pack. Come, have lunch with me, and we can discuss your new schedule.*"

"*That sounds most agreeable.*"

Recognizing the code phrase, I acted like I was casually brushing my fur back with a hand. Which I kind of did, but mostly I pulled the ear-piece out, switching it off before dropping it into a pocket.

I'd just settled back into the comfortable chair when the waitress came over with my water, setting it down before quickly bustling away to deal with a group of new arrivals who'd just sat down.

That was it then. Holde was in for the long-term at the Temple of Velshen. He'd had to pretend to be at least a mild supremacist, which had not

226

been fun to listen to, but the priestess had been a bit more low key than I'd expected.

Of course that was probably the point. If she was the main interviewer for new arrivals, they wouldn't want her to come on too strong. They wouldn't want to scare off anyone only mildly set against aliens, or those who wouldn't care one way or another.

Closing my eyes, I shook my head once to clear it. There wasn't anything I could do to investigate that right now. That was Holde's job. I had to focus on my little part in the project.

Right now that meant maintaining my own cover... and not doing things like refusing to eat the expensive treat I'd just ordered.

Opening my eyes again, I glared at the sugar disguised as food in front of me. Then I forced myself to lean in and begin eating the expensive snack as quickly as I could. Frequent sips of water helped a little with the grainy aftermath.

Within a few minutes it was gone, and I had a tablet out to check my own progress.

My luck was holding in the positive direction, at least for now. I'd been assigned to five different shuttles on my five work days, letting me install the listening devices that I'd been given before we'd left the ship.

I couldn't actually analyze the recordings. Those were being dumped into some kind of local database for Jet to pull and then delete. But I could make sure that all five were up and running, that no one had found or shut them down.

Closing that program with a finger flick once I'd confirmed that, I changed over to what I actually wanted to investigate.

Local disappearances and murders.

"Just like being on Oshflara." I murmured as I brought up the largest local news site. "Just with a less pleasant research subject."

Tapping the search window, I typed out the word I knew would make my stomach turn.

227

Searching 'Torture'... 789 articles found! Would you like to sort the results by date or relevance?

Grimacing, I selected 'relevance', then poked around for a moment before figuring out how to add another search word.

'Burns'

Search narrowing... 42 articles found! Sorted by relevance!

Picking up my tea, I took a fortifying sip while dearly wishing that it was alcoholic. Then... I brought up the first news article, tapped the auto-translate button, and then had to accept another warning that the reading could be disturbing for some readers.

Not feeling at all prepared, I forced myself to start reading all the same.

Yet another murder in our once peaceful city. The victim, Grigori Kaloyan, was a twenty five year old citizen. A hard working young man, he was employed as a line cook at the Pulsar restaurant inside the recently expanded starport.

Reported missing two weeks ago, his mortal remains were found by a farmer in the eastern quadrant during the harvest. This earnest young man had been dragged more than five miles outside of the city, crucified to a tree, and then burned alive.

I paused there, frowning, then opened another page to search what 'crucified' meant.

One stomach turning dictionary article later, and I resumed my reading.

An inside source among the local police confirmed that, despite the semi-religious appearance of the murder, that the torture was not done with conventional means. I am certain I don't need to tell the local citizens what this clearly implies.

Grigori Kaloyan was abducted by Trahcon, hauled outside of the city, and was then tortured with their unnatural powers until he was burned alive. Like a pig on a spit, they boiled away his...

I rapidly skipped ahead, breathing shallowly to avoid...

My nose flared as the phantom smell of my own burning flesh filled them.

Swallowing, I quickly squeezed my eyes shut. I had to meditate. I had to meditate.

The sounds of the staff bustling around in the back. Forks and knives striking plates. The chaotic rumble of conversation in half-a-dozen languages. A cheerful little chime as the doors opened, the call of relief of a woman entering the warmth of the diner.

"Oh! Hi Ashe!"

I jerked in surprise, blinking rapidly as I came back to the surface before I could truly submerge myself. "Sofia?"

The bartender was beaming as she walked over, wearing thick clothes suited for the weather. Her dark fur was tied up in an odd little bun, and her smile faltered quickly when she got a better look at me. "Wow. Are you all right? You don't look very good."

"Uh, just... reading the local news." I shook myself a little, trying to recover. A quick little motion closed and locked my screen, letting me set the tablet to one side. "And I think the cake was too much on an empty stomach."

She giggled, resting a hand on the chair opposite mine. "May I?"

When I nodded, she quickly sat and leaned in to whisper. "It's really terrible, isn't it? Just a bag of sugar with frosting."

I glanced around to make sure the staff wasn't nearby, then leaned in as well. "Right? And couldn't they have saved some of that for the tea?"

"You should have ordered the coffee. It's much better. Are you staying longer?"

"I can, it's one of my days off. Thought I'd try the local restaurants."

"Do you mind if I stay a bit? I was... hoping to talk to you a bit more." Her voice lowered even further. "It was nice having someone to talk to at the bar."

"Of course you can. I could... um, probably use more advice on where I should be eating."

She grinned again. "Hoping to avoid another tea and cake incident?"

I huffed, surprising myself a little by being genuinely amused. "Already calling it an incident like you know how many of those I've left in my wake."

"That sounds like a story. Or several."

More than several, and... this seemed like a good way to test my training with Holde. See if I could properly lie to someone who didn't know anything about my past. See if I could make a local contact, someone who might help me blend in.

And since I seriously doubted she was involved with the Burned Hand, without being someone I'd have to betray or hurt when it came time to resolve the investigation.

"There's quite the list." I admitted. "But now I'm curious. How many incidents have you left behind?"

"Oh, a few." Sofia leaned back, both of us raising our voices back to normal. "Trade stories?"

"Only if you tell me what to actually order this time."

"Deal!"

Five hours later we parted ways outside of the cafe, both of us grinning and promising to meet up again on my next morning off. Her because she seemed to genuinely want to be friends, and had learned edited versions of several of my better days as a conscript.

Me, because I'd learned several amusing stories of her times in the bar... and because she'd told me which parts of the city to avoid. Warned me, obliquely, that it wasn't safe to be out at night in those areas if I wanted to make it back to my hotel.

Arriving at said hotel room, I settled in to bed with a glass of something strong, convinced that I was following the right currents.

Fortified with that conviction, and a bit of alcohol... I resumed my unpleasant reading.

XXVI

By the time Rerth returned I had a compiled report ready to go, something that seemed to impress her. She read it quickly while I stood at the foot of the hotel's bed, waiting patiently for her to finish.

"At least one deceased victim found per year, every year, for the last decade." She shook her head, sitting comfortably on the bed. "Ashahn's blood. And all of them were abducted, tortured with fire, and then killed?"

"As far as the local security forces could tell." I replied. "Well, as far as the reporters could tell. Half of the deaths were only ever investigated by the pirate groups that the victim belonged to."

The agent huffed. "Have you been able to look into the local security agency at all?"

I grimaced. "According to Sofia, that's my local contact, they're less security and more mercenaries. They *try* to keep the peace, I'll give them that, but actual investigations are something they only do if the family pays them."

"Or if the pirates or mercenaries actually cared about their missing member."

"Or then." I agreed. "Most of the actual investigations were done by local reporters instead. At least until they vanished."

Her eyes narrowed at once, glancing up from the report to me. "Vanished?"

"Vanished." My weight shifted uneasily. "I, uh, think we found the right colony, Rerth. Two men, both Human, wrote most of the articles I drew from to compile that. They were blood-siblings. The first one wrote the first eight articles. Then he apparently vanished, and what was left of him was found a week later."

Rerth's tarah rose. "So his packmate investigated, discovered what happened, and wrote the ninth and tenth articles. Then he vanished as well."

"Yes."

232

"How long after?"

"Uh," It was hard to remember the exact dates, they were in the report, but I managed to dredge it up after a moment. "About a month after article number ten, I think? It should be in section three."

Her hand shifted, one finger moving to set the report scrolling. She nodded after a moment. "His last article was thirty-five days after his report on his blood-sibling's torture and death. Someone is carefully silencing anyone who looks too closely into such things."

I cleared my throat. "Section four should be a rough map. The areas around each of the three temples is... not safe for aliens to go into. I also marked the last sighting of each victim, and where the body was supposedly found."

"The areas to avoid. Are those from your contact, or personal experience?"

"Both. Sofia warned me about those areas, and none of my assigned routes for work go into them. I checked the schedule and the map too. None of the Human employees have stops in there, only the Trahcon drivers."

Both of her tarah rose further in interest. "...well done, Ashe."

I couldn't help but smile, feeling the heat in my face and chest at the genuine praise in her voice. "I'm sure there's more, but that was what I was able to find quickly."

Her voice turned dry, "Define 'quickly' for me, little shark. Have you been sleeping?"

"Um... a few hours a night?"

"I knew it." She snorted. "You haven't jeopardized your cover as a deserter desperate for work and stability, have you?"

"No sir. Um, my coworkers think I'm drinking to cope with the pain of my injuries, so does my contact." I admitted. "I may have exaggerated what happened to me on Trinity to lead to that effect."

Rerth tapped the tablet in her hands, closing the report before setting

233

the device aside. "Giving you an excuse to drink heavily during your reading, and to explain your lack of sleep I assume."

"...yes sir."

My elder huffed. "As happy as I am with this information, that doesn't mean I'm not concerned that your first recourse to hard reading is to drown yourself in alcohol. You need to ease up on that."

I heard my tones become defensive. "I don't drink *that* heavily Rerth. I never have more than one, maybe two drinks."

"Yes, but you make sure they're the strongest you can get your hands on." She countered. "But that's a topic for safer harbors. Holde didn't provide any new updates, what do you have in his field?"

I relayed what little information had come through his interview a few days ago. Apart from that I didn't know anything either, apart from the morning pings telling me he was still alive. She didn't look surprised at the lack of information there, or concerned that her bond was working alone.

Of course she hadn't on Yashun either. They'd probably sailed down this exact river a dozen times. If anything, infiltrating temples and priesthoods was probably quicker and simpler than trying to sneak in to openly criminal organizations.

"How's Jet?"

"Content to be in a supporting role, and continuing his digging through the spaceport's security system." Her eyes met mine. "Your attackers arrived three days before us, and have not left so far as we know."

Oh. That was... expected, I guessed. They were people we had to find and interrogate if we could.

But that didn't mean I wanted to run into them on my own, armed or not.

"Understood." I said quietly.

From her expression she knew exactly what I was feeling. She didn't push, instead just sailing on to the next current. "How much longer do you have before your shift starts today?"

I glanced at my wrist-comp. "Four hours."

"Good. Your cover is desperate for credits, correct?"

I nodded. "Very, considering how much I spent on the gun and shield belt. Plus the drinking and hotel fees."

"Then you wouldn't mind taking odd jobs to help bring in some money. Especially if it involves driving and manual labor."

Ah. "You have a buyer for weapons, and I'm driving whatever vehicle you rented?"

"Yes."

Two hours later I was changed into my work uniform, shield-belt and gun hidden beneath the top. My hands were on the wheel of a rental truck, carefully navigating the narrow streets while Rerth lounged in the passenger seat. The open back had been filled with two unmarked crates we'd offloaded from the shuttle, each of which supposedly contained two dozen obsolete rifles.

Moving them hadn't been too bad, with the hangar's equipment. At least until Jet had started amusing himself by offering commentary on our technique from his hidden place inside the shuttle's cockpit.

"He has full control of the hangar cameras." I complained, turning down the next street. "He could have come out to help us."

Rerth shrugged, "We hardly needed any assistance, little shark. It would have been a foolish risk despite our confidence in his skills. That, and you need to get used to the way he is."

I thought I was used to it. I just didn't like it, especially when I was a little on edge from everything that was going on with this project. When I was finally doing real, important work. When I was being included in a full infiltration to locate criminals.

...the lack of real sleep probably wasn't helping either.

Shaking my head a little, I resolved to get myself some tea or coffee before my shift. "We're just about there. I think that's it, up ahead."

Leaning forward, she nodded after a moment. "The Broken Arm. Odd choice of names for a gunsmith."

I could only agree, carefully pulling the truck over into the sleet covered parking zones in front of the walk. Its momentum left us rolling along, my foot gently tapping the brakes until we finally slowed to a stop right out front.

"Orders, sir?"

A tarah rose, then fell back down. "Go inside and tell them I'm here. I will make sure no one gets any ideas about taking the cargo."

Nodding once, I killed the motor and handed her the activation key. She pocketed it, watching in amusement as I braced myself before throwing the door open.

Apparently I should have braced myself harder. That, or worn something to cover all of my skin

Frigid air immediately sank its fangs into me, making me gasp out a curse before I could slam the door shut. Rerth's laugh was the last thing I heard before I hurried around the front, racing for the store entrance.

Thankfully someone must have been waiting for us; they threw the shop's own door open for me as I darted into the promised warmth.

"Thank you." I gasped, already ringing my hands together. The store's interior was a bit more open than the one I'd made my purchases from, with all of the goods secured behind the counters, but it was blessedly warm.

"Ashahn's blood it's too cold to be out today."

The man who'd opened the door for me had been smiling, but at my words his expression twisted into a scowl. He was about my height, though far more broad, and looked a little like a heavier set Ramos. They even had the same styling to the fur around their lips.

He muttered something in a language I didn't know, then lifted his voice to call for someone.

A moment later another man emerged from a back room. A tiny bit

236

shorter than the other man, he was pleasantly lean, with skin the color of the coffee Sofia had introduced me to. The fur on his scalp had been shaved down in the way I wished Rerth would let me do again, but the wild beard of fur ruined his potential attractiveness.

I did think I got the joke of the shop's name though; his right arm was entirely bronze and silver, whirring quietly as it moved.

"Once broken, now fixed." He confirmed, clearly noticing my attention. "A good life lesson for everyone involved."

I was about to reply when the other man growled more words that I couldn't follow.

The other man gave him an irritated look and barked something authoritative in reply. His assistant, I assumed, scowled a bit more but slunk off to the back room without another word.

"Sorry about that. He didn't like your choice of language. Or deities."

"It's fine. I'm... well, used to that kind of thing."

"I'd imagine." He sounded understanding, but not really sympathetic. It was an odd combination, but he went on before I could really think about what it might mean. "You a customer?"

"Just a driver." I said, offering Rerth's cover identity. "Ghai'thoz paid me to bring her here for some kind of sale."

The fur above his eyes rose a little. "Huh. Was expecting her, but not a driver. Who are you, and why is a bus driver helping move guns around the city?"

"Ashe'lori." I didn't really like being the only one on the team without a cover identity, but Rerth had little faith in my ability to actually respond to one.

I'd wanted to argue, but a rather disastrous training session on the way here had rather proven her point.

"And, well, I need the money. She offered to pay me double what I make in an hour just to drive her over and help with the loading."

There was an amused little huff. "Can't imagine you get paid much. Can't blame you for looking for more options. She actually a Trahcon, or she another grayborn like you?"

"Trahcon." I replied.

"She prejudiced?" He asked.

"Uh, not that I know, no." I shook my head. "I don't think she likes Thondians much from what she said when we were drinking last night, but I don't think she has any issues with Humans. She was polite, didn't make any comments about the fur or my species in general."

He eyed me for a few moments before nodding slightly. "Good. Normally I wouldn't trust an independent, but things are going to get crazy here with the wars. Bring the truck around the back, we'll get it offloaded and get her paid so she can pay you."

"Thank you!"

One more trip through the frigid morning air and we were parked behind the shop. The polite owner and his impolite assistant both helped get the crates off with the help of a small lift. They were quick and efficient, hardly speaking as we moved the crates into a secure room in the back.

There the assistant opened them up, inspecting the guns one at a time while the owner motioned for Rerth and I to stand nearer to the door.

"How much do you owe the driver?" He asked.

Rerth rolled a shoulder, "Promised her one twenty for four hours of work."

"You pay her yet?"

"No."

He let out a deep grunt. "You wait in the truck. I'll send her out with your payment when we're sure the guns aren't fakes, rigged, or trash. She'll have her cut."

Rerth eyed him, expression sour. "I don't stiff contractors."

238

"Don't care." The man replied flatly. "Your kind isn't pleasant to mine here. Do things my way, and we might do business again anyway. Understand?"

She upgraded her scowl, quivered both tarah as if restraining them from rising in anger... but spun on a heel and stalked outside all the same.

I shifted my weight as the door closed on the wind, shivering a little. Both from the temperature and because I wasn't really sure where this was going.

We stood there in an awkward silence for a while, the only sounds coming from the man checking each gun one at a time.

"Does she have more?"

The sudden question startled me, but I managed to shrug in the Human way all the same. "Um, I don't know to be honest."

He studied me for a moment, then glanced to his assistant. "...I don't like this, but we're going to need those guns. You charged her thirty credits an hour?"

"Yes?" I couldn't help but make it a question.

His cybernetic arm whirred and clanked as he reached into a pocket, pulling out a heavy loop of coins. Unlocking the ring holding them together, he ticked off several before settling them in his flesh and blood palm. I nodded slightly when he hit one hundred and twenty, then frowned when he paused, shifted his hand to his other pocket, and pulled out another forty-credit marker.

"Here. Your cut. Give the rest to her."

I took both the loose chits and the ring when he offered them. "Um, what's the extra forty for?"

"Down payment. Be back here tomorrow, at this time. You'll get another eighty to move a truck to another store. Address is 572 Canal Street."

"... Harshk's?"

"You know it. Good." He tipped his head toward the door. "Get the

239

gray to tell you if she's got more arms, and it will be worth your time."

"Um, sure. But why me?"

He paused for a moment, then looked a little sheepish. "No grand conspiracy, girl. I need to move product, and I can't drive a crawler to save my life. Andre can't even drive a regular car. Thirty an hour's half what a moving company would cost me."

I blinked, then smothered a smile. "Oh. Um, should I be worried that I'm undercutting them?"

"I won't tell if you don't."

And with that, I managed to make my second set of local contacts, entirely by accident. Rerth was pleased when I came back out to tell her the news, and immediately told me to go through with it. She'd support from a distance.

I'd made local contacts, found potential proof that the Burned Hand directly operated on Nueva Genova, and even managed to impress Rerth. It was an exceptional start to my first two weeks on my first real mission.

That was probably why I started to get more nervous with each day that passed, just waiting for the crashing wave of my bad luck to catch up with me.

XXVII

Over the next three weeks, things slowly settled into a routine.

After my initial 'trial' period, I was scheduled for six hour shifts for five days a week. It was dull, easy work, and I was consistently given the morning assignments. That was fine with both Rerth and I, since it gave me plenty of time to spend on my real job in the evenings.

I spent two or three nights a week meeting with Sofia, being introduced to some of her fellow bartenders, and generally getting caught up on what life was like here for the average Human. It was both relaxing and informative, though at Rerth's advice I didn't try to pry into any of the disappearances I'd read about.

I didn't ask about them with my new 'side-job' either. I kept my mouth shut, took the money, and didn't ask questions about what I was transporting.

Evidently that was exactly the kind of person that they'd wanted for the job. By the end of the first month I was the go-to driver for several small stores that wanted to quietly move goods around the city. Using Rerth's rental truck, I got to meet quite a few store owners and local citizens in the Human sections of the colony.

Most importantly, I got to meet the men who owned the gun stores, and get a feel for how worried they were all getting.

"That's got to be significant." I distracted myself as I drove the rental truck west, heading into the more built up zones where what passed for a local government operated. "You'd think they'd be excited. More pirates and more refugees flooding in should mean more business."

One or two of them did seem to be thinking that way, but the rest...

"...the rest are stockpiling weapons, and I don't think it's to sell them to pirates. Not with the way they're coordinating, stockpiling."

I'd started to pay more attention to the local news after Rerth had directed me to expand my research in that area. At first it had honestly seemed like a waste of time, but each day I spent watching the morning reporting before work had left me feeling like something wasn't quite right.

Embarrassingly, it had taken me most of the month before I'd realized why.

"Three major news sites, and not one of them has mentioned anything in the Trahcon neighborhoods. No fun pieces on priests doing good in the community, no picking out new art to showcase. No talking about crime, or fires, or car crashes." I drummed my fingers on the wheel. "It's like they're pretending those areas don't even exist."

Rerth had agreed that was more than a little concerning, but it fit with what we'd quickly learned about how the locals handled coexistence with aliens.

The short version? So long as you weren't Trahcon or Thondian, you were perfectly welcomed by the Human majority. You could take any job you wanted, be treated like anyone else, and generally not have any problems.

In contrast, Thondians were apparently barred from even leaving the starport, and Jet said he had yet to actually see one on the security cameras he'd hacked.

As for the Trahcon...

Well, today's buyer for Rerth's guns had refused to even see her in person. Oh, they wanted what she was selling. Wanted it enough to overpay even.

But only on the condition that she hire a local to do the delivery and pick-up.

"Which fits in with everything else I've been seeing." I gently applied the brakes, sliding to a stop at an intersection. "I think I've exchanged five or six entire words with the Trahcon drivers at work."

Not that I'd talked much with my Human coworkers either. None of them seemed sure of having a Grayborn among them, and it was the rare morning where I'd get more than a polite greeting when I showed up for work.

Still, it could have been worse. I hadn't been insulted, or assaulted, yet.

My foot eased down on the accelerator, rolling me onward. "Little victories, Ashe. Little victories. Time to focus though, station is just up ahead, and you need to call Rerth."

I drove to within a block of my destination before pulling into a parking zone, leaving the motor running for warmth. A few quick taps had Rerth's voice emitting from my wrist-comp.

"You've arrived?"

"A block away." I said. "Waiting here for your signal to go as ordered."

"Good. I'll call them and handle the negotiations. Remember, Ashe. Be as polite as you can, and answer any questions they have about me." She paused, sighed, and then added. *"And whatever you do, don't get overly defensive about your relationship with me."*

I swallowed. "I'll do my best."

"I'm not asking you to play the supremacist, little shark. Just don't come across as an Imperial patriot, advocating for peace between the species."

"I've been doing all right at that so far."

She huffed quietly. *"Yes. Over drinks, in casual settings with your contacts. People who aren't likely to notice or seriously care if you're still a bit hung up on the nation you just deserted from. This is different."*

True. This was the local security agency. People trained to investigate, interrogate, and to learn the truth. The kind of group I'd be sailing away from in any other circumstance.

"Play to your strengths. You're a semi-alcoholic deserter desperate for money. If they get too pushy, fall back on your need for credits."

"...do you really have to call me a semi-alcoholic like that?"

There was a soft snort. *"Don't get defensive about the truth, little shark. Be ready for my signal, and remember what to do in the wake of the deal."*

243

"Yes sir."

Closing the channel, I let my head fall back against the seat. Settled in to wait, I ended up watching the light traffic roll by for a quarter of an hour before Rerth finally pinged me with a message.

Deal struck, they're ready for you at the side entrance.

Shifting the truck back into drive, I carefully pulled back into the street. Rolling past the front entrance to the Security Headquarters... sorry, according to Sofia, it was the local *Police Headquarters*, I pulled into the side-lot as instructed. I'd hardly slowed to a stop near the doors before three Human men in winter clothing came out, one waving for me to pull ahead to the parking zone in the corner.

Waving back at him, I followed those instructions as well. Once I was parked I pulled a new pair of gloves on, and then wrapped a thick scarf around my face before getting out.

"Right on time!" The man who'd waved at me called. His own features were mostly covered by cloth as well, letting me see bits of pale skin already turning red from the cold. "These two will get everything unloaded, you can come inside to wait."

"Thank you!" I called back, hoping that my voice remained even. Going into a security station was about the last thing I wanted to do, but I couldn't think of an excuse not to. "Please tell me it's warm in there."

He laughed, falling into step with me as I walked toward the doors. "Just because we're cops doesn't mean we're barbarians."

A little glad that my weak joke had worked, I was equally relieved to reach the promised warmth.

Inside proved to be a small waiting lobby, with a larger security station to check anyone who wanted to go farther into the building. There was only one other man present; a very heavy set one lounging behind the station who barely offered us a glance when we came in.

"It'll be a little bit." The man who'd walked with me said. "The Inspector is still arguing with your employer about the final payment. Take a seat, did you want anything to eat or drink?"

244

I shook my head, reaching up to pull my scarf down. "No thanks, I managed a quick dinner before I came."

He started to nod, then seemed to pause when my face came into view. "...sorry, I didn't mean to stare at the scars."

My scars? I blinked once, absently reaching up to touch my cheek before quickly letting my hand fall. Were scars a bad thing for Humans to have? I couldn't remember that being a thing, and Sofia had never said anything...

"It's fine. They're on my face, so it's hard to avoid looking at them."

Green eyes blinked a few times, then he seemed to force out a quiet chuckle. "I guess that would get you used to people looking at them. Sorry, where are my manners. I'm Officer Alexis Korolev."

"Ashe..." I forced myself to pause like other Humans did between the two halves of their names. "...Lori."

"It's good to meet you, Miss Lori." His own hands rose, tugging the cloth mask off. Underneath he proved to be rather handsome in a way I'd have called feminine on a Trahcon; he had strong features, bright blue eyes, a powerful jaw, and he'd shaved all of the fur the seemed to grow around men's lips.

He hadn't quite shaved the fur on his scalp as well, but it was cut short enough that it didn't look nearly as ridiculous as mine did.

I finally took the offered seat, glancing out of the windows to see the two other men still just standing around by the truck. Officer Korolev followed my gaze, letting out a frustrated groan at the sight.

When he rose his voice again it was to call to the man behind the security station, the language yet another one I couldn't even begin to follow.

The larger man looked incredibly put out at whatever was said, glaring a little before picking up an old fashioned phone. While he growled something into it, Korolev turned back to me.

"Sorry about that." He sighed, walking back a few steps to sit down opposite me. "There's supposed to be someone out there with a lift already."

"It's all right." I assured him, remembering another Human joke I'd heard more than once over the past month. "I'm being paid by the hour anyway. Take as long as you'd like."

That got me another genuine laugh. "I'd be glad to, but we're all salary here. Inspector will have a fit if it ends up taking too long. Still, since we have some time, do you mind if I ask you a few questions?"

Fighting the urge to swallow, I forced myself to smile and nod as if I was completely fine. "Of course not."

"Thank you. How did you end up working for a gray?"

He lost a bit of handsomeness for the slur, even if it was the most mild one for a Trahcon. "She saw me in my day job's uniform at the hotel we're both at, and asked me if I was available for secondary work. We talked over drinks to work out a deal."

"And your day job is...?"

"Shuttle driver." I paused, then amended. "Sorry, uh, *bus* driver."

"Ah." Korolev nodded agreeably. "So she needed a local driver, makes sense. Why did you go through with it?"

"I needed the money." I said.

"Job doesn't pay well enough?"

I shook my head, "The pay's all right, I think, but... I mean, you can hear my accent, can't you?"

He tipped his head. "You sound like an Imperial gray. Deserter?"

"...something like that." I swallowed, glancing away and hoping it looked natural. Like a woman ashamed of what she'd done, but unable to go back and change things. "What little money I had got me here. Paid for the hotel until I could find a job, but now I need more to keep my room there."

"Why not find an apartment?" He asked.

My hands spread helplessly. "That's why I'm taking her jobs. Trying to get enough for a down-payment. All the ones I could afford right now are...

246

too close to areas I'd really rather avoid."

That made him grimace. "Yeah. I know what you mean. If you do need help, there are good loan companies here. We could point you in the right direction, get you free from working for that woman."

"It's fine." I shook my head. "It really is. She barely speaks to me, pays on time, and I get to meet lots of people. There's worse side jobs to have. And it's not like it's going to last forever. She'll move on eventually."

The officer stared at me for a long moment, then blew out a quiet breath. "All right, all right. Just a bit of friendly advice, Miss Lori? Don't be so quick to trust the grays out here."

I saw a chance to ask a question of my own, and hopefully cut off his interrogation before he could dive deeper. "I know. I've... read a few news articles."

His attention sharpened at once. Those blue eyes narrowed, his posture becoming tense. "What kind of articles?"

I lowered my voice, "Um, the ones about disappearances near the Trahcon zones. I'm not about to go anywhere near them. The only reason I trust Ghai'thoz is because she's not from here."

He stared at me, hard, for a few more seconds... then lowered his voice as well. "You're a smart woman, Miss Lori. Stay smart, and forget what you might have read."

"I will." I replied softly. "I just want to start over, and find a nice apartment in the northern zones."

"...it's the best area."

For once, my manipulation actually seemed to work. We spent another ten minutes discussing the better apartment complexes up north, and I thought he tried flirting with me a bit.

It was kind of awkward, he complimented my fur instead of my scars or my muscles, but I thanked him all the same. I was debating about whether I should reciprocate the compliment or not when the men outside signaled that they were done, and another officer came out with a sealed envelop.

247

They opened it for me, letting me count the credits, and then quickly ushered me out the door.

I drove away with a final wave to Korolev, making my way back toward the hotel. For the first few blocks I drove in silence, then carefully pulled into a side street to find a parking zone.

After that I spent a good thirty minutes carefully checking every bit of the truck's interior to see if they'd left any listening devices. Rerth had made very sure that I remembered to do that in her usual way; she'd repeated that order every chance she got all morning.

Only once I was sure they hadn't, or as sure as I could be, did I call Rerth.

"Status."

"We're paid." I replied. "They asked a lot of questions about why I was working with you. I diverted worse by saying I didn't trust the local Trahcon thanks to the news."

She hummed quietly. *"How did they react?"*

"He got real wary real fast. Told me to forget what I'd read, and to never trust the locals. Or go anywhere near them."

"Nothing else?"

I rolled a shoulder, even if the call was voice only. "I've got several leads on nice apartments in the northern part of the city."

Rerth snorted. *"What was their reaction to our working together?"*

"I think he was trying to pressure me into quitting. Or maybe pressure me into admitting you were terrible. Or something." I bit my lip, frowning as I got the truck's motor going again. "I'm not sure, but I don't think I gave him what he expected."

"Or wanted, maybe."

"Maybe. Orders?"

"Back to the hotel for tonight. Jet and I are putting together a

248

potential infiltration, and we'll need an escape driver ready if a storm brews up. I'll give you the details when you return, make any excuses you need to not go out with your contacts tomorrow."

"Understood, sir."

XXVIII

Rerth decided that the meeting needed to involve all four of us, which meant it had to happen in the shuttle. She and I joined Jet inside of it just after lunch, while Holde attended by a secure call.

"I'm in a lovely little diner a few blocks from the temple." He was on voice-only, speaking just loudly enough to be heard over the murmur of conversation in the background. *"There's nowhere in the complex itself I trusted for this."*

Rerth exhaled, pacing back and forth just as her bond might have. Jet and I watched from the same seats we'd once used to support her from a distance, turning slightly to let her past whenever she changed direction.

"Listening devices?" She asked.

"Everywhere, including my room."

I winced while Jet huffed, his voice dry. "Such upstanding speakers for the Aspects."

"We knew that." Rerth waved a hand, dismissively flicking one tarah. "We have several issues to discuss in relation to the plan I am forming. Our principle problem is the expected one; the Admiral of the Void Fleet is losing patience."

"Already?" I asked. "It hasn't even been two months yet."

Jet snorted. "They're Void Fleet. You have to be impatient to even be allowed to join."

"While I agree with the sentiment, for once I think this is justified." Rerth shook her head. "The standing orders from the Torlah are to avoid any major military action near the Ascendancy's border. The last thing she wants is for them to be able to claim we're invading. That could be used to pull the factions back together and end their civil war."

Holde didn't sound convinced. *"True, but it's one battle-group attacking a planet known to harbor pirates. Pirates who have begun raiding*

250

the Ascendancy directly as it is."

"Yes, but I got the impression that Lord Obdel'rilem has already drawn the Torlah's attention for his attack on the Group of Five, and not in a pleasant way. I think he wants this wrapped up as quickly and cleanly as possible."

"Oh." I said, thinking that I got it. "He wants to be able to justify what he did."

She nodded without looking at me. "I don't share that priority, all I care about is the resolution of our project. That being said, if we don't give the Admiral some sense of progress..."

"They'll sail in, every gun firing in the hopes of dealing with this themselves." Holde's tones were sour. *"Just like last time."*

"That is my fear." Rerth agreed. "I'd have preferred to wait another month for our first major action, but if we give them something we can buy ourselves more time to investigate thoroughly. Jet? You said you had a breakthrough over the past few days, and a working theory with evidence."

He stirred in his seat, fur rippling with the movement. "There's been a definite increase in the numbers of priests coming through the starport over the last three weeks. Arrivals only. There's few, if any, departures. Which is interesting, because according to Holde there aren't many showing up at his temple."

"There's only been three new disciples recruited since I arrived." He confirmed. *"All of them are local hunters or huntresses. There hasn't been any new senior priests that I've seen arriving either."*

"So they're coming in, but where are they staying?" Jet asked, going on before any of us could think to answer his rhetorical question. "I used Ashe's work schedule to figure out which crawlers were headed for the Trahcon majority zones during the big arrival waves, and checked the listening devices she left in there."

"And?" Rerth demanded.

Jet held his upper hands out, palms up. "Lot of complaining about the attack on the Group of Five setting things back. Even more complaining that they had to come here during winter, and a few of them sounded concerned

251

that the short-furs were getting uppity. Their words, Ashe."

I pursed my lips, but focused on the complaints rather than the slurs. "That makes it sound like they've been through here before."

"That was the impression I got." He said. "I tracked them to the last stop in the south-east. Number Forty-Five-S. They all seem to get off at that location, which is a problem."

"Edge of the city." I recognized the code after nearly two months of working the routes. "I've been to that stop once or twice. It's not even in the Trahcon zones anymore, and the only thing out there is a couple of farm equipment stores."

Rerth slowed her movements, frowning. "Nothing that could be used to conceal a barracks? No residential areas?"

I frowned, thinking hard on my memories. "I don't think so... maybe a few rough houses, but no big apartments. No warehouses or silos either."

"That's what the map shows." Jet agreed, "They must have another set of rides to take them outside the city. Maybe there's an entire complex out there that we don't know about."

"That would make sense. If there are far more Trahcon than are publicly admitted to being on planet, it would explain why the Humans haven't rioted when their own go missing."

"Ashe?" Rerth asked.

I could only shake my head. "No one has hinted that to me. Just warnings to not trust any Trahcon, not to go near their living zones, not to be alone at night, that kind of thing. It could explain why the arms dealers are stockpiling instead of selling though. And why they keep moving guns around the city."

"And," Holde added, *"It could explain why they won't use official groups to handle those shipments. You said there's at least one or two other locals with trucks being paid to do the same odd-jobs that you are."*

When I nodded again, Rerth did as well before sailing on. "Good work, Jet. You as well, Ashe. I think it's obvious that our first objective should be determining if such a facility exists outside of the primary colony, and how

252

many people are operating out of it."

"And if they're working with the Burned Hand, or if they just share a passion for torturing aliens to death." I guessed.

"Yes." She confirmed. "Once we have its location, numbers, and allegiance, we can determine if we need to bring in the Void Fleet or conduct further research. If no such facility exists, then we will switch back to a general search for your attackers from the hotel, Ashe."

When Jet and I both nodded, and Holde made a sound of agreement, she went on to ask, "Holde, how integrated are you into the Temple?"

"I've charmed several of the mid-ranks, and the Hunters and Huntresses think I'm the greatest Guide alive."

Jet rolled his eyes while I smothered a grin. Rerth merely smiled before asking, "Good. Do you have any duties that would assist us?"

He hummed in thought. *"Not just yet. They're training me up to act as the junior sorcery instructor for the other disciples, so I have limited access to the local systems. Nothing that would truly aid a break-in though."*

"What about the senior staff? Their names, duties, offices?"

"I'm already compiling a list of who is handling which duties. What are you thinking?"

Rerth made another of her little turns, gliding past our seats. "Cover and a potential distraction. Do you know which one of them is in charge of security?"

"Yes. Am I distracting them so that you and Jet can burgle the local network?"

"Yes. Can you keep them busy all night?"

I blinked, then felt heat rise to my cheeks when I realized what she meant.

Holde merely chuckled, *"She's a younger Guide whose packmates are all most of a century older. There's definitely a chance she may be in the mood for company. Can I have a few days to work her up to it?"*

253

"We'll make our move two weeks from today, just after sunset. You have until then."

"Confirmed. Will you need anything else from me? I'm due back shortly."

Rerth paused her movements, clearly thinking. "No. Make certain that she isn't in any position to respond to any alerts or warnings that may come in that night. Make your usual preparations to abandon the area if the situation collapses."

"I'll be ready, love."

The line cut out after that, leaving the three of us to handle the rest of the planning.

"Jet? Bring up the map of the Temple of Velshen. Overlay what I found in my walks around it with what Holde was able to report from the interior."

He brought it up on his screen, making me get up to look over his shoulder as Rerth did the same on his other side. One of his long fingers began tapping various locations as he rotated it around.

"It's not a good target, Rerth. Cameras are all over the place on the exterior, and there's just as many in the interior courtyard. No way we can scale the wall and move in through there."

Rerth reached out a hand as well, pointing. "There. That side entrance. It has a loading dock, and Holde's explorations don't show additional cameras in those hallways. That's our entrance."

Jet was already shaking his head. "There's three cameras on the loading bay."

"Yes, but it has an access panel that you can override. And if there's a truck in that stall, it'll block two of the three cameras, and the third one is within arm's reach of that corner."

"...could work." He admitted. "We'll need a second vehicle to block that exterior wall camera to let me climb up there though."

Her head tipped toward me. "Our escape driver will position her vehicle there. We'll use it to block that view and give you a bit of a boost to access the bay camera."

I cleared my throat, venturing a thought. "Um, I don't think they'd appreciate seeing a Human driving a car through the area. Or getting stalled next to their temple."

"I still have my disciple robes. I'll do the initial driving, and pose as if I've had a break-down trying to get back to the temple." She replied before pausing, a slight frown making her tarah lower. "That does complicate you being in position to get us out. If anyone investigates they will undoubtedly react to you."

Jet rolled a shoulder. "She could conceal herself?"

A sharp shake of her head. "Risky. No. She'll come in with us, and hold the doorway from the inside. We'll have to position a secondary vehicle elsewhere for the withdrawal."

Go with? Into the temple?

A little part of me was excited to be trusted to go with this time, but my mouth still went dry from nerves. "Is that really better than them finding me outside?"

"Yes, because we *need* that doorway to be able to get back out." Rerth said. "If anyone locks it down we would be trapped inside. If you are guarding it, that will allow me to run ahead of Jet to provide him a clear channel to sail through."

Our smallest packmate stroked the fur on his chin, nodding in agreement. "Assuming this map is accurate, I should be able to find a full terminal in the offices right in the offloading area. That should be enough. Well, unless they're so paranoid that they have completely separated networks."

"We will cross that river when we reach it." Rerth said firmly. "Ashe will cover the doorway and watch for anyone approaching from a side-entrance. I will advance to the primary entrance to the offloading area and watch from there."

"Workable." He replied. "How are we going to get a truck stuck there

255

to block those initial cameras? Sabotage?"

"Given our time constraints, I don't see another option. We have two weeks to learn the schedule and burgle whichever local group handles the local freight. We identify which truck will be used that day, add a remote command, and cripple it so it cannot leave."

I risked speaking up again. "Isn't that kind of a gamble? Won't they just call a tow vehicle?"

Rerth's grimace was plain. "Yes. This is why I don't like rushed jobs. If the Aspects are with us, than the truck will be there late enough into the evening that its removal can wait until morning. If they are not..."

"Then," Jet shrugged both shoulders, "We're stuck coming up with a new plan. Maybe inserting Rerth in as a Disciple recruit again."

"No. I already don't like that we've had to repeat that plan with Holde. If this insertion fails, then we will try for one of the other temples."

"Um," I shifted my weight. "We don't know anything about the other temples. And we don't have Holde on the inside to give us the layout."

"No, we don't." Her gaze turned to meet my own. "How fortunate you have two weeks to do as much investigating in that area as possible."

I opened my mouth, closed it, and then sighed a little. I'd been hoping to do more investigations into the local disappearances. There had to have been far more of them than the few I'd written my first report on; those had just been the most obvious ones.

Well, it would just have to wait, I supposed.

"Yes sir."

XXIX

Rerth drove the stolen van around the temple. It was a utility model, its treads biting nicely into the snow covered streets, and had more than enough space for Jet and I to hide in the back.

The last couple of days had been nothing but furious waves of preparation, with only tiny lulls of pure stress in between. Everyone hanging on each update from Holde. On Jet's discoveries regarding the supply schedule.

His slipping out of the starport to attach a tiny explosive to the truck scheduled to bring food to the temple the day of our raid. Then, when that had gone well, Rerth arranging a traffic collision to delay its arrival for a precious hour in the hopes of leaving it stuck overnight.

Getting into our gear in the back of the van, Jet thumbing the activation button on his little bomb to melt a critical piece of the truck's motor. Hopefully stopping it from being able to start at all, leaving it stuck in the loading bay, and not being obvious as sabotage.

It had to look like a standard breakdown, and it had to still be stuck there.

"...it's still in the bay." Rerth reported from the front, the words nearly making me gasp in relief. "No sign of anyone lurking around."

Jet tightened his belt, weapons and tools clanking quietly. He was dressed in the light armor of an Intelligence officer. Its tight form and unmarked helmet made him look sleek and deadly. Especially in comparison to my shuttle driver's uniform.

I didn't like not being in armor, having to rely on a shield belt and a few small bracers over my thighs, but Imperial Conscript armor was anything but subtle. If we had to run for it, Rerth and I could at least blend in with the local citizens. Jet would...

Ugh. If things seriously became storm-wrecked, Jet would stay behind in his armor to hold them off as long as he could.

"There wouldn't be. If there's an ambush waiting, it'll be inside. Ten seconds to our track failure." He noted. If knowing he was our designated rear-guard had bothered him, he'd never showed it. "Counting now."

I stayed quiet, bracing myself for what was coming next. Jet must have been counting a little faster than me; he set off his next little bomb when my mental numbers had only reached two.

The van promptly lurched as the treads on the right side snapped. Rerth swerved a little bit in that direction, playing the role of a driver doing their best to get off of the road before she became completely immobile.

"...and we're in place." She said once we'd lurched to a stop. "Jet, be quick about it. The temperature is dropping fast."

"Already on it." He pushed the back door open just enough for him to vanish outside. It hadn't even closed behind him before Rerth was similarly sliding out of the front, hissing in discomfort as she did.

Leaving me alone, in the dark of a shut down van.

"It's not a metaphor." I whispered, tugging my scarf up and over my mouth. A second check made sure my earpiece was in place, and my vision goggles were secure around my neck in case the lighting was disabled.

"You're actually an important member of the team this time. Be ready to get out at the signal."

Or to be ready to make a run for the escape vehicle; the old rental truck waiting just one street over in a public parking zone.

I didn't quite jump when Jet came across comms a minute later, but I did gasp at the sudden words in my right ear. "*Camera is locked; all they'll see is a still image. Ready to breach.*"

"*Go.*" Rerth ordered. "*Street is clear. Out and follow.*"

Swallowing, I pushed the door open and hopped out. My elder was already racing ahead of me, her breath coming in puffs of steam as she vanished around the loading dock's corner. Boots crunching in the snow, I ran after her as quickly as I could, getting into the space before any ground-cars could come by to see me.

That part worked, even if I wasn't fast enough to stop the night air from sinking its frigid claws into my skin.

The loading bay wasn't all that big; there was just enough space for one truck to offload its cargo. Jet was already farther ahead, working on the door, Rerth shivering behind him.

"Cover behind us."

"Yes sir." Drawing my pistol, I turned to stare back at the exit. A moment later I felt Rerth's back pressed against mine; each of us watching a different direction.

"Ashahn's blood it's cold." I whispered after a few tense seconds of silence, already unable to help from blurting something out.

"Quiet. Focus."

I nodded, hoping she wasn't looking to notice how badly I was shaking. Hoping it was just from the cold, and not nerves. Not from knowing that, if things went wrong, I could be tied to another chair while someone played with sorcerous fire.

Clenching my jaw against a roll of my stomach, I focused on the dim light coming from the street while Jet continued to work on the door.

"...and there it is. Rolling it now."

I started to turn, only forcing myself to stop at the last second. I had to keep watch behind. That was my job.

The sound of metal wheels turning lasted for just a few seconds before Rerth said, "Stop it there."

"Stopped. Locked. Heading in."

"Moving in."

"Moving in." I repeated quietly, backpedaling as soon as I felt Rerth's warmth leave my back.

Six long steps brought me from a dark loading bay to a dimly lit storage room. A single glance let me see two small carts for moving crates around, a pair of doors, and a heavy cargo container waiting to be loaded to our right.

"Jet, office." Rerth nodded to the middle of the doors. "That should be the primary entrance, I'll be through there. Ashe?"

"Other side of the container." I nodded. "Secondary door."

She flicked one tarah in approval, robes bustling as she strode away. For my part, I followed Jet towards his own door, but turned to get around the container instead of following him into the supply manager's office.

There was a fairly broad space on the other side of the container. It was honestly a bit excessive considering that there was only the one loading door, and I slid that observation aside to remember for later.

Right now I had to focus on the small doorway just to the left of the cargo container.

"Service door." I murmured to myself, settling in with my back to the crate. "Connects to the passages in the exterior walls, Holde says they're filled with gardening and cleaning equipment."

It was a swing door, which was good because the hinges were on my side. Anyone coming out would leave me concealed, letting me shoot them from the back.

Considering that I still hadn't improved being 'mediocre' when it came to my aim or combat skills, that was probably ideal.

Waiting for Jet to hack his way into the system was ten times as stressful in person. It seemed like years instead of months since I'd been supporting them all from the shuttle. The place I probably should have still been, and where Rerth definitely would have preferred me being, if we weren't so pressed for time.

"No." I whispered even lower. "You're her packmate. She brought you with because she trusts you to handle your duty. Prove her right."

It would have been easier to prove her right if not for the silence. Whatever Jet was doing was quiet enough that I couldn't hear him, and after his initial report that he was starting his hack, there wasn't anything on comms either.

Rerth was completely silent as well. Both of them could have vanished and I wouldn't know until it was...

Ugh.

I shook my head, flexed my fingers around the grip of my pistol, and forced myself to lean back. To settle in, to relax, and to just do my job without overthinking everything.

A painfully long two hours went by before Jet finally said anything. *"Security is very tight, but I have limited access. I'm starting my search."*

"Hall clear." Rerth said at once. *"No movement."*

I licked my lips to wet them, easing my weight from side to side to try and relieve the tension in my legs. "Side door clear. No movement."

Neither of them said anything further, leaving me to remain tense and alone in my little corner. The tiny stretches helped a little. Distracting my brain and giving me something besides a closed door to focus on.

Working my way through my legs, I did partial lunges, a few calf raises, and balanced on one leg at a time. Once I ran out of things I could do without really moving, I shifted over to my arms.

I made it about three minutes into stretching them before my usual luck showed up, and my elbow collided with the crate to my side. Gasping as the entire limb seemed to go painfully numb, I frantically shook it out, silently praying that neither of my packmates had heard the quiet clang.

Neither one of them reacted over comms to reprimand me, which was good.

The echoing thud I heard from inside the container wasn't.

"...what?" My lips barely moved, my eyes staring at the flat wall of metal.

I was entirely ready to convince myself I'd imagined it when there was a second, louder noise. Two much louder clangs that definitely reached Jet's ears.

261

"Ashe!" He hissed. *"What the fuck are you doing?"*

"It's not me!" I shot back, gun already half up and aimed at the container. "There's something inside the container!"

Rerth's snarl cut him off before he could reply. *"Check it! Both of you!"*

The bark got my gun properly up. I kept it roughly aimed at the container as I walked back toward the front of it, feeling a little better when Jet emerged from the office with his own pistol pointed at the same thing.

It didn't look like anything that should have had something in it. Just a completely standard, boring, transportation container meant to slide neatly into the back of an equally dull ground-truck.

"I'll have a nullification grenade ready." He murmured when we were shoulder to shoulder, "I'll cover it, you unlock it. We'll open it just enough to see, but be ready to slam it shut."

A few cautious steps brought me closer to the now-silent box. Reaching up, I tapped the lock controls once to set it from blue to red. The quiet clank of it disengaging came a moment later... and was quickly followed by louder sounds of movement from within.

I don't really know what I expected when I tugged it open just a few inches.

A torrent of gunfire maybe.

A blast of sorcery to slam the crate's door into me.

Pretty much anything but the rolling stench of waste that emerged, along with a chorus of pathetic sounding groans.

"...fuck." Jet groaned. "Ashahn's fucking blood. Rerth? It's not an ambush, but we've got a problem."

I hesitated for a second, then leaned in just a bit to see what he meant.

A single light in the ceiling let me see the dull eyes of a dozen or more Humans and Naulians staring back at me. A few of them were wearing rags, but most didn't have anything at all. From the way they'd been grouped up I guessed they'd been huddled for warmth. Their fur was uniformly long and greasy, matching the evidence of where they'd been unable to avoid stepping in their own waste.

They must have been stuck in the crate for days, at least.

And... Ashahn's holy blood. None of them could have been my age.

When one of the closer ones, a young Naulian boy shakily stood up to stare back at me, others following his lead, I realized I was wrong.

None of them could have even been *hunters*.

"Fuck." Somehow I managed to whisper the word.

"What is it?"

Rerth's impatient demand managed to get Jet speaking again.

"We've got a dozen children locked in the crate." He reported, "Humans and Naule. I think two of them are already dead in the back. They're in bad shape."

I found my voice as the boy took a few shaking steps toward me, giving me a better view of the dark letters stitched across his shaved neck. "They've got tattoos on their throats. Colony names. Imperial colony names. Uh... I see Colony One, Icar, Vor'flara, Pan'vos..."

Her snarl was pure lightning and fury. *"Jet, get back in the office and rip out every bit of data you can get. Don't be subtle, just be fast. Ashe? Get them out of the crate and see if they can move. Then I need you to... I have incoming."*

Comms went instantly silent. I was about to turn to face Jet when the boy, his black fur so matted it would probably have to be shaved off, managed to speak.

"Help... please..."

Jet hissed, already backing away. "Get them out, get one of them watching Rerth's door, and get the rest ready to run."

263

Left with no real choice, I turned back to the boy and waved him forward.

He didn't come.

I repeated the gesture, "Come on, out. All of you. We're getting you out of here."

He hesitated, only for a darker skinned Human girl to carefully step around him. Her legs were shaking a bit, but from her height I guessed she was one of the oldest present. The tattoo stitched across her throat read 'Altair'.

"...I don't know if we can run." Her voice was quiet. Weak, not quiet because she intended to be. "I don't know how long we've been in here."

Dammit. "Help me get everyone out here. It's very cold, so stay huddled up. Keep everyone quiet, we can't let them know we're here."

True to her prediction, she was probably in the best shape of them. Three others, including the boy who'd spoken to me first, were just about able to walk on their own. Maybe, just maybe, they could get up to a jog.

The rest of them were barely able to stumble out before falling into a new pile. Nearly all of them were crying, something that wrenched my heart. A few even tried to grab onto me, to stop me from walking away when they all emerged.

"I'm just making sure." I whispered, counting them as they came out. Seven Humans, six Naulians. "Stay close for warmth. We'll get you out of here soon."

The Aspects alone knew how. Our escape truck could, *maybe*, fit them all in the back... but the back wasn't covered. In this weather I didn't think many of them would make it to warmth. Or where we could even take them to find warmth.

"...no choice." That murmur was for my ears alone, once I'd forced myself to walk into the crate to check the two forms that hadn't gotten up. Hadn't moved.

Two Naulian boys, their necks proclaiming them both be from Ban'vos. Citizens from the great fortress world on the far side of the Empire.

264

Heirs to a legacy of resilience dating back to the First War of the Compact. Dead in a frozen crate on a world in the Reaches, hundreds of lightyears from home.

They should have been with their childhood packs. Learning. Playing sports. Pretending to be warriors, holding the line against the Federation. Or even dreaming of deserting, running off to the splinter kingdoms, or to join the Scarlet Tears in the Far Reaches.

Anything but this.

Why?

Why were they here?

Why?

Shaking myself, I backed away from the bodies. I don't know how I kept control of my stomach. How I avoided simply heaving up everything amid the stench and horror of what I was looking at.

I barely remember stumbling my way past the children, making it to Jet's place in the office.

"Th-they're out." I stuttered. "C-can't run. Orders?"

His helmet jerked up from where he'd been staring at the screen in the little room. "You're collapsing? Dammit! I knew... no. We need our truck. Get it, get it over here. I'll find-"

The sudden shrieking of an alarm above our heads cut him off.

I think he started to swear, but the sudden explosions from Rerth's direction cut that off as well.

As Khash, Aspect of Luck, visited his curses on us yet again.

XXX

I'd never been involved in a real battle before.

True, I'd been in fights. Had my fair share of sparring matches. Been beaten nearly to death. That kind of thing.

But I'd never been through anything like the storm that exploded inside the temple.

If it hadn't been for Jet, I'd have locked up as everything went insane. Those kids who could start screaming wasted little time in doing so, the alarms continued blaring, and I could hear shouting in every direction.

"Move them back!" Jet's shout made my entire body twitch. He hadn't quite nailed Rerth's commanding tones, but he got close enough for my training to kick in. "Behind the crate!"

"Behind the crate!" I shouted, motioning for the children to move. "Behind the crate, go!"

The cacophony must have given them a jolt; pretty much all of them managed to get moving. Only two still needed help, and the older members dragged them along without me having to say anything.

But not all of them were moving in the right direction.

"Don't go-" One of the Humans, the poor boy was clearly out of his mind with fear, simply ran out into the docking zone without stopping. "-outside! You'll freeze!"

Another one or two might have tried it anyway, but the eldest girl used her longer legs to get ahead of the others. She blocked the way with her body, practically tackling a Naulian boy who tried to get around her anyway.

"Ashe! Eyes on the entrances!"

Jet's shout had me yanking my eyes around, pistol coming up in both hands. "Good! I'm triggering our emergency beacon!"

266

"You sure!?"

"Rerth's not-"

A priest wearing nothing more than sleeping shorts barreled through the doorway. Half of her torso was covered in burns, face set in a furious snarl. Blue-white fire was coalesced around both of her tarah. When she saw us, it began to brighten in color, flaring out as she began to direct it.

The horrid memories of my own flesh burning filled my nose, my body locking up again.

Jet didn't have that trauma. He started shooting at once, his pistol rattling off a short burst.

I don't know if she simply hadn't seen the gun, or had been too focused on attacking. At least one of his rounds slammed into her shoulder, red splattering the wall behind her.

She screamed, flailed back, the fire vanishing.

Belatedly yanking my own trigger, I didn't do much besides blow a few little craters in the wall. For his part, Jet seemed to correct his aim, putting his next burst into her chest.

The priestess managed a barrier in time to save herself, the rounds skipping away from the sorcerous protection, but she'd apparently had enough for now.

She scrambled away, clutching at her wound, vanishing through the doorway she'd just come through.

"We can't hold here." Jet growled, "Get them into the storage hall! We'll find a place to hold up, then you'll need to make a run for the truck! Take the lead, I'll cover the rear!"

"Sir!" I replied on reflex. "Children! Let me through!"

The Aspects must have been looking out for the rest of them; they'd managed to get behind the crate, all cowering near the doorway I'd been watching over earlier.

I tried to sound confident, but my shaking hands probably ruined the

267

effect. "Follow, but stay behind me, all r-right?"

Twelve sets of eyes nodded as I ran past them. A quick yank on the door got it open, letting me plunge into a dark hallway. Lights automatically popped on around my third step, letting me see plenty of general tools and spare parts neatly lined up along the walls.

A glance behind me showed the children following along in my wake. I didn't let my eyes linger too long on their terrified features. If I did, they'd probably see just how badly I was trembling.

Focusing on the hallway ahead let me keep going. Let me pretend I didn't hear Jet shooting again. Let me pretend that there weren't more dull thuds booming in the distance.

We didn't end up running very far. The hallway ran for maybe fifty yards before it ended with a solid wall. To either side was a doorway; the left one a standard entrance that should open to the gardens, the right a heavy security model that would take us out onto the streets.

"We can't go left." I heard myself whispering out loud. "That's the center of the temple, no easy way out. Have to check what's across the street here."

It would be cold. Deathly cold, but going into the inner gardens would be straight up suicide.

I raised my voice, finally managing to speak in even tones "Stay back from the door! I'm going to see what's outside!"

If the kids said anything it was cut off by the cacophony of Jet's gun. He must have been in the hallway behind us now; the confined space making it agonizingly loud.

I flinched while the kids whimpered, clutching their ears and huddling closer to each other in fear.

Swallowing, I managed to punch the door lock with my left fist. It flashed to indicate it was disengaged, letting me hit the other button to send it rolling open.

Frozen air immediately stabbed into my eyes, skin, and filled my lungs. Dim streetlights made the snow and sleet on the streets glow a dismal white, giving me just enough to see by without pulling my goggles on. A single step outside let me look in both directions.

There wasn't any traffic. Just the useless crawler we'd used to get here far off to my right.

"*Ashe!*" Jet's shout across comms made me flinch. "*Find them cover out there! Now!*"

"D-diner!" I stuttered back, "Across the street! It's closed!"

"*Shoot out the window and get them inside! They're grouping up, I can't hold them off again!*"

"Sir! Children! Follow me!"

They did. I have no idea why they didn't all break and run for it the moment they were outside, but they stayed close as I ran out into the street. It had to been agonizing on their bare feet. On their bare skin.

I lengthened my strides, getting across the street as fast as I could. The door was, unsurprisingly, locked. At least until I followed Jet's order and simply shot out the latch, sending it bouncing open... sand also setting an alarm screaming somewhere.

Oh well. Ashahn knew that there were probably already a hundred calls to the local security forces. One more wouldn't really change anything. If they were going to respond at all to the crisis in a Trahcon district then they'd already be on the way. If they weren't, one more alarm wouldn't change things.

I hoped.

"Inside! It's warmer in here, come on!"

They were already staggering in past me. More than half were being helped or outright carried by their stronger companions. The oldest, the Human girl, quickly led them into the kitchens to take cover. Or just hide. Either way, it was probably the best spot for them at the moment.

"Jet! We're in the diner!"

Instead of replying, my packmate simply came running out of the

269

doorway we'd left. One hand held a pistol, the other three helping propel him along as fast as he could.

"They're coming!" He growled, skidding to a rough stop next to me in the doorway. "I still can't raise Rerth or Holde, but I could hear fighting."

I swallowed, desperately fighting down the urge to retch. "Orders?"

"We need to get out of here." His helmet shook sharply. "Get the truck or hijack the first big car you see out there, bring it around. I'll keep the children alive."

"B-but-"

"Go!"

I was back out in the cold, getting up to a full sprint within a few heartbeats.

It was strange. I was terrified nearly out of my mind. I could barely speak, my stomach was churning madly... but some part of me could still think as I ran.

Could still do the bitter math.

The Void Fleet was lurking just outside of the system. Jet's emergency beacon would ping the local communications system, override a channel, and then be broadcast to the local FTL buoy. That wouldn't have taken more than a few minutes.

If he'd really triggered it right away, the flagship had probably already received the signal. The Void Admiral would have to make the decision to come in, then tell the rest of the fleet, then they'd have to get their engines fully powered up for the quick faster than light race into the solar system.

All of that would take at least an hour. Probably longer, depending on how far they were, and how favorable the hyperspace currents were today.

And that would only put them into orbit. It would take them longer to actually get troops down here to save us.

"An hour or two." The words came out between panting breaths. "An hour or two."

270

We had to survive for at least that long...

How?

I made it to the street corner, turning north just as the cracking pops of gunfire began sounding off again. There was enough of it to make me think that Jet wasn't the only one shooting anymore; a thought that made me start running a bit faster.

Jet would know the how. He had to.

I couldn't let my packmate down. Couldn't let those poor children down.

"Find the truck. Find the truck."

It was one block ahead, and then just to the right. Not that short of a run... in normal weather and times, at least.

I don't know how much of my shaking was from fear, how much was from the effort of running, and how much was from the freezing temperatures. I had to slow down several times to avoid slipping on patches of ice, and once slammed my shoulder into the side of an apartment building when I couldn't keep my balance.

It was a miracle I didn't accidentally shoot something when that happened, and I made sure that my finger wasn't on the pistol's trigger after that.

Lights were popping on all over the place by the time I made the next street. Packs being woken up by the chaos, staring out of windows as they tried to figure out what was going on.

I turned right, doing my best to ignore the eyes I could feel on me. Praying that none of them sent sorcery at the armed Human running through the snow.

Those worries were washed out of my thoughts when I came around the corner to see a shuttle crawling its way past the truck. Its colors proclaimed it to be from the same company that I worked for, and the driver was already bringing it to a stop at the intersection.

It was huge. It would be warm.

I knew how to drive it.

My feet were striking the pavement before I really had a chance to think about it, cutting across the front before the driver could get it back into motion.

To my shock he actually opened the side door when I came around the side, one hand raised warningly before he saw my face. I recognized him; he was one of the regular night drivers who came in when my shift ended. We hadn't exchanged more than a handful of greetings, but I knew his name.

"...Lori?"

"Sho." The first step up and in left me standing directly under a heater, and I couldn't stop a gasp of relief. Taking a quick look told me that he didn't have any passengers, thank the Aspects for small favors. "...uh, I need your bus."

He stared at my gun, not quite pointed at him, then flicked his tarah when the distant sound of gunfire picked up. "What in the Aspects' holy names is-"

Something exploded, cutting him off and making us both flinch.

"I n-need your bus!" I half-screamed, fixing the direction I was aiming. "They had kids! I have to get them and my pack out of here!"

Ozone filled my nose, and I nearly pulled the trigger before I realized he'd just called up a barrier to protect himself.

"Dammit Lori! What kids? Who's fighting?"

"The temple! The temple had starved kids!"

He gaped. "That doesn't make any sense. You've lost it, you need to-"

I shoved my free hand into my pocket, yanking my nullification grenade out of it. His expression finally shifted into real fear when I jammed a thumb down on the primer, holding the little orb against my chest.

"Out!" I knew I didn't sound stable when I screamed again. "Get out

272

Sho!"

His pointed hand rose, the other removing his restraints. The scent of active sorcery faded as he carefully got himself free from the driver's seat. I climbed the rest of the stairs, getting out of the way so he could get off.

To my eternal relief he didn't try anything. He didn't make me use the grenade or the pistol.

He just got off, and quickly started jogging to the nearest apartment.

The moment he was outside I turned the grenade off before I wasted it, jamming it back into my pocket. My pistol followed once I'd flicked the safety back on, giving me two free hands to grab the shuttle's controls.

It obediently lurched into motion when I pushed down on the accelerator, absently shutting the door as I turned left.

"Jet! I've got a shuttle crawler, on my way!"

"Hurry!"

My foot pressed down harder. The crawler's heavy motors obediently increased the speed, the heavy treads biting into the stone as I picked up speed.

People were starting to emerge on the street, shouting at one another, pointing to the temple. A few waved at me, or tried to motion for me to stop; I ignored both in favor of keeping my focus on the short street I was hurtling down.

I took the turn at decidedly unsafe speeds, barely avoiding slamming into one of the streetlights.

Just ahead was the flashing lights and chaos of two ongoing battles.

Jet had left two bodies in the street, but was still exchanging gunfire with someone hidden inside the doorway we'd used to get outside. At least two more shooters were up on top of the wall, wildly spraying fire in a way that would have gotten them a demerit in any conscript's drill.

Much farther down the street was a far more colorful engagement; a dozen shades of blue were flaring and vanishing as a battle of pure sorcery

273

occurred. Bits and pieces of buildings or cars appeared and vanished as they were flung around; distant figures bobbing and weaving in the lights.

"Rerth?"

The first gunshot hitting a window behind me made me hunch in, focusing on slowing down without ruining any of the treads.

"Jet!" I shouted. "I'm here!"

"*Open the side door!*" His gasp was pained. "*Sending them out!*"

The shuttle finally crunched to a stop in front of the diner, covering them with its bulk.

For their part, I don't think the priests realized that I wasn't just a regular shuttle who'd been unfortunately caught in the crossfire. They stopped shooting entirely, and I was pretty sure I could hear someone screaming for me to get out of the way. That there were criminals attacking the temple.

I opened the door on the diner's side with one hand, my other frantically checking my shield-belt to confirm that it was running.

Children of two species came stumbling out of the diner the moment the door was opened. I clenched my hands around the wheel, using every ounce of self control to not scream at them to move faster. They couldn't, and I knew it.

I lost control of my lips when Jet came staggering out after them. "You're hit!?"

"*Yes!*" His snarl had heat rise to my neck.

Any reply I could have offered was cut off when the priests finally realized that I wasn't just an unfortunate passerby.

Gunfire began smashing holes in the windows on the right side, making me flinch and the children scream. I ducked my head as best I could, praying to every Aspect, keeping my eyes on the mirror to see when Jet was aboard.

At least until a round slammed into my ribs. The shields kept me alive, but they didn't do much to stop the air from being driven from my lungs.

I was still hacking, trying to breathe, when Jet's shout came from inside. "Drive!"

My foot slammed down once again. We began lumbering forward as the snow began to truly fall, as Disciples and Priests of the holy Aspects did their best to kill us.

XXXI

We pulled away from the chasing group of priests fairly quickly. Between Strike spells and gunfire we lost most of the windows on the right side, and all of the ones on the back. The children's screams trailed into crying, Jet bellowing for them to lay on the floor.

His return fire through the broken windows added to the din. "Go faster!"

"Trying!" I shouted back, feeling my bruised ribs protest the deep breath I'd had to take. "There's more fighting ahead!"

"Head for it! That might be Rerth!"

Another round cracked through the air too close to my ears, making me duck on reflex. Desperately wishing that I had a helmet, all I could do was try to crouch low in the seat and keep accelerating towards the skirmish up ahead.

It was really hard to tell who was fighting who, or even what was going on. The sorcery being thrown around was kicking up so much snow that it was creating a giant bank of fog in the street. Here and there natural fire burned in orange or cherry red, while the unnatural blues of sorcerous flame flared in and out.

All I could tell was that the battle had moved another block or two north of the temple's entrance, and that they'd left several burning stores in their wake.

I had to ease off on the speed when we hit the fog. The last thing I wanted was to run over Rerth or Holde.

"Rerth!" Jet's pained voice sounded in both my free ear and the radio in my other, giving it a very odd echo. "We're in the shuttle! Where are you?"

If our eldest could hear him, she didn't respond.

I didn't add my voice to his. I was too busy swerving around the first body in the middle of the street, nearly running us into a bathouse to avoid

276

running it under the treads.

At least I had enough presence of mind to look down as we passed it. The black and red robes of a full priest were still smoking from the flames had burned their owner alive.

Enough of the windows were broken that the smell reached my nose, and what little self-control I had left finally snapped.

I managed to aim my retching towards the stairs. Mostly.

By some miracle I managed to swerve around the next body by driving us half up onto the walk, then yanked the wheel hard over to avoid what looked like several wounded civilians trying to get away from the fighting.

Just beyond them was the actual fight; gunfire snapping back and forth across the street. Both sides had blown out the windows of a pair of stores, and were now using them as cover while they dueled. I couldn't see any of the shooters. Couldn't see any bodies in the street either.

"Rerth!" Jet tried one last time, and then cursed when she didn't respond. "Blood of Ashahn. Hit the horn!"

My thumb jammed down on the button. The sound of the warning booming out from the roof made the gunfire sputter to a stop. I expected it to start up right away... only for it to stay quiet for nearly twenty seconds. As if both sides had just been chastened by an irritated elder, and were now giving us a polite moment to drive past before they resumed trying to kill each other.

Spitting some of the taste out of my mouth, I managed to clear my throat. "Roll forward a bit?"

"Slowly."

A very gentle little push on the accelerator did that. We slowly crawled down the street, my head swinging left to right as I tried to see which side had our packmates.

The front of the shuttle was about halfway past the shot out restaurant when I saw several priests in a variety of robes carefully exposing themselves from their cover. All of them were holding shotguns and rifles, and looked to be shouting in our direction. I couldn't hear them, but a few began waving

277

their arms in clear gestures for me to speed up.

My heart hammering in panic, I spun the wheel around, desperately turning before they could see that a Human was driving. Khash was blessing me for once; they didn't start shooting right away, so they must not have seen just who they were letting past.

Moving diagonally across the street, I didn't need to hear Jet hearing me to hit the horn again to press down on the button once more... and in the ruins of a convenience store, I saw two figures cautiously poke their heads out. I waved as frantically as I could, praying that I was looking at Rerth and Holde.

Jet one-upped me by shoving the back door open on that side and shouting out, "Get in dammit!"

Rerth and Holde didn't look good when they emerged. The robes that I'd last seen Rerth in were in tatters. Only the bottom half was still intact, while the upper sections looked like they'd been both burned and torn into scraps.

That left her better than her bond, who had one arm around her neck as she hauled him into the snow. Holde was entirely nude, leaving red footprints in his wake. His chest and arms were...

I turned my head and heaved for a second time.

"Go! Drive!" Rerth's snarl had me jam my foot down, hands absently turning us back to drive straight down the street.

I was still hacking at the pain of my own stomach bile burning my throat when the priests finally realized we weren't civilians trying to get through.

The kids had recovered enough to start screaming again when gunfire erupted once more. My packmates began retaliating in kind while I focused on driving, praying that none of them thought to throw sorcery at the treads. Or shoot out the motor beneath my feet.

Either the Aspects were with us, or they were simply too exhausted for more spells; we got up to speed quickly, leaving them behind when we plunged back into the falling snow.

"Wh-where!?" I called back once we were a few blocks away. "Where are we going?"

"The port!" Rerth replied, her voice coming more through my commpiece than my free ear. Either she'd gotten hers working again, or Jet had given her a spare radio. "Get us to our shuttle! Jet, how bad is it?"

"Can't move the fingers on that arm. Getting dizzy."

"Iriahn's fucking... dammit. Sit down. Bind your wound, then help get Holde settled. Ashe! Are you hit?"

I shook my head, "Shields stopped it."

"Good. Two of the children are, I'm tending to them! Alert me when the pursuit begins, and turn the heat up! There's too many broken windows back here to keep it in!"

When.

Not if.

I pushed my foot down harder, getting us up to speeds that Fythe would have been comfortable driving at. My hands shook a little, some little voice telling me I wasn't nearly as good as she was. That my reactions wouldn't be enough if something came out of the snow and mist.

If only she was here, then she could...

Teeth ground on one another, my head shaking sharply. What was I doing? Fythe *wasn't here.* I had to focus on the pack that was with me, not the ones that I missed.

I had to focus on my driving. Not on the smell of my own vomit, on the pained cries of children.

The city itself forced me to slow down after a few minutes. The straight run we'd been on gave way to winding streets far more packed with parked vehicles, and the occasional local out and about on a late night errand.

"...this is wrong." I heard myself mutter. "Where are the security forces? They should be swarming the entire district by now."

279

There'd certainly been more than enough locals who witnessed the fighting. Heard it. Would have started making all of the emergency calls.

"We didn't get out of there *that* fast... they should have caught us easily. So where are they?"

Not chasing us, obviously. Maybe the priests had engaged them when they'd shown up? The tension between Trahcon and alien breaking out under the stress?

"...no. The aliens here were terrified of the Trahcon minority. I still have no idea why, but I can't see the security groups engaging in a gun battle. Then again, the priests themselves had proved that they definitely would. Maybe they'd be on edge. Shoot first."

Rerth looked exhausted when she walked up to stand beside me, her voice flat. "Ashe. *Stop* muttering out loud."

I snapped my mouth shut.

"Stop thinking, focus on driving." She ordered.

"Yes sir. Um... how are-"

Her snap was instant. "Ashe! Eyes on the road!"

"Sir!"

I sped up a bit, then had to slow down mere moments later to avoid crashing into a cargo hauler at an intersection. That start-and-stop pattern held true for the next ten minutes as I struggled to keep us on the fastest route to the city center.

Rerth was much the same. She stayed by my side, saying nothing for several minutes, then vanished into the back with a final order for me to focus. Then she came back, rested a hand on my shoulder in silent support for another minute... and then she vanished again. Probably checking on the others.

On the children we'd taken from the temple.

I shook my head, forcing myself to focus on the road as ordered. Not on the fact that two of them had been shot, and that another had run out into the snow on his own.

I hadn't seen him when we'd pulled out. When we'd been driving.

I was quietly praying that he'd found shelter, warmth, and safety when I got my first sight of flashing yellow and red lights in the distance.

Quickly easing up on the speed, I called out, "Rerth!"

She must have already been walking forward again. She appeared beside me within a breath, eyes narrowing at the glow. "How far are we from the port?"

"Uh, about four blocks I think. Is that...?"

"A perimeter?" Her voice was frustrated. "I expect that it is. I doubt that they will be much impressed with our Imperial credentials either. What's in this area?"

I frantically searched my mental seas. "Um... we're on the edge of the hotel district. Bars, restaurants, stores. A snowed in park."

"Stop." I didn't break so much as I simply took my foot off of the accelerator. "...I recognize that building. Which arms store is near here?"

"The Broken Arm." I replied at once. "It's back one street, then over a a half block."

"Take us there."

I quickly flicked several switches, setting the treads so that I could rotate us in place. "Um, they'll have alarms. Won't that just draw attention?"

"Yes." She allowed, "But I'm out of ammunition, as is Holde. We will break in, take what arms we can, and then resume driving. We stay on the move until the fleet arrives."

It didn't take me long to turn us around. Khash stayed with us on the quick drive backwards, and then on to the gun store; no flashing lights raced after us in pursuit, and no priests emerged from the blizzard to attack us.

Despite her blizzards being a curse, the Aspect Iothay was truly blessing us with the snowfall. It had to be making it much harder to search the

281

city, to do anything besides block off access to the starport.

Whispering a quiet prayer of thanks, I eased us into the narrow back street behind the Broken Arm. There weren't any cars parked behind it, letting me carefully roll right up to the back door we'd once carried obsolete guns through.

"Ashe, with me. Leave the motor on for the heat. Jet? Guard the shuttle." Rerth ordered. "Make sure none of the children try to get off."

"Got it." Jet sounded much better. When I stood up, glancing back, I saw him easing his way down the back stairs to better watch behind us. Far closer, and looking not at all better, Holde was sitting on the hard floor directly below one of the heating vents. What looked like scraps from Rerth's robes were only barely covering some of his wounds, and his eyes were fluttering in pain.

Or shock.

The various children were in a pile all across his legs, nearly all of them visibly crying. Even the older girl who'd been so in control before had broken down; she was curled in a ball, quietly sobbing into the fur of one of the Naulian boys.

She'd been one of the ones wounded. One of her arms was drenched in blood, the red liquid staining the boy's fur.

"Ashe." A sharp elbow snapped me around to see Rerth's hard features. "Not. Now."

"Sir." I whispered, nearly slipping on my own vomit as I followed her down the stairs. Embarrassed heat rushed to my face despite the cold. Rerth hadn't said anything, thank the Aspects, but...

Ashahn's blood this was pathetic. *I* was pathetic. The pack was relying on me, and here I was covering the stairs with vomit.

I had to do better. I had to.

The resolve didn't stop my hands from shaking, but it let me pretend that it was just from the cold when I pulled my pistol out at Rerth's order. I covered her, looking both ways as she approached the doorway.

282

I half expected her to use her wrist-comp to hack the lock, and half-expected her to simply blow it down with sorcery.

Instead she eyed the keypad, muttered something to herself, then quickly tapped out a combination.

I gaped a little when the lock flickered to blue, the door opening with a gentle shove of her hand.

She clearly noticed my expression when she waved for me to follow her in. "I wasn't *idle* when you were working. Quickly now."

The backroom hadn't changed much since the last time I'd been inside. Plenty of heavy crates and arms lockers, a few work benches, and a couple of personal lockers. Rerth ignored most of it, heading right for one of the crates that we'd brought over several months before.

Another password, probably a hidden override, unlocked it as well.

Sales must have been good, because when I peered inside nearly all of the carbines we'd sold them were already gone. There were only three left at the bottom. Fortunately each came with several clips of ammunition, and we wasted little time in grabbing all of it.

While I balanced them in my arms, she did a quick search of the room, then the small office attached to it. A quiet grunt of triumph came just ahead of her emerging with an emergency medical kit tucked under one arm, the other settling a carbine over her other shoulder.

Loaded down as we were, I didn't hesitate to follow her back outside. We quickly darted back into the shuttle, where I nearly slipped *again*, and settled the weapons onto one of the benches behind the driver's seat.

"Head west, then north." She directed once I was behind the wheel again. "Get us away from the Trahcon zones. I'm going to tend to Holde and the children, call out any security vehicles, or anyone who seems to be following us."

"Yes sir."

And with one quick reset of the controls, I had us moving once again.

XXXII

I drove us through the city, sticking to what side streets the large shuttle could fit down. I took turns at random, slowing only when the worsening weather demanded it, and generally did my best not to run into anything.

Time seemed to crawl as slowly as the shuttle was. I checked the time after what felt like an hour only to discover that it hadn't been ten minutes since we left the Broken Arm.

Twenty minutes later and we were barely moving. The heavy snowfall had graduated to a full blizzard, the wind howling through the broken windows. I managed to calm down enough to realize the worst of it was coming up from the south, so I stuck to going north as much as I could.

Keeping the closed back pointed at the wind helped a little. It still got a lot colder, even with the heaters running, but it was better than nothing.

It also let me hear that the children had stopped crying. A quick glance over my shoulder let me see that most of them had passed out, and the few that were awake were silently clinging to the others. Rerth was tending to Holde just past them, while Jet stood watch near the back doors.

He must have noticed me looking back, or else noticed how slow we were going. "Ashe, how bad are the roads?"

"Bad." I said at once, returning my attention to said road. "If anyone comes out of the snow at speed... I don't know if I'll be able to stop us in time."

I heard motion and footsteps before Rerth appeared beside me once again, glaring out at the haze of white. The city buildings were just barely visible to either side, along with parked vehicles increasingly being buried by it all.

"I was hoping that this would cover our exit from the temple when the time came." She muttered, clearly frustrated. "I suppose it still is. The next sheltered stop you can find, pull over in a way that blocks the wind. Jet will go out and find us a proper building to fort down in."

284

I swallowed, keeping my own voice quiet as well. "Are you sure we shouldn't keep moving?"

A hand waved at the window. "We're hardly moving as it is. This will stop them from sending other ground vehicles after us, and probably light aircars, but eventually they will have heavier assets in the sky."

"...and if we're the only crawler moving, we're an obvious target." I whispered, getting it. "They could just strafe us and we'd never know they were coming."

"Good to see that your mind is recovering." She replied. "We can't defend ourselves in this crate. Find us a sheltered position, little shark. We'll hold there until reinforcements arrive."

"Yes sir."

Of course that was easier said than done. My careful yet erratic driving may have kept us moving, but it had also led us into one of the more suburban areas of the city. Slowing even more let me see that there were plenty of prefabricated houses, but precious little of anything more substantial.

Grimly speeding up a bit, I hunched over the wheel and did my best to peer through the curtain of white in front of us.

Eventually we came to an intersection that had what we needed; a collection of stores all clustered around a large parking zone. Several still had their lights on despite the weather and the late hour. Pulling into the lot, I carefully drove past them before spinning the wheel hard to pull us around the end building.

The crawler crunched to a halt, the sound of the wind fading to a distant howl.

"Jet."

One arm still useless, Jet didn't hesitate to follow our eldest's command. He leaped out into the storm, leaving the rest of us to try and get the wounded and the children ready to move.

At Rerth's silent direction I picked up one of the rifles and got it

285

loaded. It felt far more natural in my hands than the pistol I'd been carrying around, though I knew that was mostly an illusion.

I wasn't actually any better with this gun than I was with the other. It was just more familiar. Standard issue. The kind of thing I'd been carrying around, if not actually using, for years.

Dammit. Maybe if I'd been given more Ah-Cycle assignments, maybe then I wouldn't be so...

"Focus." Rerth's growl had its 'you're talking to yourself out loud again' tone to it.

Snapping my mouth closed told me that she'd been right to use it, even if I had no idea what I'd actually been muttering. Hopefully nothing that the children could hear. They were rattled enough without seeing me break down anymore than I already had.

"Ready." I reported once I'd double-checked the gun. "Holde?"

"...ready." His voice was little more than a rasp, but he'd managed to get upright on his own without help.

I tried not to notice how much blood he'd left on the floor.

Or on the pole he was using to support his burned body. How he was managing to hold the rifle in his arms I had no idea. Just looking at his limbs nearly made me vomit again, and I quickly turned to look at Rerth instead.

"Painkillers... won't last long, love."

Rerth was too collected to let her tarah lower for more than an instant, but I saw the pain and fear for her bond before she got her expression under control. "You're the first out, first in. I want you sitting down the moment you find something bullet-proof to hide behind."

His smile was far more of a pained grimace. "Yes sir."

That settled, she turned back to me. "I will take the rear position. You will move with the children, make sure that they all make it inside."

Nodding obediently, I licked my lips and stepped around her to look at them all. Those who'd fallen asleep had been woken up by the others, or by

286

our conversation. They'd clearly been following every word because each and every one of them was now staring at me.

They looked terrified. Exhausted. Drained.

Swallowing, I tried to echo the tones I only barely remembered from my childhood. "Children. Um, hands together please. Everyone hold on to at least one other person. We'll be going inside as soon as we can. Stay close to me."

They hesitantly started to take each other's hands, a few of them giving me tiny nods. At my quiet urging they got themselves to their feet. I thought about trying to get them to line up, but they all seemed to crowd around me before I could even try.

"Easy." I adjusted the gun I was holding. "Um, be careful! I need to be ready to defend you."

A couple of them pulled the kids who'd been getting too close to my rifle off to the side, but those already behind me just crowded a little closer. The ones who'd been shot were woozy but upright; Rerth must have shot them up with painkillers. Probably something strong from their vacant expressions.

One of them was the girl who'd seemed to lead them. Whatever courage had let her direct the others seemed to have been drained out of her; she was pressed against me, her face buried in my shoulder. Her right arm was hanging limply, a rough patch now covering her bicep.

The other hand was clinging to my clothes, as if I was the only thing stopping her from being hurled into the sea.

"It... it will be all right." I whispered, desperately hoping that I wasn't lying to her. "We'll get you out of here. I promise."

She didn't say anything. Just hiccuped, my shirt starting to feel wet from her tears.

Ashahn's blood. What had they done to these poor kids? What was going on here!?

The anger pushed away some of the fear, the nerves. Some furious part of me wanted to find a priest and shake them until they told me what they'd been doing. Another wanted to drop my gun, wrap my arms around the

287

girl, and just hold her to tell her she was safe.

We lingered for a few minutes more before Jet finally came over the comms, *"We have a lovely bath store open to us, I'm working on getting the staff rooms open for the children."*

Holde didn't need a signal to start moving. He pushed the door open, moving as quickly as his battered body would let him. The moment he was outside I got my feet into motion as well.

To my surprise the children actually let me move ahead without getting in my way. They followed me outside, piling out into the bitter cold without more than a few whimpers. I waited just outside of the shuttle's door for them all to group again, then plunged ahead, following the broken trail of snow that Jet and Holde had left behind them.

It wasn't a long walk to the corner, thank the Aspects, and the doors were just around it.

A quaint little store selling personal and pack-sized washing tubs was wide open. The lights were dim, but it was warm enough inside. Well, it was probably cold, but compared to what we'd just left it felt balmy.

"Ashe! This way!" Jet waved an arm from the back, motioning toward a door he'd either hacked or broken open. "Staff room's warmer!"

I nodded once, "Come on kids. This way. Let's get you safe."

None of them protested. They just followed along as I weaved between the displays. I hesitated when I saw Holde stumble just ahead of us, one of his hands coming to rest on a shelf.

"Just... need my breath." He wheezed when we got closer. "Go ahead."

"Holde-"

"Go."

I obeyed.

The staff room proved to be pretty small. One table, a refrigerator, a couple of chairs, and one hard used lounge couch. The only other door was open to what looked like a restroom.

"In you go." I urged them. "The couch looks nice. Let's get anyone who's hurt on it."

It didn't take much more than my gentle coaxing to get them all into the room. Most of them curled up on the couch, or each other, without any prodding at all.

The only struggle came from the girl still clinging to me. I felt my heart sink deep into my soul when I pulled her hand off of me, whispering that she'd be all right. That I had to go back out to protect her.

I kissed both of her cheeks, tasting the salt from her tears, and gently eased her to sit down in the middle of the others. They seemed to swarm over her. Terrified to not be touching as many of their packmates as they could.

Holde staggered in just as I made to leave.

"...Holde..."

"Go." His voice was quiet. "I'll sit between them and the exit. Nothing will happen to them so long as I live."

My vision blurred for a moment. My chin jerked in a nod, legs moving without orders from my mind to get me out of the room before I had a total breakdown.

Rerth and Jet were groaning, shoving tubs and shelves into barricades. Desperate for the distraction of work, I ran over to help.

Between us we managed to lever several of them into three rough lines. One was right across the doors, blocking them off, while the other two were just a bit back to make it hard for anyone to easily break through the outer windows.

"Right." Our leader spoke when we'd finished. "Jet?"

"I'll keep the back door secured." He promised, already moving off.

I swallowed as the only one of us in proper armor left, vanishing into whatever space in the back had an exit.

289

Rerth went on, giving me direction. "Nothing in here is bullet proof, so don't linger in any one spot. Move between the displays when you shoot. If we can trick them into thinking there's more of us than there really are, we'll buy ourselves time."

"Yes sir. Um..."

"They will find us, eventually. If they branded the children they likely tagged them as well." She guessed my question without effort. Waving for me to follow, she walked back to one of the larger tubs; a full pack sized model complete with water-jets.

A quiet groan when she sat down beside it told me she was far more exhausted than she was letting herself show.

"...are you all right?" I asked, kneeling beside her.

Her bright eyes met mine, then turned to the swirling snow outside. "...no. I gave myself a boost injection, or I'd have already fallen over. I won't have much, or any, sorcery to support us with."

My hands trembled. The rifle's barrel tapped out a rhythm on the floor. "...oh."

She carefully reached over, grabbing the weapon to stop my shaking. "Focus, Ashe. I need your wrist-comp."

I turned, offering her my left arm. She quickly pulled the mesh off of my forearm before rolling it up her own. The device promptly flashed green, a tiny holographic screen declaring that Rerth wasn't me, and demanded my pass-code for access.

"...really?" I sighed when she tapped out my password without hesitating. "I just changed it. How did you already get it?"

"Jet hacked it the day after we left Altair. It sends me your new code whenever you update it."

Of course he had. I wasn't terribly surprised, but... it hurt a little that they'd done that.

A moment later I nearly smacked myself. Here we were, in a life or death situation, and I was getting offended that they'd hacked my wrist-comp.

290

I had to be in some kind of shock still.

Rerth was too focused on her work to notice. Fingers flying through my menu system to bring up the communications suite.

"...the general alert of incoming ships just went out." She seemed to relax a little. "That will be the fleet emerging.... dammit. They've shut down the main communications network. There's just the repeated warning of orbital attackers, and a warning for everyone to stay in their homes."

"We can't call for help?"

Another few taps had her shake her head. "Not until there's forces in atmosphere. Soon."

I was just about to ask her what had happened in the temple when a bright light made us both snap our heads around. The glow made the snow look like an impenetrable wall until the light swept out of view.

"They found us."

"Yes." Rerth's elbow tapped mine sharply, "Move over to the left. Remember to move when it starts. Jet, Holde. Ready yourselves. They're here."

My heart felt like it was trying to beat its way out of my chest. Getting up, I walked as far to my left as I could, crouching down behind a hot tub. That gave me a pretty good view of the front when the searchlight swept back and forth a second time.

The sound came next. That deep throated roar of engines that seemed to come from every direction at once. Its volume increased until the building itself began to shake around us.

"...are they landing on the roof?" I couldn't stop the question.

Rerth was already looking up as well, a scowl on her lips. "Likely. Listen closely in case they try to come through the walls."

"Sir." I tried to settle myself, belatedly realizing that I'd stopped shaking.

Of course, the moment I noticed my hands started trembling again.

291

Ugh. What was *wrong* with me?

I needed to-

The ceiling almost directly above me exploded into fragments. Debris hammered me about the head and shoulders, leaving me reeling back just as a robed woman dropped through the new hole in the roof.

Khash was with me in that moment. My fall onto my ass left the priestess landing just between my legs, my rifle practically pressed against her hip while her own gun was far too high; ready to shoot someone standing, not someone so pathetic as to have fallen over.

I pulled the trigger on pure reflex, some lingering training bracing it against my shoulder. The three round burst cut across her leg, showering me in blood when the limb simply came apart. She let out a deafening scream, collapsing. Her shotgun tumbled free from fingers now clutching at her shattered limb.

My finger flexed a second time, and the third life I took ended when three bullets found their mark in her head.

Shouting and more gunfire yanked my eyes away from the corpse to see Rerth shoving aside another priest's pistol. Her rifle slammed across his face, driving him back enough for her to execute him with a single shot to his temple.

Another corpse was limp at her feet.

More gunfire sounded behind us. Jet was fighting.

"Focus!" The snarl that came out of my own lips took me by surprise. "Fight!"

I'd just scrambled to my feet when the windows blew out... and more men and women stormed in to kill us.

XXXIII

I started shooting again before getting my aim settled, and managed to miss completely. My rounds punching three holes in the glass in between two of the priests rushing for the door. It made one of them duck back, but the other slammed her shoulder into the entrance to drive it open.

A bit of sorcery came with that, hurling aside the makeshift barricade we'd put in place, slowing her down by a half-step at most.

Fighting down the panic, I started moving to my right in a low crouch. Reflexes beat into me by bounce-drills letting my arms stay steady when I pulled the trigger again. My aim was better that time; all three rounds smacked into the woman's barriers, forcing her to draw up for a moment.

Rerth opened up with carefully timed shots before either of us could do anything else. Sparks and ricochets flew in every direction as the woman's protective spell did its job of keeping her alive. It held just long enough for the other priests to call up their own talents.

I flinched back behind another display tub when their spells blew out both of the front windows. The rush of the wind carried the stench of ozone and sorcery, one of them rushing towards Rerth while the other simply threw a hand in my direction.

Pure instinct had me throw myself to one side a moment before his spell hit the bath I'd been behind. He must have had real talent; the spell rammed the thing right through the space I'd been in, demolishing a shelf full of soaps instead of breaking half of my bones.

Scrambling, I fired off a panicked burst that made him duck. My second attempt was better aimed, but he had time to summon up barriers of his own; the shots didn't do anything besides spark off of his swirling protection.

"Beast!" His bellow cut through the noise of Rerth trying to hold off the other two with alternating shots, face twisting in a sneer as he began a lazy prowl toward us.

He didn't throw another spell right away. Didn't draw a gun. It was...

293

...it was *stupid*. Ashahn's blood, Rerth didn't have shields, or even a barrier, and my shield-belt wasn't visible. She hadn't thrown a single spell yet, so they had to know she was exhausted.

They could have just killed us both without any real effort.

They were just like the two who'd attacked me in the hotel.

Killing us easily wasn't enough.

They wanted to take their time about it. We had to suffer. Had to understand just how pathetic we were, how angry they were that we'd ruined whatever plans they'd had for the children.

No sooner had the thought flitted through my brain than the three of them moved closer in together. Grouping up, expanding their barrier into a swirling mess of wind and power that made our guns completely useless.

Fully protected, they began a quick prowl forward, clearly looking to get into the best position to start on the torture and pain. I kept backing up until I was beside my packmate, desperately licking my dry lips.

Rerth had stopped shooting by then, and instead seemed to be counting off the steps as priests drew closer.

"Ashe! Now!"

It took me half a heartbeat to realize what Rerth meant. Then my hand plunged into my pocket, yanking my nullification grenade out.

A panicked jab activated the little orb.

A quick spin of my thumb dialed its timer all the way down.

Rising, I threw it at the priestess like I was clearing a Strike-Wave ball. She couldn't have been more than two or three yards away, her eyes widening in horror when she saw the bomb hurtling at her face.

I think she tried to drop her barrier, tried to bat it away with a Strike, but the time ticked off before she could do more than make it start to jerk sideways.

A subdued *whump* preceded all three of our enemies recoiling in pain, their tarah lowering as they stumbled. Whatever spells they'd been holding to protect them vanished, leaving the trio with only their thin robes for protection.

Rerth flicked her rifle to fully automatic, then made a quick sweep right to left while holding down the trigger.

Three bodies hit the floor. Two of them were deathly still, one was screaming breathlessly and rolling around. Just beyond I saw a fourth person look around the edge of a broken window, spot the bloody mess, and then quickly duck back.

"Get to the back." Rerth snapped, a single extra shot cutting off the wounded man's cries. "Reinforce Jet!"

I jerked, belatedly realizing that I could still hearing fighting behind us.

"Go!"

"Sir!" Scrambling up to my feet, I took off at a run. My long legs meant it didn't take me very long to rush through the back door, entering some kind of narrow storage space. I must have gotten my second wind because I didn't have any problems lengthening my strides as I ran through the dark hallway.

I was just about to run through the far doorway, into what looked like an open loading dock, when a form appeared in it, clearly intending to sprint up to the front.

The priest and I had enough time to widen our eyes in mutual alarm before we slammed into each other. Our legs got tangled as we both tried to stay upright, bodies twisting as we fell onto the hard floor. We both let out sounds of pain, then started scrambling.

His hands were free, which let him grab my rifle before I could do more than try to lean back. Panicking a bit, I wrestled for the weapon but my grip wasn't nearly as steady. We rolled back and forth several times, fighting for the thing, banging ourselves into each corner of the doorway in the process.

He managed to twist my rifle out of my hands, but my panicked

295

flailing knocked it away before he could try to turn it around on me. Rolling again, I managed to get on top, practically sitting on his chest as I fended off a punch aimed at my throat.

I think he tried to buck me off, but for once being Human was working to my advantage; I was a lot bigger and heavier than he was. Half-running on training, half-running on panic, I parried a second punch with my forearm, then swung a fist down at the base of his tarah.

In training spars you were supposed to pull the blow, or turn it into a slap on their cheek.

I didn't.

His entire body arched, mouth opening in a silent howl of pain. He couldn't do anything to stop my second punch from hitting the same spot, putting him in too much agony to even think about calling up a spell.

Then... I yanked my pistol out of its holster, and shot him in the head.

The fourth person I killed went limp with a hole in his cheek, and far too much red spreading out under his head.

Panicked gunshots going off too close to me snapped my head around before I could really react to what I'd just done. I saw Jet scrambling backward, a priestess with a long blade advancing on him. The sword was covered in silent blue-black flame... the same color I'd seen in too many nightmares.

My hand shook, my one attempt to shoot her going wide.

His better aimed rounds skipped off of her sorcerous barrier.

Her blade swung, and my packmate screamed as the hand holding his pistol was separated from his body.

I gave up shooting, scrambling for the one thing that might let us survive.

He screamed, flailing back in time to avoid a back-swing that would have opened his throat. That didn't buy him more than a few seconds as she seamlessly slid into a lunge aimed at his chest.

296

My fingers plunged under my shirt, shoving down the button on my sternum. The one-use nullifier attached to the shield-belt pulsed out with another almost silent thud of sound.

Just like her kin in the front, the priestess recoiled in pain and shock. Her killing thrust jerked away from his heart, sliding over Jet's thin armor to puncture one of his other arms instead.

I didn't kill her in one shot. My aim wasn't that good.

I shot her five or six times before she fell over, convulsing a few times before going still.

"...is that?" The words were more of a gasp than anything else.

"Last." Jet groaned, his working hands shaking as he grabbed at the medical bag on his belt. "Get over here before I bleed out."

Getting my pistol into its holster took two tries. Getting over to Jet was easier, tearing open the little bag with shaking fingers. I followed his growled instructions, pulling out a tiny canister of medical-foam and spraying it over the gaping stump that was his wrist.

My shaking got worse as his blood covered my hands, but his growling trailed off as the foam soaked into his body.

"Get me out front." He groaned. "We can't hold here like this."

I had to swing around to his left side, since both of his right arms were wounded. Getting the upper one wrapped around my waist let me help him stagger back down the hall. I did my best not to look at the body I'd left on the ground. Did my best not to flinch when I heard Rerth's rifle bark several times.

She didn't look at us when we arrived, instead resting her gun on the cashier's counter, aiming it out the front. There weren't any extra bodies, so I assumed no one had come rushing in while she'd been alone.

"Status?"

"Two..." Jet hissed in pain as I helped him sit down behind her, "...two dead in back."

Rerth glanced back, saw his missing hand, and clenched her jaw before returning her attention forward. "Just one playing games with me out front. Ashe? With me, we're going to go out and finish him."

I didn't want to. I wanted to tend to Holde, to Jet, to the kids. I wanted to fall over.

I wanted the night to be over.

"...sir." I started to bring my hands up, belatedly realizing that I'd left my rifle somewhere in the back. Swallowing, I drew my pistol instead, and tried not to notice how sweaty the grip was. "Ready."

If she noticed my missing gun she didn't comment on it. She just nodded and started walking, leaving me to follow and cover her back.

We were just about at the ruined entrance when the heavy engines throttled up above us. I half-ducked on reflex, glancing up in paranoid fear that more of them were about to blast their way through the roof.

None did. Instead I watched running lights appear as whatever aircraft was up there swung slowly out over the snow. I couldn't tell its model. It was just a rounded, shadowy shape with two monstrous thrusters kicking up its own personal storm.

I half expected it to gun us down somehow. Maybe fire a missile into the building.

I was bracing myself when the roar became deafening... and the running lights faded into the blizzard as it departed.

"...what?"

Rerth silently shook her head, paused, then let out a wheezy chuckle. "Oh. Good."

I blinked. "...what?"

"Just watch, little shark."

I did, thoroughly numb and thoroughly confused. I stayed that way for about a minute before a heavy flash of orange and red lit up the snow shroud in every direction. The dull *boom* of the detonation reached my ears a moment later.

"They're early." Rerth said, tapping her... *my* wrist-comp. "This is Agent Riah. Tracking beacon is active."

Two heartbeats later a man replied, *"Confirmed your beacon, Agent. Assault Craft on the way."*

"We require medical attention immediately, for my pack and for rescued Imperial citizens."

"Confirmed. I will route additional medics to you. Team will be on the ground at your location within five minutes."

"Confirmed."

I felt my heart rise, even as everything else seemed to sag. "...we won?"

"We lived." She corrected me without heat, still staring out into the storm. "I'll check on Jet. Go check on Holde."

"...sir."

Picking my way back to the staff room, I kept my eyes up. I didn't need to see what we'd done. I didn't even want to think about it right now. All I wanted was to check on my packmate.

Holde was still sitting in the chair when I came in, rifle in his lap. A pained smile crossed his lips, his own opening before I could speak.

"I'm all right, little shark. Sit down with the kids."

"...sir."

I managed to shuffle over to the pile of limbs on the couch. A few of them shifted over, just enough for me to sit down on the floor beside them.

Then tiny hands were pulling at me, tightening on my clothing as they held on.

I closed my eyes, exhaled slowly... and let myself go limp until the medics arrived.

299

XXXIV

The storm let up by afternoon the next day. I'd been allowed to sleep once we'd gotten Jet, Holde, and the children onto shuttles. They'd all been taken into orbit for immediate medical treatment, while Rerth and I had been escorted to the starport.

I'd been sent to a folding cot in one of the terminals within minutes of our arrival. I had tried to protest, gotten a single glare from Rerth, saluted, and trundled off to sleep.

Honestly I was kind of impressed with myself for being able to drift off as quickly as I had. The city had been under full attack by then. Engines had been roaring, gunfire sounding, and explosions had been going off all over the place.

I'd woken up only when Rerth had laid down on top of me when her debriefing had finished, both of us fading away again within moments.

When I woke up again we'd managed to switch positions; my head was resting on her chest, one of her hands slowly stroking my fur. I had no idea how long she'd been awake, and I knew better than to ask.

And besides. There were more important questions.

"...how are they?" I asked, not bothering to open my eyes.

"Alive. Holde is sedated and being prepped for another treatment for his burns. They capped Jet's wrist, he'll go back under tomorrow to prepare him for a cybernetic replacement. He won't lose the other arm."

"Good." I yawned into her skin, letting myself go limp as I enjoyed the gentle petting. "...the kids?"

She sighed quietly. "Traumatized, malnourished, barely speaking, but they're all alive. I had them put on the *Posa'vilt*. We'll be taking them back to Altair with us."

I frowned, eyes still closed. "We're going home? We haven't found the Burned Hand yet... or was she at one of the temples?"

300

"Not that I am aware of." She replied. "And we will be returning home because those are our orders. The Regional Lead on Altair got my reports of what happened on Trinity, and she wants an in-person debrief."

"Oh." I murmured. "What about Trinity's Director?"

"She is being recalled to Gathahn for questioning by the Oasis Commanders as well."

Oh. That was certainly... high level.

I cleared my throat. "Um, what about our project?"

"The Void Fleet is collating all of the evidence they're finding here. I'll be getting up in a moment to supervise. It should give us enough to go over during the trip home." Her shoulder shifted a little under me. "The Regional Lead assured me that we'll be able to resume our work, but right now the systemic failures on Trinity are taking priority."

"...oh."

It was... I honestly felt disappointed. We'd done so much work, so much sailing about the Near Reaches. I'd been nearly murdered, we'd fought a battle, and... now we were just going home? Without answers?

Rerth chuckled quietly when I muttered my thoughts out loud, her hand shifting to pat the top of my head. "This is the life in Intelligence, little shark. We don't always get clean resolutions. Still, there's every chance that the Burned Hand was here, and died with the others. We will know soon enough."

I finally blinked my eyes open. "Others?"

"Others. Come on. Up. We have work to do."

My pitiful groan made her laugh again. Her relief about our packmates being all right left her in a good mood; she was gentle when she nudged and pushed me into getting up. She even helped me clean my fur when we ducked into one of the port's public showers to finally get ourselves washed.

Once we were back in uniform, plus coats and gloves for warmth, she

301

led me to a foyer that had been turned into a command center.

There she spoke with the senior officer to arrange a ride for us. A rapid breakfast of ration bars and twenty minutes later, we were sitting in the back of an assault shuttle with a full Sword Formation from one of the Void Fleet's Wind Arsenals, flying south.

We had plenty of room to ourselves. The aircraft was meant for five times as many people as it held. It made it easy for us to talk normally, letting Rerth get me caught up on what she'd learned before she'd gotten her own rest in.

She began with the good news. "We were right. There was a major facility just to the south of the city. It was half underground, half sheltered by a forest."

I nodded, feeling more than a little relaxed to know that our theory had proven to be correct. "What were they doing out there?"

"Training in sorcery and indoctrination, I presume. Beyond that, we won't know until we can question the survivors and tear apart whatever computer network they had." Her tarah lowered in a slight frown. "This entire situation remains shrouded. There were more than four hundred Trahcon at that facility. Far more than I expected."

"Did... they resist?"

"Heavily." When I winced, she shook her head and sailed on. "Fortunately they didn't seem to be anymore prepared than those at the temples. For all of their sorcerous talent, they were completely lacking in personal armor. They didn't have many small arms either. As soon as our soldiers began using nullifiers their defense collapsed."

I could only frown. "Don't the priestly orders train with guns just as much as they do with sorcery?"

"Yes." Her frown deepened. "The only ones using guns seem to be the Disciples, and the other raw recruits. This is a very strange group we are hunting, little shark. "

There wasn't much I could say about that. It was certainly true. "Um, what about the rest of the city?"

Rerth shrugged. "According to the Admiral, the local security forces surrendered almost immediately, as did those mercenaries and pirates unable to flee the system. The local citizens yielded after a few token street fights as well. All of the resistance came from the Temples and from the facility."

Which made next to no sense to me. What had happened on Yashun was, from what I understood, the typical reaction to an Imperial invasion out here.

Everyone resisted.

Passively standing down... was more than a little strange.

I mean, I was happy that my contacts were probably all alive. I'd liked all of them, especially Sofia. None of them had deserved to get sucked into these tides. And maybe now things would be calmer here. Maybe the tension that had led to so many warnings about going out alone, about going too near certain areas of the city... maybe that would calm down as well.

"Do you think the locals were hoping that we'd clear them out for them?" I asked.

"It's possible. From what I was told, someone hacked the emergency transmissions shortly after I checked them, telling everyone to not resist, that the Empire wouldn't be able to stay long term." A quiet huff broke apart her words. "Which is true, but it's not the kind of clear thinking I would have anticipated on a world like this."

"...I mean, someone could have been smart enough." I pointed out, "It's weirder that everyone actually listened. Right?"

"True enough, little shark." she shrugged. "Probably an Ark Fleet asset keeping watch over their lost colony in the hopes of returning. Interesting, but outside of our project."

From there, she filled me in on what had happened to her at the temple. It was about what I could have expected.

A Disciple had been up and about, maybe on late-night cleaning duty as a punishment. Rerth had ducked back into a side-hall, then jumped the other woman just before she could enter the loading dock we'd been in.

She'd choked her out within moments, but had been spotted by

303

another priest farther down the hall. Knowing we'd needed more time, she'd led as many of them away as quickly as she could, using flashy and loud spells to draw attention.

Holde had heard the chaos, knocked out the woman he'd been tasked with seducing, and then ran out to help. The two of them had engaged in a running battle to the front door, plunged out into the cold, and had to draw up short when Holde had been caught by a River-Fire spell. Rerth had killed his attacker, dragging her bond into the same building we'd found them in.

I frowned a little, thinking on what she'd told me. I was still doing so when the shuttle landed, our escort forming up around us as we got off.

Rows upon rows of bodies greeted us.

Choking, I brought a hand to my lips at the sight of them. Some had been partially covered by blankets, but most of them were just... laying there. Dozens upon dozens of corpses arranged in neat lines in the snow. Here and there they curved around shattered trees, or small craters, but for the most part they...

Went on all the way to the broken doors leading into a nearby hill.

If I hadn't been standing right next to her, I wouldn't have heard Rerth's tiny exhalation. Her frustrated little huff as her own eyes flicked over it all. Quickly averting my own eyes, I found men and women in Imperial armor sailing through the area.

Some were standing watch, others were carrying weapons, yet more were carrying...

Ugh. They were carrying more bodies to add to the neat little lines.

An officer in the star-field uniform of the Void Fleets approaching was a welcome distraction. Fixing my gaze to the black visor of their full helmet, I didn't let it stray as they came to a stop just before us.

"Agent." A woman's voice greeted us. "You're early. My men are still imaging the dead for you."

"Arsenal Commander." Rerth replied. "So I see. Have the numbers changed since your last report?"

Her head tipped slightly. "Seven more wounded prisoners expired this morning. We're down to fifty-two survivors, three hundred and twenty-two killed in action."

"And you're certain that none of the senior leadership survived?"

"Those that didn't go down fighting committed suicide the moment their fate was clear." The officer paused, then shook her head slowly. "They used the Wrath of Ashahn, Agent. I've never heard of that spell being used since the Second Airalon War."

Rerth's tarah rose in surprise. "...the Wrath? None of the priestly orders even *teach* that spell anymore. You're certain?"

Armor creaked in a somewhat helpless looking shrug. "I can't think of another spell that detonates quite like that. Not one that kills the user in the process. I put it in my reports."

"...good. Was there anything left of their bodies that we could use to identify them?"

"Ashes and burnt bones."

I shifted uncomfortably. I didn't feel nauseous, though the Aspects alone knew that wouldn't last. Not if I let my eyes wander away from the woman I was staring at.

"Damn." Rerth exhaled. "Perhaps their systems will have something. Continue pulling everything you can from them."

The Arsenal Commander nodded once. "We have specialists already on it."

"Any sign of other prisoners, like those we found at the temple?"

Another quick shake of her head. "Nothing. No signs of slaves, no evidence that aliens were being used as target practice."

I winced.

"...you all right, Rifle-Experienced?"

The officer's question surprised me nearly as much as the fact that she

305

used my full rank. "Um, yes sir."

Something in her posture made it clear she didn't believe me. Rerth clearing her throat drew our attention back to her, "My packmate has had prior experiences with this group. They were not kind."

"That I can believe. Did you require anything else?"

Rerth waved toward the rows of bodies. "I'll do a walk and inspection. See if any of them match our targets. My packmate will follow in your wake until I call for her."

And with that, I spent the next hour and a half following around an Arsenal Commander of the Void Fleet as she inspected the base her formation had helped attack.

It was... strange.

Not in their actions. They were tending to their own wounded, cataloging the supplies taken from the base, or else stripping out anything useful. Nothing I hadn't helped do once or twice, as part of the practice of tearing down a temporary field fortification.

What was different was the quiet, relentless way they went about it. There was none of the good humored joking of conscripts. What little banter was confined to quick comments and soft chuckles. None of the women were showing off their strength, none of the men were cleverly handling multiple tasks at once.

They were professionals, not conscripts, and it showed in something as simple as breaking down an enemy facility.

The officer clearly noticed my attention, speaking to me near the entrance to the underground portion of the base. "You've never been around a Wind Formation, have you?"

"No sir." I admitted. "It's... different, watching Guides work."

There was a quiet chuckle. "As it should be. There wouldn't be much point to keeping us elders separate if we all acted the same. Come, I think your own elder is done with her inspection."

Looking up let me see Rerth waving over several soldiers, pointing

306

out a body. She followed that by turning our way, a clear beckoning motion summoning me to join her.

I kept my eyes up until I was beside her, and only when she nodded at the corpse did I look down.

It was a man. Had been a man. A blanket covered his chest, but even through it I could tell that something had caved in his torso. That or he'd simply been shot so many times that there wasn't much left.

"...I don't know him."

"Neither do I." Rerth extended a finger, "But I believe you know his packmate."

Blinking, I looked to where she was pointing.

"Oh. Oh!" I leaned in, peering down at the rippled skin of his left hand. The burns extended to his wrist, ending in a perfectly even line that could only have been deliberate. "You think he was one of hers?"

"He's the only one with burns like that here, and what's left of his robes marked him as an Elder Priest." She nudged the body with her boot. "He's no Elder, but I assume he was in command here. At least until a suit of power armor got a hold of him."

I winced at the mental image. "Oh. Um, was there anyone else here?"

Another wave of her arm toward the next row of bodies. "Your attackers from the hotel are both over there. Did you want to see them?"

"I... no." I swallowed. "No. I'm all right."

She rolled a shoulder. "If you're sure. We'll be taking their bodies with us, along with his. Perhaps a full autopsy will give us something. If nothing else, it serves as confirmation that all of this is truly connected. We aren't chasing shadows in the moonlight."

"...yes." I let out a slow breath, taking in a deeper one.

The cold air was crisp, biting. The scents of burnt wood, plastics, and blood filled my nose.

"I think..." My voice dropped lower. "...I think we won this round. Didn't we?"

Rerth put her hands on her hips, humming without looking away from the body at our feet. "We still don't know what they were doing here. What they were doing with those children. The why and what of everything that happened on Trinity."

"But... we stopped them here. We shut it down."

Her lips curled slightly. "Yes. Yes we did. You're not wrong, little shark. We won this round. Now let's go home, settle in to a safe harbor, and make sure we win the next one."

I took another breath, nodding firmly. "Yes sir!"

Epilogue

We had to stop over in Trinity on our way back to Altair. Not because we wanted to, but because the *Posa'vilt* was in dire need of fuel, provisions, and some general maintenance.

It also gave us a chance to get Holde and Jet checked out by the highly experienced doctors there. Not that the ones on the ships hadn't done good jobs, they had, but Trinity had the best medical teams in the Near Reaches. As wary as she was of setting down there, Rerth wasn't about to deny her packmates the chance to see them.

She regretted it almost immediately.

The four of us had been chatting about which model of cybernetic hand Jet should pick when her wrist-comp had pinged with a priority signal. The little consulting room we'd been in had gone silent at once, three of us turning to look at her while she read.

It was easy to guess it wasn't good news when one of her trademark scowls appeared before she'd finished.

"I have been summoned to meet with the Void Lord." Her jaw clenched. "Ashahn's blood, I was hoping he was in orbit."

I grimaced as well, "Am I going with?"

The disappointment must have been a little too obvious, because her voice turned wry. "I would think meeting with one of the eight Void Lords would be more important than going drinking with your fellow Conscripts."

"Um, yes sir." I agreed, "But my fellow conscripts don't scare me like he does."

Jet snorted, "She's got a point, Rerth."

Rerth rolled her eyes slightly before turning back to me, "It's a personal summons for me alone. That does not mean you're free to wander the city."

My hands quickly rose in surrender. "I remember the rules, Rerth. I'm not to leave the hotel restaurant, I'm not to be alone, I will not have more than two drinks, and I will be back here to escort Holde and Jet to the shuttle in four hours."

"And?"

It was my turn to roll my eyes. "I am better than an unblooded conscript. I will not take any of them to bed."

Jet snickered, while Holde grinned in amusement. I gave them both a half-hearted glare that merely saw the men laugh harder.

Rerth chuckled as well, standing up from her seat. "Good. If I am not back on time, head back to the *Posa'vilt* regardless. Holde?"

Her bond nodded, still smiling. "If you're late, I'll make sure the Captain has the ship ready to leave by tomorrow."

She leaned down, giving him a quick kiss. Then she ruffled my fur, then Jet's fur, earning her glares from us both before she vanished through the doorway.

I'd just gotten my fur tied back when there was a knock at the door. Holde's call for it to open saw Ekan poke her head inside.

"They're too cowardly to knock themselves." She informed me, deadpan as ever. "I got tired of waiting."

Huffing, I pushed myself to my feet. "Of course they are. Let me know if you need anything."

Jet snorted, "One little engagement and suddenly she's the one who can help us if we need anything."

Holde smiled. "I think it's adorable."

Heat rose to my cheeks. I made a quick retreat before I could say anything else, or before the teasing could get worse. Ekan ducked back to give me room to come out, falling into step beside me as we got moving down the hospital's corridors.

"How are the books?" I asked.

"Pleasing to own." She replied, glancing at me. "I am... surprised. You actually bought them for me."

"I owed you for what I did."

"You did." Ekan agreed, "Thank you."

"You're welcome. How bad are Noro and Uru today?"

She nodded ahead, "As they usually are."

The rest of pack Thun was waiting for us in the lobby. All of them clearly amused, watching my two friends express their nerves in their own ways. Noro was pacing as best he could, while Uru seemed to be talking non-stop at Tevi.

It was a little odd to be going out in our uniforms. A bit disappointing, I'd have liked the chance to look good. And, well, the chance to see all of them dressed up too. Sadly there wasn't much point to bringing down our personal clothes when we'd be leaving planet by midnight.

That and we were just going to the restaurant on the hospital's ground floor, rather than finding a proper bar.

"And there they are." Tevi called in relief. She'd clearly gotten tired of being monologued at by her packmate. "Come on. Drinks await!"

There was a quick rumble of approval from everyone, and soon enough all nine of us were packed into the nearest elevator. To my lack of surprise Noro and Uru quickly edged their way over until I had one of them on either side.

To my surprise it was Noro who managed to be bold first; he almost shyly took one of my hands, then quickly brought it up and around his shoulders. Smiling a little, I pulled him a little closer, not missing Uru's pout when she noticed.

She quickly mimicked him, leaving me walking with my arms lazily draped over them both when we reached the lowest level.

The second surprise of the night was that the restaurant was actually quite busy. It was going to be most of an hour before we could be seated, and

311

so we ended up in the equally crowded bar space. Most of Pack Thun split off by then; leaving me with just my two companions at a high table in one of the corners.

It was a nice little place. Well decorated with stylized paintings of the various Trinity outposts. Nice, but you could tell its comfort and decoration wasn't really a priority. It didn't have the same exuberance that I was used to from Imperial bars.

That wasn't really surprising considering it was attached to the hospital, and was probably mostly meant as a nice place for the staff to unwind after their shifts.

"I still can't believe you drink Homeworld Hurricanes." Uru said, looking more than a little impressed as I sipped at the brightly colored drink.

"They're good." I enjoyed another long sip before settling the glass down. "They're very good."

"And one of them would knock Noro out for a week." She teased.

"Hey!" He protested, quickly setting his Void-Star down. "I'm not a lightweight!"

Uru grinned. "I didn't say you were."

I smiled, watching as the two of them bickered while I sipped from my drink. Eventually they ran out of wind and started haranguing me for more details about what had happened on Nueva Genova. I'd given them the broad details, but had held off describing the actual fighting.

Not because I hadn't wanted to, but because I'd wanted to do it when I had alcohol in my system. It seemed to help me forget just how horrible it had all been.

Either I was a better storyteller than I thought, or we were all just a bit past buzzed because they cheered or gasped at every twist and turn in the story. It took me most of an hour to get through the entire thing, our drinks going empty by the time I was finished.

"I can get us more." Noro quickly volunteered. "Same ones?"

Uru nodded eagerly. "Yes!"

"Hey! No kissing her with me gone." He growled. Well, tried to growl. He sounded like an angry little Meshicon; far more adorable than terrifying. "Ashe? Another Hurricane?"

"Something lighter, please."

No sooner had he slipped off than Uru slid off her own chair, grinning as she took a few steps closer to where I was sitting. "May I?"

Snorting in amusement, I brought a finger up and pressed it against her lips. "I will let you both kiss me at the end of the night. Be good until then."

Her tarah lowered in a pout for a brief moment, then rose. It was the only warning I had before she playfully nipped at the tip of my finger.

"Hey!" I yanked it back before she could do anything else. "No foreplay either."

"You're the one who put it there." Uru grinned.

I gave her a droll look, then carefully got to my feet as well. "You mind if I go to the bathroom before Noro gets back?"

"Sure, I'll walk with you." When I opened my mouth to protest she quickly got her own finger up, pressing it against my lips. "Nope! I'm not getting tortured by your terrifying packmate because I let you go off alone."

Huffing, I gently pushed her hand away. "Fine. Come on then, or he'll panic when he gets back. Hopefully the table will be ready by then too. I don't think I can drink another on an empty stomach."

It was getting more than a little crowded. There must have been plenty of work shifts letting off, and so we had to carefully thread our way through the mass of people standing around and chatting over drinks.

I let her take the lead; she was far less shy about nudging people out of her way than I was. Plus it gave me an excellent view of how she fit into her uniform's pants, and I was definitely intoxicated enough to stare far longer than I probably should have.

"Of course I picked the table on the opposite side from the

bathrooms." I muttered out loud, carefully following her around a group of doctors arguing about some new treatment. "Good move, Ashe."

The Hurricane must have been stronger than I'd thought it had been. We were about halfway to the bathrooms when I realized I wasn't quite walking a straight line. Not that Uru was doing much better; she'd started pausing every few steps, shaking her head, and then clearly focusing on remaining upright.

"She only had a Solar Wind." I blinked as the thought swam through my brain. "Those aren't strong at all."

Some instinct started trying to prod at me, tried to get my attention.

Then something poked me in the side for real.

I twitched, stumbling before a strong hand grabbed my arm. I turned to stammer out an apology, and found myself staring at the unamused face of an Elder in civilian dress.

And... and something was still poking my side.

I managed to look down in time to see something being yanked out of my belly, a silver device vanishing into the woman's pocket.

"What...?" My left leg buckled, sending me into her chest. "...drugged. You drugged me."

I felt her mouth against my ear as she spoke, so quietly that it couldn't be heard over the rumble of the crowd.

"Obviously, *beast.*"

My heart tried to lurch into panicked hammering, but everything was going gray. An attempt to push her away just saw my right hand flail against her chest. All she did was lean back a little, holding me, clearly waiting for the drugs to really sink in.

I tried to call for Uru. For help. For anyone to notice.

My tongue felt like it was covered in sand. My throat was closing. I could barely breathe, much less scream.

314

She ignored my useless motions, smiling as she looked into my eyes.

Ahshan's blood. She must have seen my panic. My horror.

She was enjoying it.

"You have no idea what you cost us." She whispered, tugging my arm over her shoulder. I tried to let my legs buckle entirely, to simply collapse so that someone would notice.

Someone did. They took my other arm, yanking it up over their shoulders.

"Too late, beast." A man whispered into my other ear. "You wanted answers, didn't you? Want to know just what you did?"

No. Not like this. Not like this.

"You will learn, beast." The elder hissed as they began carrying me through the crowd. Just another drunken conscript being helped back to her quarters. My eyes started to roll back.

The last thing I saw was a quiet commotion in the direction of the bathrooms, people rushing toward someone who'd collapsed.

Uru.

They'd drugged our drinks too.

"You will learn, beast. You will learn."

They had me.

They had me.

I let out a final whimper of fear... and everything went black.

315

Appendix A: Imperial Leaders

The Torlah (Empress) – Kradahr'iston'nirand

Origin: Gathahn   **Gender**: Female
Packmates: 7   **Age**: 376

Empress Kradahr came to power in the wake of her predecessor's aggressive advances into the Near Reaches, and has settled well into the role. Far more conservative than her expansionist precursors, she has shifted the Imperial focus away from aggressive invasions and declined reopening the wars with the Federation or Concordat. Instead she has directed the bureaucracy towards the various colonial zones, working to expand Imperial territory with a focus on peace and security.

That being said, she is not averse to adventurism when the opportunity presents itself, and fully supported the attack and conquest of Earth. She also has standing orders for at least two Chahshti'tahza and their forces to remain on the spinward frontier in case of trouble, or openings, in the Reaches.

The Chahshti'tahza (Void Lords)

The most unique aspect of the Imperial Government is, unquestionably, the Eight Chahshti'tahza. Translated formally as Void-Lord, or occasionally as Space-Lord by those seeking to give them a less grandiose title. They fulfill an unusual trifecta of roles; they are the highest Court in the Empire, they represent the potential pool of heirs for the Torlah, and they act as pseudo-independent military leaders. It is the last duty for which they are best known within, and without, the Empire.

Riv'ahvith'srong
- The eldest of the Chahshti'tahza, he plans to retire within the next decade to spend what time he has left with his pack in quiet relaxation. A renowned sailor who commanded the defense of Vos during the last war with the Federation; his masterful defense earned deep respect from his Regnon opposition who consider him one of the greatest Imperial Admirals in history.

Packmates: 2   Male, Age 483
Status - Stationed at Pan'vos.

317

Norop'fel'delarah

- An unusual Chahshti'tahza, Norop is more well known for her perfectionist logistical talents than any tactical prowess in space or on solid ground. She has reconfigured her personal fleet into a mobile repair and refitting force that is fully capable of supporting up to three other Void fleets far beyond the Imperial frontiers. While her name is not celebrated by the Imperial public or respected by her enemies, her peers consider her value to be incalculable, and dread the fact that she is likely to retire soon.

Packmates: 6   Female, Age 481
Status - Stationed at Ban'vos.

Grine'obdel'rilem

- Considered to be Riv's only rival for greatest Trahcon admiral of the age, Grine has spent most of his career in the Near Reaches battling pirates and would-be warlords. One of the few Imperial Trahcon who can accept working with aliens as an equal, his fleet has the highest percentage of Naule of any military force, and he is the de-facto expert on the Reaches in general.

Packmates: 2   Male, Age 428
Status - Currently commanding the Trinity Fortress.

Histh'akam'nirand

- A first ever case of a packmate of the Torlah being a Chahshti'tahza, she shares Kradahr's cautious military approach and conservative politics. She does, however, posses a bit of a Huntress's wanderlust even in her advancing years, and often leads multi-year expeditions into the Airalon Wastes alongside the Imperial Watch.

Packmates: 7   Female, Age 365
Status - In reserve; refitting forces in the Imperial Interior.

Troda'bahl'gekkot

- Rising to her rank after the conclusion of the last Imperial-Federal War, Troda has had a fairly quiet career. Respected but not renowned, her only action of note was to take her fleet into the Near Reaches to prevent any Ascendancy interference with Sever's invasion of Earth. The Thondians, wisely, did not test her forces, much to her personal frustration.

Packmates: 4   Female, Age 350
Status - Commanding patrols in the Contested Region.

Kahm'dovdel'vorzu
- Like Troda, Kahm was named Chahshti'tahza at an awkward time; there were no wars to wage, and the new Torlah was disinclined to start any new conflicts. So far she has spent a quiet career patrolling the various borders of the Empire, keeping an eye on their neighbors, and adjusting the composition of her fleet to her liking.

Packmates: 9   Female, Age 341
Status – Patrolling out of Shaidan.

Hedel'zor'saver
- Notable for being the only active Chahshti'tahza to have a background as a commando. While not well known to the public, he earned his rank thanks to leading several clandestine raids into the Holy Concordat to conduct sabotage, assassinations, and general espionage. Most of his heavy warships are on loan to his peers, allowing him to focus on the light forces and commando teams that are his specialty.

Packmates: 6   Male, Age 301
Status - In reserve; refitting forces in the Imperial Interior.

Sever'ahmiar'delarah
- The current heir-presumptive, well known as one of the most aggressive leaders within the Empire. While she built her reputation and achieved her rank by engaging pirates in the Near Reaches, it was her command of the invasion of Earth that cemented her place in the public image. While not official, it is widely known that the Ark Fleet has a half-billion credit bounty for anyone who can assassinate her.

Packmates: 11   Female, Age 276
Status - Currently assisting the Imperial Watch.

Appendix B: Imperial Warships

To use a stereotype, Imperial warships come in two flavors; light cruisers and heavy cruisers. While frigates and destroyers do exist, and massive dreadnought battleships do as well, the vast majority of Imperial combat ships can be described as a cruiser of one kind or another.

Most Imperial ships are built with the idea of spending moderate to long periods of time away from port, capable of carrying at least one year's worth of supplies for the crew. The Void-Ship type cruisers have even longer legs and can operate for multiple years without resupply, though the crews usually begin to wear down if not given at least some time on solid ground.

Appearance wise, Imperial cruisers are built as elongated trapezoids, something like a gold bar. Support ships will have blunt prows with forward facing hangars, while combat ships will have them angled to form a point either downwards near the keel or directly ahead. Most will have an observation/recreation deck outside of the armor that some aliens mistake for a bridge along the top.

Lighter vessels are more variable in their appearance depending on the builder, but most Trahcon ships favor sharp angles on their exteriors, but with softer, more rounded bulkheads on the interior.

Main Battery; rail-assisted torpedoes (modern), spinal mass-drivers (older vessels)

Secondary Battery; heavy railguns, long-range missile batteries

Point Defense; light railguns, laser arrays, short-range missile batteries

Light Warships

Comets; One of the smallest hulls considered a warship by the Empire, Comet type vessels are fast, lightly armed scout ships intended to emerge from FTL at the outskirts of a system, make a high-speed run collecting information, and then get out. They have very powerful sensors and network assets, along with massive engines, but their armament usually is limited to point-defense equipment.
- Named for deceased Trahcon sailors.

Lurkers; Built on slightly larger scales than Comets, the Lurker designation is given to light ships that are intended to conduct much longer-term reconnaissance. Often featuring dampening equipment for stealth purposes, they will linger in the outer reaches of solar systems, soaking up information before jumping out to report.
- Named for nocturnal creatures.

Escort: The smallest vessel designated for open combat, the Escort types are roughly the same size as most other species' destroyers. As the name would indicate they are almost exclusively attached to larger formations with the purpose of expanding a fleet's point defense and detection range.
- Named for sea-life.

Destroyer: Unlike most foreign destroyers, which are usually jack-of-all-trades vessels, Imperial destroyers are designed solely to hunt down and kill enemy craft equal to or smaller than themselves in size. Fairly maneuverable, they are well armed for close-in fights, but lack the endurance or heavy weapons required to punch above their weight.
- Named for weather events.

Patrolship: A variation of a destroyer which, unusually for the Imperials, sacrifices nearly all of its endurance in exchange for more armor, shielding, and heavier weaponry. While FTL capable, nearly all are assigned to single systems which they rarely leave.
- Named for weather events.

321

Line Vessels

2nd Rate Liner: A 'light cruiser' to any other race, to the Imperials it's the weaker, cheaper version of their primary warship. Most often used as a flotilla leader for Destroyers to cover their operations, or to command Patrolships in system defense fleets.
- Named with ships of a 'class' designated with a letter, with their names starting with that letter.

Long-Ship: A variation of a 2nd Rate designed for long range cruising and patrols beyond the Imperial borders. They make up a significant portion of the Void-Fleets and the Imperial Watch, and are the most common ship seen outside of the Empire.
- Named for metals/elements/materials.

Brawler: Usually a 2nd Rate whose few heavy mounts have been removed for additional close-range turrets or point defense weaponry, occasionally larger versions have been built with increased armor. Essentially a larger destroyer, built in response to several centuries where the Concordat focused heavily on frigate-corvette production.
- Named for deceased military leaders.

Hunting Ship: Heavily armored and shielded, Hunting Ships are virtually unarmed in order to make room for the massive equipment required to create a Null-Sphere where ships cannot flee to FTL. Incredibly expensive to build and a priority target for enemies, their deployment is strictly controlled.
- Named for mountains.

1st Rate Liner: Equivalent in size to a heavy cruiser or small battlecruiser, the 1st Rate is the core of the Imperial Fleet. Designed to be a well rounded vessel with good endurance, there is very little that a 1st Rate cannot be asked to do in any given circumstance.
- Named with ships of a 'class' designated with a letter, with their names starting with that letter.

Void-Ship: Effectively the 1st Rate equivalent of a Long-Ship, they are exclusively reserved for the Watch and Void-Fleets thanks to their increased size and cost.
 -Named for stellar events.

Capital Ships

Carrier: Nothing like alien vessels intended to deliver fighters and bombers, Imperial Carriers could be better described as Space-To-Ground Attack vessels. While they do posses point defenses, their primary purpose is the carrying of strike craft, elite ground forces, observation satellites, and C&C equipment.
- Named for cities/arcologies.

Command-Ship: While carriers are optimized to support a planetary invasion, a Command Ship is optmized for an Admiral and their staff. Usually built on a lengthened Void-Ship's hull with the additional space given over to expanded quarters and communications equipment.
- Named for solar systems.

Dreadnought: The largest type of vessels built, Imperial Dreadnoughts are slow, over-armored behemoths designed to take an impossible amount of punishment and continue fighting. Despite not being quite as well armed as their alien counterparts, numerous opposing admirals have been disgusted to watch a dreadnought so battered as to be combat-ineffective leisurely jump out system as its core citadel remained perfectly intact despite the fact that it appeared to be floating wreckage.
- Named for planets.